THE
WAR
BEYOND

By Andrea Stewart

The Drowning Empire

The Bone Shard Daughter
The Bone Shard Emperor
The Bone Shard War

The Hollow Covenant

The Gods Below
The War Beyond

THE WAR BEYOND

The Hollow Covenant: Book 2

ANDREA STEWART

orbit

orbitbooks.net

This book is a work of fiction. Names, characters, places, and incidents are the product of the author's imagination or are used fictitiously. Any resemblance to actual events, locales, or persons, living or dead, is coincidental.

Copyright © 2025 by Andrea Stewart, Inc.

Cover design by Lauren Panepinto
Cover illustration by Sasha Vinogradova
Cover copyright © 2025 by Hachette Book Group, Inc.
Map by Rebecka Champion (Lampblack Art)

Hachette Book Group supports the right to free expression and the value of copyright. The purpose of copyright is to encourage writers and artists to produce the creative works that enrich our culture.

The scanning, uploading, and distribution of this book without permission is a theft of the author's intellectual property. If you would like permission to use material from the book (other than for review purposes), please contact permissions@hbgusa.com. Thank you for your support of the author's rights.

Orbit
Hachette Book Group
1290 Avenue of the Americas
New York, NY 10104
orbitbooks.net

First Edition: November 2025
Simultaneously published in Great Britain by Orbit

Orbit is an imprint of Hachette Book Group.
The Orbit name and logo are registered trademarks of Little, Brown Book Group Limited.

The publisher is not responsible for websites (or their content) that are not owned by the publisher.

The Hachette Speakers Bureau provides a wide range of authors for speaking events. To find out more, go to hachettespeakersbureau.com or email HachetteSpeakers@hbgusa.com.

Orbit books may be purchased in bulk for business, educational, or promotional use. For information, please contact your local bookseller or the Hachette Book Group Special Markets Department at special.markets@hbgusa.com.

Library of Congress Control Number: 2025941417

ISBNs: 9780316564830 (hardcover), 9780316564854 (ebook)

Printed in the United States of America

LSC-C

Printing 1, 2025

For every reader who has found a place they belong within the pages of a book

CRESSIMA
ALBANORE
KASHAN
BATAAR'UN
BAY OF BAREXI
TAMBOR GULF
XIAZEN
THE SANGUINE SEA
PIZGONIA
THE SOUTHERN CONTINENT

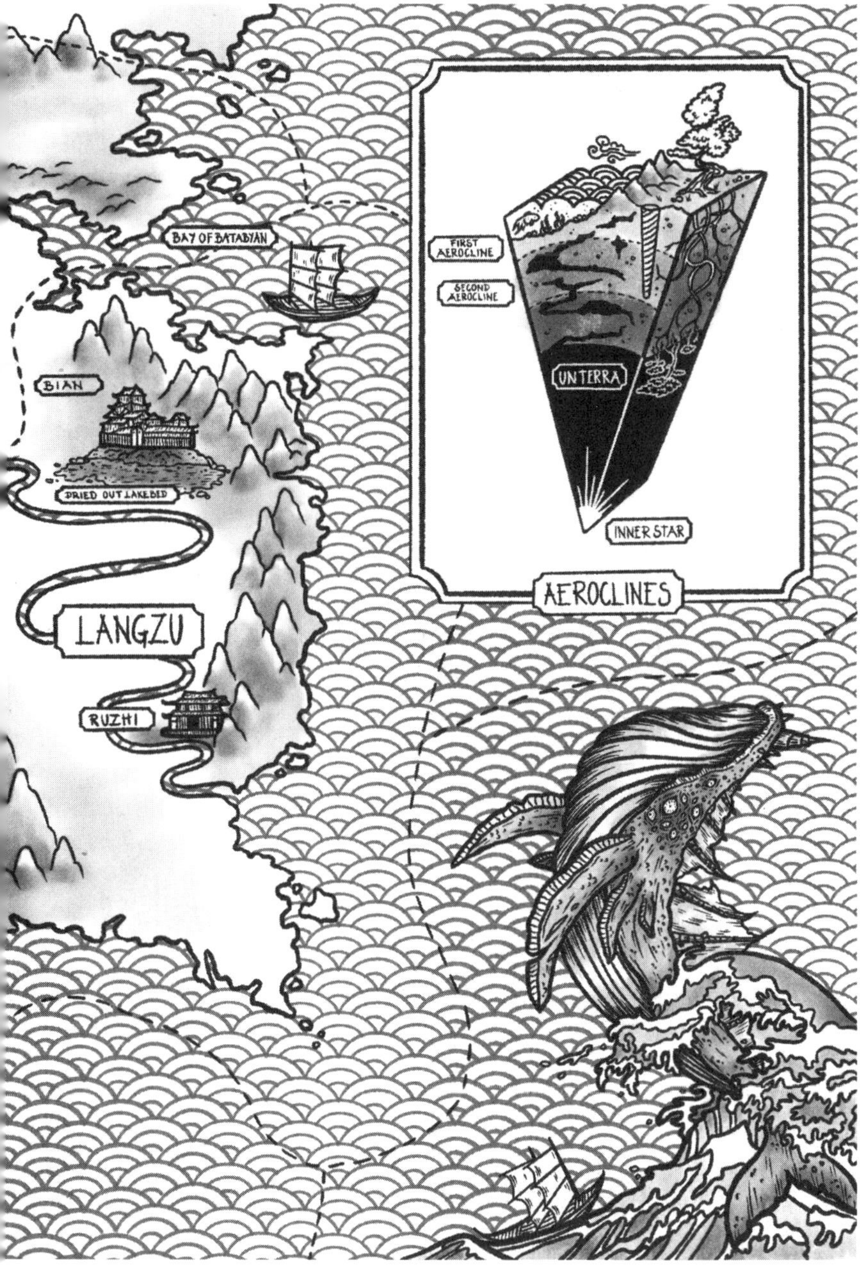
BAY OF BATABYAN
FIRST AEROCLINE
SECOND AEROCLINE
UNTERRA
INNER STAR
AEROCLINES
BIAN
DRIED OUT LAKEBED
LANGZU
RUZHI

The Gods Below
A Summary

Hakara

In the distant past, mortals broke the world. They cut and burned the giant Numinar trees, feeding the branches into their machines to distill the magic within. When the land above became uninhabitable, the mortal Tolemne made his way to the hollow center of the world. There, he made a bargain with the god Kluehnn. In exchange for religious control and a regular tithe of god gems, Kluehnn agreed to magically revitalize the surface of the world, one piece at a time.

Hakara is an orphan, responsible for her younger sister, Rasha. When the black wall of restoration approaches, promising to heal the realm while altering half the residents and disappearing the rest, she flees with Rasha for the border. In the chaos, Rasha gets left behind and Hakara awakens on the other side.

Ten years later, Hakara is working as a sinkhole miner, saving money so she can return to find her sister. When she sees a god gem just past the second aerocline, she manages to hold her breath and grab it, but the sinkhole begins to collapse. She puts the gem between her teeth and accidentally swallows it.

Hakara becomes supernaturally strong and escapes the sinkhole. This ultimately leads to her capture by the Unanointed, a ragtag band of rebels who need her help to stop their realm, Langzu, from being restored. Their leader, Mitoran, tells her that in exchange, they'll help her find her sister.

Now Hakara is one of the Unanointed, her mission to search out corestones that will help make Langzu livable again without restoration. They bond her to an altered who can summon aether – the magical air past the aeroclines.

Hakara meets Thassir, a large, winged altered man. Hakara has never been able to take a hint, and although he clearly dislikes her, she's able to convince him to help on their next assignment.

The assignment goes terribly wrong as they are ambushed by godkillers. Hakara's partner dies and Thassir offers himself up as a bonded partner in the midst of battle. Together they finish the job, retrieving the corestone. Thassir wants to break their bond immediately, but Hakara talks him into staying when they discover the location of another corestone, one they'll have to intercept godkillers to take.

They take heavy casualties. Hakara snatches the corestone but an aspect of Kluehnn appears. Thassir kills the piece of Kluehnn, though he's injured in the process. Hakara tends to Thassir's wounds and discovers he is a god.

When they return, the leader of the resistance, Mitoran, informs her they are planning to raid a den in Kashan for a corestone. Thassir tells Hakara not to go. But the Unanointed are the only ones who can help her find her sister. And then Thassir says the thing that always makes Hakara angry: in all likelihood, one way or another, Rasha is dead. And it is not Hakara's fault. But this time, she cannot find a way to deny it.

In a fit of confusion and hurt, Hakara leaves the Unanointed and breaks her bond with Thassir. But one of Mitoran's agents finds her and tells her Rasha is alive and in the very den that the Unanointed will be raiding. Hakara has to save Rasha. Unable to find Thassir, she bonds with another altered.

Hakara finds her sister in the den, but Rasha doesn't need or want rescuing. It's been ten years and it's far too late.

Rasha spares Hakara but kills her bonded partner. Fleeing from the fighting, Hakara and her team find themselves in an undisturbed part of the den, where they encounter Mitoran. Mitoran claims to have found the corestone and says she will lead them out, but they realize that in reality she is Lithuas, an elder god. She's working for Kluehnn, and they need Hakara to infuse the corestone to enact restoration.

Hakara starts to go through with it. She's lost Rasha, she has no bonded partner, she has nothing. But instead of infusing the corestone Mitoran gives her, she swallows it. Her mortal body can't handle this rush of power. She falls and sees, as though in a dream, Thassir. He's fighting back the godkillers, he's fighting against Lithuas.

He re-bonds her and tells her that she cannot give up. She's the most stubborn woman he knows. And then he... kisses her? Magical air is pouring into her and it feels odd. She rises to kill this den's aspect of Kluehnn and passes out.

She awakens. They've averted restoration but the Unanointed are in tatters. Thassir admits he knew Mitoran was Lithuas, a confession that sends them reeling away from one another. But Hakara takes control of the Unanointed, to continue their original mission of defeating Kluehnn. She'll do what she does best: make trouble.

Rasha

After Hakara is separated from her when they are children, Rasha awakens in a new and changed realm, herself changed to have horns and claws. In spite of her frightening appearance, she is still just a child and is lost without Hakara. She waits, but Hakara doesn't return. When a recruiter from a nearby den offers her a place, she finally leaves and gives herself over to Kluehnn's faithful.

Ten years later, Rasha is living in the den, hoping to become a godkiller. Her request is finally granted, and she is assigned a burrow where she will compete against her fellow converts in a series of life-or-death trials.

The first trial weeds out most of the converts. Rasha makes her first kills, finds herself physically stronger than she expected, and survives. She is promoted from convert to neophyte. When Sheuan arrives and invokes her right to an advocate, Rasha is assigned to see to her needs, which takes time away from her training. Sheuan and Rasha travel to see the Queen of Rasha's realm, and on the way, they form a tentative relationship, which is shattered when Sheuan eventually leaves her.

Rasha returns for the second trial. When she defends two of her cohort against the burrow's bully, they agree to work with her. Their task: to retrieve a key from a dangerous creature in a cave system and escape. It's a near thing on the second trial, but Rasha and her two allies are the only three from their burrow left standing.

There is one final trial. They must kill a god.

The den comes under attack. Rasha spares Hakara during the fight. Hakara kills this den's aspect of Kluehnn.

Rasha disobeys Kluehnn and speaks to the god she's sent to kill. What he says throws her into doubt. The gods do not want to take over the surface world; they merely want to live. Although she completes her final trial, Rasha has committed blasphemy. Neither of her cohort turn her in.

Mullayne

Mull seeks to follow Tolemne's Path to the center of the hollow world, hoping the gods below will save the life of his chronically ill friend, Imeah. He's invented filters that should allow them to descend below the aeroclines and not be poisoned by the magical air there. Imeah is ready to enjoy what's left of her life, but Mull can't let her go. On the descent, they discover some of Tolemne's writing, carved into the wall.

Mull's filters hold as they pass through the first aerocline. He sees the footprint of some creature, but he's uncertain if it's real. He does not mention it.

He reviews the documents he's brought with him, comparing them to Tolemne's writing. Something is off about their measurements. Just as he's figuring it out, the camp is attacked by giant lizards. No one dies, but their food is half eaten. When Mull confesses that he saw a footprint, everyone is furious. They take a vote to leave or continue on. The vote is narrowly in favor of continuing.

The second aerocline layer is longer than Mull expected. His cave expert starts to act strange and then murders another of the crew. Her filters have failed. They are eventually able to subdue her, but this means their filters are all failing. Mull has spares, but there aren't enough for everyone.

An argument ensues about whether they should continue or turn back. They continue on, but encounter a third aerocline. There shouldn't be a third aerocline. Everything says there are only two. They sleep before venturing forth, and Mull awakens to find himself alone with his right-hand man and Imeah, his gear ransacked.

He insists on pushing on. This is the farthest anyone has been. They have to know. They have to see. They pass into the third aerocline and their filters immediately begin to fail. Mull and his friend get into a fight. Imeah helps him to kill his friend.

Now it's just him and Imeah. Delirious, they find one last encampment, but this one looks like it's incoming rather than outgoing. History says Tolemne died in the realm of the gods. Mull wants to continue, but Imeah convinces him to return to the surface or no one will know what they've discovered. And Imeah? She can think of worse ways to die than trying to make it to the realm of the gods. He's given her the beautiful chance to see something new.

Mull finally lets her determine her own fate, and makes his way toward the surface.

Sheuan

Sheuan, Mull's cousin, is in his workshop, wreaking mischief. She's upping the price on some of his items so she can pocket the difference. While entertaining a guest, she stumbles upon the prototypes of Mull's filters. She vaguely grasps the implications, but she's late to the Sovereign's party ... which she hasn't been invited to.

At the party, she searches for evidence that her father was framed for embezzlement. After maneuvering her way past multiple checkpoints, she is confronted by the Sovereign himself while she's going through his study.

He's impressed that she made it this far. She demands to know whether her father, the former trade minister, was framed, but the Sovereign says that doesn't matter. Her father was executed. Information, even proof, is malleable. No one actually wishes to challenge the Sovereign's rule.

He makes her an offer – would she like to redeem her family name? If she finds out why restored realms cut off trade and communication and stops it, he will give her the trade minister position. If she fails, he will dissolve her clan. He does not offer her any resources. Of course not.

Sheuan's mother pressures her into taking the Sovereign's offer. Sheuan must figure out a way to get past the barrier and go to Kashan.

With Mull's filter, she's able to make it through. But she's lost the Sovereign's seal, and the godkillers at the border turn her away. Desperate, she remembers Kluehnn's precepts and invokes the right of sanctuary. They have to assign her an advocate. She is assigned Rasha. She begins her research by traveling to see the Kashani Queen, a trip during which Sheuan and Rasha become intimate.

Upon meeting the Queen, though, it is apparent that Kluehnn is in control and the Queen is a puppet. During a struggle with one of the priests, Sheuan is thrown into a pit of black smoke. Rasha rescues her.

Her return to Langzu doesn't go as well as she'd hoped. She only has theories about why restored realms cut off trade. That's not what the Sovereign asked for. So Sheuan leverages the only thing she has left: the filters. The Sovereign asks if the filters are used to protect from alteration or death during restoration.

Sheuan isn't sure. Of course, she can't get into contact with Mull to check – he's off on his quest. But she has his notes. She reads through them, and notices feathers growing from her back, a souvenir from Kashan.

Theoretically, the filters could work to prevent alteration. They would be hoarded by the heads of the clans, doled out by the Sovereign to those who hoped to survive restoration. Unwilling to give this power over to him, Sheuan returns to Kashan, hoping to fulfill the original conditions of her bargain.

Failing to find any new information, she finally accepts that the only way to save her family is to give up the secret of the filters. She retrieves Mull's journal and tosses his notes into the fire, determined to stop serving her family and to start using her gifts for herself. Her life is her own. And she must make decisions she can live with.

She meets with the Sovereign and assures him the filters protect from restoration. Her cousin has gone on an expedition and has not returned. He's dead, which means she is the only one who knows how to make the filters. She will make them for him in return for a place at his side.

Nioanen

Nioanen's story opens in the far past. He is one of the seven elder gods and is retreating from a battle against Kluehnn. His best friend is the shapeshifter god Irael. The retreating gods settle into a remote sanctuary on the surface world to regroup. They can sustain this if they just keep fighting Kluehnn off, if they just maintain their borders. Even so, Nioanen worries: will they all someday grow too tired to fight back? And then Irael curls at his side as a cat, tells him that he should rest, and he sleeps.

Years later, and Irael is still curling at his side as a cat to sleep, but does not creep away in the night. Nioanen finds he does not mind. There are fewer worshipers now and battle is in the air. One of the gods has refused to eat and has wasted away into a breeze. Don't go that way, Nioanen begs Irael. Irael assures him he will not. Irael wraps one of his hands into Nioanen's hair. Live, he tells him. And then he kisses him.

The battle is lost, their sanctuary taken. Nioanen and Irael are on the run. In spite of the danger, they agree to stay together. They settle into the human world. Irael is in a woman's form, and she is pregnant. They are not the only refugee gods who have started a family. Irael notes that their child will be born on the surface, unknowing of their true home. Irael suggests the name Thassir and thinks their baby will have wings.

Thassir is born and grows into a child, and Irael brings news that others of their brethren have been hunted down. They've settled in for the night when they're attacked by godkillers. Nioanen tells Irael to run with Thassir, and he'll stay behind to fight them off.

Nioanen kills the two godkillers who attack, but then finds out there were more, and they've slain both Irael and Thassir. Nioanen wishes he were dead, but he promised Irael he would live. So he uses his magic to change himself, turning his wings black with the ashes of his loved ones and dulling his godly aura. Becoming Thassir.

THE
WAR
BEYOND

I

Hakara

11 years after the restoration of Kashan
and 572 years after the Shattering

Langzu - in the wilds

The Shattering had little regard for where people lived, their social ties, the jobs they were working. Some woke to find the earth shaking beneath them. Some slept while it happened, their rooftops collapsing onto their bodies. Houses were cleaved in half, families were separated, the ground opened, and the aether rose from between the cracks.

When the dust finally settled, cities had been leveled, governments thrown into disarray. And all the realms of the world became isolated.

The stars wheeled about in the sky as a bloody corpse covered me like a heavy, fleshy blanket. The only breathing I could hear was mine, which was good, because a moment ago, the beast I'd been fighting had been breathing as well – large, rasping breaths that filled the hot night air.

"Still with us?" Dashu's face appeared above me. It was spinning too. As I blinked, his features began to align. Bronze skin, gently curved nose, dark eyes, high cheekbones. My gaze focused on the enamel flower hilt of his sword, the white blossoms as delicate as his blade was sharp.

I struggled to sit up, trying to shove the still-warm body off me. Soft, pale flesh gave way beneath my palms, antennae-like filaments brushing against my fingertips. But beneath that was a solid, weighty bulk. "Lithuas? Is she . . ."

"Escaped," Dashu said.

The whole entire reason we'd gotten into this fight in the first place. "We need to go after her. Send scouts. Keep her in our sights." I scanned the surrounding landscape and saw only the remnants of a battle long-since ended. She'd been *right there*. I remembered the smirk on her face.

He was shaking his head even before I'd finished speaking. "She's a shapeshifter, Hakara. We tried. She's long gone. I saw the aspect fall on you. Are you well?"

I sagged and then wiggled a little, mentally cataloging my injuries. "Still among the living. Didn't pass out this time."

He held out a hand to me and I took it. The world spun a little more as I righted myself, the earth beneath my feet crunching. Had a fair bit of it covering my clothes too, probably some in my hair.

"Don't say that like it's an accomplishment." Alifra's voice cut the night. She stood next to Dashu, her russet hair pulled into a bun, blood spattered on her boots. "There's not as much cause for you to pass out when you're not acting as our bruiser."

Reflexively, I touched the patch I'd sewn over my heart. The two crossed swords. I knew what it looked like – as if her words had struck me in a way that pained. Maybe they did. This fight had been my idea, my fault. And we had nothing to show for it except the dead aspect and more injured Unanointed. I let my hand drop, lifting my chin. "We killed one of Kluehnn's aspects, didn't we?"

The second one since we'd raided the den at the border of Kashan. What a mess I'd made of things. Some leader I was proving to be.

Should have seen the ambush coming from the very beginning. But when Alifra and I had traveled to a nearby town to contact a woman in the Unanointed's spy network, I'd spotted Lithuas there in the guise of Mitoran. She'd been at the market, asking after unearthed corestones. Was I supposed to leave her be? She'd used her shapeshifting abilities to take over the Unanointed, to subvert them to her cause and to Kluehnn's. Using us to find corestones so he could enact restoration.

So I'd followed her, in spite of Alifra's protests, and then I'd ordered my remaining Unanointed to attack. I could still see the smirk on Lithuas's face as she'd turned to us on the road, as her gray hair had melted to silver and she'd drawn her sword. And then at a quirk of her finger, an aspect of Kluehnn and three godkillers had come roaring out from between two boulders.

She didn't need to eliminate us. She only needed to weaken us. The fewer of us there were, the less chance we had of causing trouble. And she'd succeeded.

A figure at the edge of my vision leapt into the sky before my eyes could settle on him, black wings spread. Thassir still followed us, had still joined in the fray when we were in trouble, but I'd not spoken to him since he'd admitted he'd known what Lithuas and Kluehnn were planning. I could still feel his presence in my head, like someone had glued a string there and pulled it until it itched. I knew without asking that he'd been on the ground, waiting, wanting to be sure I wasn't hurt before he returned to the skies.

As though he had some ownership, some right to me.

He should have told me everything when I'd discovered he was a god. He was the offspring of two of the most powerful elder gods. Which meant he was old, older than the rise and fall of kingdoms. I'd thought that if I ever met such a god, they would be grand, overpowering, like trying to gaze into the brightness of the sun.

Gazing at Thassir was like looking into the depths of a sinkhole.

He'd let Lithuas hide him from Kluehnn's wrath, agreeing not to interfere with their plans. He'd kept to that terrible bargain, allowing realm after realm to be restored without ever lifting a hand or doing anything to stop it. And everyone had suffered for it.

Dashu wiped his blade clean and then sheathed it. Beyond him and Alifra, I saw three slain godkillers and the surviving Unanointed, already tending to their injured and their dead. Dashu exchanged a glance with Alifra before turning his attention back to me.

"The fight could have been worse for us. But it also could have been better, and we've lost two more people. What do you think we should do if we happen upon her again?"

Alifra tucked her small crossbow onto her back. "Will we be ready?"

Bah. I knew what they were getting at. All the subtlety of spitting camels, those two. Thassir could chew through godkillers when he was really into the swing of things, but Lithuas was one of the seven elder gods. You didn't get much more powerful than that. We needed to kill her to truly cripple Kluehnn's efforts. And to kill her, we needed to work together.

And that was the problem, wasn't it? Couldn't use the god gems if my arbor wasn't summoning aether for me to breathe in.

And if I couldn't use the god gems, I wasn't a very good bruiser. Oh, I did my best. I was a mediocre fighter, hovering only a hair above poor by pure strength and determination. I had none of Alifra's calculating smoothness, none of Dashu's deadly grace. But I could take a beating and keep going.

I winced as I took a step. Seemed I hadn't escaped completely unscathed. I was bruised as an overripe piece of fruit bounced off the back of a cart. With the god gems, I could move as quickly as a god, be as strong as one, obtain invulnerability for as long as I could hold my breath. And I could hold my breath a good long time. Even in a fight. It was what I'd trained for. "You want him to act as my arbor again." They wouldn't be asking me for this if they knew.

"You have to make a choice," Dashu said. It was like they were flanking me, cornering me with their words. "Whatever happened between the two of you, you need to either break the bond and choose another arbor or reconcile with him."

"I don't like either of those choices." In truth, I wasn't sure which was the better one.

"You don't have to like them," Alifra snapped. She cast an arm toward the Unanointed, a few of whom were obviously trying to catch snatches of our conversation. "Your team is relying on you, but so are *they*. You want to lead them? Then lead. You can't let personal feelings get in the way."

I looked to the sky. Personal feelings seemed a light way to put it. I shook my head, leaning on my knees. And here I was, keeping Thassir's identity secret – protecting him. Realms lost. Lives overturned. Could he have stopped all of that? He could have tried. "Ah, fuck it. It's not just personal feelings." I checked for listening ears and leaned in. "Thassir doesn't have an aura, but he's a god. He's not an altered. I found out after the orchards. I saw his blood. It shimmered."

They both stared at me.

"Do you understand why I might not want his help? Do you understand why I *do*?"

I watched all the implications filter through their minds, wondering if I'd looked as bewildered, betrayed, bereft. Alifra licked her lips. "Did he know about Lithuas?"

"Yes. She knew his parents. She spared him in exchange for him agreeing not to interfere with Kluehnn's plans."

I knew what they were thinking; I'd followed this path in my own mind. The gods were dangerous. They were selfish. They'd come to the surface world to take some piece of it for their own. I didn't trust Kluehnn, but that didn't mean I trusted the gods he fought against either. And a god who was this old, who'd chosen no side? How trustworthy could he be? He'd saved my life, he'd stood up to Lithuas when none of us had the strength. I couldn't be sure he would do it again, if given another chance. Would he hesitate when we all needed him the most? As he had for so many years?

Dashu made a small sound of disgust. "Break the bond, Hakara. Find another arbor. He's a god. We're the Unanointed because we don't follow Kluehnn. We don't follow *any* god. The altered were once mortal. He never was."

Alifra stared into the distance. "He knew. And he saved himself. Just think. Lithuas was right there within his reach. One stroke of a blade and he could have slowed restoration, thrown Kluehnn's plans into chaos. He could have spared so many lives. My daughter . . ." She stopped, her voice choked with anger.

They were right, both of them. But that was in the past, and I had to consider the future.

"I don't think he wants followers or wishes harm on us. He avoided us until I roped him into our schemes."

"Maybe he's just waiting for the right time," Dashu said darkly.

"He's old. Very old," I said. "Terrible strategist if that's true."

Alifra walked away from us, pacing a circle before returning, her breath tight. We both waited as she gathered herself. "He could have helped people, but he chose to help himself instead. We may not know if he wants power, but we do know he's a coward. Worst case, we're letting a viper into our nest. Best case, we're letting in someone who could abandon us at any moment but who could also be of immense help."

"I don't think he's a viper," I said softly, reluctantly.

Dashu looked between us both. "I can't say I'm so sure."

Alifra flexed her fists. I knew the feeling. Wished I could punch the big winged man myself. But he had saved us, in the end. She didn't meet Dashu's eyes when she spoke. "Aqqila has so many stories about the gods, and not all of them are bad. Didn't Irael give that orator chance after chance when everyone else had given up on her? She became a queen. You tell me that one all the time." Wasn't sure if she was trying to convince Dashu or herself.

He crossed his arms. "So you would welcome him back in spite of his lies. You're fine with him being magically linked to Hakara and always knowing where we are."

"I didn't say *that*." Alifra gave him an exasperated look. "Wouldn't be placing bets on his loyalty to us outweighing his loyalty to *her*. Not when they're face to face again. But he's useful."

I hefted my bloody spear, the one I'd driven into the eye of Kluehnn's aspect. Felt a little bit less alone, seeing my struggle reflected in them. "Now you see where I'm at. We need him, but we can't trust him. Any help he chooses to give us right now, I haven't asked him for." I remembered the way we moved together, the way he always seemed to know where I was going, how he drew the aether right to where I needed it.

There was a part of me that wished he'd make the first move

instead of lingering at the edges as though afraid of my reproach. If only he'd say the words that would make me *understand*, that would help me forgive him.

I didn't know what those words were. If they existed at all.

Dashu tapped the enamel hilt of his sword, his jaw set as he looked to the skies. "Talk to him. Decide what we can trust him with. Our choices are not good and Lithuas is still out there."

I sighed. "I'll talk to him once we find a spot to rest."

I left them there as I moved through the Unanointed, doing my best to offer reassuring, encouraging words. What would Utricht have said? He'd been my arbor before Thassir, and had always seemed to know what to say. He'd made me feel comfortable after only a few days, and that was feat enough as it was. I wasn't him, but the Unanointed seemed to appreciate my words. Our ranks were diminished even more now. Seventeen after this fight.

We stopped at the edge of a stunted grove of trees and set up the tents. I could feel Alifra and Dashu's eyes on me, four sharp little prods that pushed me to keep my word. Thassir landed just out of view when the last fire was down to embers. And I was still awake, and *I* wasn't a coward, so I set my jaw, took a lantern, and went to the edge of camp.

Looking at him directly, this close, was a shock. He didn't look any different from the last time we'd spoken, and maybe I'd built him up in my head to be more frightening. He stood on the fringes, twenty paces away from the last tent on the perimeter, his large black wings tucked around his body, his mouth in a permanent frown. He was carrying his own pack of supplies, though he had no blanket or bedroll. Not like he needed them with his wings and this unexpected heat. A few small spatterings of rain were all we'd seen of the end of summer.

I found my gaze drawn involuntarily to his mouth. Generous, but not overly so, the gentle curves I'd once thought I'd seen tip into a smile. Those selfsame lips had pressed to mine back in Kluehnn's den, had breathed aether from beyond the third aerocline into my lungs. The soft touch of them, the fire that had joined the one already burning through my veins. The feel of his hands at my back and my neck, gentle and firm. He'd *kissed* me, and I'd kissed him right back. I'd wanted him, with a desperation that had surprised me.

Then again, I'd been dying and halfway out of my mind. Everything had looked hazy, draped in gold, Thassir's sword somehow engulfed in silver flames.

Now I wasn't dying, and nothing between us felt right. "I need your help scouting the way to the mines."

Thassir was wearing the arbor patch Dashu had made him in the same spot I wore my bruiser one, mirrored, like we were two different views of the same person. He lifted a foot like he was going to take a step closer, and then decided better of it. "I can do that. Hakara..."

I closed my eyes, as though that would somehow shield me against his words. I wasn't sure why hearing him say my name felt like a shard of glass between my ribs. Always with the accents in the right places. How could I have missed it? The gods seemed to know – every language and who spoke which. "Don't... don't give me platitudes. What you did was wrong. Or what you *didn't* do, really."

"Yes."

I let out a little breath, glad at least that he'd not moved on to excuses. I wasn't sure I could have borne that. But where did we go from here? I wasn't sure. "You should have told me. You should have told me everything."

His voice was a velvet whisper. "Are you sure?"

What would I have done, if he had? I'd have turned from him. I wouldn't have had his help in the den. But I'd deserved the truth from him. I'd known he was a god and I'd been willing to let that go. I'd been willing to get past it. But this? Doing nothing while Lithuas schemed? "I don't know."

I opened my eyes and stared into his, wishing we could communicate silently, the way Alifra and Dashu seemed to. I needed so much more from him, but I could sense he wanted something from me too, something I was unable to give, and we stood there like two islands across a stretch of ocean. No way to bridge the gap.

"I can find Lithuas for you, if you want me to. I can't explain why, but we – she ..." He stopped, leaning his head back as if he could tip the words back down his throat. "If I'm near to her when she uses magic, when she shifts, I can sense her." He stretched it out to me like a peace offering.

I lifted my hands. I had no godkilling blade, nor a god's powers to kill another god. "Would you kill her, if we found her?"

Thassir stayed silent, and when he finally spoke, his voice was a low rumble. "All you have to do is ask."

All the fear came crashing in. I wasn't meant for this, being a leader, being needed by so many people. I'd never made wise decisions; I'd only ever made decisions I'd thought would lead me back to Rasha. I licked my lips, my mouth dry. "We should break the bond."

"If that's what you want," he said, his voice even.

Some treacherous part of me didn't want that at all. Some treacherous part of me wondered what it would be like if I stretched out a hand, if I led him to my tent, to my bed. I wondered if he would let me. The world was going to shit, why not try? Would I think about his eyes and the press of his mouth while he was moving inside me, or would I think about the way he'd stood aside and let countless people be slaughtered?

And then what? Would it be like it was with Altani, my old

mining partner? Just two broken people trying to use small moments to deny bigger problems? What was the point?

I reached for him anyways, because what was I if not a fool who never learned her lesson? To my surprise, he flinched back. It gutted something inside me, a spoon plunging in and scraping away, leaving a hollow, painful sensation.

I swallowed, trying to push past the feeling, to pretend it hadn't happened. "Get us to the mining camp tomorrow. Get us there safely. And then find me Lithuas."

2
Hakara

11 years after the restoration of Kashan
and 572 years after the Shattering

Langzu - the sinkhole
mines west of Ruzhi

Sinkhole miners can often be found playing cards and smoking bung-rou on their off time. It's a sweet-smelling, pungent herb that gives a person a feeling of floating, of well-being, though it can leave a nasty headache in its wake. Yes, overuse of it does lead to death, and it decreases the lung capacity of divers, which can also lead to death, but there is such a high fatality rate among miners for just doing the job itself that many of them see this as adding a feather to a brick on the scales of mortality.

I didn't know where else to hide them.
The familiar smells from the mining tents wafted toward me – the smoke, the latrine ditch, the metallic scent of freshly turned earth. Heat shimmered the air over the tents, cloth

melting into the golden grass of the hills beyond. The camp was in a midday lull, few people out and about, which suited my purposes perfectly. The sinkhole mines closer to the Kashani border hadn't been as productive lately, and most miners, including Guarin, had moved on to this new field west of Ruzhi.

I could feel the tug of Thassir's presence in my mind, and with it, another tug, desperate and fearful, pulling me onward. I couldn't find and sneak up on Lithuas with all the Unanointed in tow, injured and tired. And I needed to find her. Quickly, before she got too far away and Thassir was no longer able to track her.

I'd never asked Guarin for anything; I'd prided myself on that. I'd taken every sour word he'd ever thrown at me, shooting back my own rejoinders, working twice as hard as anyone else on the crew. Even when I'd only been a child, I'd set my jaw and risen to every challenge he'd set me. I hadn't felt I had any other choice.

Now here I was, ready to ask *favors*. That was how hard up I was. Couldn't do it for myself, but maybe I could do it for others.

We were hidden behind a cluster of speckled boulders, their surfaces hot to the touch. A lizard stared back at me from a crack, head tilted, the sun too bright for even his liking. I glanced back at my ragtag band of Unanointed. "All of you stay here. I'll come back if it's safe to approach."

Thassir ruffled his feathers, his expression dark.

"What?" I gave him a long look. "What do you think is going to be more conspicuous – me walking in there by myself, or me walking in there with a giant winged altered? You stay here. These are my people, nothing's going to happen to me."

I straightened my belt, my gem pouch conspicuously light, and ducked out from behind the boulders, making for the road. I'd been partially truthful. Sure, sinkhole miners were my people, but that meant they were like me, which meant they were a distrustful, twitchy lot.

Still, it was a shock to walk into a mining camp again, to recognize Guarin's tent, to see people I knew milling about. And when I darted past them, head down, and pushed aside the tent flap, it was an even greater shock to see Guarin sitting on a cushion at his table, looking the same as when I'd left him.

It shouldn't have surprised me. I hadn't even been away that long. Was I expecting him to have grown a beard, his eyebrows sprouting new white hairs, his back stooped and worn? But so much had changed *for me*. I'd stepped away from this camp and into a completely different life, one where I'd learned my sister didn't need or want rescuing from me and where I'd tested myself against Kluehnn and bound myself to a god.

Didn't feel like I quite knew myself yet, but felt like I was starting down a path to understanding.

"*Hakara?*" The cup in his hand dropped from senseless fingers, and he swore as the hot tea pooled in his lap. He glanced up as he wiped hopelessly at his crotch, making sure I was still there and he hadn't imagined it.

My eyes felt hot, my throat itchy. I was ... crying? And I couldn't bear the thought. I hated Guarin. He'd always stood in my way.

But then he was rising from his cushion, looking like he'd pissed his pants but not caring. His thick hands gripped my shoulders. Not quite a hug. Never that from him. "You're alive? I thought ... they took you. The godkillers."

I wiped my tears away with the heel of my hand, hoping he took it for wiping the dust from my eyes. "They did. Or they tried to. But then I fell in with someone worse." My tongue felt like a leaden weight in my mouth, but I needed to say it. "You ... it wasn't you that stopped me from getting to my sister. It was never your fault." It was the closest I could come to apologizing. I supposed we were alike in that manner.

His palms were warm weights on my shoulders, keeping me grounded. The look he gave me was half curious, half pitying. "You found her. Rasha."

"I did. She's alive." I wasn't sure what more to say. She wasn't here with me. She never would be. She'd chosen a path that led away from me and I'd chosen a path that led away from her. She had told me, in no uncertain terms, that she blamed me for not coming for her. And I'd forgiven myself for that, for being just a child, for being weak and unbearably *human*. But *she* couldn't forgive me, and I still wasn't sure how to handle that. "It's fine. She's alive. I'm alive. That's what matters." He was still holding me. I pushed his hands away. I had Lithuas to think about now. I had the Unanointed to think about.

A brow lifted, wrinkling his bald pate. "Is it really?"

"Of course it is."

He stood there in silence for a while, his gaze boring into me. "So ... you spend half your life trying to find your sister, you find her, she doesn't want you, and that's all fine with you?" He let out a disbelieving huff. "You've always been like this."

It was easier to feel angry than sad or out of sorts. Anger was an anchor, because when you were angry, at least you were sure you were right about something. "Been like what?"

"Unable to face things. Just running past them. Look at what you've blamed me for, year after year."

Wished I could fit my hands around his stout, thick neck. "You think I'm a coward." The air in here was marginally cooler, but the words burned coming up my throat.

"What? No. I think you're a fool. That's different."

Figured, that we could only be at peace with one another for the span of twenty breaths. I put up my hands and he flinched. I lowered them. "I didn't come here to fight."

"Could have fooled me."

I forced my breathing to slow. "I'm here to ask for your help." Gods, how I wished I wasn't here for that. Here to humble myself before this man who had saved my life but in doing so lost me a sister. "I *need* your help."

His eyes narrowed, his chest heaving. "You said you'd fallen in with someone *worse* than godkillers. Who in all of Langzu is worse than godkillers?" His eyebrows shot up as he found the answer to his own question. "Oh. That would make sense for you, wouldn't it? Should have spotted it as soon as you waltzed into my tent."

"What in all the realms do you mean by that?"

"You've always looked for fights to pick, so why not throw your lot in with the group that's picked the biggest fight in all of existence? Going up against the one true god. Kluehnn help me, that's it, isn't it? You're not dead. You're just as close to it as you can get. One of the Unanointed."

It was my turn to grip Guarin by the shoulders. "Keep it *quiet*. We raided a den. It went poorly for both sides. I can explain, but right now, I need a place to stash my fighters. We were betrayed at the highest level, so we can't use any of the safe houses. We have to find a new one. And this is the only place I could think of to come."

He closed his eyes, briefly, as though searching for some internal strength. "*Your* fighters. You're their leader now, aren't you?"

"Best they could do, pity for them." I waited as he gathered himself, trying to appear casual, like this didn't matter at all, when it was everything to me. It was all I had left.

His beady-eyed gaze found mine. We stared at one another until he put a hand to his forehead and rubbed the lines away. "How many of 'em?"

I let out a breath. He was considering it, and I knew if I pressed, he'd agree. The first barrier had been crossed. "Nineteen. That's all that's left of the force we took on the raid. It's a fresh sinkhole field, maybe you can—"

Guarin held up a forestalling hand. "Don't tell me how to run things." His lips pursed. "We can absorb that number. Not enough crews working these sinkholes, and the dens have been pressing the Sovereign for more money to be allocated to mining." A tap of finger to chin. "They'd have to mine every so often to keep up appearances. It's not safe work."

"Neither is fighting against Kluehnn."

"And they can attend to those duties and to these?"

I did some mental calculations, went over who we had left, who might be a good diver and who would be good at setting. "We're still regrouping. They just need some downtime until I can find them another place to go."

"And you?"

I shook my head. "I have someone else to chase." Lithuas, bright in the forefront of my mind.

"They can't stay here forever. I'll have no problem turning them out if they prove too much trouble or if they stay too long."

"That's fine. I'm fine with that." Always kicking my problems down the road. Not that I had another choice.

A whiff of a breeze and a beam of light as the tent flap opened again. I whirled, expecting a miner, my heart jumping at the thought that it might be Altani, my old partner. Instead, Alifra popped inside. She wasn't supposed to be here.

"Is there trouble?"

She eyed me. "Maybe. Heard part of your conversation. I couldn't help but notice your count of people we needed to leave here. And that it included Dashu and me."

I blew out a disbelieving breath. "You're checking in on me? When I specifically told you to wait?"

"And you're planning to take Thassir – *only* Thassir – who

can I remind you we just decided was not trustworthy, and go chasing after a god?"

Guarin's face was either melting or withering, every feature laden with furrows. I held up my hand. "It's not as bad as it sounds." I mean, honestly, it was *worse* than it sounded, but he didn't need to know that. Alifra had her hands on her hips, her mouth pressed into a discerning frown. I was reminded, suddenly, of my Maman.

I pushed past my initial urge to dodge that sharp-eyed gaze. "You can't come with me. The spy network. We've only just started reconnecting it, and you're the best person we have to manage it."

"And Dashu?"

My lips fumbled. "I don't know. I suppose I thought of you two as . . ." As what? One person? I wasn't sure how to finish that sentence, or how to define them.

Evidently she wasn't sure either, because spots of color darkened her dusky cheeks. "Someone else can manage the messages and the network." She must have been real thrown off by my comment, because there was no wry rejoinder following.

"Who? Who have we got left that can do that? They've got to be able to manage people, to read and to write."

I think we all realized it at the same time, our gazes drifting to Guarin just as he lifted his hands, as though his palms could prove a physical barrier against our words. "I can take in your people and hide them, but manage your *spy* network? Absolutely not." Sweat beaded on his upper lip, made his bald pate shine.

Alifra went to the shelf, took a teacup from the stack, and poured herself a steaming helping. "We could pay you," she said casually.

I tried not to let the question show on my face. *With what money?*

Guarin took a step back, putting himself neatly into the corner. "If they caught me, I'd be dead."

I scratched at the back of my neck and felt Alifra's gaze. She was handing it off to me. If we pursued Lithuas with our entire team – the bruiser, the arbor, the vine, and the pest – we'd still be small enough in number to sneak up on her. And if I was being honest with myself, I *wanted* them along. Our chances were better. I shrugged. "Well, if you get caught hiding Unanointed, you'd be dead. They can't really kill you twice, can they?"

He sputtered, a hand to his chest. "They could torture me!"

Alifra took a sip of the tea, let out a little sigh, then placed the cup on the table. "Twenty parcels every thirty days, paid after the first thirty days."

It was a royal sum, and I did my best to keep my expression even, like I knew where the money was coming from. But Alifra had as good a read on Guarin as I did. As much as he wanted to stay out of the larger politics of Langzu, as much as he claimed he wanted to keep his head down, I could see now that he genuinely cared about me.

And the money was good. It was better than good.

"I suppose," he said slowly, with the air of a man convincing himself, "the Sovereign's enforcers would torture me anyways." He pulled a stained handkerchief free from his pocket and wiped the sweat from his forehead. "Wished you could stay." He shoved the cloth away and held out a dusty hand. "You always *were* my best diver, Hakara."

I gripped his fingers, feeling the meaty, familiar heft of his palm in mine. It was the only praise he'd ever given me. He was a right bastard, Guarin.

But then again, maybe I was too.

3
Mullayne

11 years after the restoration of Kashan
and 572 years after the Shattering

Langzu - a cave system west of Ruzhi

The deaths of Tolemne's family are written of in vague terms — the harshness of the surface world is blamed in many texts. So scholars attribute their deaths to starvation, sinkholes, heat, fire, floods, plague, or malnutrition. What is known as fact is that Tolemne burned his family's bodies and then built them a tomb before embarking on his expedition to ask a boon of the gods, determined that what befell them should not befall anyone else.

Down here, in the dark, Mull had long since lost all sense of time. He'd forced himself to imagine more than once what life without Imeah would be like but the reality of it made him feel like his mind had turned on its side and wasn't able to right itself. It wasn't just her absence that affected him, but the feeling that a part of him now rested on fragile ground. She'd been a bulwark, reinforcing his memories and his sense of self.

Even through the painful feeling that someone had cut a chunk out of his chest, a distant part of himself thought, *So this is grief.* He'd lost Pont, and Jeeoon too. His rations were low, his determination lower. Now it was only him, the filter sticking to his sweating face as he climbed and crawled through tunnels lit by blue and green fungi.

Alone.

Every scratch and bruise was a welcome distraction, something he could turn his focus to. Every step a sensation that was not grief. It was when he lay down to rest, when he woke – these were the worst times. He wondered how long it had taken Imeah to die down there, in the thick aether. He'd asked them all to follow him to Unterra, and one by one, they'd died. And he'd kept asking them to go on, his mind always on the destination. On a cure for Imeah.

She'd gone ahead without him, into the fathomless deep. Sometimes, a bubble of hope rose within him. Maybe she'd made it. Maybe she'd gone all the way and had been granted her boon. Maybe she was beneath him, making her slow way back to the surface, her body healed of its illness.

Maybe not. He didn't deserve hope. He deserved every misery the world had to offer him – the crushing weight of the stone above him, the damp, the dark. In spite of all reason, he still thought he should have gone with her. It didn't make any sense. If his filter had failed past the third aerocline, if he'd succumbed to the aether, he would have attacked her. And there was the message scrawled on a piece of paper in his pocket – the one left by Tolemne.

On his way back to the surface.

Imeah had done her best to transcribe what she'd seen, but she only knew a few words of Old Albanoran, from Mull's own influence, so the message was choppy, misspelled. But he'd been able to piece it together. *If this is the end, I wish to be with my family.* Tolemne's family had been dead when he'd gone to Unterra, so did he wish to go to their tomb, to be with their ashes? And what did he mean by the end? Restoration?

If there was anything that drove Mull forward, it was the questions. So many questions unanswered, and he was the only one who could bring them into the light. The thought felt off, somehow, too grandiose. He touched the filter at his face. Was it failing here, past the second aerocline?

He had to keep his mind focused, sharp. Think about what he was certain was true and what was false. He knew that the books that said there were only two aeroclines were incorrect. There were three. No. Wait. There were *at least* three. He didn't know what lay past the third aerocline. He couldn't make assumptions.

Tolemne's carving that had stated the distance to Unterra – he couldn't be sure it was correct, but he could no longer assume it was incorrect. The estimations he'd made had been based on faulty information.

What use were books if they didn't tell the truth?

Something rumbled beneath his feet. He lifted his lantern, put a hand to the wall of the tunnel, and felt that same vibration.

Even with the existence of the sinkhole mines, people liked to think the earth was a settled thing. Jeeoon had taken every opportunity to disabuse his team of that notion. Cave-ins, collapses, shifting stone – she'd described the way an explorer had once gotten his body stuck upside-down in a narrow tunnel after a minor collapse, and how there had been no way to get him out because they couldn't get around the stones, and how he'd died from the blood pooling in his head. She'd said it all with a strange sort of relish as everyone else on the team had turned a little bit green.

The shaking grew stronger. Mull lurched forward, animal instinct forcing him to find safety. As if there could be safety down here. He was going to die alone. Fear stirred in his belly, mingling with relief.

At least it would be over then. The way it should have been over for him so, so much sooner, if he'd had any integrity in him. The world in front of him rippled, as though he'd suddenly dropped underwater. For a moment he thought it was the aether, and then he remembered – the failing filter. He slipped one of the straps of his pack from his shoulder, dug around until he found the extra filter. He had to clean it first. He'd forgotten to clean it. The lantern in his hand seemed to jitter. Disorientation was one of the symptoms of aether poisoning.

Something wasn't right in his head. He could recognize that, even as he knew he couldn't do anything about it.

Rocks shook loose and he darted up the tunnel. There was a cavern ahead. What had Jeeoon said about that? Was it better to be in a cavern or a tunnel during a collapse? He couldn't recall. His heartbeat drummed in his ears, his head swimming, his chest still a constant, unrelenting ache.

And then he dropped both his lantern and the filter, his foot caught a stone, and he fell. His fingers found a groove on the cave floor. The flickering light caught the edges of words in old Albanoran.

Do not trust what is written on paper. I will write the truth on stone.

Had he and his team missed seeing this carving on their way down? No one had pointed it out. Or was he even now imagining things, paranoia turning the cracks in stone to words. He traced the words as the world around him shook, pressing the pads of his fingers into rock, examining the feel of the edges. This was real. It had to be real.

The lantern guttered out.

4
Hakara

11 years after the restoration of Kashan
and 572 years after the Shattering

Langzu – the sinkhole mines west of Ruzhi

A sinkhole opened under our house in the middle of the night. There was little warning except for a brief rumble and a shake. We were fortunate our daughter was sleeping with us, otherwise I do not think we would have gotten her out in time. Our home is gone and we are safe. Now, though, our child lives in fear in spite of every reassurance. She tells me when she wakes up at night, trembling, that one day, everything will collapse. The world is too thin, she says over and over.

When my wife cracks eggs for breakfast, our daughter weeps.

We moved the Unanointed into the mining camp swiftly. There were other people looking for work heading into camp, so it was easy to filter them in without notice. Thassir lingered in the forest and fretted over the herd of cats he'd left in Bian.

"I opened the window of the safe house when I went to find you at the den," he'd explained to me. "They have a place to stay." Yes, and they were likely pissing on the sheets and scratching the chairs. He frowned. "But no one is feeding them. Someone should feed them."

"You don't have to help me if you don't want to," I'd said to him, as we stood beneath the cover of the trees. "I'm not a feral cat, you know." And after that small rejection the last time we'd been alone, there was a part of me that *wanted* him to go, so we wouldn't be in this strange, liminal place.

He'd touched the arbor patch on his shirt and kept his gaze on the branches overhead. "The corestone you swallowed. It won't pass."

"And I can't use it." I'd already figured that part out.

"It's not like the god gems. You have to be careful."

I'd waited, because there was more to this. There had to be more to this. He'd done something to the corestone back in the den. It wasn't burning me up anymore, even as it sat in my belly. But he'd said nothing else, his lips a line, his jaw moving as though he were chewing on words he couldn't quite spit out.

"When am I not careful?" I'd tossed over my shoulder as I'd left him in the trees. Lithuas might be avoiding us, but Kluehnn would send more godkillers after me. They needed another corestone and I had one resting in my gut.

I had to find Lithuas no matter the risk; that much was clear. It was the only way we could put a dent in Kluehnn's plans. Which meant I needed to be moving as soon as possible. I'd seen the last of the Unanointed to the camp, and Alifra and Dashu stood with me, awaiting my instruction.

Guarin gathered his crew, along with the Unanointed, at the

edge of camp. He was sticking his neck out for me, I had to admit. For all those long years I'd spent my hate on him, he'd been there, stubborn and cruel but steadfast. Altani stood next to him, her well-muscled arms crossed, determinedly looking everywhere else but at me. We'd once been lovers, and then something a little less than friends. Unlike Guarin, she'd stopped sticking her neck out for me, though maybe she'd had good reason.

"Thassir said he could find Lithuas for us." Alifra fidgeted next to me like a horse before a race. "We should go, before she gets too far away."

"We should," I agreed. But something kept me from giving the order quite yet.

I watched from a distance as Guarin went over the basics, assigning each of the new folk to shadow more experienced crew. It might be today, it might be three days hence. Never knew when a sinkhole was going to open up. And those first moments were crucial, when the god gems were exposed, before the sinkhole collapsed in on itself.

He found his way to us after he'd set everyone to simple exercises to train them up. Running with the ropes, learning how to ratchet and set. Breath-holding. "Things are a bit different than when you were here last." He gestured to the carts. Each one held a large wooden wheeled contraption. "Risho clan pays our salaries, and they've bought a few new machines. They act in place of setters." He frowned at them, as though they were misbehaving children, and wiped the beaded sweat from his brow. "You could stay. Here. With us."

I opened my mouth, unsure of how to respond. Mercifully, Dashu and Alifra said nothing. The words stirred memories, swirling old and settled ones to the surface. Mimi, lithe as an antelope, the set of her lips always in a half-smile. Callused fingers brushing tears from my cheeks. Maman, stern and stout, holding out another serving of goat-stuffed dumplings, the steam obscuring the space between my face and hers. We'd followed herds of camels, horses, and goats, moving from place to place as the seasons changed, Mimi offering her services as an animal doctor. Not a rich living, but a comfortable one.

It felt like a thousand lifetimes ago, that sense of safety, of being tucked beneath blankets, away from a desolate world. Guarin wasn't offering the same – he wasn't that type of person and neither was I, not anymore. But he was offering some semblance of it, and for the barest moment, I could taste the edges of it. A place to be still. And maybe not cared for, but loved, in Guarin's own strange way. Like sinking into a field of flowers.

Without Rasha.

All the warm edges of my memories turned cold. "I—"

The ground trembled beneath our feet. "Guarin!" Altani called out. Everyone was scattering, running, panicked. A hole opened up, as though some infernal beast had risen and was sucking in the earth. It grew larger faster than thought, dusty clouds rising into the air.

It was quickly overtaking Guarin's crew and my Unanointed. They darted for safety as the clouds engulfed them. I couldn't see them, but Dashu seized my arm at the very moment I realized I'd lifted a foot to move toward the hole.

He leaned in, and I felt his breath near my ear, the vibration of his speech, but I could hear nothing over the roar of tumbling dirt and rocks.

Always a risk with sinkholes. You never knew exactly how far the field would stretch, what it might swallow. Dashu's hand stayed firm on my arm as the roar dimmed, as the dust began to settle. I counted miners as they ran past me – one, two, three – a pointless exercise as I wasn't sure how many had been there to begin with.

The world stilled.

Altani marched out of the cloud, coughing into her fist, her face and clothes streaked with brown. The air smelled of scorched earth and hot stones. She turned about as though lost. "There was someone behind me. He was *right there*."

I could see the edge of the maw now, a shrouded darkness. A shout rose, echoing, from within, mingling with the last cracks of a few falling rocks.

I'd lingered only to say my goodbyes. We needed to find Lithuas. We needed to go, now, before she moved too far away.

Yet I found myself twisting my arm free of Dashu's grasp and running toward the hole. I spotted a harness on the ground where one of the divers had dropped it while fleeing. I scooped it up without slowing down. I'd been down there before, in the depths. Alone, certain I would die, all the loose threads of my life left unraveled. I couldn't care whether it was one of Guarin's miners or one of my Unanointed down there. Whoever it was deserved to *live*.

I stopped well short of the edge, testing the earth with my feet. Another shout from the hole. What was I thinking? I had nothing – no rope, no setter.

Altani materialized next to me. She met my gaze for only a fraction of a moment, and I could see in her expression all the ways I'd hurt her. And in that flash, I could *feel* it. I'd thought what we'd had wasn't serious, was only passing for us both. But it had meant something to her and I'd never tried to make things easier for her. I'd heard the words she'd said to me without ever really listening.

I swallowed my regrets as she uncoiled the rope from her shoulder and seized one of the spikes from her belt. I stepped into the harness, pulling the straps tight. With three strokes, Altani had set the spike into the ground and had the rope secured.

Not the time. Never the time.

She took the rope to the edge and peered over. A quick intake of breath. "Can't see him from this angle. Shit." I'm not sure if she proffered the rope to me first or if I grabbed it, but then I was hooking it onto my harness without a second thought.

Altani knelt by the stake, her hands on the rope. "I won't be able to pull you both up at the same time with any speed. Not by myself."

"I know." I lowered myself over the edge. I was thrown back to those mornings with Rasha, the sky a piss-yellow, the scent of smoke in the air, as I drew in breath after breath and then slid into the salty sea.

I descended, my feet against the sinkhole wall. The world dimmed, the noise from above a low clatter.

I moved with years of long practice, finding handholds on the wall. "I'm coming down." I received a faint reply, right below me. The aether might already be addling his wits. "Keep your mouth shut! You're past the first aerocline. Breathe as little as possible!"

He was on a time clock – you always were once you passed the aeroclines. The shimmer of the first one lay just below my feet. I lowered myself into it, feeling the warmth of the air creep into my pant legs, the hairs on my shins tickled by the flow of it. It ringed my waist, soft as a lover's touch, and I shivered involuntarily.

A moment of calm. A long breath as I filled my lungs from bottom to top, as I opened my mouth wide and raised my head. I closed my mouth and ducked beneath.

Hair lifted from the back of my neck, tickling my skin. Sound intensified, the scrape of the metal ring on my harness against a rock loud as though it were right in my ear. My heartbeat slowed. This was my domain, my element. Even before I'd begun to dive for abalone, I'd taken to the water with reckless abandon, worrying my Mimi every time I sat at the bottom of lakes and coves, watching the bright ripples of the surface above. "She's a fish," my Maman had told her, waving a spatula over the cookfire. "She won't drown."

But aether was more dangerous than water.

I could hear him below me, scuffing against the stone. As quick as I could, I lowered myself over the outcropping below. The man was there – someone new I didn't recognize. He was breathing. Not many could hold their breath as long as I could. He'd be aether-sick after, but if I got him out now, he'd live. I clung to the underside of the outcropping, my fingers digging into stone and dirt, before I found my footing on the ledge.

He was breathing soft and slow, trying to limit his aether exposure. His eyes were wide, his ankle bloodied, but it was his hand I focused on, pointing over the side and into the depths. Pinpricks of light surrounded us, gems glowing in the subdued light of the sinkhole. I peered down.

I wasn't sure what I was expecting. Maybe another corestone. Maybe a gem as big as my fist. What I saw instead was yet another man, farther below, halfway inside a tunnel that looked as though it had collapsed during the formation of the sinkhole.

He wasn't a miner.

The man was lying on his side, his hair brown with dust, blood smeared across his forehead. I couldn't tell whether he was alive or dead. Head wounds always looked worse than they were.

"Hakara!" Altani called to me from above, her voice muffled through the aerocline. And, to my surprise, there was a hint of fear in her voice. "If there's anyone else, they're too far down. Leave them."

He was just below the second aerocline. What was a man doing down here, where people usually didn't survive past the amount of time they could hold their breath? There was something on his face, covering his nose and mouth.

Hadn't intended to go down into the hole. Hadn't intended to linger this long. The man who'd appeared below – he was only *one man*. I unhitched the rope from my harness and attached it to the injured miner next to me. I lifted my gaze. There was a gem on the outcropping above us, red and glowing. *A gem.* My mind blazed with sudden understanding.

I tugged the line.

A wordless, strangled sound from Altani above as she pulled the rope and saw only the one man attached. But my breath was still taut in my lungs.

I couldn't explain to her what I was doing next. I pried the red gem loose from the wall and popped it into my mouth.

Who needed Thassir when aether was all around me?

The lump of the gem moved past my tongue as I swallowed. I sucked in aether, the taste of seawater on the back of my tongue, my belly fizzing as the gem reacted. I was still new to this, but it felt as though I'd done it a thousand times. An itching began at my shoulders. God arms sprouted over my own, larger than mine, more powerful, trailing black smoke. I flexed my new fingers, felt the immeasurable strength flowing through them.

It was like moving through water, my weight now irrelevant. The wall blurred as I descended, the aether still bright in my chest as I kept my breath held. I wasn't sure how much the god gem could absorb before I started falling ill.

A slight increase of pressure, of weightlessness. A sudden warmth as I passed the second aerocline. By the time I reached him, my lungs were already burning. The world swam around me, and I couldn't tell if it was the heaviness of the aether down here or the lack of air to my head.

My belly spasmed, my body trying to force me to take in air. I pushed back the need, the certainty, dwelling in that uncomfortable space as I wrapped an arm around the man's chest, pulling him in close. He was breathing. At least I wasn't doing this all for a corpse.

A rope fell from above, dangling above me. This time, Altani wasn't leaving me. I hooked the rope to my harness and tugged.

If only I'd found a green gem too, to give my legs speed, but I dug my feet into the wall and did my best to help Altani pull us up. If I breathed now, I'd lose the god arms and their strength. If I lost that, I'd lose the man I was trying to rescue. I tightened my grip, my chest burning. One foot above the other. A second time. A third. A fourth.

I risked a glance up. I wouldn't make it. There was no way.

And then someone shouted from above. The rope trembled in my hands and began to move faster. Spots crowded my vision, threatening to overtake it. I could feel my fingers slipping as my mind drifted toward the darkness, my mouth stuffed with cotton.

Hands grabbed at my shoulders, more seized my harness, and then they were dragging me from the hole, the man still locked within my grasp.

I gasped in a breath. A tidal wave of relief washed over me, the god limbs dissolving into black smoke. I rolled away from the man I'd rescued, luxuriating in the feel of air filling my lungs. Knew I had to get up soon, before the sinkhole collapsed, but I had a moment to breathe.

"I hope that was worth it," Altani huffed as she bent over me, her brows low over her eyes.

I rose to my elbows and turned the man on his back, studied his features. Didn't recognize him, but the mask still covered the lower portion of his face. I touched the cloth, the soft fibers tightly woven and unfamiliar. He hadn't fallen into that sinkhole. He'd been down there, below the second aerocline. He'd *survived*. And this thing on his face, this was the key.

"Oh, it was more than worth it."

5
Rasha

11 years after the restoration of Kashan
and 572 years after the Shattering

Langzu - the sinkhole mines west of Bian

Before restoration, Kashan held yearly games — contests of falconry, races on horses and camels, feats of strength, tests of skill. The Queen presided over these games, doling out the prizes herself. Travelers braved the barriers to see this spectacle, and a great many animals and crafts were bought and sold at the market. After Kashan's restoration, the games were declared obsolete, and indeed, the animals the mortals had used to partake had all been transformed. In a restored realm, what meaning did these contests hold anymore?

The weight of the godkilling blade at my hip felt both familiar and strange. I'd always worn a dagger there, but this one glowed with violet light, the power within a deadly, whispering thing.

Khatuya, in front of me, scratched at the back of her neck. Sweat ran into the cracks of her bark-like skin, settling into the grooves. The collar of her gray robe was damp. "I always thought I'd enjoy getting out of the dens more when we were fully fledged godkillers. Never thought I'd want to go back and just lie there in the dark."

"You always knew we could be sent to unrestored realms," Naatar said from my side. He kicked a boot into the dust at his feet, sending up a cloud. The brown scales on his cheeks folded as he wrinkled his nose.

"Well that makes me feel better about my decisions," she said dryly.

They exchanged wry looks, though I found I couldn't quite work up any humor. I was in Langzu, and Langzu was where my sister was. There was no longer an aether barrier separating us, and though I didn't know where she was, the idea that she could pop up at any moment swirled every so often in my mind, leaving me feeling slightly dizzy. I kicked at a loose rock. The mining camp was a dirty, stinking place. And though most of the tents had been packed up, leaving behind some random pieces of garbage, I couldn't imagine it had been much more pleasant when it had been at full operation.

This was where Hakara had lived and worked for ten years as she'd tried to find a way to get back to me. That was what she'd told me, at least. I still wasn't sure whether she'd been telling me the truth. I nodded toward a tent set near a collapsed sinkhole. "Let's start there."

They fell in behind me so we formed a tight triangle, our god-killing blades visible at our sides. I knew the sight we must make, our gray robes billowing behind us, the multiple white eyes sewn onto front and back. Our altered features – we must have looked terrifying to the mortals of Langzu.

Which could only work to our advantage.

I burst through the tent flap. A startled liaison looked up from his notebook, the chain that tied him to his chest of gems clinking. His bodyguard stood behind him, idly sharpening her blade. It smelled of sweat in here, the muskiness of clothes that had been worn too many times without laundering. I marched up to the man while Naatar and Khatuya began overturning the contents of the tent.

"Do you broker gems to the clans?"

It took him a moment to answer. He looked up at me with wide black eyes, his gaunt face like leather stretched over a frame and left to dry in the sun. The grooves that ran from his eyes to his jowls spoke of a hard, rough life. "N-no." He held up his box. "Everything is here. Everything is accounted for."

God gems always went missing in spots – Kluehnn knew it, we all did. But losses were to be expected, and he'd been generous in allowing these illicit activities to slide beneath his notice. It wouldn't do, he'd told me, to react with too much harshness when most of Langzu's citizens were good, pious folk.

The last time we'd met, though, he'd expressed different sentiments. A corestone was gone, and he either needed it back or he needed a replacement. I'd watched his venomous tail lash from side to side. It was time to stop being lenient.

He'd sent other cohorts to the clans, but he'd sent us here to the camp. Overturn it, he'd said. Look for any smuggled gems. Recover them. Execute the perpetrators. Make an example of them.

I took the proffered box. The liaison's bodyguard held the key out to me wordlessly, her fingers so limp it nearly dropped from them before I could take it. I knew how I must appear to her. I stood a head taller than she did, large, curling horns sprouting from my forehead, my teeth sharp. There were times I didn't mind appearing monstrous, and this was one of them. It gave me power, authority. It let me grasp them by their fear, turning them to my whims.

I turned the key in the lock and opened it. A handful of glowing gems sat in the cushioned bottom. Without asking for permission, I picked up the notebook, turning it to the latest page, comparing the logged inventory to what lay inside the box. It matched, though I'd expected it would. No one was going to leave a written record of their smuggling. "Come now." I let my voice drop into gentleness. "You think Kluehnn doesn't know that his liaisons like to skim a little off the top? That he knows gems are bought and sold in places where the perpetrators think he can't see?" I dropped the notebook, brushing my hand over the embroidery of the eyes on my chest. "He sees everything. He knows."

The liaison licked his thin lips. "It's true that I've seen others engaging in smuggling. Miners will sometimes hide the gems when they come up from a sinkhole, and the enforcers, well, they're not always thorough with their searches. Everyone benefits in little ways, you see."

I slow-blinked, my mouth pressing in a line, letting him see that I was growing impatient.

"But not me," he added quickly. "I stay well away. I know the consequences and I'm faithful to Kluehnn. Never doubted. Not once." He lifted his hands, the chain rattling once more. And then he nodded westward. "I've seen the other liaison here smuggle a couple gems. But never thought it was my business to turn her in. Just thought she was desperate. I'm sorry." He flung himself forward. "Please, may Kluehnn forgive me."

I reached down and seized his hair, my claws scraping against his scalp. Naatar and Khatuya had nearly finished their search of the tent. Clothes lay scattered, the rug upended, the mattress moved to the center. "Kluehnn always forgives. He is merciful. But his memory is long, and he cannot *forget*."

I let him go and nodded to Naatar and Khatuya. Next tent. If this liaison was telling the truth, maybe we'd find something in the other liaison's quarters. The air that breezed into the tent as Khatuya and Naatar ducked out felt like an intake of breath, a turning of one moment into another. The danger, for this man, had passed. He'd have to pick up his things, but he'd continue on, would probably pack up and move to a different mining camp, though he'd still tremble anytime he saw a godkiller.

He'd remember not to smuggle away gems, no matter how much he might be tempted.

I stopped on the threshold, an overturned book catching my gaze. Something about it felt familiar. I'd seen a copy of it in the deep parts of the den back in Kashan, in the room with the crates of books. The cover was different, but the title was the same. *The Aqqilan Empire and the Time That Was Lost*. This one was a fair bit thicker than the one I'd seen.

"Naatar. Khatuya. Wait." I heard them padding back toward the tent as I knelt and picked up the book. I thumbed the pages. There. A sheaf stuck – glued – together. My heart beat faster. If we could find another corestone hidden here, we could return triumphant to Kluehnn. He would have the means to restore Langzu. The disaster of the Unanointed raid would be forgotten. Everything could go back to normal instead of this strange limbo we'd found ourselves in.

There would be no reason to go after Hakara, my treacherous mind said. She would be safe.

With the tip of my claw, I cut an opening between two edges and pried the section apart. The liaison and his bodyguard had gone still. They couldn't stop me. Whatever happened next was inevitable.

"Yen, you old fool, what have you done?" the bodyguard whispered.

Two gems tumbled out. One red and one yellow – a rarer sort. Still, a pittance to risk a life over. I shook the book, hoping for more. Hoping that somehow a corestone would fall out, would make this next part worth it. Nothing.

I caught glimpses of pages as I ruffled through them. Someone had recorded Aqqilan stories – of gods and men and long-dead cities. An illustration flashed past – buildings carved into a cliffside, hung with colorful square banners. Something in my heart leapt. It reminded me of the flags flown during the yearly Kashani Games. I snapped the book shut, finding it somehow hard to swallow. I cleared my throat.

"Hold them," I told Naatar and Khatuya.

As they approached the cowering liaison and his bodyguard, I tucked the book into my pack.

I did not relish what came next. I was a godkiller – my truest purpose was defending mortals from their ilk, not slaughtering mortals themselves. I understood the necessity, but the whole process felt beneath me. These were desperate people, scraping the bottom of a dried-out barrel in the hopes of finding one last drop.

I drew my godkilling blade, heard Khatuya and Naatar draw theirs, the brightness of the gems in their hilts casting the inside of the tent in violet hues. "You have been caught smuggling god gems, the penalty for which is death. Your bodyguard has failed both you and Kluehnn."

They fell beneath our blades, soft mortal bodies that had only hoped for more than this dusty, stinking place had been able to give them.

And Kluehnn would remain unsated.

6

Sheuan

11 years after the restoration of Kashan
and 572 years after the Shattering

Langzu - inner Bian

Wedding ceremonies throughout the unrestored realms have evolved from the time of Shattering to the present day. Where once they were focused on words and jewels, ceremonies gradually changed to have fewer words and fewer jewels, and more inclusion of food and the exchange thereof. Or in some cases, the exchange of rare plants. As time passed, these things became more precious than gold.

Sheuan would have said she'd imagined more for her wedding day, though she'd never really been the type to imagine a wedding day at all. When she'd thought of her future, it had always been an endless string of games, of political maneuvers, of obligation and duty, clinging to the clan name that kept her and her family from falling into the streets.

And now she'd given that name up willingly. She'd done what

her mother had always forbidden her from – marrying outside the clan.

The Sovereign's hands were warm in hers, almost hot, though no sweat gathered in his palms. They were dry as the parched landscape outside. Sheuan tried on a smile, though, for some reason, it didn't feel quite right. This wasn't the sort of marriage that warranted smiles and shyly delighted looks. They both knew what they were and why they were doing this.

He could use her, she'd told him. And she was right. That didn't mean she wouldn't also try to use him. So she kept her face pleasantly neutral as they brewed the tea together, as they drank it, as they washed their faces and hands and repeated the words Kluehnn's priest bade them to.

Late-afternoon sunlight streamed in through the windows, lonely beams across the empty expanse of the Sovereign's hall. The chair on the dais was cast nearly black by the light, and Sheuan avoided looking at it. No need to appear grasping in this moment.

Guests were few, and she put on a mild performance for them. She could appear gravely honored; that seemed to fit. Some scattered representatives from the royal clans, including the Ministers of Austerity, Arms, and Archives, stood around them. The Sovereign had left the trade minister position conspicuously vacant – perhaps to remind Sheuan of her place. The hall was mostly empty. He'd wanted to cut through the formalities, he'd told her, to solidify their union without the time and ceremony these things usually took. They had bigger things to consider.

Like the filter she'd shown him. The one that protected against the poisonous aether and that might protect citizens against restoration. Langzu hadn't been restored, not yet, and they had to work quickly if they were to manufacture more and use them to their best advantage. They'd never be able to manufacture enough for everyone, not even close – some people would get them and others would not. Was it not like that for every extrinsic advantage a person might have? She eyed the people in the room. Likely he'd give the filters to them first. His inner circle.

The priest leaned forward, drawing an eye in ash on each of their foreheads. Where had the Sovereign found this fellow? He didn't keep a priest at the castle, though she supposed there must have been some lurking in the city. Kluehnn's eyes were everywhere, even, apparently, on their faces.

The thought brought a sardonic smile to her lips, and this time, she saw it answered in the Sovereign's face, as though he knew what she was thinking.

"As Kluehnn sees into your hearts, so shall you see into one another's. You are bound, body and soul, until you are remade or you extinguish."

What exactly did that mean – was their marriage dissolved if they became altered? Her thoughts froze as the Sovereign leaned down. He was a tall man, aged as he was, his back still straight and not weighed by the years. His gray hair tickled her face as he brushed his lips against hers.

It was chastely done. Sheuan wondered how he would react if she laced her hands around his neck, if she worked her fingers into his hair, if she teased his lips with her tongue. Would he react at all?

He leaned away, lashes shading his cheeks. That was it, then? She was not naïve, yet she had thought there would be something of restoration in this marriage, that sweeping black wall, bringing a cool wind and a sudden, all-encompassing change.

Servants brought out a table, cushions, dish after dish of fragrant food. Sweet duck with crisped skin, in a dark, salty sauce. Sticky rice with dried shrimp that had been rolled into balls and then fried. Cold noodles in sesame oil, sprinkled with scallions.

Surreptitiously, she watched the Sovereign as she ate, unsure of what he was thinking. Save that one smile he'd given her, she felt like she was eating alone with their guests. He didn't grace her with any further glances. The click of chopsticks, the hum of gentle conversation around her, and the steam rising from the food: these seemed her only companions.

Sheuan was still the only one who knew how to make the filters. She'd held her breath for a little while, but Mull hadn't returned from his expedition. It was the longest he'd been away. She was caught in a terrible place of hoping he was safe and hoping he would not return.

The Sovereign didn't take her hand when they retired to his rooms.

She'd never been to this part of the castle. The wooden beams formed a lattice above the bed. It smelled like cinnamon and sage, the curtains open but the sun set. A servant hurriedly left the room as they entered, a lamp on either side of the bedside lit. Everything was richly decorated, decadent in a way that Sheuan felt she'd known once, back when her father had been trade minister. The bedspread looked soft, silken, embroidered with some long-dead species of crane – black-tipped wings spread in flight. The rug beneath her feet gave with every step, mountains and clouds rimmed in geometric patterns.

The Sovereign went to the bed, his fingers working at the sash of his wedding robe, his back to her.

Sheuan hesitated. When was the last time she'd been unsure of how to handle someone? She had her own rooms, but tradition dictated they would share a room on this first night together. Rasha's face filled her mind, the sadness in her soft brown eyes a spear to Sheuan's heart. She felt that pang again, a sudden longing, the desperate feeling that everything happening now was *wrong*. She'd encountered a fork somewhere in the past, she wasn't sure where, and now she was lost, the landscape unfamiliar.

No. She was unsure. She was not *lost*.

The robe slid to the floor, white and gold elegance a puddle on the ground. He was unbuttoning his shirt. What was she supposed to do? She was used to being desired, even when others thought she was dangerous – and maybe sometimes because of it. The Sovereign had made insinuations in the past, when he'd wanted to make her uncomfortable, but now she was as a cat, sliding into the corners of the room, barely observed.

"Did you need help with that?" She took a step forward, undoing the tie at the front of her own robe.

He didn't look at her. "I am old. I am by no means incompetent." His shirt joined the robe, and Sheuan found her gaze roaming over his back. He hadn't told her not to look, and if he was going to treat her like some silent pet, then she would do what they did and observe. She'd expected thin, sagging skin, like cloth that had been laundered too many times. In spite of the silver of his hair, if she squinted she might think him much younger than he was. His shoulders were broad, his figure lean. Scars marked his lower back, valleys and hills of shining flesh.

Without thinking, she moved the two steps between them and touched him there.

In an instant, he had whirled, her wrist in his grasp, his face a hand's width from her own. A huff of breath, like a dog spotting a rival. His shoulders stiff. "What do you think you're doing?"

She wasn't sure where he'd earned those scars, or how. The stories said the Sovereign had once been clanless, had worked his way into leadership. Had he earned them during a fight? During childhood?

Sheuan took another half-step toward him, not working to free herself. She let her lips part, her breasts beneath her dress touching his bare chest. The lamplight glinted off the golden ring at the center of his eyes.

He dropped her wrist, his lip curling. "I suppose you wish something of me."

This wasn't the reaction she'd been expecting. Was he rejecting her? She knew she was beautiful; she felt the gazes of men and women alike clinging to her when she walked through a room, their attention a glittering robe that she donned as her due. Yet now the breath in her lungs turned to smoke, hot and choking.

He scoffed. "You think you are to everyone's taste, don't you?"

She'd never been so thoroughly crushed before, an insect examined with distaste before being pressed beneath the heel of a boot. She was used to unkind words, used to brushing them away like ineffectual blows as she darted in toward her targets. But she'd thought... The Sovereign was old, he had been alone. For these reasons, she'd pictured him falling upon her, ravenous. And now *she* was the one wanting, asking?

She couldn't storm off. And if she didn't consummate this marriage, her status would be in question. She had left her clan, her family. She might have gone to Mull, if he'd been in Bian. If he'd been alive.

Instead, she stood there, humiliation curling in her heart like so many dead, drying leaves. No. She firmed her jaw. This was beneath her. She tried again. "Am I not to *your* taste, Sovereign?"

His hands went to the collar of her robe. A brush of warmth and then he'd shucked it off her with the air of someone shucking corn. She still wore her dress, the room was warm, yet she felt goosebumps rise in quick succession down her arms.

"You think you know so much." His voice was soft, sibilant, as one hand slipped to her back, finding the buttons of her dress. "And you think the things you don't know, you can find out."

He undid them as he spoke, his fingers deft. "How much do you want to get to know me, Sheuan Sim?"

Was this a question she was supposed to answer? She chose something diplomatic, slightly suggestive. "I wish to know you the way any wife wants to know her husband."

"Gods below, what a boring answer." His hand rose, cupping her jaw, before sliding down her neck and beneath the collar of her dress. With a flick, it pooled around her ankles. There was no heat in his gaze as he studied her, only the clinical dissection of a doctor with a corpse. She didn't turn, aware of the angry red spots on her shoulder blades where the feathers kept pressing through her skin, where she kept pulling them out. An unwelcome souvenir from her time in restored Kashan.

One side of his mouth pressed together. "Hm."

There was something unbearable about all of this. Sheuan was used to donning different masks, different miens, different personalities. She'd thought she'd broken free, and here she was, once again wondering exactly how she should behave. What about what *she* wanted?

She put her hands to his waist, felt more puckered flesh there. Keeping her gaze on his, she pressed her fingers to his hips, sliding them beneath the waistband of his pants. He looked completely unaffected by her exploration, neither welcoming nor forbidding.

The scars ended above his buttocks, which were smooth, well muscled. She tugged him closer until their bodies touched, her breasts against his chest, his hips aligned with hers.

He wasn't the least bit hard.

The Sovereign looked down at her, the way a wolf might at a pup that had bitten his tail. "You'd think, at my age, that I've been with countless men or women. Yet I can count them on a single hand."

This whole encounter was puzzling, strange. She was his wife now. Why hold back? If he'd been with others, what had moved him to intimacy then? What did she lack? What was she doing wrong? She was used to partners melting, hot, beneath her touch, their breath quick, eyes hungry and wanting. In those bedrooms, she'd taken control, had guided their desire like a palm cupped beneath a spout of water.

Here, she tried to grasp some upper hand and found only dust, disintegrating between her fingers. "Have so few people pleased you?"

"You could say that," he murmured. He hadn't broken her gaze, his brow smooth. "I wonder what your father would think of this."

She froze. What *would* he think of this? According to the Sovereign, her father was a traitor. He'd embezzled funds. Sheuan had always had her doubts, but she'd been a child when the Sovereign had sentenced him to death. She'd let that go out of necessity, but that didn't mean it wasn't painful, a bruise that she pressed in quiet moments by wondering what her life would have been like had he lived. And here she was now, married to the man who'd ordered his execution. Even if her father *had* embezzled those funds, did that make him a greater traitor than she was?

In one swift movement, the Sovereign had removed the rest of his clothing. He stepped into her space with the confidence of a man used to getting what he wanted. When their bodies met, she felt him hard against her thigh.

She was yielding to him, her mind still a haze of guilt and confusion, lying back on the silken bedspread, unsure of where to touch him so her fingers curled instead into the uplifted feathers of the embroidered cranes. She wasn't ready, shouldn't have been ready, yet in an instant he was there, gliding inside her with the comfort of a sword sliding home. No breathless panting or mindless, roaming hands. Only a slight smile.

He *wanted* her like this. He didn't want her to play at being soft and accommodating, or to grasp his desire like a weapon to be wielded. There wasn't so much desire in his face as satisfaction.

This wasn't who she was. She was Sheuan – sure-footed, clever, the only one who knew the game being played. But he was the Sovereign, and she could only push back so much. She lifted her hands, determined to tangle them in his hair, to touch and bite and find something of the truth there.

But then he moved inside her, his thumb settling at the junction of her thighs. Rubbing in even, steady circles. Her fingers grasped uselessly as she gasped, as he settled into a rhythm. He seemed to know exactly how and when to touch her. She was the one mindless now, as he held her wanting in one hand. She wasn't sure when he'd bent down, but his voice sounded in her ear, amused. "Is this what you were begging for?" He thrust into her, again and again, until she found herself asking, please. Please.

He gave it to her, the pleasure overtaking her in a rushing, pulsing tide.

A coldness, a breeze. He'd withdrawn just as she'd finished, and while she lay there, shaking and helpless, he matter-of-factly pulled both his pants and his shirt back on. "You'll find I signed the paperwork yesterday," he said.

She was still floating, her heartbeat a drum, the space between her legs aching. "What paperwork?" Her voice sounded dull even to herself. Spent.

"To dissolve the Sim clan. We both know they aren't going to make tithe, and with you here, I have no use for them. As I am simply the Sovereign, you will simply be Sheuan." He lay back down on the bed, propping himself up on one arm over her naked body. He watched her, and she knew he was waiting for her to react. So little she knew about him, about the way his face spoke of the thoughts beneath, but this she *knew*. He'd driven a dagger into her lungs and wanted to see if she'd fight for breath.

She was the one lying here steeped in the fading echoes of her pleasure, yet she felt she'd lost this contest. *It doesn't matter*, she told herself. *What matters is that you pick yourself up.* He'd blocked her from his side of the bed, where her dress and her robe lay in a heap. She couldn't retrieve them without either crawling over him or creeping awkwardly around the bed. So she didn't move, as though her nudity bothered her not at all. She chose her words carefully, working her way back to solid ground. "It's what they brought upon themselves. If they cannot meet the standards of the other royal clans, they must be discarded."

Something like hunger sparked in his eyes.

7
Lithuas

235 years before the Shattering

Unterra - a party in the Sixth Territory

The land of Unterra spans the inner surface of the world, split into seven territories. Each territory is ruled and cared for by one of the elder gods. Each of the younger gods can trace their lineage back to one of these seven. Ayaz, the Cutter; Barexi, the Scholar; Rumenesca, the Mother; Nioanen, Defender of the Helpless; Irael, the God of Many Chances; Lithuas, the Bringer of Change; Velenor, the Glittering One. But where did the seven elder gods come from? No one is sure, but one thing is true – they are the eldest gods in existence.

The air was filled with the scent of dianeral blossoms, sweet and tangy. Lithuas made her way through the throng, the younger gods inclining their heads to her as she passed. A flicker of recognition passed through her at each face she saw. It had been a long time since any gods had died, and so it had been a long time since any gods had been born.

It was Barexi's turn to host, which pleased her. He might have been scholarly and dull, but he knew how to throw a party. It was like he stuffed down the fun, the graceful touches, the *style*, and let them come out to play for this one day every fourteen years. He himself didn't really care for the festivities; he'd probably be in his library reading a book, a drink in hand the only sign for him that he was, in fact, at a party.

Voices were raised in raucous laughter in one corner, gods lounged in a pool in another. Baskets of blossoms were placed on tables, surrounded by delicate bites to eat and glasses of sparkling tintean wine. Some pieces of conversation that flitted past her ears were petty bits of gossip regarding the gods. How many nights did Nioanen actually spend in his bed in Unterra, and was anyone else warming it? Ayaz wasn't here; was he quarreling with Barexi again? Velenor had caught a meteor and was making a blade from the metal inside – it was sure to be grand.

Most conversations, however, dealt with the mortals. And of course they did. Their lives were ever-moving, a river as compared to a stagnant pond. Generations passing in what felt like moments. And the gods couldn't help themselves from dipping a toe into that river, feeling a little bit more alive for it.

Not that Lithuas could hold herself above that. She stepped from the main ballroom into an empty hallway, trailing a hand along the carved walls. She'd spent more than one lifetime among the mortals above. She was a shapeshifting god, and could move among them easily. So while others had dipped their toes in, she'd immersed herself, pretending for years on end to be a mortal. She'd borne more than one mortal child, had pretended at love – had even truly fallen once or twice – had fought in wars. She'd famously once run into Irael, also in mortal form, without recognizing him. They'd had a good laugh over it once they'd both figured it out.

And then, in the end, she'd returned to her palace in the Fifth Territory, looking around at surroundings that had not changed at all in the time she'd been away. The Bringer of Change, the mortals called her. Maybe up there, on the above-world, that was who she was. Down here, in Unterra, she was as everyone else – ceaseless and still.

A darkened alcove opened beneath her fingertips. A balcony, overlooking a quiet garden. Someone stood with his back to her, moonlight limning smooth antelope's horns and pointed, tufted ears. One ear twitched back in her direction and the man turned.

Thick black brows lay low over eyes the rich color of sun-ripened oranges. His skin was pale, his cheekbones so sharp it looked as though the spiny back of some creature was breaking the calm surface of a lake. His full lips curved outward, hiding what Lithuas was sure were pointed teeth. He wore a long-sleeved green tunic with a cape attached by silver brooches at the shoulders. It made him appear wider than he was, more imposing.

She didn't know him.

Had a new god been born when she'd not been paying attention? Maybe during one of her last dalliances in the mortal world. They were burning more and more of the Numinars up there, and though the machines they built fascinated her, she could see the effects consumption of the living wood was having on the world above. There had been a tipping point that no one had recognized, where the wonders of the world they'd built had stopped outweighing the ugliness they were putting into it. It wasn't as pleasant to be there as it had once been, not unless she wormed her way into the richest palaces, where delicacies were served on crystal platters.

His gaze traveled over her, and he *must* have been new, because he didn't incline his head the way he should have. "Lithuas." His voice was deep and dark. He took in a breath of the night air, letting it linger in his mouth and lungs as though he were tasting it.

"I'm afraid I don't know you."

"We've not met. My name is Kluehnn." He didn't hold out a hand or offer his parentage. A glass lingered in his right hand, the violet liquid inside still nearly at the brim. "It's my first party here in Unterra."

"You must be very new."

"Not as new as you might think." He spoke to her plainly, without deference, and she found herself intrigued by it. "I've just held myself back from these celebrations." A lift of the glass. "After all, what are we celebrating? When the mortals finally cut down the last Numinars, the offshoots of their roots, the vast forests we have down here – they will die. What will Unterra look like then?"

"That's a long way away."

He sipped, regarding her from above the rim of his glass. In the dim light of the alcove, his eyes were banked embers. "Is it? We are gods. We must know that time marches ever forward and what seems far away now moves inevitably closer."

"There's still a chance things might change."

"Only if someone makes them change." There was a challenge in his voice. She should seize him by one of those horns, take him to task. But even though she was not old, she was growing *older*, and the fires that had burned in her in her youth had become smoke and ash. She couldn't stir herself to the same righteous passions. Kluehnn waved a hand at the garden, dotted throughout with luminescent plants. "The gods use the mortal world as a playground, then retreat to relative safety, refusing to do their duty. We have fallen so far. And the seven elder gods sit in their palaces and do nothing."

"You think I'm doing nothing?" She said it lightly, but laced the edges with poison. He might be interesting, but by her reckoning he was little more than a child. She could shift in mere moments into a beast that could swallow him whole. And he spoke to her like this?

His eyes widened a little. The pup realized he'd overstepped. Good. "Forgive me, I spoke out of turn." He licked his lips. "Not *nothing*. Just not *enough*."

Lithuas frowned. "You say it as though we've failed the mortals, when they were the first to act."

His head dipped then, finally. "Yes."

She found herself moving closer, drawn in by the potential here. There was anger in him, passion, a yearning. She could always feel it, the way birds knew a storm was on the horizon. And she'd not felt this sort of energy from a god in many long years.

His gaze met hers once more and he lifted the glass again. His claws curled around the stem as though he wished to crush it. The violet wine slipped past his lips. She focused on his throat as he swallowed, rapt.

He set the empty glass on the balcony railing. "The mortals should be punished. Down here, the gods moan and complain about what they've done to the Numinars, yet no one has fought back." His hands clenched into fists and an answering rage lit inside her. The mortals kept cutting and burning the Numinars for their wars, their petty desires. And the gods needed the syrup to live. Had she wandered down this hall, to this alcove, by chance?

"I'm still young," Kluehnn said slowly, regretfully. "I want to punish them, but ... I'll need help. I can't do this alone."

She'd been the catalyst before, so many times. Helping mortals wreak righteous havoc on their enemies, facilitating scientific and magical breakthroughs, turning one regime over into the next. This change felt bigger than all of them – more personal, and more *right*. She pressed a finger to his cheek, tracing the line of the bone beneath. It was nearly sharp enough to cut. The touch of his skin buzzed against hers, a vibration that traveled down her arm and settled beneath her tongue. Together they could do things – marvelous and terrible. She could focus that passion, hone it, point it in the direction it needed to go for the greatest effect. She ran her fingers to his chin, tilting it up, noting the line of his jaw, the pulse throbbing quick at his throat.

Had he known how irresistible he would be to her? Had he come to this party to seek her out? It didn't matter. She was caught, had perhaps been caught as soon as she'd stepped into the alcove.

"Yes. I will help you."

8
Hakara

11 years after the restoration of Kashan
and 572 years after the Shattering

Langzu - the sinkhole
mines west of Ruzhi

The Bay of Barexi is littered with the ruins of the pre-Shattering civilization, rusted metal struts emerging from the water like strange, dead trees. Over the years, the salt and water have slowly caused them to disintegrate, their surfaces covered in algae and mussels, while some have been hauled away by scavengers in search of useful scrap.

I rifled through the man's pack like a monkey in a garbage heap, tossing irrelevant things to the side. A pot, an extra flask of lantern oil, a measly ration of uncooked rice, and one sorry-looking side of dried fish. Alifra watched over my shoulder with bright-eyed attention while Dashu hovered nearby, shifting his weight forward and then back as though he were trying to decide if he should stop me.

I ran my hands down his person. Dashu finally spoke up. "Should we not leave him with his dignity intact?"

"Eh, calm down. I'm not going to rob him of his virtue." I heard a little breathless noise behind me. Alifra, silently laughing. I found the small leather folder that held his identification in a pouch at his belt and flipped it open. His clan seal, a dragonfly, was affixed to one side. A piece of waxed parchment lay in the other side, his name and affiliation written in rich black ink.

Mullayne Reisun. Not one of the royal clans, but one of the noble ones. The very same man who'd invented the setting machines now in use at the mines. I dropped the folio onto the pile. "Well, that settles it." I looked to Dashu and Alifra. "We can't kill him."

Dashu eyed the man on the mattress, his fingers smoothing his goatee. "Were we considering that? You did go through a good deal of trouble to retrieve him."

I lifted the filter Mullayne had been wearing on his face, my thumb rubbing the inside. There was some silk in that cloth blend, but I wasn't sure what else. "Nah, I meant we definitely have to keep him alive, now we've got him." His chest rose and fell, but sweat beaded at his brow, his mouth whispering words I couldn't quite hear. I leaned in until his breath tickled my ear. Even then, it took all my concentration to figure out what he was saying.

"Do not trust what is written."

I frowned and stepped away, his litany becoming a hushed blur once more. What kind of mad nightmare was he trapped in?

"Should we send him back to Bian, where he belongs?" Alifra asked. She sat cross-legged on a cushion, slouched over her feet in a way that I was sure would make my back ache after only a few blinks. She stretched forward, her spine a liquid thing.

I held the filter up to the light streaming in through the hole at the center of the tent. The sun brightened the cloth. Air could get through this. But aether could not. What a novel thing. "We need to stop Lithuas. What happens if she flees through a barrier? May be a simple enough matter for a god, but not for us. We'd lose precious time. But this ... this could help us, if it works."

"He's still aether-sick," Alifra pointed out. "Not like it blocked it completely."

I waved a dismissive hand. "Yeah? And he's still alive. We don't know how long he was down there for." I studied Mullayne's sleeping face, the hollows of his cheeks, the streaks of gray in his beard. "Man is smarter than the three of us combined. We take him with us, he makes more of these face things for the Unanointed."

Dashu shook his head. "He's a noble. He won't want to help us."

"He can be persuaded."

His frown deepened. "Hakara, I do not like where this is headed."

"What do you think I'm going to do, torture him? Come on, torture is messy and disgusting. Am I really messy and disgusting?"

Their faces mirrored one another, long gazes from beneath low brows.

I threw up my hands. "Look, he's a noble, right? He should have had an entourage, but he didn't. He was alone down there. He's been through something. I don't know what, not yet. I don't know what he was doing down there at all. But do you think the clans aren't afraid of restoration too? We should be working together."

"Tell that to the clans," Alifra muttered.

Altani swept into the tent, carrying a bowl of some truly awful-smelling brew. Dashu and Alifra were suddenly occupying themselves with some side conversation, their gazes steadfastly avoiding both me and Altani. And I was at Mullayne's bedside, caught. Annoyance pricked beneath my skin. Where were my pest and vine now? I knew they'd sensed the tension between me and my old setter, and they were doing nothing to protect me from it.

Altani approached and I shuffled awkwardly out of the way. Should have just ignored her. Maybe she would have ignored me too, and we could have gone on pretending we'd never known one another, had never pressed lips and hands together in the privacy of a darkened tent.

I gestured to the bowl. "Is that supposed to help with aether sickness? Glad I wasn't really awake when they were pouring that down my throat."

She only grunted as she lifted the back of Mullayne's head with the air of a bitch taking a hold of a puppy by the neck. She tipped the brew, bit by bit, down his throat. He coughed, sputtered, but drank it without opening his eyes. We had no way of knowing how bad his aether poisoning was, how long he'd been down there, how long it had been since his invention had failed, and how much aether he'd breathed in. Could be he'd live. Could be that he'd die.

"Giving me the silent treatment when you left me to rot with that godkiller? You could have said something, distracted her. I would have gotten away."

Altani let the empty bowl drop to the floor, her shoulders tight. "Gods below, you are *such* a piece of shit, Hakara. Just think, for one second, about everything that led up to that point."

I wanted to fight her. It was easier to fight. I was better at jabbing and darting away, at finding the places I could sink in a blade. Better at pushing people away than bringing them in close.

I could feel the quick glances from Dashu and Alifra, watching, pretending not to watch. I wasn't the type to hold things together, as much as they wanted me to be. I . . . didn't know how.

Oh, that was a lie. I knew where to start, didn't I? I let my shoulders relax, faced Altani full-on, my hands at my sides, palms open. "You're right."

She crossed her arms, the muscles tensing and relaxing. "Right about what?"

Felt my eyes narrowing before I could stop 'em, but I squeezed them shut and shook my head, hoping that was enough to banish the impulse. Deep breath, my gaze focusing on the wall of the tent. Maybe I'd grown, but I hadn't grown *that* much. "I was always walking a thin line between life and death, and I kept making you walk with me. It wasn't . . . it wasn't fair."

Altani's gaze was like a weight, pressing me into the rug beneath my feet. "Aye. You think I didn't care about your sister or your need to find her? I just wanted you to care about more than that. You have to know, if you'd shown me any consideration at all, I'd have taken it, even the smallest morsel. I would have been at your side, no matter the cost to myself."

"Would have followed me to the Unanointed too?" I said it like a joke, but she didn't even crack a rueful smile.

"You don't know the effect you have on others, do you?"

I had no idea what she meant. I reached out and took her hand. "I truly *am* sorry. I've been an ass."

"I believe you."

"About me being sorry, or me being an ass?"

Her lips curved then, and she opened her mouth to respond.

Thassir ducked into the tent. His gaze flicked between me and Altani, then down to our clasped hands. He didn't say a word.

I pulled my hand away. "Ah, I was just apologizing to Altani. We were partners . . ." *Partners? Why had I described it that way?* "That is, she was my setter and I was her diver. I always pushed myself too far and left her to clean up the mess. Wasn't right of me."

His raven-dark gaze trailed up from where our hands had been clasped, to my face. "Don't stop whatever conversation you were having on my account. There is ... You are ... You can do as you wish. It's not my place to limit you."

I wiped my palms on my pants, the sweat leaving dark trails on the cloth. "Oh, you're not limiting me. I mean, I know what my limits are. Ah, let's leave it." I was still sweating.

"Leave what?" Thassir's dark voice filled the tent. His face was expressionless.

"Shouldn't you ... not be here?" I attempted, weakly.

He held out a letter to Alifra. "A report from one of our spies in Bian. A full assessment of the current political situation in Langzu. She said she would spread word to others about our location, so we should be able to re-establish contact with our network with some time and effort."

His attention focused on me, and then Altani, and then back again before landing, steadfastly, on the tent wall. "You can do as you like, Hakara." As though he'd not just said the same less than a minute ago.

Why did I want to reach out to him, to reassure him? He was right. So we'd shared one kiss. We could share a lot more without being bound to one another.

Except we *were* bound to one another. I thought, unbidden, of Gamone and Keka, a bruiser and her arbor, their heads bowed together, their bond obviously stronger than just the magical link between them.

Nothing about this had to be inevitable. I was only making it that way in my head.

Alifra cleared her throat. *There* was my pest, finally. I met her gaze. She said nothing, only pointed past me. I turned to see

Mullayne Reisun laid out on the mattress, his hands clasped beneath his chest, his dark eyes red-rimmed but open. "I'm alive?" He sounded almost ... disappointed.

Me? I was relieved – not just that he was alive, but that I was freed from fumbling my way through further conversation with Thassir. "Seems so," I said. "Though you really shouldn't be. Had Irael's own luck, it seems. Now tell us – what in all the gods' names were you doing down in that hole?"

9
Mullayne

11 years after the restoration of Kashan
and 572 years after the Shattering

Langzu - the sinkhole
mines west of Ruzhi

While the dead are burned and their ashes scattered to the winds in Langzu, entombing the dead is traditional practice in Albanore. Bodies are burned and the ashes placed into urns that are collected in underground structures. According to old religious practices, these tombs are closer to Unterra and thus closer to the gods. Even though all realms turned to worshiping Kluehnn after the Shattering, the practice of entombing the dead remained the same in Albanore.

His head was a breakwater and the waves were crashing through to the shore. If Mull could have, he would have crawled away from the pain, left the nausea to swim in his stomach, separating from the sordid aches and pains of his fragile body.

But he was still bound to this mortal realm, the shapes looming above him rocking gently from side to side in a way that made him close his eyes and lick his lips. He tasted the bitter remains of herbs and the faint astringent aroma of alcohol. He couldn't remember if a rock had knocked him unconscious or if the aether had gotten to him and wiped clean his memories of the collapse.

His vision cleared until he could make out silhouettes. People. The one nearest to him was talking. He had the vague feeling he'd been saying something, his tongue thick but his mouth dry. She spoke again. "What were you doing down in that hole?"

He lifted a hand feebly, and then she was gesturing, and someone was tipping a water skin to his mouth. He drank desperately, relieved to clear the taste from his mouth. "An expedition." His voice was the rasp of sandpaper against wood. "How long?"

"Less than a day," the woman above him said. "You've been tossing like a boat in a storm. Altani has taken care of others with aether sickness before. You were in good hands." He glanced over at the big woman standing at her shoulder. She didn't look like a doctor. Straw jutted between gaps in the thin cloth of the mattress, which sank and crackled as he moved. The blanket strewn over his chest smelled like it had come fresh from a year's use on a horse.

Mull was used to poor conditions. But these ... these were *poor* conditions.

He was in a tent. And by the rough look of his captors – or saviors – the blackened fingers and sinewy strength, it was a mining tent. The cavern had collapsed into a sinkhole.

Fortunate, that the cave system had stood so long, since Tolemne's time. Unfortunate, that it had lost structural integrity at that moment. Or fortunate? He wasn't sure if he'd have made it back to the surface alive otherwise. The paper with Tolemne's message. His gaze fell on his belongings, gathered into a messy pile. His leather identification folio sat on top. He'd tucked the message behind his papers. Had they pulled those loose?

The carving. The one he'd seen before the collapse. Was it real? And if someone was altering the records, how were they doing it?

"I need to get back to Bian." If he went now, how long would it take him to get there? He needed to talk to his parents, to Sheuan. He needed to look at all his books that said there were only two aeroclines. Tolemne hadn't lived out his days in Unterra, he'd traversed the caves back up. He'd wanted to see his family's tomb again. What had he done after that? There were so many mysteries Mull needed to solve. To understand.

The woman above him exchanged glances with another, russet-haired woman at the other end of the tent. "Not quite yet."

"Why not?"

She focused on him, sticking out her hand. "I'm Hakara. And by the looks of your papers, you're Mullayne Reisun."

He stared at the dirt caked beneath her nails, his head still swimming. "You can't mean to hold me for ransom."

Hakara barked out a laugh. "This is a legal operation, funded by the Risho clan. We may not be pretty, but we're here under the auspices of the Sovereign. We're not brigands." She withdrew the proffered hand, tapping a finger to her chin. "You were saying something in your sleep. *Do not trust what is written.*"

It sent a fresh shudder through him; all his hairs seemed to prickle. He was going to vomit. Hakara, as if sensing his unease, cast her gaze about and then reached for an empty bowl. He swallowed the bile down and pushed himself up from the mattress. "Tolemne brought the ashes of his family with him to Langzu. He built a life for himself here, he gathered support for an expedition. He built a tomb for them in a cave in the mountains." The light from above pierced his eyes, lancing the back of his head

The War Beyond 65

with pain. It helped to speak his thoughts aloud, to bring them out from the clutter of his mind.

The woman gave him an odd look. "He's raving. He was down too long."

He held up a hand in her direction, his glance a warning. He needed to keep talking, to keep these thoughts moving before he lost them. Before he doubted what he'd seen, before it all started feeling like some strange, dark nightmare. "He was on his way back up. He didn't stay down. He didn't stay down there after he asked for his boon. I followed his path, but his path led back to the surface. He said he wanted to be with his family." *Before the end.*

His things. They were scattered on top of his bag. Clearly, someone had been rifling through it. They might not have been brigands, but they certainly behaved as though they were. He pulled his journal free, flipping through the pages. "I was always focused more on the path than on the tomb. Why would I need to know about the tomb? I thought it was interesting that the Langzuan people always burned their dead while Albanorans entombed theirs – but it wasn't relevant." He found the pages where he'd made notes on the tomb. A sketch of a woodcut print he'd seen of the entrance. Copied phrases that indicated where it was located. Northeast of Bian. In the mountains. Off an established road.

A map. He needed a map.

There. Swept nearly off the table on the other side of the tent. He stumbled toward it, the ground tilting beneath him. A man with sinewy bronze arms stepped to the side to let him pass. Mull only registered a confused expression before he had his hands on the map. He took it with him to the ground, struggling to focus. Slowly, the words settled into one place.

"It's near Sleeping Crane Mountain. The texts all say that." There was a note of uncertainty in his voice; he observed it as though from a great distance. Books had always been his foundation, and now that foundation was crumbling as surely as that tunnel had.

No. He had to believe in *something*. He could be wary, but if he started throwing out all knowledge wholesale, he'd get nowhere.

He traced the road, referred back to his notes. One text had mentioned that the entrance to the tomb lay in the shadow of Sleeping Crane Mountain by mid-morning light. That meant it was west of the peak, just off the road, and the old coordinates weren't the same as the new ones, which put it somewhere around . . .

His finger stopped. "I need to go there. I need to know what Tolemne did next. Because everything we know of him is wrong. It's a lie. If he came back to the surface, when did he encounter Kluehnn? Was it when he was in Unterra? We are told Kluehnn and Tolemne made a pact, and that pact led to the Shattering and restoration. What exactly did Kluehnn promise him? When? There are answers buried there, I know it." Answers to why there were three aeroclines, answers to what had happened to Tolemne in Unterra, what was happening to Imeah.

The man he'd brushed past loomed over him, casting a shadow across the map.

"That would put the tomb right by Kluehnn's den."

Another shuffle of footsteps. Hakara's voice, swimming into his ear. "Nah, that's not by Kluehnn's den. It's buried? It's in a cave? That tomb is *in* Kluehnn's den. It's in his goddam den."

For a moment, all he could hear was a dull ringing sound, his mouth gone dry as day-old bread. But then certainty came crashing back down on him. He was turning to his pile of things, he was fumbling, packing everything into his bag once more. "I have to go back to my workshop in Bian and prepare. And then I need to set out for the tomb."

The russet-haired woman spoke again, one eyebrow arched in clear skepticism. "With who? All I see is you, and you don't look fit to be doing anything."

A heavy hand on his shoulder, surprisingly gentle, guiding him away from the bag. The rustle of feathers. "Sit down," a deep voice said.

He obeyed, though he didn't have much choice. The pain in his head was so sharp he could almost taste it – like rust and wet earth. He was back on the mattress again, feeling like he'd just climbed out of that hole himself. The man who'd guided him to the bed was an enormous altered, black wings framing a stern countenance.

What in all the gods had he wandered into? He took in the blackened claws of the altered, the curved sword at the belt of the bronze-skinned man, the crossbow strapped to the side of the russet-haired woman. This wasn't some regular mining crew.

It didn't matter. "I have to go."

And then Hakara was kneeling next to him, holding a square of cloth in front of his face, straps hanging from the rubbery edges. He felt everything inside him go still. He had forgotten, in the confusion of the aether sickness, that he'd been wearing it when they'd found him. "I know what this does," she said.

It was still new, this technology. He'd not had the chance to properly test it until his expedition, and that had gone all wrong. He'd killed them. He'd killed all of them. The only thing that could make this right was if he finished what they'd started. If he couldn't follow Tolemne's path to Unterra, he could at least follow it back to the surface, to understand where and how things had gone so very wrong.

Was this truly what Tolemne had bargained for? If what was written wasn't true, then what did that mean for restoration?

Hakara was still talking, taking his silence as acknowledgment.

"You're not going straight back into danger. I didn't save your life just so you could immediately go and off yourself. You're a noble and an inventor, and we need your help."

He scoffed. "And what if I don't want to help you?"

She wasn't wearing a weapon, just several pouches affixed to her belt, but the single half-step she took toward him was filled with menace. "Let me be clear, friend. There are bigger things at stake here. You're not in a position to negotiate."

His mouth was *so* dry. He could feel the grains of dirt and dust stuck to his gums. There was something in Hakara's gaze that felt familiar, as though he'd met her at one point or another – though that was impossible. But she was not his friend. "My friends are dead."

A flicker of understanding, but her gaze was relentless. "It happens," she said, her voice light. "Not a one of my people hasn't lost someone, and unlike your friends, those they lost didn't have much choice in the matter." Each of her entourage looked steadfastly in other directions, none of them meeting his eyes. He caught the tightening of a jaw on one, the sheen of tears on another. "You have talked your way in circles. *Do not trust what is written.* What does it mean, and what sort of expedition were you on?"

And maybe it was the way she settled onto the floor near him, with the air of a bull that had set its feet to charge, or maybe it was the sense he got that beneath her bluster there was some fresh hurt too, but he found the story spilling from his lips. Not all of it. Not what the deaths of Jeeoon and Pont had meant to him. Not the votes they'd taken and the thumb he'd pressed on those scales. But the larger parts of it – the hope of a cure, the desire to see Unterra, and finally the discrepancy between his notes and the reality.

"There's a third aerocline." He pressed a hand to the creases of his forehead, felt the dust and dirt caked onto his skin.

The woman with the russet hair went still. "There's a what?"

The enormous man with the heavy jaw and black-feathered wings stood behind Hakara. He stared at her back as though willing her to look at him. She did not, the whole of her focus on Mull.

He took a breath. "We made it past the first and second aeroclines. We thought we'd get to Unterra. And then we encountered another one."

Silence met this pronouncement.

"He's mad," said the man with the curved sword. "Still aether-sick."

"And you're the Unanointed," he blurted out. He probably shouldn't have said it aloud, but they were *not* miners, and he didn't enjoy the implication that he wasn't of sound mind.

The man with the curved sword put his hand on the hilt. "Quiet."

Hakara finally exchanged glances with the winged man behind her. Why did he get the impression that they both already knew there were more than two aeroclines? She held a hand up. "No, Dashu. Let him speak. If he's spotted who we are, then his mind is sound."

Mull shook his head. "I wish I was lying. I wish there wasn't a third aerocline. We might have made it to Unterra." Instead of dying, one by one. Imeah stabbing a blade into Pont's back. Pont's body heavy atop his, the scrape of skin against stone as he wriggled free. Imeah's back disappearing into the darkness. He shut his eyes tight, wishing he could wipe the memories from his mind. "There's not supposed to be a third aerocline, and yet there was. Nothing that was carved into stone down there matched the scrolls and books I've read. One of the carvings said not to trust what was written on paper. It said he would write the truth on stone. Another indicated that Tolemne didn't stay in Unterra. He returned to the surface. To his family's tomb.

"It's there." He pointed to the map. "There are answers in that tomb and I have to go there." What he didn't say was: I have to *know*. If he'd been fed lies all his life, then what was he? A scholar of lies, of untruths, of a spun reality that glimmered and shifted, capricious and diaphanous as the clouds. He had to find out why Tolemne had returned to the surface, what had truly happened next. For the sake of his dead friends, who were murdered by the lies he'd spewed as though they were truth. For himself.

Hakara cast him a skeptical look. "He's speaking too logically. I don't think he's raving. But if that tomb is inside the den, he's not getting in without a fight."

A low grumble as the winged man spoke up. "We don't have the resources or—"

She cut him off, as though it were nothing to speak over an altered with arms as thick as Mull's thighs. "I need your help and I'm willing to make concessions to get it, but going into that den is not an option. We won't fight for you."

He was used to this. His family scoffed at his expeditions, at his desire to find Tolemne's Path. An ill-advised obsession. He'd funded each one from his personal accounts; he'd found and hired his own crews. Why would anyone help him now? His jaw shifted, teeth setting into place. "You won't need to. Just let me go. I'll do what you want, and then I'll infiltrate the den myself."

10

Hakara

11 years after the restoration of Kashan
and 572 years after the Shattering

Langzu - in the wilds, on the road to Bian

Velenor, the Glittering One, took a particular interest in the Aqqilan Empire. She forged beautiful weapons for them with blades that never needed to be sharpened. While Barexi focused on scholars, Velenor appeared to the warriors she saw as worthy in both body and soul, and taught them how to fight. These warriors passed these skills to their children, and theirs to their children.

It was the stupidest plan I'd ever heard. Infiltrate one of Kluehnn's dens, all to get a look at the tomb of some dead family? Seemed like the sort of idea a noble would have – someone obsessed with lineage and bloodlines. I kept one eye on the shape of Thassir, high above, as we marched away from the mining camp. He'd been able to sense Lithuas's presence, and by the looks of things, she was heading eastward. I wasn't sure where to. I kept my other eye on Mullayne, in case our wayward noble decided to make a run for it. Taking him with us was a risk, but so was leaving him at the mines. And I'd convinced Thassir to help me; maybe I could convince someone else.

"I understand that clan members have a way of thinking things will just magically work out for them – because, let's be honest, they usually do– but how did you think you were going to infiltrate a den? The dens are tightly controlled. The only people who move freely in and out are godkillers. Were you going to pretend to be a godkiller?"

Mull just walked stiffly at my side, as if my words were merely the nonsense twittering of songbirds. Every so often, he touched the wound on his head. We'd marched out of camp with Thassir dragging him along in a sling. It had taken several days before he'd been able to walk on his own without wobbling, but I knew from my prior experiences with aether sickness that he'd still have a right headache. Took a long time for that to fade.

"And how useful would what you learned actually be?" I dashed sweat from my brow and then lifted my pack to let some air flow beneath my shirt. Our boots crunched against dried, trampled grass. "So there were three aeroclines, not two. So what? What does that change?" I had to do a little hop to catch up to him; the man had very long legs. I sidled up next to him, until my shoulder nearly touched his. "So? You're so smart, right? Tell me."

He sighed, squinting against the sun, realizing he couldn't keep ignoring me. "Sometimes it's less about what has been done and what has happened, and more about why. It's not just about the aeroclines, it's about what happened to Tolemne, what he did when he returned to the surface, what he and Kluehnn said to one another. Why would someone want to lie about all of this? My friends ..." His voice broke. He took a sharp breath. "My friends died because someone hid this information. Of course I want to know why."

"And then what? You can't save them."

He regarded me with wary eyes, leaning away to put some distance between us. For a while, he said nothing. I held my tongue. Finally, he scratched at the stubble on his neck. "You're Unanointed. From the sorry looks of you all, you've suffered some staggering losses, though I don't know from what. Everyone can feel that we're close to restoration, so maybe it's that. Maybe you were trying to stop it. Maybe you did. It didn't come without a cost. Kluehnn says he is restoring the world. I can no longer believe that. Don't you ever just want to *know*?"

I leaned on my spear as I walked. "Just for the sake of knowing? Who has the luxury of that?" I gave him a sideways look. "Ah. Well, consider the question answered."

His jaw tightened.

"Why go to all the trouble of finding the truth if it can't help someone? We all know you're smart. Yes, I need you to make us some more of those filters, but we could also use your help beyond that. We have a loosely connected network – you'd be joining that."

He put his hands out in front of him, holding them slightly apart. "The Unanointed want to change the world. I'm content to live in it."

"Even if so much of what you've known about it is a lie? Look at you, building machines to mine more gems from the earth, creating filters for your pet projects. What if you put all those grand thoughts of yours toward figuring out how to fix our world without killing half the people in it?"

His jaw tightened. "I'm not one of your foot soldiers. I'm not interested in meddling in the affairs of gods."

Oh, was that so? "Walking Tolemne's Path? That had nothing

to do with meddling with gods? Please, I may not have your brain, but I'm not stupid."

"I was trying to help someone," he snapped at me. "It wasn't out of selfishness; I walked the Path to ask a boon of the gods."

"Okay, well now you could help a lot of someones."

His hands tightened around the strap of his satchel. "Do you ever just quit?"

"So you're saying you can't do it?"

I'd touched a nerve; I could hear it in the edge to his voice. A memory surfaced – a boy, his arms crossed, the fur at the neck of his jacket lifting with the wind. I wasn't sure if the line between his brows was a furrow or a smudge of dirt. "Are you saying you can't do it?" he'd said to me. "Scared of a little bit of water? A little bit of cold?"

"I could if I wanted to." It was the midst of winter – far too frigid for a swim – but someone had managed to drop a god gem into the crystal-clear waters of the lake, and it lay at the bottom, winking like a distant star. I couldn't remember, even then, how I'd gotten into this argument in the first place. Rasha tugged on my hand. I didn't acknowledge her, but I didn't let go, either. Maman and Mimi were both busy, leaving us to run about with the local children.

"Then why don't you want to?"

We stared into one another's eyes. He was only a little taller than me. I could take him in a fight.

If I wanted to.

Rasha stepped between me and the boy, her face screwed up in frustration. "She doesn't want to! That's enough!"

He'd been so startled by this tiny girl talking back to him that he'd opened his mouth, closed it, then turned to go. "Fine," was all he'd said over his shoulder.

How had I forgotten that moment? When had things changed so that Rasha stopped using her voice? Was it because Mimi and Maman were gone, or had I pushed us into the only roles I saw as making sense? I'd dived after the gem anyways once the boy had left, and Rasha had been forced to find Maman to dry me out and warm me, the ends of my toes gone white, my teeth chattering. Hadn't gotten the gem. Hadn't gotten anything but a tongue-lashing from Maman and a heavy sigh from Mimi. But Rasha had held my hand until I was warm again.

A hot breeze grazed my cheek, bringing with it the tickling sensation of a stray tear. I swallowed past the lump in my throat, blinking. I'd been someone else then, hadn't I? Couldn't seem to draw a straight line between then and now, and didn't really want to.

Mull was talking, unaware of my sudden changed demeanor. I flicked at the tear as though brushing away an itch. "Sure," he was saying, "it's possible. Magic is just that — possibility made real — isn't it? And the changes brought on by restoration are drastic. What if we went a less drastic route, changing the environment only slightly? What if we didn't change the people at all? That's assuming there's some level of adjustments that can be made and restoration isn't an all-or-nothing process. That's assuming I had the chance to look into it. It's not exactly my priority, especially when—"

"Wait." I felt a tug in my mind. Mercifully, the man stopped talking. I shaded my eyes and looked to the sky. Thassir was so high and away that if I hadn't known better, I might have mistaken him for a bird. He was circling, not going in any one direction or another. Alifra and Dashu stopped next to me, following my gaze.

Alifra pulled her crossbow free. "Either he's found our quarry, or we're about to hit a spot of trouble."

He started to fly in one direction, I lifted my foot to move, but then he pivoted back.

"I'm going to assume trouble. Wouldn't be surprised if there were godkillers on our tail." I drew my sword and heard Dashu do the same. And then Thassir seemed to unstick, flying further down the road. I relaxed, tucking my sword back into its sheath, and climbed a small rise.

No godkillers ahead. No hulking aspect of Kluehnn, arms and legs eating up the ground.

But we'd only gone ten steps before I saw someone headed in our direction, on a path to intercept. A whole group of someones in blue jackets, silver trim glinting in the sunlight.

The Sovereign's enforcers. Five of them.

I supposed that was better than godkillers, and if Thassir had led us here, that either meant Lithuas was among the enforcers, or godkillers were closing in from other directions. The enforcers had been too close for him to land without rousing suspicion.

All things considered, this was the best choice he could have made. But Dashu, Alifra, and I were bereft of papers. And if there was one thing enforcers loved doing, it was checking for your papers. There was a tier system to it. If you were a legal foreigner, they'd often look at you sideways, look at your papers, look at you sideways again, and then try to pin you with some petty crime until you either bribed them or gave them cause to beat you. If you weren't one of the clans, well, depended on the day, how they were feeling, and how you looked. If you were from a clan, they'd fall all over themselves to make sure you were doing well. Maybe even fetch you a cup of water if the day was particularly hot.

And if you were one of the Unanointed? You got marched into a nice little cell, interrogated, and executed at the end of it.

But they didn't know we were Unanointed just yet, and the godkillers would skip straight to execution. We had better chances here.

"Hide? Run?" Alifra whispered to me.

I shook my head. "Too late. They've seen us." A loose plan formed in my head.

"I've got papers," Mullayne said. "I could vouch for you." His clothes were just as covered with dust as ours were, the bandage on his head spotted with old, brown blood.

Did he not see how he looked? We resembled a group of brigands more than anything else. They wouldn't believe him. I grimaced, not willing to argue the point. "Maybe it doesn't have to get that far. We stop here, look like we're having a bit of a rest. Let me see what I can do." I was passably Langzuan, if you squinted. And the day was hot and bright, so maybe they would be squinting. At least my Langzuan was fluent these days.

So we sat, and waited, and had a drink or two of water in blessed silence. I pulled a few gems from my pouches and palmed them, just in case.

"Halt!" the enforcer in the lead called out as they approached us. As if we'd been moving. Didn't say a lot of nice things about them, that they were used to people running away. "Name and business, please." She was a tall woman, all leg with a short, stout torso. She stood with one hand already on her sword, her posture aggressive.

I shaded my eyes, knowing it would make them harder to see. "Long way out from Bian. Hot these days too." Before she could reprimand me for not doing as she'd asked, I gave her a quick, easy smile. "I'm Namata. All of us here are just headed to the mines. Looking for work."

She didn't change her stance, didn't relax in the slightest. On the contrary, the two men behind her reached for their swords. They hadn't even asked for our papers yet.

I gave them my best I'm-just-a-hapless-traveler expression. "Whenever a new sinkhole field opens, the supervisors are short on help. It's not been long. Thought we'd try our luck."

"You seem to know something about mining," the woman said.

I shrugged. The gems felt warm in my sweaty palm. "I've mined before. Didn't think I'd be returning to it. None of us did. We're just laborers, down on our luck."

Her gaze seemed to say, *Try me.* "Papers, please. All of you."

"I'm afraid there's been a misunderstanding," Mullayne cut in smoothly.

I gritted my teeth, hoping they couldn't hear them squeak against one another. I couldn't stop him now without making everything worse. I slid my hand toward the hilt of my sword. He'd buy us a little time, at least. Alifra was at my back, and I knew from the slight rustle behind me that she was readying her crossbow.

"Is that so?" the enforcer said.

He reached into the battered satchel at his side, digging until he found the leather folio. He handed it over.

She took it, her gaze never leaving his face. With one hand, she flipped it open before glancing down. "Mullayne Reisun, is it?"

"Yes," he said, the relief in his voice palpable. "I could use an escort."

Her eyebrows lifted. "And these people are . . . ?"

"My associates."

She flipped the folio closed again, and Mullayne put out a hand to receive it. Gods, he might have been smart, but he certainly could be foolish. He frowned when she made no move to hand it over.

Instead she passed it to the man on her left. "There's one small problem with your story. According to recent reports from Bian, from the highest levels of our realm's esteemed government, Mullayne Reisun is dead."

The click of a crossbow's ratchet sounded from behind me. "Now!" I shouted as I ducked down and tossed the gems into my mouth.

People always liked to speak disparagingly of the Unanointed. Like we were just a bunch of lunatics working ourselves into a cult-like frenzy every time we engaged in a fight. But I had to give it to Lithuas – she'd not shirked on training them. Had to be believable, didn't it? Couldn't lie effectively if you didn't throw yourself so wholeheartedly into the role that it nearly became truth. So even though she'd been working for Kluehnn, even though she'd used the Unanointed for her own purposes, we were honed to a keen edge.

What were the enforcers in comparison, living on the fatty, juicy scraps of the clans? The man to the left of the lead enforcer fell; Alifra had the crossbow reloaded before any of them had drawn their swords. Dashu flowed forward as I pulled my blade free and sprang from my crouch.

Wasn't as quick as Alifra, but I was fair enough. I clashed with the leader, and just as our blades met, I breathed in the scent of the ocean.

A fierce joy buoyed me. Thassir had known what I would do, had been there to meet me at just the right time. My shoulders and hips itched, the god limbs sprouting, giving me strength and speed. The invulnerability felt as light as a cloak and stronger than metal. I was no longer a mediocre fighter, I was divinity.

As long as I could hold my breath for, anyways.

Wasn't going to waste it. I shoved their leader back and ripped into another one, flinging him into a tree stump at the side of the road. I swung my blade down so hard on the third that she fell to her knees, and I kicked her to the ground.

And then something in my belly flared to life. A fire there, waiting to be stoked. Wanting it.

The corestone.

I hadn't known what I was doing when I'd swallowed it in Kluehnn's den. I'd only known we needed to keep it out of

Lithuas's hands, and she, one of the seven elder gods, had me at a distinct disadvantage. Temporary solution, but I'd thought it would at least buy us time. It would at least stave off Langzu's restoration for a little longer.

Instead, the stone had burned me from the inside out. It should have killed me. That was what Lithuas had told me. She could have been lying, but at that point, what need had she for lies? Thassir had done something when he'd poured that third aerocline aether into my lungs, when he'd held me close and kissed me.

I didn't know what.

I only knew that my insides felt like they were burning up again. A slower, subtle burn rather than the raging bonfire I'd felt in the den, but it was undeniable. I couldn't breathe through the pain, so I did my best to shunt it aside, to focus on the fight.

I staggered. Alifra was there with her daggers, making sure the enforcers didn't skewer me. Teasing them with her neat footwork, whirling just out of reach.

If Thassir was going to act as my arbor, then I needed him *here*. Alifra and Dashu could only do so much. I needed to take a breath, but something stopped me. I focused on the burning sensation, the weight of the corestone still lodged in my belly. There was something there. Just past the pain and the fire...

My mind fell into a vastness of power. It was like lying on my back in a field and contemplating the stars. I felt small next to it, insignificant. A fragile, papery thing as compared to the weightiness of an endless sea.

It was there, somehow just beyond my reach. I could feel the other gems reacting with the aether in my blood, fizzing into nothingness. And there was the corestone, promising so much more.

My stomach spasmed and I took a breath. The burning

disappeared along with my god limbs and invulnerability, smoke lifting from my limbs and dissipating into the afternoon sun. I was mortal once more, the corestone in my gut a thing I could easily forget about.

One of the enforcers in the back stepped toward us. Her eyes glinted. And then her enforcer uniform was melting away, along with her hair and her skin. *Shifting.* Lithuas, *here.* She was all in silver, shining blade in hand, stalking across the wasteland with terrible purpose. I shored up my resolve. I'd wanted to find her, hadn't I? But I'd wanted to find her *alone*, not with enforcers.

I moved back into the fray, giving Alifra a chance to retreat, to pester our enemy from a distance. A *click* and the last enforcer fell. Dashu was darting toward Lithuas, his curved blade moving like an extension of his arm. For a moment I could only watch their fight, the blinding speed of it, blades whipping back and forth, flashes like lightning. They made it look like a dance, their feet kicking up whorls of dust.

A gust of wind lifted my hair. Thassir's landing sent a little shock through the soles of my shoes; his black wings knocked over the lead enforcer, who'd only just found a way back to her feet. His voice was at my ear. "I'm here."

It was the four of us again: the arbor, the vine, the pest, and the bruiser. Something about this felt *right*. We could do this.

Lithuas ducked a blow from Dashu, rising inside his guard in a movement I couldn't follow. She snaked an arm around his waist, twisting beneath his arm so that she stood pressed to his back. Before I could confront her, she lifted the silver of her blade against his throat.

11
Rasha

11 years after the restoration of Kashan
and 572 years after the Shattering

Langzu - Kluehnn's den in
the hills north of Bian

Godkillers each have a den of origination, where they are "created", for lack of a better word. However, they often move from den to den, between realms, sent to wherever Kluehnn needs more of them. Wherever there have been rumors and sightings of gods.

We returned to the den near Bian, handing the gems over to our handler, Millani, with little fanfare. The rust-colored rock here felt unfamiliar, the dryness of the air so different from the damp, mossy surroundings of restored Kashan. But we moved where Kluehnn bade us to.

Kluehnn himself did not appear to praise us, as he once might have. Instead, he stalked through the deeper tunnels, venting his frustrations. I could hear his voice echoing as I left Khatuya and

Naatar in the mess hall to return to our shared room, lanterns making the rock glow red.

"The gods are beginning to organize. The realm was supposed to be restored, the people brought into line, and a new batch of altered ready to fight!"

A pause as someone responded in a low murmur.

"And now the gods are rallying and the mortals have more time to get into mischief. We put an end to this. All of it."

The voices faded as I rounded the corner and opened the door to our rooms. I lit the lamp. Three beds lined the walls, a desk and a table in one corner. Sparse, but we weren't often here. I went to my pack and lifted out the book on Aqqilan stories. The heft of it in my hands felt oddly comfortable. It had been a long time since I'd read a book.

I wasn't sure exactly why I'd taken it. An action born of impulse, a flash decision. This version was thicker than the one I'd seen in the deep parts of the den back in Kashan. I'd thought, when I'd taken it, that the liaison had removed the book from its binding, had added more pages. But when I flipped through to where he'd carved the hole into it, the stories blended seamlessly one into the next. Did this one have more stories? There was one about a lost city where most people had died of plague, which was uncovered by an explorer. There was one about a drunkard who became a Queen with the help of the god Irael and ruled over an era of prosperity for nearly sixty years. There was one about Nioanen blessing a warrior's sword to never break.

Ever since that day in the forest, when I'd spoken to the god, I'd tried to kill any doubts left in my mind. He'd said he'd been in that village for three years, helping those people. He hadn't tried to take over; he lived on the outskirts. And us, the acolytes? The godkillers? We'd slaughtered everyone in the village for the impurity of worshiping another god.

I didn't know what was true anymore. Was the thinner volume I'd seen in the den the genuine one, or the book I was holding now?

I was a godkiller. I closed the book, placing it back inside my pack. There was no place in this den that was barred to me. Even the deeper places.

We were supposed to rest. To wait for Kluehnn's orders. I took the lantern from the wall and slipped out the door.

There wasn't any rest for me, not while these doubts still kept surfacing, kept gasping out whispers in my mind. If I could put these thoughts down, if I could make them settle, I'd feel better. And Kluehnn's way was the true one, the *right* one, so anything I found would only help me quiet my doubts.

Lamps were fewer this deep, and the den in Bian seemed averse to using too many resources. So I followed the sound of voices and the creak of cart wheels. Every so often, I passed symbols carved into the walls, lines of texts I couldn't read. Tunnels ended in shallow recesses, in places a person could only crawl through. I looped back, my heartbeat low and steady, feeling almost as though I could hear the heartbeat of the world echoed in mine. I passed human and altered converts, their heads low, eyes averted as soon as they saw the violet glow of the gem in my dagger's hilt.

I wasn't sure how deep down I was, but I'd not seen the room they brought the books to yet, and I didn't dare ask anyone. I lifted the lantern and saw some carvings I recognized. I'd doubled back somewhere, so now I was close to the god room – the one the godkillers brought dead gods to, for storage.

They didn't decay, so they had to be put somewhere.

I found my feet leading me there instead, a feeling like dread curling at the back of my throat. I tried to reason it out. I knew about this room, I'd seen it briefly. The next god I killed, I'd be expected to bring it there too. It was normal. It was a part of our lives in the den. In spite of this reasoning, anxiety unfurled into my chest.

The door loomed before me, black iron set into rusted red walls. There was a keyhole, and I fumbled for the key at my belt. It turned easily in the lock and the door swung open.

Gods hung from meat hooks, the air slightly cooler and smelling strangely sweet. A breeze brushed at my cheeks – there was some other tunnel in this room through which air flowed. I closed the door behind me. I was allowed to be in here, yet my heart fluttered against my ribcage.

Wings, scales, fur, horns, roughened skin. They reminded me of the altered, yet for the most part their features were more extreme. Larger antlers, longer faces, noses that were padded like a cat's, shoulders that were too broad or limbs that were too lithe. Some looked more human, like they could hide if they really tried. They probably had.

Something about this room disturbed me. It wasn't the gods hanging like meat – they were our enemies; we protected the mortals and brought them to justice. There was something else, trying to free itself from the recesses of my mind. I squinted at the hanging gods, trying to figure out what it was. I'd been led here, and not by my conscious thoughts.

A scratching sound emanated from the corner of the cavern. My breathing quickened; my hand went automatically to the dagger at my belt. I stalked toward the sound, pushing the wing of one dead god aside so I could move past her, the feathers tickling my palm.

There was a hole in the ground, nearly hidden behind the bodies. The sound was coming from the hole. I started to lean toward it, sliding my feet across the cavern's stone floor.

A hand crested the edge of the hole, and then another, and then yet another. Kluehnn's aspect hauled itself out. This one was different from the one I was used to in Kashan, the one that Hakara's people had killed. Its legs were longer, like a hairless wolf's, two rows of four flitting across the floor in wave-like movements I couldn't follow. The back two legs on each side were capped with cloven hooves; the front two ended in hands. The body was thinner, ribs pressing against the pale skin, tendrils running in a row down its back, moving like individual insect limbs or antennae. Five eyes blinked out from a long, narrow face, somewhere between a human's and an antelope's.

There was only one spare mouth on this aspect, at the base of the creature's throat, and it licked the air as if tasting it. A flash of sharp white teeth.

All five eyes focused on me. "Rasha," the rasping voice said. "What are you doing in here, my child?"

The memory finally burst through my anxious thoughts. A horned girl with golden skin, eyes fixed on me. A hook through her shoulder. Moistened lips parting, blue eyes wet with tears. *Help me.* A mouth wrapping around a hand, devouring it. I blinked, the vision retreating. Sweat gathered between my shoulder blades; I felt as though all five of his eyes were seeing right through me to the thoughts beneath. "I . . . couldn't rest." It was the truth. I couldn't.

Kluehnn eyed me for a moment. "Perhaps it is better that you can't rest, as I have a task for you and your cohort. You did well, catching the smuggler." His voice was calm, not the raging I'd heard only moments before.

I bowed my head, trying not to let the relief show too openly on my face. This, I knew what to do with. This, I understood. "We aim to serve you."

His barbed tail lashed, and in that moment he reminded me of a lion, caged and every muscle coiled. "And that is why I must send you farther afield. Your cohort is strong, loyal."

What exactly did he mean by that? "What is the mission you'd like us to accomplish?" Others were in Bian, or traveling to country estates, raiding the houses of the clans, searching for gems they'd hidden away.

"Back in Kashan, in the den, during the attack." He stopped. One back leg trembled and then lay still. "There was an altered on their side. Big man, black wings. He was not an altered. He was a god. He lived through the attack. He escaped. I need him dead."

"The trail will have already gone cold."

It took a while for Kluehnn to respond, and when he did, his voice was soft. "Are you blaming me for not sending you sooner?"

I fell to the floor, immediately abashed. "No! I would not suggest you made such a mistake. Everyone was scattered, regrouping. Our den was in turmoil."

"He is traveling with the Unanointed. I've found them once since they escaped."

It was news to me, but then I wasn't privy to all the information Kluehnn had. No one was. The stone pressed, cold, against my cheek. "And?"

"The group of them slaughtered my godkillers and took down another of my aspects. We've lost them. I need a cohort to find this god again. A strong cohort."

Hakara. My sister must have survived the raid. I couldn't believe otherwise. Who else could wreak that sort of havoc? It still baffled me that she'd ended up with the Unanointed. I'd seen the mines, and understood a little better the environment that had shaped her recent years. But what in that environment had led her to working with one of the gods? Neither Maman nor Mimi had been particularly devout, but they still looked at the gods with distrust. Everyone knew the history: how the gods had invaded the world above and attempted to wipe mortals from its face.

"You hesitate."

I lifted my head. One of Kluehnn's eyes met my gaze; the others surveyed the hanging gods. The hands that lay palm-flat in front of me were tipped in claws. "And what of everyone who is accompanying the god?"

"They are impure. Kill them as well."

I licked my lips. I'd let Hakara go during that raid. A mercy, I'd told myself. A mercy for the kindness she'd shown me once, long ago, when we'd both been children. She'd taken care of me after Maman and Mimi had died. For two years, she'd been the only parent I'd known. I wasn't sure what I'd do if I faced her again. What if I could convince her to leave the foolish Unanointed behind? "What if there was another way?"

A staccato of feet thumped against stone. Claws pricked at my cheeks as one of Kluehnn's hands seized my face. He lifted me until I stood, my eyes on a level with his. The extra mouth on his throat worked soundlessly. "There is no other way. You will go and find this god. You will kill him and all his companions." His black eyes studied my face like he was deciding where to bite me. "There is a woman who travels with him."

My innards froze. I let him hold me, the feeling of dread pooling into every limb.

"Ah yes, you think I don't know? You think you could *hide* this from me? Me, the many-eyed god? She is your sister. And she is fighting for the Unanointed."

His hand dropped back to his side and still I couldn't move.

"Take your cohort and go. Hunt him down. Bring his body back to this room."

I swallowed, but could say nothing. My hand went to the godkiller blade at my side, the violet gem warm to the touch.

A tongue swiped out from the lower mouth, claws digging into the stone floor. "And Rasha? My sweet Rasha — know this: if you hide anything else from me, it will be the last thing you do."

12

Sheuan

11 years after the restoration of Kashan
and 572 years after the Shattering

Langzu - inner Bian

The Sovereign often lamented the inefficiency of the clans before he took control of the realm. He thought that by uniting, they could stop unnecessary administrative overlap and accomplish more. So when he took the castle in Bian that once belonged to the Hangtao clan, when he had every other clan sign agreements with him and with one another, he established ministerial positions that he doled out to those he most favored. The Minister of Trade, of Arms, of Archives, and of Austerity.

It took longer than she'd expected for the Sovereign to fall asleep. She'd learned something of the people she'd taken to bed over the years by the way they slept. Some turned away from her, shoulders sloping like some distant, unreachable hill. She'd often test these ones, placing a hand on the valley of their waist, waiting to see what they did – if they'd shrug away or let her hand sit. Others pressed against her, as if they could relive the closeness of coupling in their sleep. And a very few nuzzled at the junction of her neck and shoulder, seeking the comfort of a nurturing touch. She treated those the way a mother would a child, stroking hair and murmuring sweet-nothing phrases into their ears.

The Sovereign slept with his fingers wrapped around her wrist. She couldn't tell if the touch was possessive. It certainly didn't feel tender. It felt as though he sought the beat of her heart as a line into her thoughts. Every so often, his fingers would tighten and then relax, a twitch of his mouth, a hitched breath.

She waited until his touch relaxed, and even then she feigned rolling over in her sleep to get away. She'd almost expected him to send her back to her rooms when they'd finished with one another; instead, he'd said nothing, ignoring her completely until she'd slid into bed next to him. Then his fingers had settled around her wrist, a manacle made flesh.

There was a slight bit of satisfaction in winning this battle, in him falling asleep before she did, though it felt like the sort of conciliatory handshake one gave after thoroughly trouncing an opponent. You'd given it your best try, but you never stood a chance. Valiant effort. Fair play.

The blankets rustled as she swept a foot out from under them and set her heel on the floor, holding her breath as she listened for any sound from the Sovereign. Nothing. It had been easy for her to stay awake, his words still swirling in her mind. *I wonder what your father would think of this.*

There had been a shift in her father's demeanor, now that she looked back. She couldn't recall exactly when it had occurred, but she remembered him at the dinner table, more quiet than usual. He'd brushed his robes to the side as he sat, the star anise scent of him wafting toward Sheuan. When her mother had asked him how things were at the castle, he'd only shaken his head and run a hand through his thick black hair.

He'd always had a smile for Sheuan, no matter the difficulties he faced with the other ministers, with the demands the Sovereign made of him. Yet that night, he'd not even looked at her, staring into the bottom of his teacup as though the answers to whatever bothered him lay there if only he looked hard enough.

How soon after that had the Sovereign arrested him? How soon after that had the enforcers questioned him?

The hallway was quiet, a few guards doing the rounds. They only bowed their heads at her as she passed, her robe brushing the wooden floorboards. At least she didn't have to sneak around. This was her home now; they expected her to be here.

The door to the Sovereign's study opened with a soft creak. She lit the lamp near the door and unhooked it.

This time, he wouldn't barge in on her. This time, she'd get what she'd come for.

She closed the door behind her and made her way across the rug, the soft fibers giving way beneath her feet. The windows were dark but for a few lamps still lit in the city below, pinpricks of light swimming in a depthless sea.

The circle of the lamp's light followed her, swaying and sending her shadows creeping across the far walls of the room. The ledgers were there on the bookshelf, organized by year and date. She walked her fingers over the spines, picked one of the relevant ones, and pulled it from the shelf.

Pages fluttered as she settled onto the floor. She set the lamp to the side as she thumbed through it. Back when she'd focused on proving her father's innocence, on chasing down the one who'd framed him, she'd memorized the numbers in the clan's books – the tithes they'd sent to the Sovereign. It hadn't been intentional; she'd just spent so much time thinking about these numbers, prodding them as though they were a loose tooth, not trying to work them free exactly, but to discover the depth of them.

And there. Exactly what she'd wanted to know.

The numbers didn't match. Someone had falsified the ones in this book. Someone had taken his seal and pressed the red ink into the paper, just so. And they'd signed his name next to it.

It wasn't her father's handwriting. It was close, but she knew exactly how large his flourishes were, where he placed more pressure for thicker lines, and where he pressed less. The page... it wasn't quite the same color as the others. Sheuan ran a hand across it and into the crease where the binding was. There was an extra stitch there. It was messily done, observable after only a moment's study.

But why would the Sovereign have to be careful? He was too powerful to have to be careful. He'd said as much to her.

He was right in what he'd said. She could find all the evidence in the world that he had framed her father. She could have caught him in the act and still the clans would not move against him. All that time she'd spent, all that effort, all that will directed toward a stone wall. She'd been asking the wrong questions. She'd asked: is my father innocent? If he was framed, who had done it?

The pages lined up neatly when she shut the book; they'd taken enough care to trim them at least. Her lip curled, her disgust reserved only for herself. She wondered how she'd appeared back then – to Mitoran, to the Sovereign himself. So naïve, a lost lamb trying to sniff out the wolf that had eaten her parents.

She pressed her fingernails into the cover of the ledger, felt half-moon impressions in the leather. What she should have asked was: why? What had her father uncovered? What had made him so dangerous to the Sovereign that he'd accused an effective, intelligent trade minister of embezzlement and sentenced him to death?

When she lifted the ledger onto its end so she could see down the spine, the extra stitch was even more apparent, the faint edges of ripped paper a whisper next to the replacement pages.

Her eye caught on something else. There was something wedged in the space between the stitched papers and the spine. Carefully, Sheuan bent back the covers until they touched. The space widened. There was definitely something in there. A folded piece of paper.

Quickly, her heartbeat thumping, she went to the Sovereign's desk and found a metal seal-breaker. She knelt back on the floor, bent the covers again, and pushed the folded paper with the seal-breaker. The edges stuck a little on the binding glue. Sweat pricked at her forehead as she did her best to work the paper free. It tore – once, twice, the seal-breaker piercing one of the folds – before it finally fell to the bottom of the bound book. She seized the end of it and pulled it free.

Someone had gone to some effort to hide this. It couldn't be coincidence that it lay within this altered ledger, that anyone examining the binding and seeing the replacement pages might happen across it. With trembling fingers, she opened it.

Her breath stopped, her eyes blurring with unshed tears. It was her father's handwriting. She'd know his true script anywhere. The page smelled of ink and glue, crackling as she laid it flat. They'd sold so much after his execution to keep their estates afloat; she didn't have much left of him except her memories.

I know I am walking on dangerous ground.

Why doesn't anyone know where the Sovereign comes from? Why doesn't anyone know who he is? How did he rise to power so swiftly? We think we know the answers to these questions, but I don't think we actually do. I don't know the answer yet, but I am searching. If I am killed, it is only because I found the truth.

Sheuan might have been a little naïve, but she'd never been a fool. She held the secret of the filters. That made her valuable to the Sovereign; it made her worth keeping around. But he'd do his best to uncover how they were made. If he found out, he could produce them without her and she'd no longer be quite so useful. She'd be a liability he could easily dispose of. But if she uncovered what her father had discovered, she'd have leverage against him.

She wandered back to her rooms, on the opposite side of the castle from the Sovereign's. She'd have to move carefully. If she made the same mistakes her father had, then she'd just land herself in the same predicament: with her head on the chopping block. She'd have to discover the Sovereign's secrets before he discovered hers; she'd have to set up a failsafe that would reveal them as soon as he tried to move against her. There was information she could leverage in her search, things she'd learned from her time as Mitoran's informant. Though she'd been far below the Sovereign's ministers in the social hierarchy, rumors still filtered their way through the ranks like jewels sinking into shifting sands, their worth quickly obscured.

But if there was one thing Sheuan was good at, it was digging for secrets.

13
Hakara

11 years after the restoration of Kashan
and 572 years after the Shattering

Langzu - on the road west of Bian

Although the seven elder gods were, for the most part, friendly with one another, that did not mean they were always friends or that there did not exist some competition between them. Lithuas and Velenor once saw each other as sisters, but Velenor never taught Lithuas her famed fighting style, though Lithuas hinted on more than one occasion that she would very much like to learn. This privilege Velenor always reserved for the Aqqilans she saw as worthy.

It was an awkward situation, to say the least.

Only one of the enforcers was dead; the rest of them lay groaning on the ground, clutching at wounds, unwilling to get back up. The grass bent beneath their weight as they writhed. In her natural form, Lithuas seemed to glow, a soft light emanating from her skin.

I had her where I'd wanted her. Only I hadn't thought about who I might have to sacrifice. For the longest time, I'd thought I only cared about Rasha. But in this moment, with that sharpened edge to Dashu's throat, I felt as if it were *my* skin beneath the blade, my heart catching against my ribs as though impaled by them.

"Really?" She didn't even look at me, her silvery gaze focused on Thassir. "You're throwing your lot in with them? Now?" Her head cocked to the side, her blade unwavering at Dashu's neck. "What is it about you? You really get pulled into the most pathetic, desperate situations, don't you?"

"And you," Thassir said at my back, "thinking you will possibly have any power over this world once Kluehnn finishes his work."

She let out an annoyed huff of breath. "It was never about power for me. It's about change."

"What's the point of change if you're making things worse?"

"*Is* it worse? What could be worse?"

They stared at one another. The blade nicked Dashu's neck, a thin trickle of blood mingling with his sweat.

"It would be a shame to murder such an artist. I've rarely met a mortal who could stand against me for any length of time." Her silver eyes were edged with steel. "What do they know about you? Do they know everything?"

Thassir's jaw tightened. "They know the truth of who I am, what I am, in this moment."

Her laugh was bright as a fingernail striking the edge of a bell. "You were always such a coward."

The *click* of a crossbow sounded just behind me. A bolt whizzed past my ear. Before I could even understand what was happening, Lithuas had melted into the form of a hawk, the bolt taking out one tail feather before she surged toward the sky.

"Thassir..." I reached a hand for him, but he was too far away.

He only grunted. "She moves too quickly in that form. I won't catch her like that." He let out a breath, continuing before I could form an angry response. "But she will shift again. Lithuas could never stay in one shape for long."

I watched the hawk follow the road eastward. Toward Bian.

Dashu was wiping a spot of blood on his cheek as Alifra approached, tucking her crossbow back at her belt. "Close," he said, looking at his reddened fingertips.

She touched his cheek, her fingers light. "Can't fault me for a little envy. Maybe I just wanted her to recognize *me* as an artist it would be a shame to murder." Her smile faded as she looked skyward. "We're near Bian, and it looks like Lithuas is headed there. That could be a problem."

Dashu frowned. "How so?"

"I *may* have promised Guarin the money from one of the Unanointed stashes. I saw Mitoran depositing money there once. Kept it in the back of my mind. Just in case."

He groaned. "Which means she knows where it is too, and she might very well be on her way to make a withdrawal. You should never promise something you don't have in hand, Alifra."

"And where would we be if I hadn't?"

I glanced around at our little group. "You know what else is a problem? We're missing a certain clan noble."

Each of them cast their gaze about. Only stunted trees, boulders, injured enforcers, and desiccated plants. Alifra let out a low whistle. "We are *really* shit at this, aren't we?"

They weren't. *I* was. This was my responsibility now, wasn't it? I pressed the heel of my palm to my forehead. "He can't have gotten far. Thassir. Go find him. We'll continue on the road."

Dashu eyed the enforcers.

"Leave them." The taste of death still lingered like bitter ashes at the back of my mouth. No need to choke on it.

We were less than an hour on the road when Thassir rejoined us, dropping Mull unceremoniously into the dirt in front of me. The man watched me, his gaze defiant, as I let out a heavy sigh, lifted the flap of his satchel, and took his identification folio. He'd managed to nick it back from the enforcers before he'd run.

"No matter what you take from me, I'm still Mullayne Reisun," he said.

"No," I said, waving the leather wallet in front of him before lifting my shirt and tucking it into the waistband of my pants. "You're dead. Best you remember that. Don't forget how well it went for you the last time you told someone who you were."

Maybe it would have been better to ransom him to his family, to take the money and run. But I had to think bigger than that.

We arrived at the outskirts of Bian just as the sun was setting, a hot breeze at our backs carrying us into the city as if we belonged there. A few gazes lingered on us, but there were plenty of unsavory folk in the outskirts; what were a few more? Thassir peered past the buildings as though he could see through walls. "She changed again. She's in inner Bian."

I felt all eyes move to me. There it was again, the weight of responsibility. "The safe house is on the way there. With luck, she won't have stopped in yet. Where's the money?"

Alifra chewed on a corner of her lip. "In the basement. In a hole behind the head of Barexi. You have to move it a little."

"There are god gems in the safe house," Thassir said. "In a lockbox. I can open it."

"Fine. Thassir and I will go inside. Alifra, you and Dashu keep watch. Dashu, watch Mull."

The house itself didn't look any different from when we'd left it. A sad, sunken building at the edge of the outskirts. Thassir took a quick glance down the street before putting his shoulder to the door. A creak, a break, and it opened. Alifra and Dashu took up positions at opposite corners, Dashu's hand on Mull's arm as he led him away.

We entered.

Dust had accumulated in the shadows. The curtain at the window stirred with the breeze. The fading sunlight reached tentatively into the room, limning the furniture in gold. I tensed as something moved in the far doorway.

A calico shape hurtled from the shadows before her head encountered Thassir's shins. I swore I could hear her purr rattling the floorboards.

"Rumenesca!" He knelt to pet the animal. She hissed and swatted at his hand.

To my surprise, the cats hadn't completely trashed the place. There were a few more scratch marks on the chair legs, some tufts of hair stuck to the cushions, but nothing more than that. "They've not ruined too much here, but they've probably pissed all over the bedrolls upstairs."

Thassir frowned at me. "Cats are fastidious animals." He put a hand out to Rumenesca again and got only one lip-curling sniff from her.

You would have thought I'd insulted his favorite child. He might have kissed me, once, but I barely understood him at all. "Why the cats? Of all the things to care about. You're a god."

His wings curled around his body, the useless protective gesture of a child pulling a blanket over their head. "I told you once that I lost everything. I could only lose everything because I *had* everything. I was in love." As though unbidden, a corner of his mouth curved into a smile. "He was a shapeshifter. He liked to be a cat."

I took a tentative step toward him, felt the loosening of our bond, an undercurrent of relief. "What happened to that god?"

Black eyes found mine. "He was murdered. Along with our son. Hakara, I have not been honest with you."

As soon as he stood, I felt as though I should not have come as close as I had. A cat. A god who liked to be a cat. Even now, I could see flashes of the elder gods in my mind, the few paintings I'd encountered, the carvings in stone. "Why are you telling me this?"

He reached out, and I flinched away, felt like I should hiss. But I had no breath left in me. "Because I want to be honest with you. Because Lithuas is right. I am a coward. I have always been a coward."

I'd never wanted to be the bearer of such secrets. Such terrible, world-breaking secrets. But I knew what he was going to say before the words left his mouth. I wasn't sure how long I'd known for, why I'd wanted to keep pretending.

"I am not the son of one of the elder gods." He'd tucked his wings behind his back, but even there I could see the shape of them, the way the dying sunlight cast the black feathers in gold. "I *am* one of the elder gods. Or I was."

Nioanen. Defender of the Helpless. I couldn't say the words aloud. They felt like a joke, a cruel joke. He'd barely managed to defend *me*. I held so many pieces in my less-than-capable hands. The remains of the Unanointed in my care, a corestone in my body, and now an elder god bonded to me by magic. *Do something*, a voice within me urged. *Make this all right.*

I couldn't even make things right for Rasha. I swallowed past the lump in my throat. "You know that only makes things worse. You've done nothing. For so many years. You . . ." I stopped, my voice breaking. "You were supposed to do something."

He stood there, and if he had any reaction to my words, it was buried deep. "Everyone dies. Everyone has left me. Everyone will leave me." Finally, he looked away, and I felt the bond tighten again as he moved for the stairs. "Get the coin. I'll get the gems."

I didn't move until I heard his footsteps creaking above me. And then I was rushing down the stairs toward the basement, feeling like I was trying to escape from my own life. *Nioanen. Nioanen. Nioanen.* It was a litany in my mind as I lit the lantern at the bottom of the stairs. The basement flared to life. The cage where Buzhi had once kept me. The crates. The reliefs of the elder gods. I couldn't help myself; I lingered on the one of Nioanen. It wasn't a good representation of him, but I still traced a finger across one of the wings before my fingers curled into a fist. I pounded my hand against the stone face until my bones ached. He'd saved me, and he was offering to find Lithuas, and gods help me, I felt backed into a cave, all my choices narrowing into this one clear path. I needed to use him and his power in whatever ways he'd allow me to.

I found the heavy box of coin exactly where Alifra had seen it. Part of me was relieved, and part of me concerned that Lithuas hadn't deemed this important enough to retrieve.

Thassir was already at the door when I made my way back upstairs, a basket beneath one arm. He wouldn't look at me, though he lifted the basket a little. "Less conspicuous than a lockbox."

We nearly ran into Alifra as we went to the door. Dashu was behind her, swaying before he leaned an arm against the door frame to steady himself.

Alifra grabbed the front of my tunic. "He's off again. The noble."

I squeezed my eyes tight. "Again?"

Dashu ran a hand over his nose and mouth. "He put that filter over my face. It must have still had aether clinging to the inside." He shook his head, cocked it to the side. "Concentrated aether. He slipped from my grasp. I couldn't see what direction he went in."

Alifra lent him a steadying hand. "He went that way." She pointed eastward.

Resourceful little shit. Should have taken his entire pack off him instead of just his papers. Where would I go, if I were a wayward clan noble? Back to my family, most like. No. I'd seen the look in Mullayne's eye. I knew that look, because I'd felt that way every day for ten years – filled with a singular purpose.

"He wants to get into that den. He wants to get to the tomb. He said he needed to go to his workshop first." The sun was low in the sky, which meant our presence in the inner city would be tolerated for only a moment longer. But if we lingered past dark, we'd find ourselves packed up into one of the enforcers' carts. "Hurry."

We rushed past people carrying out their last business of the day: street vendors packing up their wares, a woman brushing dust from her stoop. The stink of unwashed bodies mingled with the smell of hot oil and sautéed greens. Nothing smelled particularly good, but my mouth watered regardless. I'd been surviving on various forms of porridge – amaranth and millet, mixed with whatever else we could find.

The gates to the inner city were still open, and we passed into a district of fine buildings, the breeze marginally cooler, bringing with it a faint scent of smoke from the dried-up lakebed, where bodies were burned daily.

Thassir kept his wings tight by his sides, his head low, that stupid basket still tucked beneath an arm.

I fell back to walk beside him, my steps quick. "Where is she? Do you know?"

His gaze wandered over the buildings, finally settling on one. I followed his gaze, and then swore, hoping I was wrong, or that he was. "Really? The *castle*?"

He grimaced, but nodded.

"What in all the depths could she be doing in there?"

"Hiding, possibly," Dashu said.

I stopped. "Which of you knows where the Reisun family's workshop is?"

Thassir ruffled his wings. "I do."

Was this how I would have to manage things from now on? Splitting our group into smaller and smaller pieces to handle problems that were too large for us all? Nothing for it. I handed the box of coins to Alifra. "Alifra. Dashu. Find some of our informants in the city and give them the money to pay Guarin. Then go to the castle. Watch it for anything unusual. We'll have to hope Lithuas holes up in there for a bit. Thassir will take me to the workshop. Dashu, you can take the god gems."

Thassir's arm tightened around the basket, his voice stiff. "I would prefer to keep them with me. You might need them."

I didn't have time to argue; I just waved Dashu and Alifra away. They nodded and disappeared down an alley. The longer we spent here, the more likely it was that Mullayne would get away. And we needed more of those filters – the possibilities they opened for the Unanointed were vast. We could cross barriers more easily, we could retrieve gems from mines ourselves, we could access the deeper tunnels of dens.

And dammit, he knew too much about us, about Thassir. I couldn't let him go free without guarantees.

I followed Thassir past whitewashed plaster buildings, their facades regularly cleaned of dust. Even the cobblestones beneath my feet were cleaner than they were in the outskirts. Clay roof tiles in red, blue, and green shone bright by the setting sun, so much that I had to squint against the glare when I looked at them.

Here, the people about their business were mostly servants, bearing embroidered patches from each of the clans. I spotted several with the Sovereign's cherry-blossom emblem. They carried messages and goods, arms laden with cloth or produce.

Still, the bustle of the day was fading as people returned home for their evening meals, which meant the streets were quickly emptying. Which meant we were soon going to stand out.

"There." Without seeming to think about it, Thassir grabbed my wrist with his free hand, tugging gently to pull me abreast of him. The dry, soft scratch of a claw at a tendon, the roughness of a callused palm against sensitive skin.

I swallowed, my belly lurching. I opened my mouth to say something, anything. But his hand came away and I saw the workshop in front of us, the door painted with the Reisun dragonfly emblem. We exchanged glances and approached slowly, quietly.

The workshop itself was closed, the workers gone for the day. But a small scratching sound emanated from nearby. It took me only a moment to pinpoint it. Down the narrow alley on the south side of the building, someone crouched by a window.

He'd escaped twice and had let himself be caught twice. I took a step into the alley, beckoning for Thassir to cut him off on the other side. Mullayne didn't seem to notice, his focus on the window, his lip caught between his teeth as he wedged the nib of a pen into the gap between the shutters.

As soon as I saw the shadow of Thassir's wing on the other side of the building, I spoke. "You're a pretty sorry thief, you know that?"

He dropped the pen, his gaze darting around for an escape. There were no easy handholds here, no gaps to squeeze through — only two solid walls and the narrow strip of street between. "I need to get inside. You want more filters? My materials to build them are here. And I have notes. Papers. Books. You can't expect me to help you if I don't have any resources. You think what I want is selfish? Foolish? Somewhere in that den, in that tomb, is the truth. Tolemne wrote the truth there. You didn't think to make filters against aether. I did. Imagine what else I could do with more of the truth – about the god pact and restoration."

I opened my mouth.

The window burst open. A familiar face peered out into the alley, glancing with a frown at me and then Thassir, before finally settling on Mullayne. The eyes of Mitoran's informant widened.

"Cousin?"

14
Mullayne

11 years after the restoration of Kashan
and 572 years after the Shattering

Langzu - inner Bian, the Reisun workshop

The Hangtao clan was once the most powerful royal clan in all of Langzu, their estates and holdings representing the largest fraction of the realm's riches. And in one bloody night, the Sovereign and his enforcers eliminated them entirely. It was a calculated attack, undertaken when the majority of clan members were in residence at their Bian estate. While most of the clan was eliminated in Bian, simultaneous attacks occurred in Ruzhi, Xiazen, and the Hangtao's country estate.

They were given no quarter and no chance to retaliate.

This wasn't exactly how Mull had planned on reuniting with his cousin. He'd imagined having far less dirt on him, for instance, and he'd imagined Imeah by his side, fully restored to health. He certainly hadn't imagined being trailed by two members of the much-reduced ranks of the Unanointed – one the rudest woman he'd ever met, and the other the biggest altered he'd ever seen.

For one of the few times in his life, he was at a complete loss for words. He could only stare into Sheuan's face, a face that seemed oddly unchanged since he'd seen her last. The same luminous black eyes, the same slight line between her brows when she frowned. He felt so much older; shouldn't she, then, *look* older? He wasn't sure where to begin, how to explain.

Sheuan put a hand on his shoulder, and he felt suddenly as though everything would be all right. She was *family* and she knew who he was and he was home, in a manner of speaking. But then her gaze focused on Hakara once more. Right. He'd brought trouble with him.

To his surprise, she addressed Hakara first. "What are you doing here?" Her voice cut through the darkening alley. "Did you find your sister?"

And now his mind was reeling again, the headache he'd borne for the last twelve days needling at the backs of his eyeballs. "You know one another?"

Sheuan took a breath, held it, let it out in one quick *whoosh*. "Never mind that. You'll get picked up by enforcers in another moment, the state you're in. Get inside. All of you."

And then she was closing the window.

For a moment the three of them just stood there in the alley. The brightness of sunset was fading into the cool blues of a new night, the heat emanating from the walls beginning to fade. What was Sheuan doing in the workshop after hours? The scraping sound of the front door seemed to unstick them all. Thassir and Hakara flanked him, as though they thought he might still try to run, Hakara taking him by the upper arm. What was her plan here? Ransom him? He'd welcome that.

Not that Sheuan or her family could pay.

She shut the door quietly behind them and turned the lock. The workshop felt like a place asleep, projects draped in cloth, awaiting the return of workers the next day, only one lamp lit behind a screen, leaving everything else to fade into grays and browns. The smell of greased metal and sawdust filled the air. By all the gods, old and new, he'd missed this place.

Only, he was used to Pont lounging in a corner, or Imeah striding in with some new book to show him, or even Jeeoon sorting through whatever scraps he had for things she could use. It no longer felt like a place asleep to him; it felt like a place that had died.

Mull slipped free of Hakara's grip, and she let him. Where could he run to now, after all?

Sheuan turned, and he was falling into her arms, gripping her so tightly he wasn't sure she could breathe. So many times, under the weight of the earth, he'd thought he'd be trapped there. He'd thought he'd never return to the surface. Even after Hakara had fished him out of the sinkhole, nothing had felt quite real, his head still swimming on the road to Bian. Yet here, now, it cleared, everything crystallizing into the ginger scent of his cousin's perfume, the firm feel of her back beneath his fingertips. This was *real*.

She was saying something, he wasn't sure what; something soft and soothing, the litany of a mother to a frightened child. He made something out – "I thought you were dead."

It wasn't until he pulled away that he noticed the tears on his cheeks. He dashed them away. What was the use of tears? They did nothing for him, or for anyone.

In spite of the shine to her eyes, Sheuan was watching him in that peculiar way of hers, as though every blink was saving some judgment of him in the recesses of her mind. Her hand was still on his shoulder, the dust he'd brought with him now clinging to the front of her dress.

Her dress.

He'd been so focused before on her face that he hadn't seen what she was wearing. Mull didn't know a terrible lot about fashion, but he could spot a finely made piece of clothing. And it wasn't just the dress. The comb in her hair was dripping with pearls, her wrists heavy with jade. This ... this was different.

Pieces started to arrange themselves in his mind. She was here in his workshop after hours, she was wearing clothes that were richer than the Sim family status indicated, and the one lit lamp was located in the corner where he'd once done his work. A place that was now separated from the rest of the workshop by a screen.

His voice felt strangely steady, given the absolute maelstrom in his mind and his heart. "Sheuan, what did you do?"

As soon as she opened her mouth, he knew she was going to lie to him. So he didn't listen – what was the point? Instead, he brushed past her, past her flailing explanations.

"Mullayne ..." Hakara's voice. He didn't stop to hear her either. No one he cared about ever called him by his full name. Not unless he counted his mother and her disappointed moments.

He drew the screen to the side.

The place was a mess. Books scattered across surfaces, a notebook with her handwriting on it, bits and pieces of discarded cloth littered over the floor. And a neat row of newly manufactured filters, lying next to the window he always looked out of to daydream.

He'd specifically put the prototype in a box, had labeled it, *twice*, as not to be opened. Of course she'd gone and opened it anyway. He should have known she would. He was wrong to think that nothing here had changed. *Everything* had changed.

"I was going to tell you," she said from behind him.

"You were going to *have* to." He ran a hand through his hair and then looked at his palm, disgusted. He needed a bath. "Are you selling them?"

"No," she said quickly. Too quickly.

"Then what are you doing?"

She hesitated, her gaze finding a spot somewhere past his shoulder. Someone else might not have noticed, but Mull knew her.

"The truth, Sheuan. *Please*."

She sighed. "The Sim clan has been dissolved. I've married."

Hakara let out a low whistle. "And married well, it seems, judging by that comb."

Her jaw firmed. "It wasn't what I wanted."

No. It was *exactly* what she'd wanted. Sheuan didn't let a chance pass her by; she never faltered or fumbled opportunities. She never could afford to. He'd seen the deft way she moved through social circles. A woman in her position within a dying clan, everyone waiting to see when they could pounce upon the corpse? She couldn't have done it without a great deal of skill. She didn't let a thing happen without a plan.

"Who?" Gods help him, he knew the answer before she said it.

Her tongue flicked out to wet her lips, her gaze casting involuntarily toward the corners of the space, as if there were an escape there he couldn't see. "The Sovereign."

There it was, still a shock after all. When he spoke, he couldn't feel his lips moving. "You leveraged the filters, didn't you? My filters?"

Her stance widened, her eyes locked onto his. "Yes."

"For mining? Exploration?"

She shook her head. "Mull, you never really thought through what they might be able to do. If they can keep the aether out, then maybe they can protect a person against restoration."

He reached out, fumbled for the chair at the desk, sitting in it before noticing there was still a book laid out on it, the pages spread. He didn't care. "*Restoration?*" Theoretically, it could work. If the aether existed as particles in the air, and restoration was enacted through aether, and alteration was initiated through breathing in that aether, then filtering those particles out would mean avoiding restoration. You might be able to come through unscathed – without becoming altered or having your matter transformed. But someone's matter still had to be transformed in order for restoration to work.

Sheuan was nodding. He'd been speaking aloud. So he finished the thought. "Just not the people the Sovereign chooses. Including the Sovereign himself."

Hakara pushed past him. "He's pitting this invention, his entire realm, against Kluehnn himself. If that's what he wants, we should be working together – the Unanointed and the clans."

Sheuan picked up one of the finished filters. Mull couldn't help but notice the craftsmanship of it, the crisp, clean lines. "Even if we distributed the secret of how these are made to everyone in the realm, there simply aren't enough resources. We can't protect everyone. I don't think the Sovereign *wants* to protect everyone."

He removed the book from beneath him, letting it fall to the floor, scattering bits of cloth in its wake. His head throbbed and he rubbed at his temples in an effort to assuage it. "Sheuan. I left you in charge of my workshop while I was gone. You were supposed to watch over the workers and sell my wares. You were not supposed to start a *revolution*."

She gave him a little half-shrug, and he knew that was all the apology he'd get from her. Her attention went back to Hakara. "Did you find your sister?" she asked again. She made the question sound casual, though Mull knew from the strain in her voice that it was anything but.

Hakara nodded. "I did. She's well."

It was a less than satisfactory answer – Mull could see it from the way Sheuan turned and busied herself with stacking the opened books on the desk. She couldn't pretend it didn't matter to her, so she was doing the next best thing and hiding her expression. He remembered a time, back when they were young children, when she cast her true feelings out for the world to see. Now, she was a closed box he only sometimes could crack the lid on.

And then everything fell into place. Her staying late at the workshop, the filters, the enforcers outside the city. "It was you. You told everyone I was dead."

She stopped, her hands lingering on a book. "I had to, Mull, it was the only way."

"And now what? Now that I'm back?"

He'd never seen such a sharp, calculating look in her eye. "I don't know. It would be better for me if you stayed dead."

She said it matter-of-factly, yet it pierced him in places still tender from the deaths of his friends. *If he stayed dead.*

He shoved aside his feelings, examining the thought rationally, and that was when he knew. It might have hurt, but she'd unknowingly done him a favor. That was how he could get into the den and access the tomb. "What if I *did* stay dead?" he said slowly. "Have me arrested," he added. "Say that I murdered Mull. I have my papers; I don't look like myself. The enforcers outside the city didn't recognize me. Do it quietly. I'll plead clemency from Kluehnn. They'll take me to the closest den."

Hakara was glancing at the shutters, the light fading to full darkness. Her foot tapped. "It's a terrible idea. You'd never survive."

"Well that would work out fine for Sheuan, wouldn't it?" He couldn't help the bitterness in his voice.

His cousin reached for him and then let her hand fall back to her side. "Why do you want to get into the den?"

So he explained, feeling much more level-headed than the last time he'd done so. And the more he spoke, the surer he felt. What he'd seen written on stone was real.

Sheuan was nodding, her expression thoughtful. "I saw a book in Kashan – it said things I knew weren't true. If there's a third aerocline that isn't mentioned in any of your books, then we don't know how much of our information has been corrupted."

"The Unanointed need his help," Hakara broke in. "I'm not sending him to his death, even if that would be convenient for you."

Thassir grunted. "There are more filters here, if we need them. If what he says is true, knowing more about why Tolemne returned to the surface and the nature of the bargain he made with Kluehnn could only help us."

"It's a terrible plan," Hakara said. "We have no scheme to get him out."

"Are all our plans not terrible?" Thassir said, his voice light. "If he's clever, let him find a way out."

Mull raised an eyebrow. "And do you really want to be dragging me along with you?" He could taste victory, just a moment away. Yes, victory meant being tossed in with criminals and then into a den for hard labor, but if he could find that tomb . . . he knew, he just *knew* he'd find the answers he sought.

"Fine." Hakara's lip curled in a grim smile. "But I need those filters and something else in return, since this works out so well for both of you."

Sheuan's eyes narrowed. "And what is that?"

"Get me into the castle."

15
Rasha

11 years after the restoration of Kashan
and 572 years after the Shattering

Langzu - in the wilds

Most of the elder gods, except Ayaz, have dallied with mortals at one time or another. Even more of the younger gods did so. Mortals once proudly traced their lineage back to the gods, their abilities to work with magic stronger than that of their brethren. As time went on, and the world changed, mortals desired and searched for this connection less and less.

The sun shone through the clouds, hot against the top of my scalp, burning the bare skin at the base of my horns. Gravel crunched beneath my feet. Moisture filled the wind, but no rain dropped, just a crackling, electric energy prickling the hairs of my arms.

Khatuya and Naatar strode behind me, their voices carrying with the breeze. "I'll ask for a bath as my reward when we return," Naatar said. I heard him scratch at the dried scales of his arms. "The weather here is terrible for my skin. I'm not used to it. Imagine – a tub with steaming water, the surface draped in flower petals, just a sprinkle of lavender oil on the surface. And a soak so long that every finger and toe is as wrinkled as an old woman's face."

Khatuya laughed. "What would the gods think if they knew you wish to bathe in flowers and not the blood of your enemies?"

"Please, we can't all have skin as thick and tough as tree bark. What would *you* ask for?"

A long, heavy sigh. "Meat. Something from Kashan. The chicken here is so stringy and tough. Maybe I'll ask that we be stationed back there."

I closed my eyes tight, and there she was again in the black depths behind my eyelids. The horned girl with the golden skin, her eyes pleading. I shook my head. Everything seemed to remind me of her lately. The infusers in the cavern just inside the den entrance, chained to the stone, reminded me of the gods hanging next to her. The glowing gems the altered placed between their teeth reminded me of the glow of the young god's aura.

But where had I seen her? Had it only been in dreams? Nightmares? It felt too real, too solid, yet at the same time I could not place it.

Five days on the road, and each time I lay down to sleep, I thought of her. I pressed a palm to my forehead. "What makes you so sure we're coming back?"

The footsteps behind me halted.

"Rasha?" Naatar's voice, soft and hesitant.

Crunching steps as Khatuya approached. "Of course we're coming back. And we'll drag that god's body back with us."

I pivoted to face her. Golden hills surrounded us, punctuated by the dark green of patchy trees. Above, a few birds wheeled in the sky. A *caw* echoed off the hills. "We've only killed one other god before."

"So?" Khatuya had to crane her neck to look me in the eye. She was short but powerful, her body compact and muscular. "What's one more?" Naatar hesitated behind her, watching us as he followed at a slower pace.

"This god was in the depths of the den. Did you not hear the whispers? He cut down godkillers like they were *nothing*. And what of the rumors of the other god? The one who fought on Kluehnn's side?"

Khatuya scoffed, tossing her black hair over her shoulder. "Rumors. No one speaks that now."

"Because they were silenced."

"Rasha." Naatar's voice was a warning. He stood behind Khatuya, his hand touching her shoulder briefly before falling back to his side. "Think about what you're trying to say."

I didn't know what I was trying to say, only that everything felt wrong. I longed for the days when I could sink into my faith, when everything felt right. I'd once believed in Hakara above all else. Then I believed in Kluehnn. And now? I wasn't sure. The world had battered at my defenses, peeling back the shell I'd kept around my heart. I'd left the book in my pack when we'd gathered our supplies and checked our blades. It seemed to weigh twice as much as everything else, the square shape of it a pressure against my back. "The gods are organizing. I've heard Kluehnn say it."

"Then it is true." Naatar shifted from foot to foot, his tail undulating behind him. "Shouldn't we keep going? Kluehnn said his aspect fell somewhere near Ruzhi. We don't know where this god will be, but if he's as powerful as you say, we should be able to track him from a distance. We can stop in Bian, refill our water and buy more supplies."

Khatuya and I stared at one another, neither of us moving. "The gods are organizing . . ." she repeated slowly.

"What if there was another way to end this conflict?" I started to walk again, just to keep Naatar off my back. Khatuya followed at my shoulder. "The gods came here to conquer the mortals. We kill them, we keep them from doing that. But it's been so many years. What if we could send them back to Unterra and seal the way? Kluehnn gets the surface, he gets our faith, and the gods are forever imprisoned."

"If you keep speaking that way, you'll be named impure." Khatuya's voice was level. She said it like a joke, but I felt the whip of those words, the fear they were meant to inspire. I opened my mouth to reply, but she kept talking. "The gods cannot get back to Unterra. They do not want to. If we gave them even a moment's clemency, they would take over the surface. Is that what you want?"

"No, of course not." Frustration welled within me. She wasn't listening. She wasn't willing to consider what I was saying at all.

"Kluehnn protects us. He protects all of us. As he wills it."

"And this is what he wills? Sending us chasing after a god when Langzu awaits its turn at restoration?"

Naatar shot me a sharp look that clearly said, *Not here*.

But Khatuya was always quick to defend Kluehnn. "He is the many-eyed god, the all-seeing."

The question I'd asked still sat uneasy in my belly. Why, if he was all-seeing, did he need our help to find and kill the gods? I knew what Khatuya would say. That it was a test. That it was always a test.

And what of the people in Langzu who were suffering, waiting for their realm to be restored? "We're altered. It's easier for us to get through the barriers," I reasoned. "Why wouldn't he send us back and forth from Kashan? Why wouldn't he have us bring food here, to help the mortals survive? He says he cares about them."

Khatuya scoffed. "Does a parent not care about their child? Yet they do not let them have sweets at every turn."

"Basic aid is not sweets. It's survival."

Her bark-covered lips peeled back. "If you wanted a soft god, you've devoted your life to the wrong cause."

"I'm not arguing with you." I let my voice drop. "I'm only confused. Why would he say that he cares so much about the mortals and then leave them in such terrible conditions? You saw the mines."

Naatar stepped between us. "Likely Kluehnn is putting all his considerable force and attention into restoration. The gods must be contained while he's doing that. We still have to do our duty. Can you imagine if they were left to wreak havoc while the mortals await restoration? Everything has its order."

Khatuya settled back, the rough edges of her bark skin lying smooth and flat, like a bird whose feathers had come to rest.

But I wasn't finished, all the tension in my body tangling into an ugly knot. I thought of the sharp white teeth of the aspect, the claws against my cheeks. Something else had been gnawing at me, something other than that golden-skinned god. "Did *you* tell Kluehnn?"

"Tell him what?" Her voice was too casual.

"You did. You told him about my sister!"

Another *caw* from above. A crow, circling lower.

Khatuya shrugged. "He is all-seeing. How could I not tell him? Be grateful I did not tell him that you spoke to a god. So you can thank me for that."

She'd nearly gotten me killed. I was lucky I still had my godkilling blade. I was lucky I still had my life. "He is all-seeing because we *make* him so!" The words tumbled out of my mouth, stones spilled on the ground I could not take back.

Khatuya's fist lashed out. I leapt back, but not quickly enough to avoid a glancing blow to my cheek. I ducked, feeling the spot where it would bruise. The next time she tried to strike, I caught her by the wrist. I squeezed, feeling my strength measured against hers and knowing it was greater.

"You are a *blasphemer*," she hissed.

"I am part of your cohort!"

"What will you do when we find this god you think is so powerful? Will you speak to him too? Let him pour his lies into your ear?"

Naatar seized both of us, pulling us apart. I resisted only a little; I didn't want to hurt him. And neither, it seemed, did Khatuya. But we exchanged fiery glances around him. I still wanted to fight, to release all the ugly words I had inside of me. But Naatar now stood between us.

"Rasha does not intend to blaspheme Kluehnn. And Khatuya's first loyalty is to our god. As it is for all of us."

I watched Khatuya take a shuddering breath, her hand moving away from the hilt of her dagger. I tried to follow her example, though the heat climbing up my neck did not cool. Naatar didn't speak for me. I'd meant what I'd said.

One of the crows had landed on a nearby log, half obscured by grass. Khatuya scooped up a stone and threw it at the bird, letting out a shout of frustration. The crow launched back to the skies, the rock thudding harmlessly against the dried, decaying wood.

She leaned on her knees and then rose, extending a hand to me. "I don't want to fight with you."

I clasped her wrist reluctantly, drawing her close enough to pat her on the back. She smelled like sweat and leather. "I don't wish to fight either." It wasn't quite the truth. I felt like Naatar always stopped our fights too soon, before we'd ever actually resolved anything.

We fell into unbroken silence as we trudged through the wilderness, each of us keeping to our thoughts. I couldn't help the way mine tumbled – from my sister, to the golden-skinned god, to the way Kluehnn had told me never to keep anything from him again. I was walking a dangerous path. Every so often, a wagon passed us on the road, giving us a wide berth as soon as they spotted the armor with the embossed eye on the breastplate.

Above, the birds still circled, and I couldn't be sure if it was the same birds that had watched our fight, or an entirely different flock.

Naatar and Khatuya had returned to good spirits by the time the sun set, gently ribbing one another about their fighting skills, the devotion of their families, the foods they preferred to eat. I didn't have the heart to join them, and I started the fire and laid out my bedroll with only my morose thoughts to keep me company.

We ate millet gruel and salted meat for dinner. "I'll take first watch," I offered, my voice raspy. Naatar gave me a nod of gratitude. Khatuya said nothing.

I sat cross-legged on my bedroll as they settled in for the night, focusing on the crackling fire. A log popped, sending a shower of sparks into the air. I was accustomed to walking long distances, and to fighting, but the tangle of uneasy feelings proved more exhausting than both these things. I hadn't been aware of exactly how tired I was. I propped my chin on my hands, my elbows on my knees.

At some point I must have dozed off; I found myself listing to the side, a bit of drool escaping the corner of my mouth, my elbow slipping from my knee. I caught myself.

A crow sat on the ground next to me, startlingly close, its black eyes bright by the light of the fire.

"Hello," it croaked.

16

Rasha

11 years after the restoration of Kashan
and 572 years after the Shattering

Langzu - in the wilds

After the Shattering, while Kluehnn was hunting down the gods, one of them, Ophanganus, appeared in a Cressiman market, hooded and veiled. Witness accounts say that when he reached the center of the market, he threw off his hood and veil and all the mortals drew back at his countenance — his long, furred face and antelope's horns. And then he drew two swords and began murdering mortals indiscriminately, crying out that they'd destroyed the world.

He slaughtered forty-six men, women, and children before Kluehnn's godkillers came and put an end to him.

My hand tightened on a nearby stone, my fingers curling around its sharp edges. The bird was close. I wouldn't miss like Khatuya had. It didn't move, its head cocking as it watched me lift the rock.

Was it the same bird that had heard me arguing with my cohort? Why stand so close to me? Its feathers ruffled. It hopped a little bit closer.

This wasn't an ordinary bird. Somehow, in the dead of night, with my cohort asleep, I felt more sure of this. I let the rock go. "Hello," I responded.

For a moment, I felt intensely foolish. I must have dreamed the bird talking, and now I was talking back to it like it could *understand* me. But then its little throat moved.

"Rasha," it said. "Godkiller."

I waited, feeling as though I were floating above my body, watching this scene play out through someone else's eyes.

"You were right," it croaked, its voice soft. "What you said. If the gods could get back below, they would retake their homeland."

I gave it a long look. "*They.*"

The crow bobbed its head, let out a little *caw*. "We."

A shapeshifter god. A cohort as green as mine wouldn't get sent after one of these, not yet. For one thing, they were the hardest type of god to find. We could scent their magic each time they shifted, but if they didn't shift, it was difficult to pinpoint their location. And each time a cohort found a shapeshifter, the shifting meant the god had two very good options: shift into something big and strong, or shift into something fast and small. Both ways meant they often escaped capture. Godkillers did defeat them, just not as often as we did the others.

I was breaking the first precept yet again. We were forbidden from speaking to gods. I could be excused the first words I'd spoken to this bird, when I hadn't known for sure what it was. Anything I said past this point would be yet more blasphemy.

I'd broken the precept once before; could I really be

condemned any further than I already was? Slim justification – I knew it. "Kluehnn tells us you wish to take over the surface, that you wish to rule the mortals and the world above."

The bird shook its head. "All we want is to live."

It felt like a dzhalobo was making its nest in the hollow of my body, tearing away at my insides. "No. The stories say nothing of that. There were gods who wanted more, who wanted to conquer. What about Ophanganus, who went about murdering mortals indiscriminately?"

"Our stories tell a different tale of Ophanganus. A tragedy." The bird's beak snapped as it caught a bug, swallowed it down. "One we could not prevent. But even if your stories were completely true, are all Kashani the same? All Cressimans?"

I pressed my lips together, annoyed. "No, we aren't. But we do share a culture."

"And you think *our* culture—"

"Glorifies death. Conquest. Oppression."

Another head-tilt. One black eye, reflecting flame. "That is how you see us? All of us? No god has ever done a good thing, lived a decent life?"

"Only Kluehnn."

"Ah." The crow watched the fire, my cohort beyond it. Somehow I knew it wouldn't shift. It wasn't here to fight. I wasn't sure exactly what it *was* here for.

It shook out its feathers. "I never know what to say to that. Imagine if you were told there was only ever one good Kashani. What would you do with that information? Would you submit yourself to death as you surely deserved?"

The gems of my cohort's daggers winked in the darkness. A dead tree curled over their bodies, its branches like reaching fingers. I tried my best to keep my voice soft. If Khatuya and Naatar woke now, I couldn't blame them for turning me in. "We are *not* the same. You're twisting my words. This is why we're not meant to speak to gods."

"For which the punishment is death. I know." It hopped from one foot to the other. "I do appreciate that you've spoken to me at all."

I took a deep breath and let it out. I should have kept my silence, but something drove me forward. "Tolemne went to the gods and asked for help. Only Kluehnn answered. No other gods did."

"Perhaps that is true. I wasn't there. But if one god can make such a decision, who is to say others cannot? If one god can work with mortals, why not others?"

My fingers curled around the stone and I hurled it. The crow let out a *caw* and leapt into the air. My rock landed in the brush. Instead of flying away, the bird landed in the tree above Naatar.

Naatar stirred on his bedroll, his tail slipping from beneath his blanket, brown scales shining by firelight. The crow waited in the tree, watching me, as I did my best to pretend it didn't exist. I slid my copy of the Aqqilan stories from my bag. I wasn't supposed to have it, but what was the shapeshifter going to do? Tell Kluehnn about it? And I needed a way to stay awake, especially with a god watching over us.

The stories inside didn't all view the gods favorably – they made mistakes, they acted in petty ways, they hindered as well as helped. The middle pages were frustratingly clipped in the middle to hold the smuggled gems, so I couldn't quite tell what those stories were about. I flipped the book this way and that, as though that might help me figure out what had lain there.

I'd nearly forgotten the crow was even there by the time I went to wake Khatuya for her shift. She slept with her arms curled by her head, knees to her chest, as though she was trying to fit herself into a spot that was smaller than she was. Her face was so much softer when she slept. When she was awake, she always had a firm set to her jaw, as though ready at any moment to make a rebuttal. I remembered the way she'd stood against Shambul, even when she knew she'd pay for it later. I remembered the way she always tried to protect Naatar, whose family didn't afford him as much grace as hers did.

I didn't want to fight her. I'd keep these doubts to myself. For both our sakes.

I reached to shake her awake.

"You cannot continue to believe two different things," the crow said from above.

Startled, I spoke louder than I intended to. "I can believe whatever I want."

Khatuya rolled over in her blankets, her black eyes blinking. "What?"

My breath caught. Had she heard that whole exchange? "Nothing. I was talking to myself. It's your turn for watch."

She pushed herself up to her elbows.

The scent hit us both at the same time.

I didn't know what it smelled like to Khatuya or Naatar; I'd never asked. But it smelled like a dung fire to me, it always had. That scent I so closely associated with home, with safety. It carried on the wind, fainter than a true aether scent, something lighter but something I could follow.

A god using magic.

17
Hakara

11 years after the restoration of Kashan
and 572 years after the Shattering

Langzu - inner Bian

Rumenesca, the Mother, always roamed the surface world with the intent of enacting some grand, sweeping plan. Instead, each time she found herself collecting orphans. She gave them a choice: stay here on the surface or come with her back to her home, where they would be fed and happy and would live out the rest of their days. Nearly all who were asked went with her, and she loved and coddled them and gave them the best her territory had to offer. There are accounts of a few who refused her — too afraid of a place they did not know, of a decision that would define the rest of their lives. But each of those few recalled, to their dying days, the kindness in Rumenesca's eyes.

"It won't be easy," Sheuan said, handing me some workers' clothes. I stripped without pretense, ignoring the uncomfortable glances from Mull and Thassir. We didn't have time for blushing modesty. Each of our plans was threadbare, hastily crafted in moments. I'd only been able to bargain three of the filters off Sheuan; she'd insisted that was all she could spare before someone might notice. I'd taken another off Mull, leaving him with only one. Four was at least enough to cover the mortals on my team, plus one extra.

The tunic and pants Sheuan gave me were plain, brown, a bit scratchy at the seams, but a fair bit cleaner than what I'd been wearing. I pulled my hair into a tail, combing through some of the tangles with my fingers.

"Doesn't bother me. If I wanted easy, I wouldn't have joined the Unanointed."

"What exactly are you looking for in the castle?"

I opened my mouth to lie, but Mullayne spoke first. He'd pulled some of the cushions from the workshop chairs to make something of a mattress, and he was laid out on them, a hand to his head. "Lithuas. The elder god. They're chasing her. She's aligned with Kluehnn. She's helping him enact restoration, and if they kill her, they disrupt his plans."

I glared at him, but he only shrugged. Maybe it was better he was going to the den, that he was doing what he wanted to. Couldn't have expected any loyalty from him. I plucked several filters from the counter and handed them to Thassir. "We're taking these too."

"Lithuas is ... alive?"

"Yes, and there's a third aerocline. Nothing makes sense anymore." I tried and failed to keep my gaze from sliding over to Thassir. Or Nioanen. Somehow didn't feel right to call him by that name, not when he'd so thoroughly failed to live up to its epithet. "She made some sort of bargain with Kluehnn to keep her own life. And now she's holed up in the castle. If we flush her out, we can take her in a fight."

I said it a lot more confidently than I felt. We could take her *if* Thassir used all his godly might against her. But I'd not seen him glow with an aura or summon his blade, Zayyel, to his hand. I wasn't sure how much of that was his disguise and how much was who he had become.

Thassir held the filters awkwardly in one hand, the basket still tucked beneath his other arm. Didn't exactly look godly at the moment.

Sheuan straightened the collar of my shirt. "I'll have to convince the guards that you're from Mull's workshop, and that I need you in the castle for something important. Maybe a repair. Just don't say anything. Let me do the talking."

I caught Thassir's gaze. "Thassir?"

He shook his head. "She's not on the move, not yet. She's still inside."

Sheuan scratched absent-mindedly at her back. "I'll come back for you, Mull. You two – follow me. Stay close." She walked with purpose out of the workshop.

I halted next to Mull before I left, hesitated. He'd made it clear he didn't want any part of the Unanointed, but what kind of leader would I be if I didn't try to recruit people who could help our cause? "If you can't find a way out yourself, we'll come up with an extraction plan. Just ... stay alive."

He nodded, his gaze distant. Wasn't sure how much he heard me, and how much he was thinking about that tomb.

Thassir and I filed into the streets behind Sheuan. To my surprise, no one even bothered to stop us. A few patrolling enforcers looked our way and then quickly glanced away again. Sheuan never stopped to show her papers or to pull rank. She just walked toward the castle without ever even making sure we were still there, her silk skirt flashing by lanternlight with each step, the pearls in her hair glinting.

Funny how just looking rich meant you could go wherever you pleased.

We found Alifra and Dashu at the tea house across the street from the castle, lingering over a still-steaming pot. Alifra bit into a millet cracker, frowned, but took another bite.

The proprietor watched us as we approached, but said nothing when we took seats at the same table, even though he was clearly closing up for the night. I should have walked around with a beautifully dressed woman more often.

Alifra tossed a few more coins onto the table. Perhaps it was the money that was staying his tongue. "We've been watching the castle. Nothing yet," she said. She eyed Sheuan. "Is it my imagination, or did our noble friend get a fair bit prettier since we saw him last?"

"Mull had more filters in his workshop, so I took them. Couldn't convince him to join us, but we got what I wanted. This is his cousin. The Sovereign's wife."

Dashu's eyebrows lifted. "She'll get you inside?"

"That's the hope."

Alifra sipped the tea and let out a pleased little hum. Then she sat bolt upright. "Thassir? What is it?"

His gaze was locked onto the palace. "We don't need to get inside. She's changed again. She's approaching the servants' entrance."

We rose to our feet as one. Sheuan's hand darted out, catching my forearm. "Wait."

I buzzed with energy, my heartbeat pounding in my throat. This could be it. This could be the chance to kill Lithuas. Finally. But I let Sheuan talk.

"If you see your sister again, tell her . . ." She swallowed. "Tell her that I'm sorry. That I wish the world was different. That I wish *I* was different."

Before I could pry, or ask her exactly *why* she was sorry, Thassir darted toward the castle, his step surprisingly quiet. I shrugged Sheuan off and followed, Dashu and Alifra on my heels.

He stopped at the corner and held up a hand. Then he pointed, slowly and carefully. I crept to his side and peered around the wall.

There was a servant, her clothes as plain as her face. She walked alone down the street; the only enforcers in sight were manning the walls of the castle, their gazes out on the city at large.

She hadn't seen us.

I beckoned Alifra and Dashu closer. We could take her by surprise if we were careful. Thassir stood still as a statue, unblinking, every muscle in his body tensed. I was out of gems in my pouches, so I reached toward the basket he held, surreptitiously lifting the lid.

A yowl pierced the night.

Lithuas's head whipped toward us, her eyes glittering. Before I could even process what was happening, she'd shifted into a hawk. High above us, enforcers shouted, running across the wall, disappearing down stairs.

Alifra's crossbow clicked. Her aim was true, but Lithuas shifted again into a deer, falling from the sky before the bolt could reach its mark, and bounded down the street toward the empty lakebed.

I grabbed Thassir's wing hard enough to pinch as I pulled him after me, enforcers behind and Lithuas ahead. "Keep that crossbow loaded. Keep her on the ground," I called to Alifra.

We chased her into the alleyways of Bian. Above us, lanterns brightened windows, sending stray beams of light trickling into the darkness. The moon above was a sliver, the stars barely visible past the lights of the city.

"You," I huffed at Thassir, "you brought a *cat* with you?"

He clutched the basket to his chest, a disgruntled growl emanating from it with every jolting step he took. "Rumenesca," he said.

And now that he said the name, it all made a horrible sort of sense. He'd named her after one of the dead elder gods, and if the stories were correct, they'd once been friends. That awful, spitting beast was his favorite, and he wasn't about to leave her behind again. I'd thought we might not be able to rely on Thassir to kill Lithuas. I hadn't counted on not being able to rely on him because he thought nothing of bringing a goddam cat with us while we chased after her. "You could have warned me!"

"You would have told me to leave her behind." His voice was annoyingly steady.

"Would you have listened?"

The echo of hoofbeats ricocheted from the walls. Was the sound fainter or was I imagining it? Swearing, I lifted the flap of the basket and grabbed for the pouches of gems. A hiss, the flash of a paw, and a searing scratch across the back of my hand. But the pouches were in my grasp. One was much smaller than the others. I loosened the top and saw a glow of yellow. Utricht had shown me the yellow gems once, when he'd explained what they all did. These ones allowed the user to manipulate time, though he hadn't told me exactly how. They were too rare for regular use. I tied the pouches to my belt.

The alleys opened up. I caught a glimpse of the deer cutting past a corner. Two more turns and the warehouses at the edge of inner Bian met my gaze, the boulders that ringed the edge of the dried-up lakebed. We could lose the enforcers in the boulders. If we weren't wandering around in the city, they had far less incentive to chase after us.

My breath was ragged in my throat, my chest tight. We were so close.

Lithuas shifted again into a mountain goat as she hit the boulders, leaping from rock to rock with a grace I knew we couldn't manage. "Alifra!" I called.

She stopped, took aim.

Her bolt hit the goat in the haunch. Lithuas stumbled, disappearing into the lakebed.

We rushed forward, picking our way through the boulders until we were out into the dusty bottom.

"She's not running anymore," Thassir panted. A dark shape moved ahead of us, limping across the barren landscape. I reached into the pouch of gems.

"Hakara!" A voice rang out behind me. It was like I'd been struck by one of Alifra's bolts. Everything in my world just stopped. Even the breath in my ears went silent.

Rasha.

18

Rasha

11 years after the restoration of Kashan
and 572 years after the Shattering

Langzu - Bian, the dried-up lakebed

There is a parable told in Langzu to children: "Barexi and the Clan Son". When Barexi came to visit the clans in disguise, a young man cornered him at a party, bloviating on topics he knew nothing about – namely Unterra and the gods themselves. Each of his supposed facts was wrong, which grated on Barexi's nerves. When the young man dared to speak on Barexi himself, the elder god could take it no longer and laid his hands on the young man, sending him back in time to a mewling babe.

While it appeared in the present to others as though no time had passed at all, the young man seemed to retain some memory of being sent back in time and the offense that caused it, because from then on, he spoke much more carefully, especially in the presence of his betters. The lesson children were to take from this was that it was important to know one's audience before speaking.

The black-winged god stood at Hakara's shoulder, but all I had eyes for was my sister. She wore brown work clothes, a clan crest embroidered onto one shoulder. But the sword strapped to her side and the spear at her back told a different story.

It seemed like forever since we'd last seen each other. It seemed like it had only been a moment.

She seemed unable to move, her gaze fixed on me as I approached, Khatuya and Naatar flanking me. The black-winged god took her arm, pointed into the distant darkness.

Hakara's mouth firmed. She didn't turn away from me, but the man and woman accompanying her stepped to her sides as she backed slowly into the lakebed. I gestured to Khatuya and Naatar, and they spread out, rushing forward to follow.

My sister drew her sword. "Rasha, this isn't your fight."

"Leave the god. I'll let you go if you leave the god."

The look she gave me reminded me of the time I'd tossed an entire egg into a stew instead of breaking it. "Which one?"

What did she mean?

She let out a bitter laugh at my expression. "We're both chasing gods, Rasha. Only I'm chasing the one that's working with Kluehnn."

I pulled my dagger free, the light from the violet gem in the hilt outlining my fingers. "Kluehnn doesn't work with gods. He protects us from them."

"Don't listen to her," Khatuya said. "She's lying."

Hakara thrust her hands to the sides, nearly dropping her sword. I wanted to tell her to hold it tighter. "Why would I lie?"

"To turn her from her faith!" Naatar spat out.

This was why I shouldn't have spoken to that god. Doubts could stay my hand. Doubts could make me fail. Part of me wanted to listen to her. I'd told Hakara we were different now, and we were, but when I looked at her, I felt like that little girl again, curled up in the blankets of our tent with my older sister a bulwark against the cold. The words she would whisper to me in the dark, the way, for those small moments, she seemed to forget she was responsible for me, and in that shared space we could laugh over terrible jokes, half delirious with exhaustion.

Hakara glanced back into the darkness and swore.

"She's still there," the black-winged god said.

My sister extended her free hand. "Rasha, you may never forgive me, and I made my peace with that. Don't really have any other choice. But if I'm not out here chasing one of Kluehnn's aspects, what do you think I'm doing?" She waved an arm toward Khatuya and Naatar. "They're free to answer too. Go on, then."

"What does it matter what you're doing?" Khatuya snarled, her dagger free.

"It matters because the truth matters!" Hakara shouted back.

Naatar closed in on the man with the curved sword. "If Kluehnn is working with a god, he must have his reasons."

Hakara dipped a hand into her pouch. I lifted my blade. She didn't swallow a god gem; she threw it into the darkness.

Its red glow illuminated the shape of a mountain goat limping away, a bolt in its haunch.

"What do you think I'm doing chasing a goat into the night? Think! You're smarter than this. If it's a shapeshifter god, what do I care? I'm not a godkiller. The only reason I could care is if that god is working with Kluehnn. And if that's not a problem for you, when the tenets of your faith tell you that there is only one true god, then what is the point of your faith?"

I wanted to tell her to shut up, but my tongue felt stuck to the roof of my mouth. And then I looked to Khatuya and Naatar, closing in on Hakara's compatriots. "The point is that I belong somewhere, and that is with my friends."

No doubts. No hesitation.

The goat disappeared into the darkness, fled beyond the small circle of light provided by the god gem.

"You're making a terrible mistake." Hakara's voice was anguished. Her hand dipped into her pouches again, and this time she did swallow a gem.

Fine. This was always the way it was going to end, ever since Kluehnn set me to this task. "Kill the winged god," I said. Khatuya and Naatar moved at the same time I did.

Hakara lifted her arms to block me, just as the scent of a dung fire hit my nostrils. Another set of smoky limbs enveloped her arms.

We felt evenly matched with her enhanced strength, her feet digging into the ground. I pressed my dagger down toward her and she pushed back. I was so much *taller* than her now, and something about this change disoriented me, made my limbs feel unfamiliar.

Too much weakness. Too much indecision. She shoved and I faltered.

Both of us knew she should have pushed the advantage, and yet she didn't. She hung back. Only a brief moment, but enough for me to get my feet beneath me again.

The two of us tossing rocks toward a pit in the sand, laughing when we missed and lifting our arms in triumph when we didn't. The yellowed sky, the distant scent of smoke. The gritty feeling of crushed seashells between my toes. And then the day I'd caught her throwing stones at a distant branch, and watched her hit it every single time. She'd *let* me win some of those games and I'd never even had the courage to tell her that I knew. After that, I'd only pretended at triumph each time I won, my heart catching in my throat.

"Fight!" I screamed, slashing my dagger at her. She leapt back, barely quick enough to avoid the blow. "You always thought I was weak, but now which of us is stronger?" I struck out again and felt my blade catch her sleeve, hissing past to kiss the skin beneath.

Blood darkened her shoulder, and though I gritted my teeth against the feeling, a part of me still wanted to brush the cloth aside, to clean the wound, the way I'd done so many times before when she'd cut her hands and feet on the roughness of barnacles.

I wanted to erase our history, and the only way I could do that was to end her. I had to.

I lifted my blade again, noting with a dizzy, distant feeling the smear of red across the metal. Behind Hakara, the black-winged god was setting something onto the ground. He was stepping toward the fight between Khatuya and the russet-haired woman.

If I didn't get past Hakara, I couldn't help my cohort. I redoubled my efforts.

She let out her breath. "I never said you were weak," she panted between blows.

She tried to push past my guard, using the length of her blade to her advantage. I kicked at her torso. She grunted, but moved with the blow, her blade falling away. "You never said it, but you *showed* it. You never let me go to the shore with you. You kept me at our tent. You let me win all our games."

"Rasha!" The scolding tone of her voice sent me reeling into the past. "You were a child."

"So were you!" I struck at her again, and our blades clashed, hers barely lifted from her side. I shoved forward, knowing that if I got close enough, I could slip my blade past hers.

"Mimi told me to watch over you before she died. Not Maman. She told *me*. Some days, that was all I had."

My cheeks were hot, a prickling sensation at my eyes. In my mind, Mimi was a round, soft shape with kind eyes, blurring into some indefinable background. "I never asked for that." My blade moved incrementally toward her thigh.

"I did the best I could. I did what I thought was right."

With a grunt, I dug my feet into the earth and pushed. Hakara gave way, flowing to the side. It took two fumbling steps for me to regain my balance. Sloppy. I'd let her distract me the way I'd once distracted Shambul. Should have known better. She pulled another gem from her pouch.

"Rasha!" Khatuya shouted, her voice panicked.

I caught glimpses in the dark of black wings, of a looming shape. She and Naatar had moved toward one another and stood back to back. The flash of a curved blade, Naatar flinching away. And the click of a loading crossbow.

I pushed past Hakara. The sharp impact of something entering my body. I couldn't move, every limb frozen. "Ah, shit. Shit shit shit." My sister pulled her sword free from my gut, dropping it, frantically placing her hands over the wound.

"I told you not to hold back," I breathed out through the pain.

And then she was swallowing something from one of her pouches, her eyes wild and confused, her hands waving over me as though she was unsure of what she should do. The scent of aether whiffed into the air above me, a shimmer between our faces. Her expression changed to one of certainty, and she lowered her palms, pressed her fingers to my shoulders.

Something *changed*.

I heard the click of a loading crossbow. I pushed past Hakara.

She thrust her sword at me and missed. I wasn't sure if she'd missed deliberately.

My gaze was focused on my cohort. We'd all heard the whispers of the black-winged god in the depths of the den, tearing the godkillers apart as though they were paper puppets. We'd killed gods before – quickly, efficiently. But this one was different. Bigger, stronger, older.

Before I could reach them, he thrust out a clawed hand. The

glow of the gem in Khatuya's dagger lit the crags of her face, her bark-like skin slack with fear. She tried to slash his palm with her blade, but he caught her wrist instead. His other hand took her by the throat.

He lifted her as I ran screaming toward him, launching myself at his wings. I seized his feathers.

Pain seared my leg. I gasped, unable to breathe past the sensation. I felt my body falling, my grip on my dagger loosening. It was happening to someone else, only I could feel the hard ground beneath my back, another jolt of fire to my thigh, the softness of the silt at my cheek strangely incongruous.

A blade flashed, resting against my neck. The sounds of fighting died. The man with the curved sword was standing over me, his lips firm and brows low over his eyes.

"Don't, Dashu." Hakara, breathless; hurried footsteps. "*Please.*"

Dashu didn't look away from me. "She will keep following us. Her god sent her to kill Thassir. She is a fanatic – they do not quit."

My sister knelt at my side and pushed the blade gently away. For a moment, I thought she would brush the hair from my forehead, the way she'd done every morning in our shared tent, her expression soft. But she reached instead for my hand, prying my godkilling dagger free.

"Take theirs as well," she said, nodding to Naatar and Khatuya. They'd both stood down when that curved sword had touched my throat, their hands raised. My heartbeat raced. We'd all be punished for this.

"Well. No way to kill a god without a godkilling dagger. And seems like something we could use. Now hold still," Hakara said. In one smooth movement, she'd gripped the bolt in my thigh and yanked it out.

A fresh wave of pain washed through me.

She pressed a hand to the wound, then called to Naatar. "Come here. Hold that until it stops bleeding." He obeyed, replacing her hand with his.

I gritted my teeth. "You should kill me. Your friend is right."

Hakara squeezed my shoulder, leaving a bloody handprint on my robe. "When have I ever done what you told me to?" She tucked my godkilling dagger into her belt – the blade I'd bled and killed for. "Thassir?"

He shook his head, ruffling the feathers of his wings as though casting off the touch I'd laid upon him. "No. She's gone. She changed." He picked up the basket on the ground, tucked it beneath his arm, and pointed. "South."

I tried to memorize the exact place he was pointing to.

Hakara lifted her hand, dusting her palms against her pants as she rose, leaving a single smear of red. Then she looked at her palm as though she'd spotted something unusual there.

"Hm. Got an idea."

She pulled the dagger free again.

"Hakara," Thassir said, his voice a warning. But when did my sister ever listen to warnings? She nicked her palm and then took my hand too. I tried to pull away, but she'd caught me by surprise. The movement only drew the edge against my skin.

And then she was holding her hand against mine, our blood mingling. "Do it." She didn't look away from me, but I saw the black-winged god let out a soft little sigh, the slight shake of his head.

A lingering moment with our hands clasped, during which nothing happened. Her eyes looked so much like mine – the same shape, the same color. A scent swirled into the air. Aether, slightly warm, surrounded our hands. Something tickled at the back of my mind.

"Now she'll know exactly where we are." Dashu still hadn't sheathed his blade. "You never asked us. One of the things that made Lisha the Orator such a great leader was that she took the time to listen to her subordinates."

Hakara beckoned to the russet-haired woman. "And was Lisha in the middle of chasing down an elder god when she asked for all these opinions?"

"Can you do that?" the russet-haired woman asked. "Hold two bonds at once?"

Hakara shrugged. "No one told me I couldn't." She gave me one last look. "And I'll know exactly where *she* is at all times too. This goes both ways. You've two choices now, Rasha. You can follow me. But I'd sooner toss all three of your blades into the Sanguine Sea before I let you have them again. And if you get too close, I'll make sure to drop them into a place you'll never recover them. Or you can run back to Kluehnn. Tell him what happened here. Beg another blade from him. I don't care. Just don't bother us again."

She put a hand to her bloody shoulder, winced a little, but walked into the darkness, the dagger at her side winking as if to mock me. The russet-haired woman dipped by me, picking up the bolt Hakara had yanked from my leg. They faded into the night as quickly as they'd appeared. A stretching sensation formed in my mind, a piece of dough being pulled from either end. I could *feel* her moving south, away from Bian.

Naatar still knelt at my side, his hand on the wound in my thigh. His tail twitched behind him, a nervous gesture. I knew he was thinking about the loss of our blades. We couldn't hide that. We weren't godkillers without them. Yet if we set off after them, we'd still lose the blades and we'd have no way to complete our mission.

"I spoke to other godkillers about the battle that killed our den's aspect. That winged god was there, a force like a hurricane wind. But he was not the only one. There were others. Unanointed mortals. It wasn't the god that killed the aspect. It was a mortal. A woman with dark brown hair, who looked mixed. Like you." Khatuya turned her gaze to me on these last words, and I did my best not to flinch.

"Khatuya, leave it." Naatar's voice was strained.

"It needs to be said, and we are here alone with no one to overhear us. We cannot follow you blindly. There can be no lies between us, or even half-truths. We are a cohort, but the only reason we made it through was because we relied on each other. The bond we have is unique, it is strong, but that doesn't mean it can't break." She held my gaze. "I know she is your sister. She is also the one who killed an aspect of Kluehnn."

I worked to tear a strip of my robe free so I could bind my wound. "That doesn't compromise me."

"Doesn't it? You let her go free back in the den and she went on to kill Kluehnn's aspect. I saw – she only enhanced her arms. You should have been able to defeat her. And if you'd defeated her, we could have found a way to kill her two companions and then take on the black-winged god."

Khatuya always liked to bite off more than she could chew when it came to a fight. "It was too much. He's too strong." I gently lifted Naatar's hand from the wound. The blood had congealed, leaving a reddened pit on my leg.

I touched the front of my armor, where there was a hole, a streak of blood across it. As far as I could tell, the wound in my thigh was the only one I'd sustained. Strange.

Naatar wiped his hand clean on his robe. "Are you trying to say that Kluehnn gave us more than we could handle? That he set us up to fail?"

"I ... No. That's not what I'm trying to say at all." Wasn't it, though? My mind was a traitor to itself, digging into all the weak explanations I'd been fed over the years, the ones I'd willingly swallowed. "He might have made a mistake. Maybe he didn't know the others would be with him."

"Then what should we do?"

I wanted to run away, to follow Hakara and her friends south, to avoid facing Kluehnn.

My chest tightened. "We should go to Kluehnn. We should warn him of what we saw, of the lies they told us about him." I took a deep breath as I tied the bandage. It did nothing to ease the fear creeping up the back of my neck, the dread that wormed its way into my bones. "We should face our punishment, whatever that may be."

19
Mullayne

11 years after the restoration of Kashan
and 572 years after the Shattering

Langzu - in the mountains east of Bian

Daily arrest log, fourth day of the third month of summer, Bian
- *Drunken loitering in inner Bian in the early-morning hours. Offender: member of a noble clan. Action: escorted home.*
- *Theft of ration tickets. Offender: citizen. Action: fined and made to return stolen property.*
- *Vandalizing a competing market stall. Offender: citizen. Action: fined and three nights' imprisonment.*
- *Murder of a royal clan member. Offender: non-citizen (no papers). Action: sent to the barrier.*

It had been far too easy for Sheuan to convince the enforcers that he was in fact not Mullayne Reisun, but the *murderer* of Mullayne Reisun, a common brigand who'd taken a noble's money, his papers, and his life. They hadn't even considered that he might be the man himself. Under Sheuan's watchful gaze, they'd taken him into custody, handed his papers – *his* papers! – to his cousin, and then tossed him into one of their barred wagons.

Was it really that easy to get someone thrown into the barrier? All one had to do was have the right credentials and dislike a person with no clan rank? It didn't seem right, or fair – and yet...

He couldn't deny this was the state he was in.

To his surprise, only two other criminals begged clemency from Kluehnn. "Not interested. I'd rather have a quick end," one grizzled woman had said. Before he could ask exactly what she meant by that, Mull was being pulled from that wagon, put into another one, and then carted over a bumpy road mostly during the night. During the day, he'd lain on the floor, trying to ignore the sound of the others pissing into the pot in the corner. Thin gruel, sips of warm water. Even in the depths of Tolemne's Path, even in all his despair, he'd still had his pen and his notebook, if not a fully functioning mind.

Here, his mind was fully functioning, and it didn't feel like a blessing. Day bled into night bled into day. It wasn't a long distance to the den, but it was a climb. He thought he counted seven days. Maybe eight?

But now it was dawn, the bleating of goats was sounding in the distance, and he couldn't tell if the strong scent of body odor was his or from one of his two unfamiliar roommates.

An enforcer banged on the bars. "We're here."

He really shouldn't have been excited to see the den, but he couldn't help the rise of curiosity. People didn't go in and then come back out. He was about to see something few mortals ever did. He hopped out first, stretching his sore legs.

An altered man stood outside the wagon, gray robes embroidered on the front with a white eye. Every visible bit of skin was covered in spotted fur; a pair of tusks curved out from between his lips. No dagger at his hip, but a set of black claws tipped his fingers. "Three," he muttered. "We could have used more."

The enforcer closed the bars behind them, the clang echoing off the mountain rock. She shrugged. "Well that's really not the Sovereign's problem, is it?"

The man only grumbled. "Line up and follow me."

Mull was already in the front. As he marched down the path after the altered, the woman at the back made a run for it.

The altered man let out the most aggrieved sigh Mull had ever heard. "Runner!" he shouted.

A soft click, and the woman fell, a bolt in her back. A gray-robed figure rose from behind a cluster of rocks farther up the peak.

The altered man pointed to the winged woman with the crossbow and then to the body on the ground. "That's what happens if you run. Some people need to be told. Some people" – he shrugged – "need to be shot." He turned and continued to lead them down the path. "And if you're thinking of trying to jump me..."

Mull had not been thinking of that.

"... it didn't work out that well for the last eight people who tried."

It was a little cooler here in the mountains, the rust-colored rocks punctuated by small patches of grass and a few trees that reminded Mull of the short, gnarled hands of his grandmother. The path they walked on split off into others, the dirt and gravel marked with overlapping footprints. They took a right fork. The scent of earth gave way to something stronger. Something quite unpleasant.

"You'll be working the latrine ditches."

Whatever excitement might have been building in Mull's gut shriveled into a raisin. "Are we not going into the den?"

The altered kept speaking. "We rotate use from the north end to the south end and then back to the north. What you'll be doing is removing the old, compacted waste and packing it into the provided wagon. We sell it to nearby farmers. So." He picked up a shovel. "A necessary task. And a glorious way to serve Kluehnn." He handed the shovel across to Mull.

Mull could hear his heartbeat drumming in his ears. He wrapped his fingers around the handle. This couldn't be it – digging out waste until he dropped from exhaustion or heat or both. He was here to infiltrate the den. "Where do we sleep?"

The altered man's eyes narrowed. "You ask a lot of questions."

"So you heard my first one?"

The altered took a half-step closer. He loomed over Mull, a growl low in his throat. "You asked for the mercy of Kluehnn. This is his mercy. Now get to work." He pushed him toward the ditch.

If Mull thought it had smelled bad from above, the scent was eye-watering inside the ditch itself. The filter he'd smuggled beneath his shirt rubbed against his skin. A part of him was tempted to wear it just to avoid the sting of each breath. They joined two others already at work – broad-shouldered women who glanced up briefly as they stepped into the filth.

Mull fell into the rhythm of it, his back aching after only a few trips up with his bucket. There was only one wheelbarrow in use; the other lay broken at the side of the ditch. He'd been so sure when he'd made these plans that they'd take him into the den, that he'd be able to sneak away and find the tomb. But there was someone in the rocks with a crossbow, and with his shoes coated in waste, he'd not escape notice. They'd smell him coming.

For the second time in his life, he found himself completely out of his depth. He'd been accustomed to all the mysteries of the world giving way to the gentle press of his intellect; there'd not been a problem he couldn't solve given time. But his mind now was blank, every potential solution discarded as soon as it whispered into existence.

What the *fuck* had he done? He was going to die here.

What a useless way to die. He'd never been devout. He didn't care about Kluehnn's missions or ideals. The only thing that really affected him was restoration, so that had been the only thing he'd cared about.

He watched the woman next to him as she stepped back down into the muck, her black hair shorn close to her scalp. She worked with alacrity, barely slowing. Someone came down the path, lifted their robes, and pissed into the trench only a short distance from where Mull stood.

He caught the woman by the arm before she could take hold of the wheelbarrow again. "Why work so hard?"

She shrugged him off. "If you prove worthy, you're granted a boon. I've been doing this for nearly a year."

The man who'd arrived with Mull snorted. "No one gets out alive."

"That *you* know of," she panted out. And then she was putting her legs into the work, shoving up toward the shit wagon.

They broke for a meal around noon, their supervisor giving them a bucket to wash their hands in, and then small meat-filled buns when they were finished. They were eating in the shadow of a boulder, Mull savoring each bite, when a cohort of godkillers appeared down the path.

He was on his feet before he'd realized he was scrambling. There was no mistaking them: the fluid way they moved, the daggers at their belts, their embossed leather breastplates and fine robes.

The one in the front had a pair of large black and white wings, which he spread when he was ten paces from the workers. The godkillers behind him stopped. "You." He pointed at the woman with the short-shorn hair. "Your efforts will be rewarded. You have been chosen to descend and speak with Kluehnn."

She fell to her knees, her food forgotten. "Bless the many-limbed god. Bless his many eyes."

Mull shrank back into the shadow of the rocks as they took her. The supervisor was there, too, licking at one tusk, his brows low. "Well that's one less worker for the ditches. They'll overflow if they keep that up."

"Where did they take her?"

A blow struck Mull across the cheek, so quick he barely registered that it was the supervisor who'd hit him. He stumbled, struggling to keep his feet beneath him, his face throbbing.

"Too many questions!" the supervisor barked.

By the time night fell, Mull was a collection of bruises, blisters, and aching muscles. For a moment he hoped they would be ferried into the den, into the shelter of a cave. Perhaps he could sneak away while everyone slept. Surely there wouldn't be someone with a crossbow in the narrow confines of the tunnels.

But the supervisor merely pointed them to a bank of bedrolls beneath a ledge, out here in the open air, nestled into a bed of gravel.

"There are sentries set around the perimeter of the den, and they can see in the dark better than you. So unless you want to end up as a nice pincushion, you'll get some rest."

Mull waited until the supervisor had retreated to his own bedroll, somewhere up the slope. He heard the rustle of wood, the faint crackling of a new fire. "How many do they take for Kluehnn?"

The broad-shouldered woman sighed. "Risana was the first

I've seen. They don't take them often. But she got what she wanted, eventually." She rolled over in her blankets, her back to Mull. The man who'd arrived with him only grunted.

When he heard the breathing of the other two even out, Mull stepped out of his bedroll, his mind whirring. He couldn't escape, he knew that now; besides, escaping would mean giving up, and he wasn't ready to do that. They'd taken Risana into the den.

He couldn't work that hard. It wasn't because he didn't have the will for it. He had plenty of will. It was his body that wouldn't cooperate. Maybe if he stayed here for a year, he could build the sort of strength that she'd had. But he didn't have that long. The whole realm would be restored by then, and the tomb might be buried beneath the magic of new growth.

Well, his body wouldn't cooperate, but his mind was always willing, and as soon as the opportunity had presented itself, he'd left despair by the wayside. He might not be able to work harder, but he could always work smarter.

No sentry manned the latrine ditch. He gathered materials from the ground, from the refuse pile. Scant bits of metal and rope and wood. Not what he was used to at his workshop. But it would be enough.

Blisters opened as he turned the broken wheelbarrow over, pulling and poking at it to find the issues. The supervisor's fire was out; he must have gone to sleep hours ago. A discarded wheel was buried beneath a burned stretch of cloth.

There was something soothing in the work, something familiar. Tired as he was, his palms burning, he was able to forget for a moment that he'd thrown himself into this predicament wholeheartedly, that he might never come out of it. That his cousin, Sheuan, had agreed to the whole thing a bit quicker than he would have liked, in spite of knowing how dangerous it was.

The sliver of the sun crested the horizon. Mull tested the

broken wheelbarrow. It was bulkier than it had been before, the wheel smaller, but it worked.

"Hey!" The supervisor's voice bounced from the rocks. "What are you doing down there?" He slid down into the ditch and reached for the wheelbarrow.

"Don't touch that," Mull snapped back. Everyone always ruining his things by touching them. Using the filters to protect against restoration – it was absurd, Sheuan had never tested it. Not that there *was* an easy way to test that, he supposed.

The supervisor was glaring at him, though he hadn't, thank the gods, touched the wheelbarrow.

"The biggest problem with this broken wheelbarrow was the wheel. I replaced that and the cross-brace."

One fur-covered arm reached out and seized one of the handles. "This isn't what you were told to do."

Mull lifted a hand. "Wait! You said you needed more workers. This helps. This gets more done." The supervisor wrenched the wheelbarrow away, the newly affixed wheel creaking. "I'm trying to help you!"

"You think you're so smart?"

Mull gritted his teeth, swallowing back the worst of his retorts. "I'm not stupid."

"Yeah? Then why are you *here*?"

He froze. There really wasn't anything he could say to that. The expedition down Tolemne's Path had been a mistake. This was also a mistake. Maybe he wasn't smart, at least not in the ways that actually mattered. He hadn't found a cure for Imeah. He hadn't made it to Unterra. He hadn't even managed to make it inside the den.

"You stay where you're told to stay."

When the first blow struck his knee, it felt to him like a natural conclusion. He didn't even raise his arms to defend himself.

Instincts kicked in after the third blow, when he curled inward, his hands lifted over his head.

"Didn't that one just get here?" a voice drawled. "Already causing trouble, is he?"

A shift in the light as the supervisor moved to the side, his shadow retreating from Mull's eyes. The winged woman who'd taken Risana into the den was adjusting her robes after using the ditch, her godkilling dagger at her side.

"He snuck away from his bedroll last night."

"Trying to escape?"

When the supervisor didn't answer, Mull shouted back, "No. I did that." He pointed to the wheelbarrow.

The godkiller strode over to them, then bent to examine the wheelbarrow. "Interesting." She took one handle, lifted it, and moved it back and forth, the wheels creaking. But his repair held. "Looks like he fixed it. With garbage."

"I didn't give him permission to go digging in the refuse pile."

She ignored the supervisor, her attention turning to Mull. "Can you read?"

"And write. Multiple languages." He bit his tongue. Her eyes narrowed. He'd give himself away like this, but it was hard not to feel some hope, and with it, a trickle of pride. He met her hard-edged gaze, doing his best not to flinch. Her irises were a dark hazel, the pupils contracting as her brow smoothed.

"I'm taking another away from you, I'm afraid," she said to the supervisor. "Kluehnn will want this one."

The altered man swore, casting his club to the dusty ground. "How am I expected to do my job?"

"If need be, get in there with the rest of them," she said lightly. And then she was touching Mull's arm with surprising gentleness, helping him to his feet.

He'd *done it*.

The next moments were a haze to him, his mind swimming with success. He gathered only slim impressions – the maw of the den's mouth, the coolness of the air inside, the many white-stitched eyes against gray cloth. She led him to a small bathing chamber, where she found a fresh set of clothes for him.

He took a moment to breathe when he was alone, hiding his filter beneath the gray clothes, the white-stitched eye staring at him. No warmed bath here, no soaking tub. But he relished every dip of the ladle into the barrel, the feel of the cold water sluicing over his skin. He was in the den. Once he got his bearings and figured out what they wanted of him, he'd find the tomb.

The altered entered without knocking. Thankfully he was already dried and dressed in the gray tunic and pants, his filter tucked up against his skin. "Eat this." She approached with no further preamble, something small and white held in her hand.

For a moment, he hesitated. "I'll get to ask a boon?"

"You will be rewarded."

That wasn't *exactly* what he'd asked. But he couldn't really see a way to refuse. Better to earn himself some favor through compliance. Her hand grasped his chin before he could take the piece of food from her. He opened his mouth, startled, and she placed it on his tongue.

He chewed and swallowed before he could think too much about it. It had the softness of steamed bread, with a sweet and gritty paste in the middle. A sticky residue lingered on his teeth. He swiped his tongue over it.

"Follow me."

"Are we going to see one of Kluehnn's aspects?" Mull dared as they walked through the tunnels. The floor sloped down, and soon he lost any sense of how deep they'd gone. Lanterns lined the walls at regular intervals, illuminating the faces of strangers as they passed. She didn't answer him.

Finally, they entered a vast chamber, stalactites dripping from the ceiling. The floor was lined with cushions, a wooden altar taking vague shape from the darkness at the other end of the hall.

She led him toward it.

Two other godkillers stood there, violet gems winking at their waists. Her cohort. She must have spoken to them while he'd bathed, because they said nothing, only watched as he approached.

A pit appeared in the floor, as wide as Mull was tall. The godkiller stopped at the edge, her cohort on the other side.

He knew, from his studies, that Kluehnn's aspects often existed deep underground, ascending to speak to his followers or to perform one function or another in the den. His step slowed. The godkillers watched him, expectant.

He peered over the edge. Only darkness met his gaze. The longer he looked, the more he realized: it wasn't the depth that created the black, but a cloud, a haze, a mass of smoke. It moved, shifting like the surface of the ocean. His mind went immediately to the descriptions of restoration, the black, smoky wall sweeping over the landscape and overtaking both man and animal alike.

"Is that where Kluehnn—"

A palm touched his back. The light prick of claws.

And then the godkiller shoved him into the hole.

20

Sheuan

11 years after the restoration of Kashan
and 572 years after the Shattering

Langzu - Inner Bian

Every ruler of every realm owes a tithe of gems to Kluehnn as part of the god pact. In Langzu, this is the Sovereign. And the clans, as stewards of the land, owe a certain tithe of gems to the Sovereign. Thus, mining crews are sponsored by the clans and the liaisons are appointed by the Sovereign. Given that gems always go missing during this process, sold and bought by the clans, the system isn't exactly airtight, and records are loosely kept.

Sheuan had done what she could, in secret, to ensure her family wasn't entirely out on their own. But what she could do felt so vastly inadequate. A few houses purchased here and there, places to hide, to lie low. Word sent through others so she would not be seen associating with the clanless. Her mother sent no word back. She thought about her mother sometimes, her grim determination to save their clan, a stone gripped in a steady hand. That stone was now so many grains of sand. What did she have to live for now?

It wasn't her problem to bear. She had to remember that.

As the Sovereign's wife, she had access to her own coffers, though they were much smaller than his. Anything she spent, she made sure to funnel through other channels, so any bookkeeping would point the Sovereign in other directions. Some deep instinct told her she was living with a predator, and though she didn't think she was quite a prey animal, she knew he'd turn on her once she'd lived out her usefulness.

Dust scuffed up as she strode down the street, the hot air oppressive as a weighted blanket; she blinked against the pressure on her eyes. She licked her lips; they still felt parched in spite of the water she kept drinking. She didn't look back, though she could feel the presence of two of the Sovereign's enforcers at her shoulders. It was becoming increasingly difficult to find time alone.

And she knew they'd report to the Sovereign what she was doing.

Mull's workshop was as she'd left it. She could almost feel his presence there, the feel of his thin-framed body as she'd hugged him goodbye. Workers glanced up as she entered, gazes lingering on the enforcers before they returned to their tasks. The Sovereign wanted as many filters as she could produce, but she was the only one who knew how to make them and she couldn't share that knowledge without increasing risk.

The enforcers made as if to follow her into the shop, but she held up a hand. "Absolutely not. You wait outside. There are two entrances and one of you can watch each of them to be sure I'm not in any danger. But you'll get in the way inside and be a distraction to my customers." Both of them – a man and a woman – shifted on their feet, exchanging glances. The woman opened her mouth to speak, but Sheuan talked over her. "He's probably told you not to let me out of your sight. I'm not asking you to shirk your duties." She rapped her knuckles on a nearby workbench. "Am I in any danger in here?"

The closest worker lifted his goggles. "Aye, if you don't keep your hands to yourself and watch your step. Sometimes someone drops a tack, and the saws are sharp, so you need to give everyone fair space."

"Will you protect me from saws and tacks?" Sheuan said to the blue-clad enforcers, her brow lifted.

The woman hesitated, wiped the beaded sweat from her forehead. "That's not—"

"Not your duty," Sheuan finished smoothly. "Since I'm safe from everything in here except my own carelessness, you can wait outside. As I've requested." She let the threat linger in the soft end of her sentence – did she need to make this an order? – and waited.

They did as she asked, shuffling back into the street and letting her close the door behind them. The Sovereign might have told them to watch her, but the Sovereign was in his castle, and she was here, and only a half-step in rank below him.

She turned to the corner where Mull always sat, now cordoned off with screens. The silhouette of a woman shadowed the thick paper. Sheuan ducked behind a screen.

Her mother stood there, peering out from between the closed shutter slats. She whirled as soon as she heard Sheuan's footsteps. There was something gaunt about her, though her arms looked no thinner than they had before. Sheuan couldn't decide if it was the light or the way the white robes of mourning washed out her mother's skin tone, melding with the white in her hair. There was something muted about the way she regarded Sheuan – whereas before her gaze had always been sharp, discerning, it now felt wrapped in gauze.

"My uncle . . ." Sheuan began.

"Dead," her mother finished. "The Otangu clan have had their revenge."

Sheuan fished in the satchel at her side, handing a purse to her mother. More coin to tide her family over. "I'm sorry. Use it to give him a proper funeral." It seemed as though it had only been a few days ago that her uncle had argued with her mother in the garden, lamenting the money spent on Sheuan's training. And now he was dead. Just as he'd feared.

Her mother's thin lips pressed together. "Don't pretend you have regrets. This is a consequence of what you've done."

Bold of her mother to assume she didn't have regrets. Sheuan hadn't been fond of her uncle – he was too loud, too brash, too caught in old ways. She often did have regrets, but that didn't mean she would do anything differently, given the chance. Some regrets she could live with more than others. "I made a judgment call." She'd said all this before; she wasn't sure why she felt the need to keep defending herself to her mother. Old habits. "The Sovereign was never going to restore our clan. But he was willing to raise me up, and me alone."

Her mother let out a soft huff of breath, her hands curling like claws at her sides. "Yes, of course. You had to do what was advantageous for you. Individual over clan and even family. Your father was the same – feckless, irresponsible, thinking only of increasing his status without considering how to mitigate risk."

Strange, how the words could still sting. She was the Sovereign's wife, her mother just some clanless old woman. Maybe it was because Sheuan truly hadn't wanted anything bad to befall her family. She found herself reaching out, wanting to unclench her mother's hands, to feel the touch of that weathered palm against hers. "You have to understand, I didn't have control over our clan's dissolution. I didn't ask for it. I couldn't prevent it."

There was no softness in response. Her caress only met the outside of her mother's unyielding fist. She found herself pivoting, a response she couldn't quite control. "You said he was irresponsible. What exactly was my father doing before he was executed?"

If eyes could spit venom, her mother's would have. "Getting involved in things he shouldn't have. He—"

Raised voices sounded over the noises of the workshop. Someone had entered. Sheuan frowned and drew one of the screens aside to exit, ready to send the enforcers back into the streets. "Stay here," she said to her mother.

It wasn't the enforcers. Mull's mother and older brother stood in the doorway, their gazes searching the corners of the workshop, as if he was hiding in them. Every time she saw Kiang, she wondered that he and Mull were brothers at all. They were of similar height, but Kiang was broader. He'd taken to shaving the hair on his head to a close stubble, probably to disguise where it had gone thin, and his beard was iron gray and a little longer than Mull's. While Mull always seemed to be drifting halfway between this world and a place Sheuan couldn't see, Kiang seemed undeniably grounded, his thoughts existing in the here and now. Mull strongly resembled his mother, down to the sharp cheekbones and thin arms.

Sheuan inclined her head to them both. She'd known they'd be by sooner or later, but she'd hoped it would be later. "Ah, the Reisuns. Can I assist you?"

"Mull hasn't come home yet," his mother said, her lips pinched. "He said he was visiting one of the daughters of the Temiki clan at their estate in the mountains of Ruzhi, but we've not had word from him since."

Kiang stepped in front of her. "You've generously managed his workshop while he's been gone, but we cannot expect you to do so indefinitely."

Oh, Sheuan knew this game. The polite ousting. This wouldn't do, not when the Sovereign was expecting her to produce more filters. Just as well – she could out-polite the best of them, maneuvering her way straight back to where she wanted to be. "It's been no trouble for me. The Reisun clan must have so many matters to attend to, not the least of which is finding their wayward son. I can continue to manage the shop until he's found."

"You must be busy with your new position." Kiang's gaze trailed over her gray silken dress, the crossover neckline secured by a silver belt in the shape of a blooming cherry branch. She'd declined a robe – it was too hot in the streets – but she'd allowed the servants to do her hair, to place a silver comb in it that trailed pearl beads. They clicked against one another each time she moved her head.

"I'm never too busy to keep a promise to a cousin and good friend." She stopped, hesitated as though she wasn't sure about what she was going to say. "Mull told me not to tell you ... but it's been so long since he's been gone."

"Tell us what?" his mother asked.

"He didn't go to the Temiki clan. He went west of Ruzhi. He went to look for Tolemne's Path."

"Again?" Kiang's face was a study in quick-changing emotions. First surprise, then annoyance, frustration, and ultimately concern. "That *fool*."

Sheuan had never liked Mull's brother, but she couldn't deny he cared about Mull. As did his mother. Her chest ached. The next part would not be fun. "I think something must have happened to him. I've not had word from him either, nor any of his companions."

His mother clutched at her collar, leaning heavily into her elder son. "We have to find him. We have to send search parties."

"Caving is dangerous." Sheuan let that hang in the air. "As is traveling the roads. I'll check with the enforcers to see if they've had any word. I'll have them follow up with you." And they'd say Mull was murdered, just as she'd planned. Best let someone else handle giving the unpleasant news.

Kiang grasped his mother, holding her upright. "The Reisun family can take back management of Mull's workshop until we find out what happened to him. I'll speak to Imeah's family — they might know more."

Sheuan went swiftly to a table of refreshments for the workers, pouring a mug of water for his mother and returning to the entrance. She waited until she was sure the old woman had a firm grasp on the cup before letting go. No need to add pottery shards to the tacks on the floor. "Mull left the workshop in my hands. You'll find it's become more profitable since I took it over, and all the money earned will continue to go to your clan. Find some satisfaction in that."

Kiang gave her a skeptical look. "You are the Sovereign's wife now. Haven't you other things to do?"

"What I do with my time is my business, not yours." She let that hang in the air. She might have once been the daughter of a failing royal clan, but she wasn't anymore. And the Reisuns weren't even royal status. They were noble tier. She outranked them in every possible way and Kiang had overstepped. He blanched as the realization washed over him.

"Yes, of course." He bowed, keeping his arm around his mother. "Please, accept our congratulations on your recent marriage."

She could always sense conversational opportunities; they hung before her like ripe peaches, ready to be plucked. Mull was the sort of conversationalist who was content to let someone else lead, unless she landed on a topic he had some special knowledge about. Kiang always needed to be in control. Growing up with someone like Mull could do that to a person – Kiang would always feel insecure about his intelligence. She could lean on that, if she chose to, on his embarrassment, his desire to recover. "Thank you. I've been learning so much more about the Sovereign. His rise to power was quite remarkable. He must have been quite the diplomat." She intentionally kept things vague and just the slightest bit wrong. Not that she had some new, startling insights. Other than that first night they'd spent together, the Sovereign had paid her little attention.

Kiang scoffed, taking the bait. "Diplomat? My father told me what it was like. The Sovereign came out of nowhere, he built the enforcers from the ground up."

"Oh." The slightest drop in tone, as though she was mortified to be caught saying something incorrect. "He must have trained his enforcers quite thoroughly. He's often said that he values those closest to him and wants them to improve their skills."

Kiang was shaking his head before she'd finished, releasing his mother to cut a hand through the air. "My father was there when it all happened. The Sovereign's specialized enforcers are very good at getting information they shouldn't. Too good. Unnaturally good. But you should ask the Risho clan about that. They helped the Sovereign in his rise to power. That's why he promoted them to royal tier."

Kiang's mother gripped his loose hand. "Be quiet. You shouldn't speak such rumors." Her gaze flicked to Sheuan and she understood the look to mean *especially not in front of her.* "Thank you for looking after the workshop for our clan." And then she guided her son away, as though he were a wayward child.

The door shut behind them. A few workers who'd stopped

to listen returned to their work. Sheuan tried to remember their faces, just in case. Never could be too cautious about who was listening in and who was paying attention.

Kiang's mother needn't have worried too much about the rumors her son was spouting. Sheuan already knew about the enforcers and their ties to magic, but the bit about gleaning information – that, she hadn't been aware of. She'd always assumed the magic they used had something to do with their ability to fight.

She scratched absent-mindedly at her back, felt the pinfeathers there, the downy softness of new growth. Each time she caught the feathers growing, she pulled them out, and each time she pulled them out, they grew back. There was something satisfying about scratching there, feeling the ridge of some unknown structure pressing against the skin.

Her fingernails came away bloody. Quickly, before anyone noticed, she rubbed them against the palm of her hand. A bit of flaking redness remained. She flicked at it as her mother emerged from Mull's workspace.

This time, her mother caught her hands in her own. To Sheuan's relief, she didn't look at them, didn't catch the hint of blood still clinging. "You should wait," Sheuan said. "Wait until I'm gone and the enforcers are gone. Then you can leave." She pulled to free her hands, but her mother leaned in, her breath tinged with the sweet earthiness of loquat tea.

Her voice was low in Sheuan's ear. "Don't think I don't know what it is you're doing."

"What do you think I'm doing?" Sheuan couldn't keep the peevish tone out of her voice. Her mother's hands squeezed hers so hard she could feel the bones beneath the soft wrinkled skin.

"You must stop digging. If you want to keep your life, you must stop."

21
Lithuas
220 years before the Shattering

Unterra - a home in the second territory

The fauna and flora of Unterra are far different than what we find on the surface of our world. There aren't many specific descriptions — while we suppose some mortals made it to Unterra, only one or two have come back. But those who have returned described masses of glowing roots from the Numinars above, birds with iridescent feathers, equine creatures with cloven hooves and shimmering green coats. And above it all, in the very center of our world, the inner star.

Nioanen's home lay nestled in the giant, swirling roots of a Numinar. Shoots of the enormous tree arose from the gently glowing roots, sprouting into a miniature forest. The home itself was small, modest. It didn't have the sprawling grandeur of Barexi's palace, or the spiraling towers of Irael's castle. Every time it was Nioanen's turn to host a party, he let them all gather outside no matter the weather, and scowled at anyone who dared complain. Lithuas glanced up as she approached. A layer of cloud cover obscured the inner star, the green curve of Unterra's landscape disappearing behind the mist.

She'd gathered support from the younger gods first. It had been easy to rile them up, to get them thirsting for vengeance, for retribution on the mortals. She'd waffled over approaching Nioanen for a long time, but if she could get him on board with Kluehnn's plan, the rest would fall into line. Even Ayaz respected Nioanen, though he might bitch and moan at the way others deferred to him. "He's such a steadfast bore," he had drawled to her at the last gathering he'd hosted, running a finger over the edge of a dagger. A smattering of glittering gold scales marked his cheekbones, swirling across his shoulders and down his back. His tail lashed as he spoke, the end of it sharp as a blade. "I don't know what Irael sees in him."

"Even Nioanen doesn't know what Irael sees in him."

"More accurate to say he's completely oblivious to it. Irael is too flighty for actual courage; that shapeshifter will forever pine in silence."

Lithuas wasn't so sure, but then, she could smell change in ways others could not. While others saw the same thing occurring day in and day out, she knew there was no consistency in the world except inconsistency.

She knocked on Nioanen's door. According to the gossip she'd gathered from the younger gods, he was currently in residence. She never personally kept track of these things.

It took a moment for him to answer. Other than their yearly gatherings, the elder gods seldom spent time with one another. They were solitary by nature, keeping to their territories, the younger gods flitting from one to the next like flocks of birds migrating from lake to lake.

Somehow, she was always startled by how tall he was, his golden-brown wings filling the space left open by the double doors. If she'd had to guess at what his home looked like from his appearance, she would have assumed soaring ceilings, wrought-iron railings, tablecloths threaded with gold and silver. The aesthetic beyond him spoke instead of warm and dark places, the soft, musky interior of a nest. Worn but plush cushions, a stout table, rugs strewn in seemingly random patterns. He had to duck to get through his own doorways.

He'd spent too much time among peasants.

Without a word, he stood to the side to let her pass. She was in the form she used most often, the one that reflected her depictions in the mortal world above – a woman with silver eyes and bright silver hair. She brushed past him and settled into a chair by the front window. It sank beneath her weight, cradling her. He offered her a glass of syrup, which she waved away. She was fortified enough.

He sat in the chair opposite her, the tips of his wings grazing the faded rug. She arranged her skirts, opened her mouth.

"I'm not interested," Nioanen said.

She narrowed her eyes at him. "Then why did you invite me in?"

"Someone has to put a stop to this foolishness before it runs out of hand. And you seem intent on letting it run out of hand. Change is not always good, Lithuas."

Her name on his lips always sounded like a reprimand. It made her want to shift into a porcupine, to lift her spines and hiss. She was not younger. She did not need to be brought to heel. "You've not even heard me out."

"I've heard enough from others. You think I sit here alone all day, that I never mingle with the younger gods?"

She cast him a sardonic look, wishing she'd asked for a glass of syrup now, just so she could lift it in his direction. Instead, she inclined her chin. "Defender of the Helpless."

"They're not helpless, and you cannot keep stirring them up this way. I hear you've fallen in with one of them."

"Kluehnn. He's the one proposing action, yes."

"And you're supporting it. Be careful who you throw your considerable weight behind. Did you know that some of the younger gods have disappeared lately? Have you taken the time to hear what's happening within your territory's borders?"

Ah, well this she *hadn't* heard, and it irked her that Nioanen knew something she didn't. She'd not had the time to wander her territory; she was traveling to other places, here and across the sea, trying to gather support for a series of offensives. "Younger gods disappear sometimes. They go above ground, they make fatal errors, they challenge one another to foolish actions."

"Yes, but these disappearances haven't been spread out in the way you might expect. Who is this Kluehnn? How much do you know about him?"

In truth, she didn't know much, but she didn't appreciate Nioanen's prying. "He's new. Sometimes that's what it takes to initiate change. Someone who thinks in different ways, who doesn't see the barriers we always put into place. The ways we tell ourselves we *can't* act."

"Assassinating the mortal leaders? You think that will bring about any actual change?"

"Yes. They cannot be allowed to think they can act with impunity. We sit down here and drink the syrup from the Numinar roots. And above, the mighty trees are being cut down, one by one. How long will these roots survive?" On an impulse, she reached out, touched his knee. "I am not content to let our kind die out without fighting for a chance at life."

He tossed her hand away as though it were a spider, ready

to bite. "I cannot be compassionate toward a need for reckless violence."

"Purposeful. Necessary." She could feel everything unsaid between them. They'd failed in their duties too, though they had good reason to abandon them. The mortals had made their sacrifices pointless.

His lip twisted, as though he'd bitten into something acidic. He might have been handsome had he not so often looked sour. "You won't stop, will you?"

"The proposal Kluehnn drew up with my help is solid. We put together five teams of four gods, each one with a shapeshifter, an augmenter, a changer, a maker. We assign them neighboring realms. They assess the situation, move in quickly, kill whoever is ruling."

"And if the realm is ruled by a council? If it is ruled by a gathering of their elders?"

"We kill all of them. It sends a message – we will not tolerate the desecration of the Numinars."

His wings ruffled; dust rose from the windowsill. Outside, a faint pattering of rain darkened the root passing just below the glass. "You cannot control the message. They won't take it as a warning. They'll take it as an act of war."

"And you would rather do *nothing*." She pushed up from the cushion, suddenly discontent to be cradled by it. "How well has that worked for you?"

"Lithuas, *please*." He sounded so weary, she was nearly soothed into sitting back down. "We are friends, yes? I understand your urgency, your need for change. But you don't know this Kluehnn. Let us all meet, the seven elder gods, and discuss solutions."

It sounded so level-headed. But how many times had they tried this very same thing? Seven elder gods in a room, arguing and debating and changing nothing. It was always easier to settle back into old patterns. They were a cart stuck in a rut in the road, rocking back and forth but never breaking free. "You're always the first to leave these discussions."

He looked to the window, shifting in his seat. They both knew he preferred his solitude, that he couldn't bear these conversations for too long. Nioanen had only ever been stirred to passion when defending those weaker than himself; he didn't know what to do when faced with the verbal daggers of his peers. He couldn't summon Zayyel to his hand nor did he have the same eloquence Irael or Barexi did.

She prepared to launch another verbal barb, hoping she'd find one that would dig deep, that would make him understand. But he straightened, his gaze suddenly fixed, like a cat spotting a bird just out of reach.

He shoved himself from his chair, wings drawn tight to his body, and swept past her. Lithuas blinked. "What—"

A loud knock cut her off.

Nioanen opened the door, and a god with cat-slit pupils, claws, and black-striped fur stumbled in. Moisture clung to the ends of his whiskers, his shirt stuck to his torso. Wet pawprints marked the rug at the entry. A young god, one Lithuas remembered from the past several gatherings.

"Yanera went missing." He was gasping, leaning against the inside wall, legs trembling. "But I found her. I found . . ." A wrenching sob.

Nioanen tucked a wing around the god. Lithuas could feel the warmth from his feathers even two steps away. The impulsive part of her wanted to touch them, but she kept her hands still. Perhaps Nioanen was right, and she needed to tend to her own territory. Had others disappeared there?

"What did you find?" Nioanen's voice was low and soothing.

Lithuas almost expected the god to shake himself, to send droplets of moisture smattering across the entry, but he only stood there, quivering and miserable. "I found *half* of her. Just her arms and her upper torso. It ... There were *teeth* marks on her spine."

Nioanen took his arm. "Did you leave her there? You shouldn't have left her there. Were there signs of life in the body?"

There was always a chance to find the rest of Yanera, to piece her back together. A shudder of revulsion coursed through Lithuas. But if the god had been eaten? If she had been consumed?

There wouldn't be anything left to find.

22

Hakara

11 years after the restoration of Kashan
and 572 years after the Shattering

Langzu – on the road to Xiazen

Among the gods, there are promises and there are blood pacts. A promise is binding, leading to the death of the god that breaks that promise. A blood pact, if broken by anyone party to the pact, leads to the death of all the gods involved. A blood pact can also be used to bind gods beyond those initiating the pact.

I could feel the difference in the two bonds, though I wasn't sure exactly how. I worried at it like a loose tooth as we made our way south. It wasn't that the bond with Thassir was slack and that the bond with Rasha tugged at the back of my mind the farther we traveled. Each had something that was close to a *taste* when I focused on it – bright and tangy for Rasha, smoke and pine sap for Thassir.

After I'd hurt her and then thrown her back in time to save

her life, I'd known I couldn't let her leave again without knowing where she was. Knowing that she was alive. It had been such a near thing. I could still feel my blade entering her body, that moment of panic before I'd remembered the yellow gem and what Utricht had once said to me. *I've seen one used once. Took away a killing wound as though it had never been there.*

Dashu's hand wrapped around my upper arm. "Careful." He nodded to the hole I'd been about to step into. "Ground squirrels." He let go as I hopped around it, his gaze studiously focused on the distance. Thassir wheeled above us, waiting for us to catch up before he moved unerringly southward. Always south. Lithuas hadn't slowed since we'd lost her in the lakebed.

And neither of my earthbound companions was speaking to me.

Yellowed grass cracked beneath my boots as I dodged another hole, clods of baked, uneven earth surrounding it. The vegetation rustled as squirrels darted away from our approaching party.

Sweat trickled between my shoulder blades. Each time I asked Thassir if we were gaining on Lithuas, all he would say was, "We're close," before his eyes narrowed and he found some excuse to walk or fly away. And this response, when I thought about it, didn't really answer the question, did it?

We'd used some of the Unanointed coin to hop on various wagons on our way south, but sometimes our wayward shapeshifter led us too far off the road for us to ride in comfort. As she had now. I wondered if she, in the form of some slinking cat, was grinning to herself as she thought of the trouble she was causing her pursuers.

For some reason, that was all I could imagine her as right now – a cat. A troublemaking creature with little compassion for those it caused trouble for. As though she could hear my thoughts, Rumenesca let out a small growl. I was tempted to shake the basket I carried, but honestly wasn't sure I had the energy.

"It's my turn," Alifra said, holding her hand out.

I pulled the makeshift strap over my head, noting the damp streak it left across my tunic. "I won't argue with you."

The scent of the ocean drifted over the hills, and I watched Alifra's posture tense, her expression tightening. She tried to hide it with her movements, slinging the basket over one shoulder, tucking a hand over the lid.

I wasn't sure what to say. She'd confessed to me, right before we'd raided the den, that her daughter had drowned when they'd made the crossing. That she had nearly drowned too. I thought of her waking on the sand, her arms empty, the anguish – all mixed with the scent of decaying seaweed and the salt on her lips.

"If Lithuas takes to the sea—"

"I'll be fine," Alifra broke in. "As long as we find her."

I knew that feeling too. The emptiness of the landscape, the still air – it made it all too easy to fall into your thoughts. Moving helped. Doing things helped. But if I stayed still for too long, I thought about the stiff-backed way Maman had walked away from Rasha and me both, the slump of her broad shoulders, the stoic way she hadn't even turned for Rasha's tears. She was going to make it through the barrier, she'd explained. She was going to find her family in Cressima and then bring them through. But she wouldn't look me in the eye as she said it, only patted my shoulder as though that would help me understand.

I hadn't begged. I hadn't cried. Maybe I should have.

I took out my water skin, swished it, and swallowed hard past the lump in my throat. "We'll find her. She may be an elder god, but there are only so many places in the world she can run to."

And if she ran to all of them? If we cornered her at the ends of the earth, a place where we both were forced to stillness? No – I wouldn't be still. I'd be fighting her. I'd kill her, and then I'd focus on protecting the Unanointed, on finding some way to help Langzu survive without restoration.

Alifra watched Thassir in the sky as he caught an updraft, becoming a spiraling speck. "I used to start fights, back then. It helped. It brought everything into sharp focus, had me feeling an actual part of my body. Like I was here and present and away from everything that had come before." She lengthened her stride, her gaze on the crest of the hill, where Dashu waited for us. "I can't do that anymore. I'm more sad than angry, see?" One shoulder rolled in a half-hearted shrug.

"My sister—" I started.

She shook her head. "Don't apologize to me. I understand not being able to … let go. And Dashu – he understands too, though he might not say it." Her mouth quirked in a grin. "Let's ask him about the feud between Barexi and Ayaz. He cannot tell that story straight. It'll give us both something else to think about. Hey! Dashu!"

I hurried to catch up to her.

"How did Ayaz end up cutting Barexi to pieces? Seems a bit extreme," she said, shouldering him.

He frowned, a stern expression that only made his fine brow more noticeable. "I've told you this story many times," he said.

"Hakara hasn't heard it."

A moment's hesitation, and then his face brightened at the thought of a new audience. "Well, it all began when Barexi argued with Ayaz that cutting things away never improved them." He rubbed his fingertips against his goatee. "But I suppose that doesn't explain why Barexi argued with Ayaz in the first place. Ayaz decided to murder a mortal Barexi was watching over and cultivating. Not that he didn't have his reasons – he said the mortal should be pruned for the health of his family lineage, which, of course, Barexi intensely disagreed with . . ."

Alifra gave me a knowing look and I did my best not to crack a smile.

Thassir landed next to me just as Dashu was describing the way Ayaz had scattered the pieces of Barexi across the realms.

"She's coming back this way." His gaze was locked on the crest of the hill, his wings spread so that the feathers almost draped over my shoulder. I'd refilled my pouches, even if the one that had held the time gem was now empty. We could do this. We could fight her and win.

"Any indication of godkillers or aspects?" Alifra pulled her crossbow free, finger tapping against the metal ratchet.

"No." Thassir flexed his claws. "But I didn't see her either. She may not be in her human form."

I strode toward the crest of the hill, drawing my sword, my other hand ready at my belt. "We take the high ground. Stay close."

The port town of Xiazen opened up beneath us as we summited, a city that blanketed a gentle valley. We weren't on the road, but I could see it snaking out from between the buildings, a thread pulled loose from a quilt of blue tile rooftops. And that quilt itself merged into the glittering sea beyond, white sails dotting the water, nearly invisible even when I squinted. Here, closer to the sea, a breeze blew the yellowed clouds further inland, leaving free patches of brilliant sky.

Grass crunched beneath my boots with each step.

I didn't see Lithuas. "Where is she?"

Thassir scanned the horizon. "I can't be sure. I can only sense her when she shifts or uses magic."

Alifra gave a little shrug, though she set the cat basket down and lifted her crossbow at her shoulder. "Could be she's turned herself into a ground squirrel and is hoping to sneak past us. Maybe" – she eyed Thassir – "we should let the cat out. It could chase her down."

Thassir's wings pulled tight to his sides. "You are joking." His voice was flat, the unspoken *You had better not* a heavy implication that came with a side serving of violence.

Alifra let out a small, delighted laugh.

I held up a hand. A dark speck had appeared in the sky, traveling rapidly toward us. I squinted against the sea's reflected light. A bird. There was a brightness to it, a glow just underneath the wings.

I pointed. "Thassir?"

Out of the corner of my eye I saw him shake his head. "She's still not used any magic."

"Well what in all the depths is that creature then?" It drew closer, and I didn't have to squint anymore to see the glow. Dread pinched at my belly. "Alifra. Shoot it down."

She sighted with the crossbow. "Still too far. It's got to get a fair bit closer if I want a good shot at it."

The glow was orange and flickering; the wings of a bird took shape. It dropped lower in the sky. I suddenly understood.

It wasn't magic the bird carried, nor any god gems. It was a branch. A branch that just happened to be on fire. And here we were, standing on an entire hilltop covered in bone-dry kindling.

"Oh shit," Alifra breathed.

My heart jumped. "Thassir! Take her out of the sky."

His wings swept out just as I started to run down the slope, the scent of the sea mingling with the sweetness of dried grass and old wood. I'd be giving up the high ground, but how much would that matter if Lithuas burned us all to a crisp? She wasn't coming here to fight us. Why bother when she could let wind and fire do the work for her?

I remembered watching her train the Unanointed fighters, praising efficiency of movement, expending the least amount of energy for the biggest results. What did she care for a land that Kluehnn was hoping to restore?

"The road!" I called to Dashu and Alifra. It was wide, the surrounding area cleared of vegetation. If we wanted to have a chance, we needed to make it there and into the city.

I caught sight of Thassir above us, flying toward the falcon. Each beat of his black wings flattened the grass below him. My feet pounded against the hard-packed earth, grass brushing my knees, catching my bare elbows. I couldn't stop to scratch.

Thassir dove for Lithuas. Even if he managed to seize her, she might drop the branch. A flash of white and she darted to the side, narrowly dodging his claws. Without pausing to recover, the burning branch clutched in her talons, she snapped her wings out and glided over the grass.

The branch grazed the top.

It was like touching a finger to a house of cards. The grass collapsed into licking flames. I skidded to a halt and Thassir rolled into the ground near me, unable to correct his momentum. His black wings sent up clouds of dust. And then he somehow managed to get his feet beneath him and sprang from slope to air again.

But he'd lost time, and he simply wasn't as quick as a falcon was.

A bolt zipped through the air, but a sudden gust of wind waylaid it. Alifra swore. Lithuas dropped the branch before Thassir could reach her, and then with a flick of her wings she was off toward the city again. Thassir pursued her.

"Hakara!"

Alifra and Dashu were trapped on the other side of the rapidly spreading flames, smoke nearly obscuring them from view.

I pointed downslope. "Make for the road! I have to go after her!" I didn't wait to see if they obeyed.

I followed the dark shape of Thassir's wings, sprinting toward the ocean and the dockside town that marked the very end of this realm – and our last chance to catch Lithuas before she ventured into the sea.

23
Hakara

11 years after the restoration of Kashan
and 572 years after the Shattering

Langzu - Xiazen

The Great Upheaval occurred 161 years before the Shattering. According to historical documents, the gods assassinated nearly all the world's leaders in a span of ten days. While this threw governments into disarray, heirs were quickly chosen, successors appointed, and other than a new distrust in the gods, life returned mostly to normal.

The acrid scent of smoke filled my nostrils, my eyes watering as I ran after Thassir's shape in the sky. Couldn't see Lithuas, but that didn't matter as long as I could see him. We had to catch her before she could flee across the sea. She was a shapeshifter and an elder god – there were ways she could get through or around the barrier. Ways we didn't have access to.

And then what?

Air burned in my throat, my chest aching. She'd go to the

southern continent, she'd take over any rebellion they had brewing there. She'd use them to find more corestones. And then she'd help Kluehnn restore that realm and this one both.

We had to stop her. We had to kill her. It was the only way.

Thassir's wings shadowed the ground as he moved unerringly toward the city rooftops. I did my best to keep up, the ground beneath my feet uneven. I wasn't sure we'd be able to defeat her with just the two of us. Thassir might have once been Nioanen, but it was clear he wasn't that elder god anymore. I didn't know if he had the power to kill her, even if he tried.

My shirt clung to the dampness of my armpits, the air stickyhot and moist. The road was right there, a wagon stopped at the side as its occupants gawked at the fire behind me. I turned my face to the sky, looking for Thassir. My heart jumped. He'd disappeared. Had I lost him completely?

Something seized my arms. I tried to twist. My feet left the ground; my stomach felt like it was still tumbling down toward the road. I kicked.

"By Unterra, stay *still*," a voice growled. Thassir.

I would have felt relieved if there was more between me and the earth than several spans of empty air. I did my best to remain still, to be the sort of limp cargo I saw hawks carrying to their nests. The smell of smoke was thicker up here. I tried to look back, to see if Alifra and Dashu were safe.

Thassir grunted with effort, sounding very un-godlike. "If you keep that up, I'll drop you." His claws pricked my skin and I froze.

The rooftops of the city appeared below us, a dizzying array of tile, interspersed with cobblestones.

"Where is she?" I scanned the streets below. People wended their way through thoroughfares, alleys dark and littered with refuse, the smell of fish mingling with smoke. Xiazen was the size of Bian, bolstered by trade, the ships a quicker way to move from one part of the realm to another. I tried to pick out a pattern of movement, to find someone who didn't fit. There were a few altered in the crowd below, the mortals moving around them like water around river stones. I tried desperately not to think about what would happen if I fell.

I held my breath as Thassir readjusted his grip. "She shifted. Main thoroughfare, far as I can sense. Lingering magic right below us."

Main thoroughfare — the street leading out of the city and all the way down to the docks. Someone had once possessed the foresight to pave it wide, as if they'd known what Xiazen would one day become. Wagons joined people, the buildings on either side lined with merchants' stalls.

Lithuas wouldn't be wearing Mitoran's face. Not while trying to hide. There. A woman making her way determinedly toward the docks, not stopping to look at any of the stalls, her footsteps hurried. "Lower. Drop me there." I pointed ahead of her. "Woman in the straw hat, just past the green stall."

"I see her. I'll cut off any escape."

A brief moment of warmth for him blossomed in my chest. He'd known what I'd wanted him to do. There was a part of me that yearned for that sense of unity — the one we had when we fought, the bond slack, the aether there whenever I needed it.

Voices rose in alarm as Thassir swept down, the sounds carried on the ocean's breeze. He tossed me from a bit higher than I would have liked. I staggered, my knees nearly giving way. I pivoted just in time to see him land.

And there was the woman in the straw hat. Her face was broad and brown, her arms wrapped around a covered basket. Tendrils of graying hair peeked out from beneath her hat. She wore an apron with smudges of old brown blood. Her eyes widened as we locked gazes.

Yes. I had her. I stood between her and the sea.

She glanced behind her to see Thassir moving rapidly through the crowd. If the other altered were river stones, he was a boulder pushing his way upstream. Mortals scattered so as not to touch the night-dark feathers of his wings. His glower could have melted glass.

Lithuas did the only reasonable thing she could. She darted toward me. I reached out for her arm. Someone jostled me in their haste to get away from Thassir. I stumbled and she slipped out of my grasp. I gritted my teeth as I caught myself. Maybe we were not as aligned as I'd thought. Couldn't draw my sword. Not here, not where the Sovereign's enforcers might be lurking around a corner.

I chased her down the street.

She was surprisingly quick for such a short body, darting into an alleyway, disappearing around a corner at the end. I hoped Thassir had taken to the skies again, so he could keep a better eye on her path. I caught a glimpse of her straw hat as I followed.

"Right!" Thassir called from above.

I tore down a road to my right, nearly running into a man carrying a basket of laundry. I spun around him. Where? There. The flash of a foot into another alley.

She moved through the streets like she knew them. And I'd already been running before Thassir had hoisted me into the air. I pulled a green gem free of its pouch and swallowed it. He must have spotted the movement, because the ocean scent increased, the fizzing in my belly beginning just as I took in a deep breath of air.

I'd hold this breath if it was the last thing I did.

Smoky god limbs encased my own, sending me hurtling down the alley with the speed of a galloping horse. I had to bring my hands up to stop from slamming face-first into the plastered wall ahead of me. I pushed off from it, pursuing Lithuas down yet another alley. My lungs burned, protesting the lack of air after an already-strenuous run.

A dark shape dropped into the narrow alley ahead of the woman. Thassir, falling like a stone as he pulled his wings to his sides. The cobbles seemed to shift beneath my feet when he landed.

Lithuas stopped, pivoted. I let out my breath, my smoky limbs dissolving into the air. Her face paled. She didn't smirk. She didn't shift into her true form. She only stared, one arm still wrapped around her basket, the other raised in a gesture of surrender.

And that was when I had the first inkling we'd been played.

Thassir stalked toward the woman, and she shrank back. "She paid me to run," she gasped out. "She gave me two parcels. I couldn't turn that down."

This was the problem with living among desperate people – they were always willing to do something a little unscrupulous and a little dangerous for some coin. Couldn't say I was any different or any better.

My companion was less forgiving. He loomed over the woman. "What did she look like?"

Her lip trembled. "A sailor. She had a scar over her eyebrow. Black hair, shaved on the sides. Dark green sleeveless jacket that fell to her knees."

At least the woman was thorough. I gestured to Thassir. "The docks. Now." Without thinking, we met one another at the opening of the alley and I hopped into his arms. He leapt into the sky. Wind sheared past us, the scent of smoke thicker. I caught a glimpse of fire carts on their way out of the city, laden with water barrels and scythes.

We landed at the docks and, without speaking a word to one

another, split up to search. A green sleeveless jacket. A woman with a scar. She'd shifted earlier, but she hadn't shifted since then, which meant Thassir would have lost track of her.

Glares followed me as I shoved my way past sailors and fishmongers. The harbor at Xiazen wasn't small, each dock laden with ships. I scanned for green.

A hand seized my arm.

I whirled, ready to fight, fingers clutching instinctively for the hilt of my sword.

Dashu, with Alifra just behind. He'd taken custody of Thassir's cat basket; it swayed at his side. He pointed back toward the city. "There's a sailor murdered in an alley a little ways back. They just discovered her. There's a crowd gathering."

Enforcers would be on their way. My mind was hurtling forward, rusty gears grinding against one another. "Did you see her? Was the dead woman wearing a sleeveless green jacket?"

Alifra nodded. "Aye, she was."

"She didn't take just any shape, then. She took that woman's place. She's on a ship. She's already on a ship." I searched the docks. "We have to get Thassir. We need to get out of here. We need a boat. Now. Before enforcers start investigating."

Dashu hadn't let go of my arm. "Hakara." His voice was low. "You should stay here. In Xiazen."

I pulled away. "What?"

"You are now the leader of the Unanointed. They need you here, leading them, making sure they have something to hope for. And following Lithuas across the ocean . . ." He trailed off. "It may not be the wisest course of action. For you."

The wooden boards of the dock creaked beneath my feet as I shifted, torn between two places. I could feel the tug, the need to find Lithuas. The one thing I *knew* would change our world for the better. She was an elder god, and she'd betrayed not only mortals, but the gods as well. "I have to stop her. Before she does it again."

He'd pitched his voice as soothing, as though he was trying to reason with a stubborn child. "Alifra, Thassir, and I can chase her. Have you forgotten? She is looking for another corestone and you have one. It's one thing to stop her here, in Langzu. We don't know what things are like outside of this realm. We don't know if Kluehnn has more aspects in the southern continent, we don't know if Lithuas has more allies."

And she could have *fewer* allies farther south. We didn't know. We couldn't know. I could stay, but Guarin was better suited to managing our spies, our people. I had always been a one-edged blade, uncomplicated and single-minded. If I drove myself forward, after Lithuas, I knew my task. If I stayed? I wasn't Utricht, with his easy familiarity. I wasn't Sheuan, with her quick charm and clever mind.

Something yawned open inside me, a sinkhole so vast I didn't know the depths.

They'd chosen the wrong person.

A flash of green met my gaze, almost obscured by the sun glittering off the waves. I grabbed Dashu's shoulder, wordless.

A sailor smirked at me from the deck of a ship that was rapidly exiting the harbor. A sailor wearing a green sleeveless jacket, black hair shaved at the sides. I took note of the ship, the shape of its sails. Damn Thassir! Where was he when I really needed him? I could feel he was close, from the bond, but he wasn't close enough. "She's on that ship. We need to follow that ship. Alifra . . ."

She was already moving away, down the docks, her gaze sharp, stopping people, asking questions. My bond with Thassir slackened, the bond with Rasha still taut at the back of my mind.

And then Alifra was gesturing to us from another dock, and Thassir was there at my side. "She's on a boat," I said breathlessly. This was the closest we'd been since the lakebed at Bian. "Thassir and I can—"

"No." Dashu cut me off. "Too risky. We do this together. If we're quick, we can catch her today, out on the water."

Alifra was halfway up a gangplank when we arrived, arguing with the captain. Several sailors on deck watched us with curious gazes. "Ten parcels for a quick trip?" She scoffed. "You're going to the anchor anyways. What's it hurt to take a few more people? Do you want me to throw in an arm and a leg, too?"

The captain, a lanky fellow with black hair and the tilted-head attitude of a curious crow, pointed at Thassir. "That looks like three people in one," he said.

Thassir graciously took the cat basket back from Dashu. A faint meow sounded from within. "I also have a cat."

"You're not helping," Alifra muttered to him. "Five parcels," she countered.

"The cat will work while she's aboard," Thassir said.

The captain cast him a skeptical look. "Not every cat is a good ship's cat."

Thassir's feathers bristled. "She is a good cat. The best cat. In all circumstances."

We didn't have time for this, nor did I want Thassir starting a fight over one of his cats. Again. "Pay the man eight parcels and have done with it."

"I didn't agree to eight," he protested.

I slid past Alifra on the gangplank, putting my foot on deck. "You can take eight or you can pay two to have someone scrub blood off your deck."

"You're trespassing! That's illegal!" The captain's hand tightened around his belt knife. Really? If that was the first complaint his mind went to, we were going to have an interesting time on this trip. I wondered how he felt about the legality of elder gods.

I did a quick scan for enforcers. If they'd arrived, they'd be at the alley with the dead sailor first. "Do I look like I care about the law?" I knew I probably smelled like sweat and fire, my boots still dusty and the muscles of my arms tightening as I gripped the hilt of my sword. The gangplank dipped and I felt Thassir's presence at my back.

"Fine. Eight." The captain's face paled, his gaze focused on Thassir. He was one of those people that looked big from far away, and even bigger up close.

"And that's a good bargain for you, make no mistake." I squinted out at the sea. I could still see the boat that Lithuas had fled on, the sails filled with wind. "Now follow that ship. We've work to do."

24
Rasha

11 years after the restoration of Kashan
and 572 years after the Shattering

Langzu - Kluehnn's den northeast of Bian

The mortals didn't always cut down the Numinars. There are records, stretching far, far back, that show entire cities being built in and around the roots and branches of these trees, their vast canopies sheltering the buildings below. No one knows for sure who first discovered that magic could be extracted by burning the tree's branches, but the mortals went from burning the dead branches, to creating machines that could better extract and capture the magic from those fires, to creating machines that would allow them to burn the living branches to extract magic. They began to cut down the trees.

And with each step along the way, the mortals lost more and more respect for the gods.

T he empty spot at my belt was a constant thing, a lightness I couldn't stop being aware of. I'd only recently earned that blade, and now it was gone, in my sister's possession. Even as we trekked back toward the den, I could feel Hakara's presence in the back of my mind, moving farther and farther away, a tenuous stretching. My bandaged thigh ached.

"Your sister bested you again," Khatuya said, a slight limp in her step.

I squinted up at the sky, the setting sun searing the horizon a deep red. A bird flew in a widening circle above us. I had the sneaking suspicion it was the crow, but I was too tired and heartsick to do a thing about it. "She didn't best me last time. I let her go."

"She bested you." Khatuya's voice was firm. "If there was a winner in that contest, it was her. And now she's taken all our blades."

Naatar put a hand to my arm just as I'd opened my mouth to respond. He spoke softly, so I had to quiet myself to listen. "You know where she is now. And if she was telling the truth, that means you know where *he* is. Maybe that will be enough."

We fell into silence as we walked, though I could still feel that tension between me and Khatuya. Would knowing where Thassir was be enough to escape punishment? Not likely. I'd lost the fight, I'd lost our blades, and now we were returning to the den with nothing to show for it, and a bond that meant Hakara would know I was coming. I hadn't seen a better option than returning to the den, but I wasn't sure if Kluehnn would view the situation the same way. The sun slipped below the horizon, the world growing suddenly colder. "Will you tell him?"

It took a terribly long time for Khatuya to answer. "About the bond? If he asks, I will. That is my duty."

Naatar sighed. "He'll find out, one way or another. Better he finds out from you."

Somehow, it was harder to argue with Naatar, who spoke without anger and whose words had the uncomfortable ring of truth.

It took us seventeen days to get back to the den. My bond with Hakara was an itch in the back of my mind. What I didn't tell Khatuya and Naatar was that in the early mornings, I felt that bond snap closed. In those few moments between sleeping and waking, it was as though she was next to me. I could feel the tickle of her breath against my hair as she wriggled from beneath the blankets to go dive in the ocean, the familiar fear squeezing my chest. If she died, I would be alone.

She'd never admitted that was a possibility, she'd never prepared me for it. So that fear lingered over my head and my heart, because I didn't know how to survive without her. During those mornings, I found myself reaching for her hand beneath the blankets and finding only cold, dew-clad grass.

Millani found us soon after we made our way back to our chamber, just as we were wiping ourselves free of the dusty road. She entered without knocking and looked us up and down. Her gaze landed on the empty scabbards at our sides. "Kluehnn will want to see you." The three of us rose. "No," she said. "Only you, Rasha."

Dread flooded my veins as she led me through the rusty tunnels to the room where Kluehnn's aspect met with his devotees. He was already crawling up from the hole in the floor when I entered, was out when Millani shut the door behind her. He dashed toward me, his hands and feet slapping against the stone floor. "You lost your quarry," he hissed. "And all three of your blades."

I fell to the floor, prostrating myself, one of his clawed hands visible through the curtain of my hair. "Forgive me, Kluehnn."

The hand disappeared, and then pain blossomed at my scalp as claws seized one of my horns, yanking me upright. "You failed."

He pulled me in close, and something pricked my leg. The barb on his tail. A small trickle of blood, then a burning sensation running down to my feet.

"Are you going to kill me?"

He leaned in close. "I don't discard those who are still useful to me. Tell me you have something for me other than excuses and failure."

I gasped as the burning grew stronger, as it traveled to my ribs. It felt like someone had cut a piece of my skin loose, had peeled it back, and set fire to the veins beneath. "You poisoned me."

"Tell me something I don't know, little one."

For a moment, I resisted. Some deep instinct inside of me pressed to the surface, some remnant of the love and admiration I'd once held for my sister. But those feelings were bones, hollowed out by the years, brittle and disintegrating to dust at the slightest touch. My fingers were aflame, every careless brush against them making me suck sharp breaths. Time shuddered in and out of existence, the pain the only thing that seemed real. Why should I protect her? I'd given her one moment of mercy and that had been a mistake. She'd taken my knife. It was *her* fault I was here, suffering Kluehnn's punishment.

"The god was not alone. He was traveling with three mortals, all skilled fighters."

One of his arms circled me, and I realized I'd begun to slip, my limbs melting toward the floor. Another arm lifted, a claw caressing my cheek. Past his face and his black eyes, his barbed tail hovered, blurring in my vision.

"Very good. What else?"

"One of them ... was my sister. You were right. She is still with him."

The hand didn't pause in stroking my face. I felt the hard shell I'd built for myself cracking and breaking. Tears ran hot down my face. Beneath it was something soft and vulnerable. "Let me go. Please. Please stop."

He pressed into that space, relentless. "You still love her, you still want to protect her. As strong as you've proved yourself in these trials, you are still a weak thing. You cannot be ruthless, as hard as you try. You are the flesh of rotting fruit." His hand gripped my chin, every place his fingers and his claws touched screaming with pain.

He was right about me. I was not and could never be like Hakara. I could not even pretend. When anyone got close enough, they could see that the shell I'd built was a false thing. But as the poison raced through me and down to my legs, I realized this: a soft thing could not break. He could press and I would yield, and when he was done, I would fill those spaces back in.

No matter what he did to me, I would remain myself. And that was still strength. I licked my lips, my mouth pulsing even with that small movement. "She bonded with me. They used magic. I can tell you where she is. I can tell you where *he* is."

A held breath. His gaze flicked across my face, landing every so often like a fly in search of sustenance.

And then he was lifting my robe, his mouth lowering over the wound he'd given me. I felt the prick of a hundred tiny teeth, light against my skin. A probing tongue, soft and hot.

Relief traveled over me in waves, the pain and fire draining away. When he pulled his mouth back, the place he'd stung me was red and raw. I fell to the floor, all my strength gone.

That connection in my mind stretched even now, as Hakara traveled farther and farther south. I closed my eyes and pointed. "She is that way. And if I still have my bearings, that means she's headed south. She's far, and drawing farther away by the moment. They're going toward Xiazen."

All of the lips on Kluehnn's mouths pressed together. "The

Sanguine Sea. They may cross if their quarry does. And she'll cross if she hasn't found a corestone here." Then he seized me by one of my horns again, dragging me across the floor toward him.

I was still weak from the poison, unable to resist, my hands scrabbling uselessly. "What are you doing?"

"You lost three godkilling blades. You must be punished." The mouth at the base of his throat fastened around my right horn, teeth coming together, tightening until the pressure was painful, more than I could bear.

I heard the *crack* before I felt it. The sound echoed in the small space. I couldn't see, couldn't think. A throbbing pain followed, traveling through my skull. Wave after increasing wave. Another bite, a terrible sucking sensation. Blood trickled down my scalp, mingling with the fiery pain of teeth scraping against bone.

He was eating my horn, sucking out the marrow, blood dripping from his mouth onto the cold stone floor. I wanted to scream. I couldn't take a full breath. I was nothing except pain and horror and fear.

I wasn't sure how long I lay there, clasped in Kluehnn's arms as he devoured part of me. It was his right, my dizzied mind told me – after all, he'd altered me. He'd given me these horns. They were his to do with as he wished.

At last, he drew away, leaving me there on the floor. Without another word to me, he retreated into his hole, the rasping sound of his claws against stone echoing before finally disappearing into the depths.

Naatar and Khatuya found me halfway back to our room, hauling my weak and sweating body across damp stone. Two mortal devotees almost stopped to help me before they saw the wound on my head, blanched, and strode quickly away.

My cohort had no such hesitation. Wordlessly, they lifted me, carrying me back to our door. Only one of the lamps inside was still lit. It filled the small space with a wan, warm light. They sat me on my bed and Khatuya lifted the hem of my robe. I hissed as the cloth brushed over the wound on my leg. An echo of pain traveled up to my shoulder before dissipating.

Water dripped as Naatar dropped a washcloth into the barrel in the corner, as he wrung it out and approached. He knelt and pressed it against the wound. The coldness of it gave me some relief, banishing the stinging fire. I swayed to the side and found Khatuya's shoulder against mine. She was warm, smelling of oak and cinnamon.

"Your family has always been devout. Was it easier for you? Was any of this easier for you?"

"I don't know." Her fingers traced the lines of my shoulder blade in a soothing motion. "My parents lived their lives in the service of Kluehnn, and I just followed their example. Becoming a godkiller after I was altered seemed the right thing to do. I had no reason to do anything else. But I don't know what things are like for you or what it's like to have someone you love on the other side."

I wanted to tell her that I didn't love Hakara, that I didn't *know* Hakara. I only knew the person she'd once been. Instead, I said, "This was my fault."

"Yes," Khatuya said. She brushed a piece of hair from my eyes, tucked it back behind one of my horns. She started to reach for the other, the bloody wound where my horn had once been, but then drew her hand away. "But we are still your cohort. And together we are strong."

I couldn't bear it. *We* were not strong. She couldn't speak for me. I pushed Naatar away, rising to my still-unsteady feet. "I need the latrine ditch."

Khatuya touched my back. "We have a pot in our rooms, you don't need to—"

"I need some fresh air. Alone." I batted away their useless, fluttering hands.

It felt like the longest walk I'd ever taken, each step a burning limp, stopping every so often to lean against the wall and catch my breath. Twice I felt the odd carvings beneath my palm, my fingers dipping into letters and symbols I didn't understand.

When I put my head down to breathe, blood caught in my eyebrow. I limped past the infusers and their altered handlers, the glowing gems dropping into baskets. I limped past carts and mortal servants and into the warm night air. The moon was full, silver light tracing stunted trees and boulders.

I made my way down the path, past the latrine ditch where the convicts were finishing their work for the day. Not knowing exactly why, I climbed up the slope of the mountain. Everything hurt; more than once, I was reduced to crawling.

When the lanterns below were pinpricks in the darkness, the crow found me. I heard the flap of its wings as it descended, its talons scratching against a nearby stone. "Rasha." It fluttered its wings once, twice. "You look terrible."

A breeze cut through the air. It felt like a knife against the exposed nerves of my severed horn. I hissed, gritting my teeth against the throbbing pain. "Never mind that," I said when I could speak again. "You said the gods would go back to Unterra if they could. That they would let us shut them into the center of the world if someone showed them the way. That you are not all the same."

Kluehnn had broken me open. But I'd survived. I'd yielded before him and it hadn't changed me.

I thought of the books in the depths of the den, the things Kluehnn said that didn't seem to meet his actions. I'd long wished to be more like Hakara, but Hakara would have spat her defiance at Kluehnn. She would have stood in my place and she never would have given way. She would have died.

But here I was, still alive, still thinking and breathing. And wanting answers.

"I want to know more. I have to know more. Tell me everything."

The crow blinked. "Very well."

25
Sheuan

11 years after the restoration of Kashan
and 572 years after the Shattering

Langzu - inner Bian

The clans fight over territory, estates, and even skilled labor, but nothing is treated so much like a trophy as the artifacts they have gathered from a pre-Shattering world. The most prized of these is a chair carved of dark wood, the seven elder gods winding around its surface. It has passed from clan to clan through the years, stolen in the middle of the night, taken during a raid, bargained and paid for in negotiations. For a long time, the Hangtao clan had possession of it. When the Sovereign and his enforcers took control of Langzu, they also took the chair. It sits now in the Sovereign's castle, in his great hall, a reminder of the bloody night that wiped an entire clan clean from the slate of history.

Filial piety aside, Sheuan hadn't ever been good at listening when people told her what to do. She had listened to the needs of her clan, yes, but *technically* she didn't have a clan anymore. So what would following her mother's dictums do for anyone? If her mother told her to stop digging merely to protect Sheuan's interests, well, Sheuan counted herself a better judge of her interests than anyone else.

Mull's brother had given her more than he'd intended to. He had said she should ask the Risho clan if she wanted to know more about the Sovereign's rise to power, about his ability to pull information from others.

And of all the fortunate coincidences, it just so happened she was already well acquainted with someone from the Risho clan, and it just so happened she owed this someone a favor. A younger scion, but one she understood, one who was malleable.

Nimao of the Risho clan sat across from her on a cushion in the castle's informal meeting room, a place that was meant to put visitors at ease instead of showing off the Sovereign's power. The walls were painted in cherry blossoms rather than tigers, idyllic scenes of picnicking families next to rivers that ran blue and clear of silty floodwaters. The tea in the cup in front of him was still hot, but he'd only lifted it to his lips to blow on it once, before absent-mindedly setting it back down. He had half his hair tied up in his customary bun, the rest falling flat down his back. Such a pretty man, with the sort of lips that made her thoughts tip into the obscene. And as for *his* thoughts?

She could practically *hear* them.

The last time they'd been together, she'd unbalanced him – something he'd quite enjoyed. So much so that he'd forgotten she wasn't supposed to be at the Sovereign's naming-day party. And now she was here, dressed in the finery of the Sovereign's wife, a silver cherry branch pinned to her breast. It was quite the turn of events. He wasn't sure how to react, and she let him sit in that discomfort without saying a word, as he opened his mouth, shut it, lifted the teacup to blow on it again and then once more forgetting to drink from it. She clearly outranked him, which meant she was supposed to speak first. But he was also her guest, which afforded him certain privileges, and perhaps Sheuan herself was unsure of what decorum dictated here. After all, her clan had been on the brink of disaster, and she'd always been something of a novelty at parties – perhaps she hadn't been raised correctly.

She hid her smile with the rim of her teacup. What was the point of having power if you couldn't have a little bit of fun with it?

But then footsteps sounded from behind her, and Nimao rose to his feet. Sheuan pushed herself up.

Liyana Juitsi entered, fingers swiping at her hair, readjusting briefly before she let her hand fall back to her side. She was a lovely young woman, her crowning feature the long, lush lashes she fluttered at every opportunity. When she looked at men, when she made a particularly funny joke, when she made a particularly cruel one. She was lithe as a sapling, her skin smooth and unbroken by freckles. Words like "statuesque" had been invented to describe women like Liyana. Sheuan wondered, if she tipped the girl over, would she shatter into so many bits of porcelain?

Nimao's face broke into a relieved smile. This time, Sheuan wasn't sure if he was pleased that she'd remembered the promise she'd once made to introduce them, or relieved that there was now a third party to this awkwardness.

Liyana bowed to her. "I am Liyana of the Juitsi clan. I'm so glad we could meet . . ." She trailed off, unsure how to refer to Sheuan. *Sovereign's wife* seemed a mouthful. Consort? Not exactly her role. And she didn't technically have a clan anymore.

"Sheuan," Sheuan said. "Just Sheuan."

Liyana's shoulders relaxed. "Sheuan," she said, relieved.

"But we've met once before." She might as well have shoved the girl into a Cressiman snowstorm. Each and every lithe limb froze.

Liyana blinked, an action that reminded Sheuan of nothing so much as one of the blinking dolls mothers bought for their children in the marketplace. A stiff, exaggerated action. "Oh, of course we have. I must have forgotten."

"It was memorable for me. You stepped on my foot."

Lips moved soundlessly, a wordless whine escaping her mouth. And again, that exaggerated blinking, all as a flush crept up her cheeks. She swallowed, tried again, her voice thin. "I'm terribly sorry. If I didn't apologize then, I should have. Please" – she bowed, and then bowed again – "please forgive me."

Immensely satisfying, given that Sheuan had been the one to apologize during that long-ago party. But she didn't do this just for a bit of fun – that would be wasteful. Embarrassment and discomfort could be wielded as well as any dagger. "Ah, but you should forgive *me*."

A small, muttered protest from Liyana.

"I haven't yet introduced you to my other guest. Nimao of the Risho clan."

To her credit, Liyana recovered quickly, smiling and bowing. Sheuan watched them both sizing one another up, an action so obvious on Nimao's part that it was painful to witness. Liyana, at least, had been taught some subtlety, flicking her gaze over the man so quickly he could hardly notice, disguising it with the movements of her hands.

Sheuan gestured to the table, where a third cup sat waiting. "If I proved unmemorable, I hope you'll at least remember him."

"Oh, I don't think I could forget him." Eyelashes fluttered,

Nimao smiled, and she let them have at it while she sipped her tea and occupied herself with frowning at the dregs. They talked, and sipped, and talked some more.

Gods below, she'd seldom heard more vapid conversations. The weather, their families, the state of their estates. If there was a spark between them, it was kindled on damp wood.

She interjected after a while, just so they wouldn't start to feel she was some voyeuristic third party, a dog watching a couple undress. Both seemed to appreciate her peppered-in commentary, and both, disappointingly, agreed with everything she had to say.

Sheuan wondered exactly how the Sovereign could stand it, after all these years. Was that why he'd found her interesting?

At last the tea grew cold, the dumplings the servants had brought in had been devoured, all except the very last one – Nimao's manners had extended to that at least – and Liyana rose. Nimao followed, daring to take her hand in his. "I'm so glad we could be introduced," he said.

"As am I. I'm having a dinner party in two days. I'll send you an invitation."

They both moved to leave, but Sheuan touched Nimao's arm. "Stay a little bit. I've something to ask you."

She watched and waited until Liyana left the room, until the door was shut and latched. Then she whirled, seizing Nimao beneath the chin, her fingers resting lightly around his throat.

"Sheuan . . ."

She didn't let him finish, tightening her grip marginally, pushing him back toward the cushion he'd only just vacated. His eyes were wide, his hands out to the sides, helpless. "Pushing" was a rather strong word for what she was doing. Guiding? He gave way to the slightest touch, letting her have this mastery of him.

There was a time this sort of control would have thrilled her. Not that she wasn't thrilled now. But it was like observing a mountain through the haze of a veil. Everything felt muted. She couldn't help but think of Rasha, the bright clarity of her eyes, the brush of those clawed hands against her skin. It was more than that, though – it was the brief flash of her smile, the way she'd seen past Sheuan's tricks and had still wanted to know the person beneath. The touch of warmth she'd felt cooled as she remembered the way she'd left Rasha, the way she'd shut her out. She'd had to do it; there was no way she could have stayed in Kashan, and Rasha wouldn't come with her.

Sheuan had wanted her to. It would have caused worlds of trouble for her, for her clan, but she hadn't been able to help wanting it. What could they have become, in a quiet space of their own?

She shook the thoughts from her mind as she guided Nimao back to sit on the cushion. So maybe she didn't feel the same thrill as she had back in the workshop, what felt like a lifetime ago, but that didn't mean she couldn't pretend. And Sheuan was very, very good at pretending.

She leaned over him, his face close to hers, until he could feel her breath across his cheeks. She held him there by the neck as she ran her other hand over his body, groping him roughly.

His breathing quickened, his hands splayed at his sides, elbows locked as he held himself upright. "Your husband," he said. "You're married. To the Sovereign. And we . . ." He trailed off, his lips parting.

Oh, for the love of all the green plants in the realm – there was something so pathetically *simple* about the man that it almost circled back to endearing. She nearly felt bad about all this. She pressed her chest against his, let her lips brush the space next to his mouth. "We shouldn't," she finished for him. She moved her hand down his neck, pressing her thumb lightly into the hollow above his collarbone. His pulse leapt beneath her palm. "You owe me, Nimao."

"Yes." An ecstatic whisper. "Anything."

Quickly and deliberately, she pushed away from him, seized her teacup, and dumped the now-cold liquid onto his lap.

He gasped and sputtered and looked like nothing so much as a fish that unexpectedly found itself hauled onto dry land.

She stood over him, her skirts brushing against the floor. "The Sovereign's special enforcers. How did your family help them when he was making his bid for this realm?"

"What?"

She spoke again, more slowly and forcefully. She wanted him to answer while he was confused, before he could come up with any convenient lies. "How did your family help the Sovereign's special enforcers? Tell me now. As you said – anything."

He brushed at his lap, still bewildered. "My family helped to usher those enforcers into places they didn't belong. It was about access to people. Important people."

"What happened after that? After they gained access?"

Nimao frowned, his generous mouth a pout. "What's this all about? I don't know what the enforcers did. I wasn't there."

"Did they hurt anyone?"

He shook his head, vehement. "No, nothing like that."

So. It was magic then. She could put the pieces together in her head. Magic that helped them get information from people without hurting them. That would have given the Sovereign a stark advantage. Hm. Interesting. Nimao moved to rise, and she put a hand to his chest, stopping him. "How did the Risho clan become acquainted with the Sovereign? Your clan was noble before the Sovereign promoted you to royal status. So how did a noble family connect with someone of no rank?" She pointed, dragged a finger to his sternum.

Nimao licked his lips. "He smuggled god gems. The Risho clan was an important customer."

A smuggler. Of god gems. It made sense – the Sovereign had never seemed particularly devout. There was a nave in the bowels of the castle, fallen into disuse, and only a few religious relics scattered throughout the building. A relief of Kluehnn's all-seeing eye in the dining hall, a painting of one of his terrible aspects in the room the Sovereign used for his formal meetings. She pieced together what she knew of Langzu's recent history. "The Hangtao clan found out," she said slowly. "Through an informant or sloppiness, it doesn't matter, they realized the Risho clan was purchasing a goodly number of god gems from this smuggler. They used it to pressure your clan, to get concessions from them that they wanted. But that didn't sit well with your family. They were willing to do many things to get out from under Hangtao's thumb – including partnering with a criminal."

Nimao said nothing, which she expected. He'd let something slip that he shouldn't have, and now he was sullen and quiet. But she could tell, from the brief flinch, that she was correct. The Hangtaos had been the most powerful of the clans before the Sovereign had taken over. With the help of his enforcers, and probably with the assistance of the Rishos as well, he'd eliminated the Hangtao clan entirely in one bloody night. Which had left a convenient opening amongst the royal tier.

It made sense for the Risho clan and the Sovereign to work together – they'd had a common enemy. Was this the information her father had had? The Sovereign wouldn't care if his trade minister knew about his sordid past, nor the Rishos' greed for god gems. It seemed far too mild a piece of information to execute someone over. But it was a start, like uncovering the rooftop of a buried city. Her instincts told her there was more beneath.

She knew she wouldn't get anything else from Nimao, so she held her hand out to him, helped him to his feet. He looked completely out of sorts, still trying to piece together exactly what had happened. She resisted the urge to pat his cheek. "I do hope things between you and Liyana work out."

This time she didn't guide him anywhere; she led him to the door as he followed her like a little lost lamb. She opened the door to let him leave.

One of the Sovereign's special enforcers stood there, a silver cherry blossom pinned to the collar of his jacket.

Sheuan hadn't heard him approach, hadn't heard even the creak of a floorboard from the hallway. Yet here he stood, gaze indiscernible. Had he heard anything? If so, what exactly had he heard?

"The Sovereign wishes to see you. Now."

26
Hakara

11 years after the restoration of Kashan
and 572 years after the Shattering

Langzu - on the Sanguine Sea

Trade at the anchor has slowly diminished over the years, though both Langzu and Pizgonia stand to benefit. Goods are sometimes lost in the barrier. Trade agreements are old and out of date. Payments have been slowly adjusted upward, but changes are not nimble, and the goods available have never remained the same. The governments of Langzu and Pizgonia have made revisions through handwritten notes sealed in oilskin packets; however, several exchanges are necessary before anything can be agreed upon.

Practically, it works thusly – goods are secured to wooden floats and then attached to two of the chains at the anchor. One from the originating side and one from the other side. Someone pulls the chain taut to signal the goods are being sent over. The other side pulls the chain from their side until the float of goods (hopefully) appears, and secures the chain from the other side to the platform on their side. Payments are marked numerically and are sent with the preceding shipment. It's a delicate system that is gradually breaking down, one tiny piece at a time. Soon, trade between the continents may become a thing of the past.

The winds died down soon after we left port. And in spite of the captain's reassurances, his ship, *The Birdeater*, was not the fastest in Xiazen. I watched the sails of Lithuas's ship recede into the distance a little at a time, day after day, until we could no longer see it.

We were moving, yet it felt like we were still.

The cabin we shared was small, *The Birdeater* clearly not built for guests. So I spent most of every day pacing from stern to prow and back again. Thassir had let Rumenesca free, and she roamed the bowels of the boat. If she survived on mice and rats, I didn't see it. I only saw him feeding her scraps from his own meals – bits of dried fish and the tentacles of squid. On the third morning, I slid from my hammock, the sway of the ocean making my head swim, and crept up to the deck before the crew woke.

Alifra was there at the stern, staring out over the uneasy sea, the water dark by early-morning light. Her russet hair was loose, a cloud swaying around her head with the wind. "Sometimes I think I can't bear it," she said, her gaze never breaking from the ocean. "The loss. That ending of possibilities, what should have been. But then another moment passes, and somehow I'm still here."

I rocked from foot to foot, the tension from my bond with Rasha pulling at the back of my mind, that bright and tangy feeling that reminded me of the way she glared at me each time I made a bad joke. She was still alive, but she was also gone. I swallowed, my throat tight. "Does it ever get easier?"

"In some ways, yes. But the pain remains."

A small part of me wanted to stand with Alifra at the railing, to feel the spray of the waves and sink into my thoughts. But the larger part of me wanted to keep moving, to leave the moment behind. I'd forgiven myself for what had happened to Rasha. Wasn't that enough?

I wished the ship were a hundred times bigger. A thousand. "How long until we reach the anchor?"

Alifra let out a sigh. "Another five days if the winds pick up. Who knows how long if they don't."

Five more days on this boat, with no place to go except pacing the deck. I could go back to the cabin. Find Dashu. See if he'd spar with me. I'd lose, every time, but at least I'd be doing something.

I left Alifra at the rail and made my way back below decks. The narrow space below the door was dark, which meant Thassir and Dashu were still asleep. I should let them sleep. No sense in waking them up so early. Except I couldn't stand the stillness. So I took the nearest lamp from its hook and opened the door.

A woman sat on the floor of the cabin.

I'd never seen her before in my life – not in Xiazen, not on this boat, not anywhere. Her clothes were odd, a cut I didn't recognize, the neckline square, the hem asymmetrical. Small flowers had been embroidered around the neckline, the shirt topped with a short and colorful vest, made entirely of square patches. Golden ear cuffs curved around the top of each ear, her linen pants loose and flowing.

She looked up at me in alarm, her shoulders hunching, her back arching. Her brown hair was the same wood-oak color as her skin, loose ringlets falling to her shoulders. Vivid green eyes caught mine. I didn't only have no idea who she was, I had no idea where she was from.

I had my sword drawn before I'd even remembered unsheathing it. Black wings ruffled as light from the lamp reached Thassir's eyes. Dashu stirred.

"Who the fuck are you?"

Her nose twitched, as though she'd smelled something she didn't like. She rubbed at the side of it with her wrist. "It should be safe out here." Her voice was muffled, thick. She cleared her throat and tried again. "We're in the middle of the Sanguine Sea, yes?"

I didn't lower my blade. Dashu poured out of his hammock, the flower hilt of his sword in his hand as though it had been there while he slept. "Answer her question."

The woman licked her lips. "Are we?"

We stared at one another. Dashu caught my gaze, an eyebrow raised, one shoulder rising in a confused shrug as he pointed the blade at the strange woman. "Not her. *You* answer *her* question. Who are you?"

I believed I'd said "Who the *fuck* are you?" but this was clearly not the time for finer points.

She didn't rise; she stretched right there on the wooden boards, her arms laid flat in front of her. "Gods below, it's been almost a century. I don't . . . It's Talieluna. You can call me Talie."

"What I should be calling you is dead, because that's what you're about to be if you don't explain."

She yawned, as though my threat bored her. "You're not a godkiller."

Dashu and I spoke at the same time.

"You're not—"

"How are you—"

We both stopped. He spread his fingers, allowing me to go first.

"How are you here? Did you stow away?"

A voice rumbled out of the darkness. "No." Wood creaked as Thassir tipped out of his hammock. "I see her for what she is. A shapeshifter."

I watched as she ran her hand over her face and then over her hair in a gesture that felt oddly familiar. I set the lamp down on a side table, but kept my sword raised. I'd seen that gesture before, though not in a human form. It struck me, clear as a mountain spring. "You're . . . a cat. You're the cat that Thassir took from the safe house."

"I am a god," she said, in the sort of self-satisfied manner that told me she must have been a cat for a very, very long time. She'd been living off scraps, shitting on the streets. We'd carried her from Bian to Xiazen in a *basket*. Really, there was no cause for smugness. Well maybe a little on that last bit. Why do the walking when someone else could do it for you?

"Rumenesca," Thassir said, crossing his arms. I wasn't sure if he was angry or confused, or both.

"Ninety-eight years as a cat," she said.

His lips pursed. "And you spent nineteen with me."

"Nineteen?" The word burst from my mouth. I wanted to punch him. "When were you going to get a clue? When you'd had her for thirty-five years? Fifty?"

He had the gall to turn his nose up at me. "I took very good care of my cats."

"You took very good care of a baby god."

Talie finally rose to her feet, her nose crinkling. "I'm older than you are."

"And your life experiences consist primarily of sleeping in beams of sunlight."

She lifted a finger. "Now that isn't entirely true."

Dashu sheathed his sword, evidently certain that any danger had been prematurely assessed. "Stop. Both of you." He took in and let out a deep breath. "Fine. There are no godkillers aboard that we know of. But what are you expecting us to tell the captain and his crew?"

Now that she was in her natural form, and we'd established what she was, I could see that faint glow surrounding her, nearly invisible, but there if you looked. A god's aura. There was something soft-edged about her, something that felt a little like looking at a lamp through the mist.

"They may not notice. And they can't do anything about it. Not in the middle of the sea. They've got goods to get to the anchor, and goods to retrieve. They won't stop to deal with me."

The doorknob turned. All four of us whirled to face the door.

Alifra entered. For a moment, all she did was stare. Then she wisely closed the door behind her. "When I prayed for a distraction after several days at sea, I did not expect a stowaway god to be the distraction." She eyed Talie up and down. "The cat. You were the cat we were carrying. A shapeshifter."

At least that forestalled some long and awkward explanations.

Alifra didn't launch into questions; she didn't draw her daggers or her crossbow. She simply shrugged. "We should get you fed. I can't imagine you've eaten well when you were a cat. I'll bring some food over from the mess and then we can talk."

The three of us sat in uncomfortable silence until Alifra returned, her arms laden with a bowl of rice topped with a healthy serving of fish and pickled vegetables. Talie took the bowl with grateful hands, digging into the food with a wooden spoon.

We watched her as she ate.

"She should turn back into a cat," Dashu murmured. "This raises too many questions. We can't hide her, and if she's safe from the godkillers sensing her out here, then she can change back without anyone noticing."

Her ears twitched. "I can hear you talking about me. This is a very small room. I understand that me being a cat again would be more convenient for you, mortal." She did not say it in a conciliatory way.

Dashu's face went still, then he straightened, made for the door, and left. He closed it softly after him, but it might as well have been a slam by Dashu's standards. I'd only seen him lose his temper once, when I'd goaded him to it, and this was something more than that.

Alifra caught my gaze. "I should—"

I held up a hand. "No. I should. You stay here." I was their bruiser. It was my responsibility. I left the three of them in the cramped cabin, Talie still eating like she'd not had a proper meal in fifty years. Come to think of it, she probably hadn't.

Dashu was on the deck, his sword in hand. Two of the crew were now awake, and they watched him from the corners of their eyes as he moved from one form to another. It was hard not to find your gaze trailing to him when he fought – the fluid movements, the whip-quick flashing of his blade. It wasn't just fighting; it was art.

I drew my sword. "Care for a sparring partner?"

"Not really." He grunted as he spun, one foot stopping his movement and becoming the pivot point for another.

I drew my sword anyways, tossing it from hand to hand as I moved from foot to foot, trying to get limber.

Dashu paused mid movement, eyeing me. "You and I both know we're not a match, not like this."

"I've been improving." Couldn't exactly keep the indignation from my voice.

"I don't feel like teaching."

"Well, I feel like being taught." I lifted my sword, keeping my knees loose. "So which of us wins when there's one of you and one of me?" I struck out, and he batted my blade to the side. "If I attack, will you stand there and refuse to teach me?"

I darted to the side, slashing at his shoulder. One moment his shoulder was there, the next my sword was finding only empty air.

"That's enough, Hakara. Leave it."

"Is it?" I circled. "Something is bothering you and you're pretending no one is noticing." I thrust my sword at his torso. His blade locked with mine and his foot lashed out. I stumbled, and leaned hard on my weapon, our hilts sliding together.

We were close now, close enough that he could lean in. "We have two gods with us now. It's dangerous for all of us."

I pushed, trying to unbalance him. "Danger never seemed to bother you as much as it does now. Even in the Otangu orchards you were cool and collected. If we are fighting a god, we need gods on our side."

"The Unanointed were doing fine before."

"No. You weren't. I'm not fond of where we've gotten ourselves either. But the more I find out about what is truly going on in this world, what has happened, *who is to blame*, the more lies I uncover. Lies I've believed my whole life."

A flick of his wrist, and he was free, dancing away. "I don't believe the lies. I have the old stories, after all. I am the keeper of them. I know the gods were not all as Kluehnn makes them out to be."

He wanted so badly to be Aqqilan – the way his ancestors were Aqqilan. I could see it in every story he told, the way he repeated the words to himself while he sharpened his sword, a family heirloom he'd never let out of his sight. But I'd had to let so many things go, and I understood I couldn't trap myself in the past. I struck out at him – once, twice, three times – searching for an opening. It was like he was surrounded by a cage of metal, one I couldn't quite see. "Yes, and you grew up in Langzu."

He leaned on his back foot, his brows low. "What are you trying to say?"

"You've still *heard* the lies – that the gods came to the surface to overthrow mortals, to take this world for themselves. That they are all selfish and that Kluehnn is the only one who cares. You think those haven't seeped into your mind and into your heart? How many times can you hear a thing repeated before it punctures your defenses?"

A sharp counter-attack, one I barely managed to block. He bared his teeth. "I am not so weak."

"Who taught you those stories? Was it your mother? Your father?" I leapt back, dodging a slash at my belly. "Did they rap your knuckles each time you got them wrong? And when you played with other children, children who weren't Aqqilan, did they tell you *their* stories? Did you look at their unbruised knuckles and wonder if maybe, just maybe, your parents were the ones who were wrong?"

Two quick moves I couldn't follow. My sword went clattering across the deck. A foot hooked my knee and I fell. The hard boards of the deck met my back, pushing the breath from my lungs.

He was over me, a hand pressed just below my neck, keeping me down, the point of his sword hovering above my left eye, his breath heaving. Black hair curtained his eyes.

For a moment, I struggled to breathe. But I used what little breath I had to speak. "You say you didn't believe the lies, but it doesn't mean they haven't touched you." I wheezed. "It doesn't mean they haven't made some part of you ugly. And you cannot . . ." I stopped, felt his hand loosen. "You cannot live free of it if you don't know that it's there."

He fell back, rocking onto his heels. "I don't have to like her."

I pushed myself into a sitting position. "No. You don't. But we're all a little ugly inside." My collarbone was still sore, and I rubbed at it to soothe the ache. "Better if we admit it to ourselves. Let's figure this out together, right?"

Dashu rose to his feet, sheathed his sword, and helped me up. "It was my uncle who told me the stories. My mother and father were dead. And he never beat me." His lips pursed. "He never needed to."

I didn't pry further as we made our way back below. I'd done enough prying in one day. Best let it rest.

I opened the door to the cabin. Talie sat on the floor, the cleaned bowl in front of her. She was licking her fingers and lips, rubbing at the space around her mouth. Alifra and Thassir stared down at her. She was talking, uncaring whether her audience was actually listening.

"There's quite a lot of us. Shapeshifters in other forms. Half your feral cats are shapeshifters, my friend. We go where we please and people still toss us scraps. Don't think I don't know who you are by now, Nioanen."

Dashu, Alifra, and Thassir all froze.

I lifted my hands, as though I could stuff the noise back into her mouth.

She continued, checking her fingernails. "Wouldn't have risked shifting otherwise. Fact of the matter is, you stopped restoration, and that's given the hidden gods hope."

No one else was asking questions, so I stepped in, my voice too loud in the crowded space. "Hope for what?"

She met my gaze, her green-eyed stare like a spear. "Enough hope to organize. To fight back. And we need all the help we can get."

27
Sheuan

11 years after the restoration of Kashan
and 572 years after the Shattering

Langzu - inner Bian

When the mortals first began capturing magic from the Numinars, they used it to heal wounds, to create food, to strengthen their buildings. But there will always be conflict — among mortals as well as among gods — and there will always be those who seek an advantage. So the mortals began to use the magic to build innovative, terrible weapons. If magic could feed a people better, it could also be used to kill a people better.

Sheuan did her best to store the enforcer's face in her memory as they made their way to the Sovereign's study. She'd been too occupied with her clan, with the filters, with the sudden reappearance of Mull. If these enforcers had access to magic, then that was a weapon the Sovereign had that she did not, and knowing their exact numbers could only serve her in the future.

And it was a distraction from her anxiety. Her limited interactions with the Sovereign had been something of a relief. She'd left their last encounter as unsettled as Nimao had left theirs. Now he was requesting to speak to her. Rather urgently, judging by the pace of the enforcer.

He opened the door to the study and then stepped aside to let her pass.

She thought she much preferred the room at night. It was still beautiful by day, the shutters half closed to keep out the heat, the sunlight gleaming in bars across the elaborately threaded rug. One shutter was completely open, letting in a warm breeze. Perhaps it was because, at night, the Sovereign hadn't occupied it.

He seemed to take up more space in the study than he physically occupied, so that Sheuan stopped, hesitating, a good distance from his desk. He stood behind it, by the window, his attention half on her and half on the city outside. A thin bar of light stretched across his eyes; he squinted, accentuating the line between his brows.

It wasn't until the enforcer's footsteps creaked down the hall that he spoke. "I need more filters. You're moving too slowly."

"If I knew the quota you were trying to fulfill . . ."

He shook his head, still not looking at her. "I can give you no quota. It changes, depending on circumstances. And circumstances are always shifting."

She'd watched various clan members arrive and leave the castle, meeting with their Sovereign. Some left looking satisfied, some disappointed, some with no expression at all. No matter what he did, the clans would gossip. Rumors would spread about the filters, the favor of the Sovereign, about restoration and the possibility of escape. With the manufacturing of the filters at the workshop, she'd not been able to keep as accurate a track of the people the Sovereign was bestowing favor on as she would have liked. She could understand the appeal of Mitoran's approach, with her spies in so many places. But there was no one she could trust, not yet.

He turned from the window. A brief flash of gold in his eyes before the shadows overtook them. "Why not have someone assist you?"

"It's a complicated process. I'm not sure many could manage it."

"Surely you and your cousin are not unique amongst the whole of Langzu. I find that hard to believe." His voice was smooth, soothing. But she knew his tone often belied his words.

"I wouldn't dare suggest that, especially not with you standing right before me."

His lip quirked. He appreciated the attempt at flattery, if not the flattery itself. "Are you truly suggesting that I join your efforts?"

"It's a good deal of work." Was she . . . flirting with him? She didn't know what to do with this man. Really, she was embarrassing herself, wasn't she? Her words were all hard-edged and unwieldy.

He swiped a hand across his desk, his fingers landing lightly on a stack of parchment, a spider coming to rest. "And you're working so hard that you had time to meet with Liyana Juitsi and Nimao Risho."

She struggled to keep the flush from rising to her cheeks. Of course he would know – they'd had to come in through the castle's only entrance, past the Sovereign's enforcers. Her movements were always watched, she *knew* that. Fine, though. Let him think he'd caught her out. "Do you wish me to maintain our family's social ties, or not?"

One lower eyelid twitched before his face was flat again. Something about what she'd said didn't sit well with him.

What? Family? They were married – that was what they *were*. Technically, at least.

"You could maintain social ties more easily if you gave over charge of the filters to someone else."

It really bothered him – that she had this knowledge and he didn't. But as long as she held the secret, he couldn't get rid of her. He needed her. And that needled him. She couldn't help but needle him further. If he wanted her confused and compliant, what would happen if she gave him the opposite? Could she press him until he snapped? What would she discover? She let out an exasperated sigh. "If I had to slow down to show someone how to make the filters, I wouldn't be meeting any quota, real or imagined, and who knows when restoration will be?"

He lifted a few pages of parchment, peered beneath, then let them fall again, apparently bored, not even mouthing at the bait. "It's better to invest the time now for a more productive outcome."

How direct should she be? Or should she continue to circle, let him speak plainly first? She didn't know what course of action to take with him. A stray cat passed by the open window, stopping to clean its face. She wasn't sure exactly how a cat had gotten onto the rooftop, except that cats seemed to always manage to get to places they weren't supposed to be. It made her think of the winged altered man with his cat in the basket. An opening presented itself to her, and she squeezed into the gap. "Kluehnn will get word of this, sooner or later. You've been distributing the filters to the royal families. Some of those family members are devout."

"I haven't been giving filters to *them*," he snapped back quickly.

It was a vehement response, one she grasped, recorded, and filed away. So . . . it wasn't just a lack of faith he suffered from. He *actively* disliked those who were devout. She waved a hand, pretending she hadn't noticed or cared. "Regardless, people talk. Families talk. Do you want Kluehnn to figure out a way to get around the filters? What's the use of all the work you're doing now, if you're allowing him time to counteract this measure?"

"Hm," was all he said.

"Keep the secret to me. Minimize the risk."

For the longest time, he just stared at her. She studied his features yet again: the gentle, sloping brows, the white hair with a few last strands of black, the slightly curved nose. It was like trying to find purchase on a cliffside. She didn't know what he thought of her words.

"Why did you want to meet with Nimao and Liyana?" His voice was the soft padding of feet on a plush rug.

She had an answer at the ready – the truth. Or, at least, part of it. "I made a promise to Nimao before I became your wife. I told him I'd introduce him to Liyana. I wanted to keep my word."

The Sovereign pivoted around the corner of the desk. There was something about the way he approached her that made Sheuan feel suddenly exposed, like she should be maneuvering to put that desk between them, or making her way to the door. She forced herself to stillness as he lifted a hand and wove his fingers into the unbound portion of her hair. "Honorable, to keep a promise like that. Honorable, for a woman who would let her family fall into ruin for personal gain."

Maybe it was because his words held an echo of her mother's, but couldn't help but respond. "My family was already falling into ruin. Nothing I did would have stopped that."

His fingertips brushed her scalp, and she shivered. "How like your father you are," he murmured, brown eyes fixed on hers. "It would be sad to see you end up like him."

Sheuan wondered if he could see her pulse, the steady thrum of blood rushing through her veins. She kept her breathing slow, even. "Oh," she said, her voice light, her gaze as sharp-edged as his. "I could never be quite as clever."

28
Hakara

11 years after the restoration of Kashan
and 572 years after the Shattering

Langzu - somewhere in the Sanguine Sea

Irael was always an inconstant god, one who flitted from place to place, unable to stay in any one form for long. The only steady thing about him was his heart. Every mortal that he loved, he loved until they died.

To say that Talie's revelation was like dropping an explosive within our tight-knit group would be an understatement. "Nioanen?" Alifra had hissed, turning away from Thassir until she stood with Dashu. "*Nioanen?* The *elder god?*"

Thassir didn't respond. He didn't even glower or ruffle his wings. He just stood there like someone had carved his countenance from stone, his gaze fixed somewhere above the door frame. I had no idea what thoughts were going through his head, or even if there *were* any thoughts.

Dashu's voice filled the silence. "Hakara. Did you know?"

When I'd answered with only a small, sheepish shrug, Dashu had taken Alifra's hand and led her out of the room. Their footsteps creaked on the deck above us.

"Well." I'd fixed my gaze on Talie. "You could have, maybe, I don't know ... left that to another time?"

She'd shrugged and swiped a finger through the dregs of her bowl before sucking on it. "They would have found out. At least now they've got nowhere to run and no one to tell."

So much for all that hard emotional work I'd done with Dashu during our sparring conversation. Both Alifra and Dashu avoided the three of us over the next several days, only returning to the cabin to sleep. Talie didn't change back, though she crept above deck during the night to get some air and stretch her legs. If anyone noticed the extra food we were eating, they didn't dare confront Thassir with it.

And I watched the horizon, waiting to see signs of the ocean barrier, circling the edges of the ship like a caged tiger.

Truth be told, I was in two minds. I had my own reasons to resent Thassir, despite everything I'd said to Dashu. It was one thing to be a god, hapless and hopeless on the surface, hunted by others. So many of them had been born there, had done nothing to deserve the ire of the mortals except rumor and superstition and an old pact between a god and a person no one even really knew. But Thassir? *Nioanen?* He'd been there when it had all happened.

Gods below, I needed to get off this ship. Still nothing on the horizon except the dark sea and some clouds. Behind me, a few sailors moved, adjusting the sails at Captain Falin's direction. I didn't even know if Lithuas was still out there. I could feel the bond between me and Thassir. When I closed my eyes and concentrated, I knew exactly where he was. Just below my feet. Probably quietly arguing with Talie again.

A voice startled me from my thoughts. "Talie is missing." I whirled. Dashu, scratching at the side of his goatee. "We need to find her. Before she causes trouble."

"Thassir is looking below decks. Alifra and I will look above." I made for the steps below deck. She'd been restless, I knew, and I couldn't blame her. The cabin was small, and while she made her way above at night in a hooded cloak, when most of the crew slept, the isolation still had to chafe. She'd been a cat for nearly a hundred years. Sure, she'd had some company in the form of other shapeshifting gods, but if they'd all been trapped in their forms – well, it was enough to make anyone stir-crazy. The floorboards shifted beneath my feet. I wasn't sure how the crew would react to a god in their midst, if they would notice, how quickly they'd notice. They'd certainly notice they hadn't seen her before. There just weren't that many people on board.

They'd try and throw us all overboard, wouldn't they? I was going over that hypothetical fight in my mind when I opened the door to the cabin.

It took me a moment to parse what I was seeing. Thassir crouched, wings hunched low over his back. He held out a hand with a bit of dried meat to a bedraggled-looking calico on one of the support beams over the hammocks. Talie. Or Rumenesca, in this form.

I pressed my palms into my face. "She's not out and about in her natural form. She just decided to shift."

"She wanted more freedom, and it was better to shift before we crossed the barrier. We don't know where the godkillers will be."

"Lithuas?"

"She's shifted twice. She's shifting less now – we may lose her. Her trail leads up to the barrier, as far as I can tell." His shoulders slumped. "I miss my cats," he said, his low voice almost plaintive. Rumenesca leaned toward his hand, sniffing the offering at his fingertips. With delicate teeth, she pulled the meat away, retreating like a lion with its kill. The soft rumble of her purr filled the small space.

I watched Thassir watching the cat, his black eyes reflecting the room. "Are you done?"

He didn't respond, reaching out a hand again. Rumenesca hissed, but tolerated him as he stroked the soft fur of her neck with the back of his knuckles. "Please. You know I'm not a cat now. Nioanen, your people need your help."

He pulled away.

"You cannot keep pretending that you don't matter." She took one last glance at him and darted out the door.

The ship swayed. I'd never been on a boat before, and I wasn't braced. My legs wobbled, sending me careening into Thassir's side. He stumbled but didn't fall.

His wing, however, snapped out for balance, hitting the door of the small room and slamming it shut. The lamp guttered.

"Must have hit a swell," I said when the movement reduced to a gentle swaying again. His chin lowered, his gaze dropping to where my hand still rested on his arm. I patted his bicep like it was merely a tree I'd leaned against, and maneuvered around him toward the door, heat rising in my chest. In such a small space, I still brushed against his feathers, no matter how tightly he held them to his sides. It reminded me of a time, what seemed like a lifetime ago, when I'd blown on those feathers to dry a wound.

I yanked on the handle. It didn't move. I pulled again, harder.

"I must have hit it a little too hard. Let me." Thassir's hand closed over mine, and then opened to allow me to escape. I felt the bond overlap in that brief moment of contact, the stretching feeling disappearing. He pulled on the handle, his teeth bared. Nothing.

I gritted my teeth. "Trapped by a cat. Of course."

When he turned to look at me, he was too close. I could feel the warmth of his skin, the musky scent of his feathers thick in my nostrils. I remembered how soft his hair was, how it felt to run my fingers through it. "Does this make you feel better?" he said. "Biting at everyone within reach?"

Everything I'd held inside, all the swirling questions, the disbelief, erupted up my throat. "I've been more than fair. I haven't ignored you the way Alifra and Dashu have. And you act as though I'm snapping at you with no reason. You let so many people die. You did nothing about it. You *knew* Lithuas and Kluehnn's plans and you just . . . let them carry them out. How could you look into the eyes of all those hopeful Unanointed and know you were letting them go to their deaths?" It felt like lancing a wound.

"Don't act as if that bothers you." He leaned down so our faces were nearly level. "You were content to find your sister and to leave the Unanointed to their fate. To let restoration take Langzu. How are we different?"

I lifted my hands, clenching my fists. "Because you always had more power than I did!"

"Maybe it's easier to be angry with me than it is to be angry with yourself. Would you really have fought if you were in my position? If you'd watched Rasha die, if you'd watched everyone you cared about die? If you had nothing left to live for except a promise that you wouldn't fall to despair?"

There, in that small, confined space, the anger in me drained away, leaving a wellspring of something cold and delicate. This wasn't just about all those hopeful Unanointed. He'd looked into my eyes and known *I* was going to my death, and still he hadn't told me the truth. He'd prodded and cajoled, but in the end, he'd let me go.

But he'd also come back.

"You are the worst woman I've ever known. You know that? You're rude. You're insufferable. You never stop to think before you speak." His face hovered close to mine. My gaze flitted to his lips, slightly parted, the warmth of his breath against my cheeks.

This close, the bond was quiet in the back of my mind. I found his eyes again, raven-dark. He'd lived so many lifespans before mine. He'd seen the rise and fall of realms, of empires. And here he was, keeping to himself, tending to his cats, his godly aura dulled. The lamp dimmed briefly, nearly out of oil. I didn't dare lean toward him, knowing deep down that he'd lean away. "Thassir." I could barely draw breath. "What aren't you telling me? What are you afraid of?"

His eyelashes fluttered against his cheeks. Some wall within him slowly shuddering into the ground, finally giving me access. He opened his mouth. "I wish I could tell you. I made a promise, and I—"

The door flung wide with a thud. "Ah, you're awake." Alifra stood in the doorway, Dashu at her shoulder.

Thassir pulled away, so swiftly it was as though he'd not been nearly chest to chest with me, his lips a breath away from mine.

"We're at the anchor point," Alifra said. "Time to tell our erstwhile captain we're having a bit of a mutiny."

29
Mullayne

11 years after the restoration of Kashan
and 572 years after the Shattering

Langzu - the den northeast of Bian

Years after the Shattering, which crumbled machines and buildings into dust, intrepid inventors still tried to piece together the creations of their predecessors. One such person, Botaieus the Clever, managed to find, through wheedling and searching and a good deal of financial output, the scattered components of a machine said to extract magic from Numinar wood. He reconstructed it based on old drawings and diagrams. Through another series of acquisitions, he obtained a comb carved from a Numinar.

Witness statements say he started up that machine, the gears whirring to life, and without further preparation or pretense, dropped the comb into the business end. The machine groaned, grinded, and spat out a black cloud of smoke before emitting a high-pitched whine.

What happened next, as eloquently stated by his

assistant, was that "He blew himself the fuck up." Botaieus may have been clever, but he was not wise, and this unfortunate incident was used in academies in more than one realm to point to the importance of safety standards in experimentation.

Mull had always thought himself capable.

How quickly the den had disabused him of that notion. Or perhaps it had begun in the dark, on Tolemne's Path, where every decision he'd made seemed only to send his friends further into danger. Stupid, ruinous Mull, with his head in the clouds, never seeing where he was putting his feet. Or maybe it was that he hadn't cared who he was crushing along the way.

But he *had* cared.

Black-ticked fur covered the backs of his hands; the end of his nose felt softer and wetter. Every movement seemed to bring to life some fresh new horror. Each time he thought about it, he squirmed in his chair, and every time he squirmed, he felt the newness of a tail. He tried not to think about the fur covering his body, his face, the way two of his teeth were now so long and sharp they nearly jutted from his mouth.

No one in these caves seemed to notice his discomfort, the way his feet tapped or his chair scraped. They'd placed him in what they'd called the archives, though they weren't like any archives Mull had ever known. The cavern was filled with books of every type and language. He'd been given confusing instructions, phrases he was tasked with marking, before he passed the books on to someone else. They'd given him books in Albanoran, in Kashani, in Langzuan. The godkillers had questioned him right after his transformation was complete, while he still lay gasping on the floor, aftershocks of pain racking his body. What languages did he know? What could he read? He'd told them everything without a second thought.

The archives were filled with nooks and screens, obscuring everyone's tasks from everyone else. The far wall had some openings to the outside that let in light and air, though they were shuttered at night and in the early mornings, when mist cloaked the foothills. The alcove Mull sat in was lit by a single lamp and almost entirely blocked by a screen. An aspect of Kluehnn was painted on the dark surface, the pale-faced creature graced with three extra sets of eyes, three mouths, and two sets of wings. Antennae-like tendrils extended from its forehead and along its back. This aspect was shaped like some sort of grotesque caterpillar, multiple short arms and legs holding its body upright. It wasn't the sort of view Mull was used to when he worked.

That life felt to him now like a dream, something he could only grasp in the hours before waking. All his woes from then felt petty – his annoyance at his older brother, his exasperation that his parents never fully backed his curiosity, the subtle pressure to settle down and marry. He'd funded his expeditions himself, but his clan had provided the seed money for his workshop. He'd uncovered Tolemne's Path, but he'd had the coin to pay for those ancient tablets; his parents had paid for his language tutors. Mull had always thought himself capable, but he'd built up small woes to be grand antagonists, enemies he had to fight and struggle past in order to fulfill his dreams.

Of course he'd imagined he could do anything he set his mind to, he thought bitterly, when he'd lived a life of such relative ease.

He paged through an old Kashani book, the dialect so ancient he barely recognized it, cross-checking with the list they'd given him of the phrases he needed to mark. He wasn't even sure why he was doing as the godkillers had asked, except that he had nothing else to do and nowhere else to go.

He had never heard of alteration being reversed. In all the reading he'd done, in all the research, alteration was an immutable process. He couldn't imagine what his clan would say if he tried to return in this new shape, his hands heavier than they'd once been, fur covering his face and body, a tail curling around his legs. He'd not even been able to bring himself to look for his reflection anywhere. He didn't want to know exactly how he looked now — as if knowing would wipe clean his memories of his old self.

He couldn't be the son of a noble clan, not anymore. Altered existed at the fringes of Langzuan society. There was no place for him with his family, and this was a truth that stung more painfully than his consistent failures. He had really thought he could infiltrate this den, that he could find the information he sought and then saunter back into his old life — bereft of old friends, but still the selfsame person.

He was a fucking idiot, that was what he was.

A section caught his eye — a phrase he'd seen on the list the godkillers had given him. *The hollow inner sanctum, where the gods lived. He* took one of the painted strips of parchment and tucked it into the page. His feet tapped against the floor, his tail moving without his consent. He'd nearly flipped past the page when he saw something else.

Unterra exists just past the third aerocline, a place where all manner of creatures live, and one becomes lighter than air.

The third aerocline. The *third*. He'd never seen any mention of this in a book, and now here it was, in this old Kashani text the godkillers were asking him to mark. He could almost feel Imeah next to him, her hand on his shoulder as she peered at the book. "Well that's interesting, isn't it?" she would have said. "There's not supposed to be a third one."

Pont would have sighed from the corner. "It's a mistake. Just a misprint." Always the skeptic.

And Jeeoon? She would have kicked her feet up onto a table and asked when they were going to leave on their next adventure. She had to source their supplies, you see.

For a moment, it felt so real to him that he lifted a hand to place over Imeah's. He found himself patting his own empty shoulder.

They were gone – all three of them. Jeeoon and Pont dead, and Imeah lost to the tunnels underground.

He was not dead, nor was he lost.

Gods below, had he forgotten the entire reason he'd come to the den? He'd come here to infiltrate it. And no, he hadn't intended to become one of the altered. He'd never wanted that. But he was here, inside the den, with unprecedented *access*. That was exactly what he'd wanted, wasn't it? And instead of doing something about it, he'd been puttering along, doing everything the godkillers asked of him. He was still alive and he was here and he'd promised himself the deaths of his friends would mean something.

He could feel the rusty gears of his mind creaking into motion. They'd changed his body, but they couldn't change his thoughts. Those were, and would always be, his own. If they were asking him to mark these sections, that meant the phrases they'd given him might also be linked to other truths Kluehnn wished to suppress.

New, frantic energy surged through his veins. He'd already wasted too much time. He had an entire stack of books here, and though his understanding of older dialects wasn't great – except Old Albanoran – there was still information he could glean.

Was there a way out of the den and back to Bian? A way to share the knowledge he found? That, he wasn't sure about. But it was a problem he could manage in the future. He might have lived a softer life than he'd realized, but that didn't mean he couldn't rise to the occasion when things became more difficult.

He had no journal to take notes in, so he did his best to memorize the section. There was a third aerocline and once, a long time ago, they'd known this. He seized another book, flipping through the pages, looking for the key phrases. There was a bit that claimed the god Barexi had had five children with a mortal wife, another that included a description of Unterra and a fearsome creature with mottled gray fur that roamed its woods.

What were they doing with the marked pages? And why?

Mull leaned his head around the edge of his screen. He couldn't see anyone else's workspace, but he could hear the scratch of pens against paper, the cut of a trimming knife. Were they removing those pages? Replacing them?

Why?

"You." An acolyte appeared from behind a screen, long, spiraling horns nearly scraping the ceiling. Her gray robes brushed the floor as she strode toward him. "What are you doing?"

"I need to go to the latrine ditch."

The acolyte waved a hand. "Then go. Don't linger."

Mull set his jaw and set off toward the entrance of the archives, moving to the side to let a convert with a cart of books pass by. He'd come down here for a reason, and he'd let despair drive him for too long. Somewhere in this den was the tomb of Tolemne's family. He'd promised his dead friends he'd find it. He'd promised himself.

This alteration? This changing of his body and of his life? It was a setback, nothing more. He'd find that tomb. He'd find out why Tolemne had returned to the surface and what he'd done.

He'd find the truth.

30
Rasha

11 years after the restoration of Kashan
and 572 years after the Shattering

Langzu - Kluehnn's den northeast of Bian

There are few accounts of the life and accomplishments of Runata, a renowned philosopher from Cressima. Instead, accounts always focus on her capture and execution — a terrible, violent affair during which she was placed in an empty arena and an aspect of Kluehnn himself devoured her alive, piece by piece. Do not poke further into the past, these accounts seem to say, lest you end up like her. So what was her crime? The few records that do exist say only that she asked very pointed questions. If the gods were so powerful and wanted to take over the surface world, why had they not initiated an organized attack? If Kluehnn wanted the best for the surface, why not give them all fair warning of restoration? Questions, it turns out, can be more than mere annoyances. They can be a power to be reckoned with and silenced.

My hands itched for my blade. I found myself waking most mornings reaching for my belt, only to find the knife sheath empty, no violet glow cast across the etched brown leather. I ate little, slept too much, my injuries still causing me pain. I'd strained myself by climbing up the mountain to talk to the crow, and I could now only put a little weight on my leg before I hissed in pain.

On the third day after Kluehnn had punished me, Millani strode into our room, her gray robes brushing against stone. "Khatuya, Naatar, I'm to brief you – we've received reports of several gods gathering nearby. Higher up in the mountains. You're to engage with them, bring back at least one. Alive or dead."

She passed them each a new blade, the light of the violet gems winking off the ceiling.

I pushed myself to my feet, though every muscle in my body felt like it was on fire. Millani's yellow-eyed gaze fixed on me, her red tail lashing. "Not you. What do you think you can do without your godkilling blade?"

"Then I'm not to receive one?"

"No. If you want your blade back, you'll have to earn it. You were leading your cohort. You are the one responsible for their loss."

"I should still be with them. They need me."

"Kluehnn's orders." She beckoned for Khatuya and Naatar to follow her before pursing her lips at me, as though I were a problem she didn't particularly want to be dealing with. She tossed a simple wooden crutch at the foot of my bed. "Report to the archive after worship. You're to guard the conscripts."

"For how long? When will I be able to return to work?"

She ignored me, the door closing behind her, cutting off any further answers.

I sagged back onto my bed, pressing my palms to my forehead. The pain in my head had retreated to a dull ache. I still dreamed of Kluehnn's teeth at my skin, his poison coursing through my veins, and then woke drenched in sweat, everything still aching.

The crutch helped with the limp, though each jolting step toward the nave still caused me pain. Worship didn't revive me the way it usually did. Kluehnn's offering slid down my throat in a tasteless lump. The crow had said the gods hadn't come to the surface to conquer; they'd come because they'd been driven out of Unterra by Kluehnn. They'd been forced to live in a land that wasn't their own, hunted by mortals and Kluehnn alike. And then Kluehnn had created the altered and the godkillers, and those godkillers had killed the last of the gods that had been born underground.

The crow had allowed me to ask questions after he'd finished telling me what he knew, as my wounds ached and the lights from the den winked in the darkness. Even in that one conversation, I'd found he didn't have the answers to everything. Why would Kluehnn drive the gods out from their homeland? He didn't know. Why did Kluehnn want to keep the bodies of the gods? He wasn't sure. How could I trust him? I didn't have to – it was enough just to listen.

And that was the part that really bothered me. The crow didn't push his answers on me. He only responded to the questions I'd asked, in narrow, polite terms. It contrasted sharply with everything I'd been told of gods. I might have been able to still dismiss this crow as an outlier if I'd not also spoken to the god in Kashan, the one who'd watched over that village without an expectation of anything in return.

I wasn't sure what, if anything, I should do with this information, but it stirred around in my mind, the dregs of a teacup that was never fully emptied.

The archive lay through a series of tunnels, higher up in the den – a cool, dry cave with glass lanterns fixed into the walls. The far wall opened into a cliff face, windows carved into the stone to let in the light; metal shutters affixed on either side of each opening. The warmth and sunlight brushed my skin, a breeze from the windows tickling my neck. It smelled sweet and dusty, like dried earth and yellowed grass. The room was sectioned off by screens, alcoves providing even more privacy. Footsteps and the scratch of pen against parchment echoed through the space.

An altered man in a simple robe nearly ran into me at the entrance. Black-ticked fur covered his face; the end of his nose was black. "Ah. Sorry."

I limped back, trying to feel angry and failing. All I could feel was pain shooting up my leg. "Are you here to show me the archives?"

He shifted from foot to foot. "No. I'm just a conscript. A murderer who begged mercy."

I couldn't help my raised brow. "And you're here in the archives?"

"I'm educated," he said defensively. "I work hard. They rewarded me." He glanced over his shoulder. An acolyte was approaching, a tall woman with spiraling horns. "Excuse me. I'm going to the latrine." He slipped past me.

"Rasha," the acolyte said as she approached. She didn't incline her head, didn't show me the deference I hadn't realized I'd become used to. She walked me through the archives. "You'll be in charge of the conscripts and converts here. Watch over them. Make sure they're on task."

"And you? What will you do?"

She gave me a startled look. "I'm being transferred. The gods are organizing, and Kluehnn needs more of us handling logistics and supplies." She gave a quick nod of her head before leaving me to this simple work.

So he'd chosen her over me to handle logistics. An acolyte. It shouldn't have stung – this knowledge that I had fallen so low in the hierarchy. I'd spoken to gods. I'd broken our first precept. As soon as someone found out, as soon as someone told Kluehnn, I wouldn't belong anywhere in this hierarchy. But I had survived three trials, had killed my fellow acolytes, had faced down my sister, and *this* was what was left for me? For a moment I just stood by one of the windows, looking out into the hot, dry day, a mouse with large ears scurrying across one of the rocks outside. I was gripped by the sudden urge to launch myself out that window, to tear my robe from my body, to run into the wilds and leave this all behind.

A reckless fantasy, no more.

I limped from one end of the archives to the other, listening to the sound of knives cutting paper, books being clapped shut. Every so often, someone would ask leave to go to the latrine. It chafed, like a belt drawn too tight. I was accustomed to fighting, to traveling long distances. Now I was confined to this space, my leg burning with each step. And with nothing else of consequence to do, my mind kept turning to the crow.

Why? Why would Kluehnn drive the gods out from Unterra?

It plagued me that the god couldn't answer any of my questions about Kluehnn. It seemed that neither mortals nor gods knew much of him. Shouldn't the gods know more? Shouldn't *I*, as someone who'd worshiped him? Who had loved him like a father?

I picked up a book from a stack outside one of the screens, leafing through it. It was all in Langzuan. I'd learned to speak bits and pieces of it, but I'd never learned to read it. I tossed it back onto the stack and chose another. This one was in

Cressiman. Another was in Albanoran. I watched, surreptitiously, as one of the workers emerged with a stack of discarded pages and placed them into a crate. She returned immediately to her work.

I might not fling myself out the window and take off into the wilds, but was anything truly keeping me here, in the archives? The converts all seemed to be working. I limped, hesitating, to the entrance and lingered there. One of the workers passed me with a cart, taking it further into the tunnels. Where were they going? And why take the books deeper down?

No one admonished me. No one seemed to notice me at all. I slipped away and into the tunnels, following the path I'd seen the cart take, my crutch sliding across the uneven ground. It was slow going, and painful, but two thoughts drove me forward: someone might notice I was missing from the archives, and I needed to *know*. A part of me still hoped there was a reason for all of this, for the discrepancies; that once I found out what was happening in the den, I'd fully understand and could go back to being one of Kluehnn's faithful.

I'd needed Hakara when we were young, I'd leaned on her, trusted her, never doubted or questioned her. And when she'd disappeared, I'd replaced her with Kluehnn. Now I was drifting and uncertain, my path unclear.

The air cooled the deeper into the den I wandered. I'd never walked these tunnels before; I'd never had a reason to. And it was easy to get lost down here if you weren't familiar with the way. Darkness filled the tunnel before me, the lamps on the wall unlit. I took one down, lit it with the tinderbox in my satchel, and crept forward.

Water dripped somewhere ahead. The tunnel divided, one leading off to the right. No lanterns lined the wall that way. I squinted. There was ... something strange about that tunnel.

Acting on impulse, I blew out the light in my lantern. It took a moment for my eyes to adjust, but then I saw it.

The tunnel was emitting a faint glow.

My hand at the wall, I ventured toward that light.

The tunnel curved nearly all the way back around, opening into a small cavern. I sucked in a breath. Boxes lay in this room, golden light gleaming from between the wooden slats. I knew what it was, but I had to see. I opened the lid of the nearest box.

Yellow gems – more than I'd ever seen, even when we'd conducted our raids on the mines. They'd said the yellow gems were the rarest, yet here were more than I could count, even given an entire day, filling box after box in a cavern deep inside the den.

The sound of a scuffed footstep set my heart racing. I whipped about, raising my lamp before remembering I'd blown it out. No one was there.

Slowly, carefully, I limped back out of the cavern and toward the fork in the tunnels. Someone was muttering around the corner, a man's voice, low and soft. I crept closer, trying to make out the words. He was speaking in a language I didn't recognize.

I could wait it out, see if he would leave, before returning to my post. But that meant someone was more likely to notice my absence. Or I could try to move past him, hoping he didn't know who I was and wouldn't be able to later identify me. The crutch made that unlikely.

Wait. I'd heard that voice before.

I stepped out from behind the bend in the tunnel.

The man who'd nearly toppled me earlier, the former convict, stood in the tunnel, his hand to the wall, brushing over a set of carved symbols there. Without thinking, I reached for the blade that was no longer at my side, grasping only empty air.

I lifted my crutch like a weapon as the man finally saw me, a lamp in one hand, illuminating his sharp white teeth, the golden fur around his eyes. I stood a full head taller than him, and in spite of the crutch, I must have looked a sight, materializing out of the darkness, the area where my horn was missing still red and raw.

I pointed the end of the crutch at his throat. It wasn't much of a threat, but I could give him a good whack on the head with it. "You said you were going to the latrine. What in all the realms are you doing down *here?*"

31

Hakara

11 years after the restoration of Kashan
and 572 years after the Shattering

The Sanguine Sea - the anchor point between Langzu and Pizgonia

Trade manifest: five boxes of winter melons (value 50 allos each), one box of assorted glazed pottery, packed well (value 200 allos), one box of medicinal herbs (value 150 allos), a purse of forty-five parcels to pay for Pizgonia's next shipment to Langzu, and one complaint letter lamenting the quality of the last shipment of tea.

Our captain, Falin, did not take the news of our mutiny well. "This is *my* ship," he sputtered, his face red. "When I took your money, that didn't mean you were welcome to take my entire gods-damned ship and sail it into the barrier. I granted you passage, nothing more."

The maritime barrier was impressive, I had to give it that. A wall of roiling mist rose toward the clouds, dissipating into the air somewhere higher than I could comprehend. Down here, near the surface, the barrier looked like one continuous wave, crashing against itself. People who complained about the lack of trade with Pizgonia really had no idea how hard it was to cross such a barrier, did they? Sailors who had been to the anchor point must have gritted their teeth each time they heard someone say that passage could be easy if only someone took the time to figure it out – with the unspoken implication that the sailors were neither smart enough nor forward-thinking enough to do so.

A tattered flag flew from the anchor point – the Sovereign's cherry-branch crest against a golden background, the colors faded and the ends tattered. It was a broad wooden platform, sloshing high above the waves, metal rings affixed around its perimeter. This close to the barrier, I could smell the aether, feel the mist against my cheeks. Falin had dropped our ship's anchor at our command, and we rocked close to the platform.

"How often does a ship go through the barrier?" I asked Alifra as I joined her at the rail.

"They don't." She pointed at the mists, nearly having to shout over the crashing water. "The barrier's short, but the sea is more than just choppy inside it. The only way goods get across is using the anchor. There's been no reason to send people through. When was the last time you saw someone from Pizgonia? Any of the folks you see are almost certainly descended from people who crossed before the Shattering. People like to claim they've been through the barrier, but as far as I know, it's just that – a claim."

"You'll break the ship," Falin shouted from behind Dashu. Dashu had his blade out, the point held at the captain's chest. The other sailors stood at a distance, hands raised. "This is my livelihood."

I pointed at the anchor. "The goods make it through, don't they?"

"Battered and bruised," Falin said. "And even if the ship makes it, we won't. There's the small matter of the aether. Unless you can breathe it without harm, we're in a whole lot of trouble."

It felt like my gaze moved of its own accord, much as I tried to keep it under my control. Thassir – Nioanen. The altered had a greater resistance to the aether, but the gods could breathe it without becoming intoxicated.

Thassir lifted his gaze to mine and I felt suddenly locked in place. How much did I tell this man? Thassir had put his life in my hands when he'd told me the truth, and now I had to acknowledge some responsibility for that life. "We have our ways."

Four filters – that was all we had.

I turned to the crew. "All of you who wish to can disembark at the anchor point. It may take a few days, but another ship will be along and can take you back."

They bristled, and suddenly I was reliving that hypothetical fight in my mind. Guess sitting on an empty wooden platform at sea didn't sound so appealing to most folks. Hands hovered near the hilts of knives and daggers.

A cat came skittering across the deck, black tail a bottlebrush. She stood between us and the sailors and hissed.

One of the sailors barked out a short laugh. "Oh, as though that'll keep us from tossing the lot of you overboard."

She shifted into a panther as big as a horse. Claws flexed. A massive tail lashed. The ship listed to one side. Someone screamed.

"A god!" another shouted.

So much for keeping others' secrets.

"Right. Well. Off you go then." I drew my sword and waved it at them. They moved to the rail and one by one took the rope down to the anchor. The platform wasn't small, and we left them with several barrels of water and supplies, but it would be an uncomfortable wait, especially if it began to rain. They'd live, though.

Falin stopped at the rail, gazing down at his crew. He pivoted back toward us, hands up, brown jacket swaying about his ankles. "You need someone who knows something about sailing."

Alifra pointed to her and Dashu. "Both of us know how to sail. We can handle it."

He shook his head. "You don't know *The Birdeater* the way I do. I won't go. This is my ship. I go with the ship. Even if there's a god on it."

Talie stalked toward him, growling.

He stood his ground, though his face paled.

Thassir held up a forestalling hand. "Let him stay."

I dug around in my satchel, handing one filter to Alifra and one to Dashu. I didn't need one, not when I'd be downing god gems, and neither did the two gods with us. I held one out to the captain.

He took it, holding it the way a fisherman might a sharp-toothed fish.

Thassir frowned at me.

"What? So it's fine for him to stay, but not fine to make sure he lives?"

"That's a very sought-after artifact."

"I'm not about to let the man die just because we're taking his ship. We're going to take the boat through using the anchor chains. Lower all the sails, bind them. The wind inside the barrier can only hurt us. It's not the best plan," I admitted. I turned my head to watch Dashu put on his filter as Thassir went to the rail and Alifra moved to the sails, beckoning to Falin. "Don't you have any Aqqilan stories about people winning out in spite of terrible odds? Woman comes up with half-assed plan, still succeeds through luck and a simple unwillingness to die?"

He stared at me for a long while before responding. "I will be sure to pray for us all."

Alifra gave a half-shrug, calling at me over her shoulder. "It's better than the other plan you were tossing about." My other plan had been just to hold my breath and go alone through the barrier using one of the anchor chains, sending the other three back to Langzu. All of them had protested, even Talie.

The sea was shallower here. Our predecessors had, through a good deal of effort and some sort of unknown ingenuity, placed the anchors on either side of the barrier, attached the chains. Every so often, someone had to come out here and dive to replace them. If they could do it, so could I. I'd been the best diver in Guarin's company. Of course, that would have left me alone on the other side of the barrier, with quite a distance to go to shore, a whole host of potential issues between me and safety. Sharks, storms, exhaustion, hunger. "Did you really only think through the very first part of this?" Alifra had said, shaking her head. "And what if you made it to land? What did you expect to do then, all by yourself?"

I'd opened my mouth, shut it, and then thrown up my hands. "Fine. We take the whole boat. We mutiny."

Which wasn't really what anyone wanted.

"Thassir?"

He turned his head this way and that, his gaze on the ocean, as though listening for some distant sound. Finally he drew back from the rail. "She's on the other side. We have to follow."

He sprang from the ship's deck, his wings spread. The sailors gave him a wide berth as he landed on the platform and examined the instructions on the raised metal plate in the center. He unhooked two of the chains and hopped back onto the ship. "Each time goods cross, they go with two chains – one from their side and one from ours. It's how trade is maintained." He hooked the one for the return onto a ring at the mast that held some rigging rope.

I hefted the heavy chain, the metal cold and wet in my hands, the moisture seeping through my shirt and into my shoulder. I focused on the task ahead, steeling myself for the journey, remembering how it felt to be buffeted by aether in the barrier between Kashan and Langzu. This would be a little different. I had to be prepared for it. The chain lightened, clinking sounding over the roar of the barrier as Alifra and Dashu lifted sections of it.

I gritted my teeth as I tugged the chain. It didn't move, but then I didn't have the strength in me yet. "We need rope. We should tie ourselves to the mast. Then let's pull up the anchor." I pointed at the captain. "You. Get below deck. Find yourself someplace secure." I didn't have to tell him twice. "You" – I pointed at Talie – "change yourself back into a cat and find a good corner to wait in. We can handle this up here. When we come through to Pizgonia, I'd rather keep you a surprise. Lithuas knows she's got one god on her tail. She doesn't know there are now two." She nodded, shifted back into a scruffy-looking calico, and padded her way down below.

I barely noticed as Thassir helped Dashu and Alifra tie themselves to the mast. But then he was there, a hand on my arm. Quickly and quietly, he unwound the rope and tied it around himself before knotting the end around me. He stood behind me, lifting the last of the chain from the deck.

Facing down the wall of mist, I reached into one of the pouches at my belt and pulled out a small, glowing red gem. "This isn't foolish, is it?" My voice sounded small over the roar of the waves. I wasn't sure why I was allowing myself to be so vulnerable in front of *him*, but I'd staved it off for so long and now, this close to crossing, I felt myself folding.

He bent down, his lips near my ear. "You are Hakara. You

have killed two aspects of Kluehnn. You have stood against godkillers and survived. You have been past the second aerocline. We do this together. We go south to Pizgonia, we find Lithuas, and we stop the cycle. All you need to do is pull."

"All I need to do is pull," I said. I tilted my head to the side and nodded. "I can do that." I tipped the gem past my lips.

A quick breath, a brief touch of claws against my hair. "Just . . . don't draw more than you have to."

Before I could think to ask what he meant, a puff of aether materialized around me. I breathed it in, felt the god arms grow to encase mine. Strength flooded through me, something in my belly fizzing. I pulled. And behind me, Thassir, Dashu, and Alifra did the same. The chain ground against the rail of the ship and the boat moved toward the roiling sea.

The boat jolted as it hit the barrier, though I kept my feet planted and my breath held.

"According to the stories, there's a lull part way through the barrier here, a place of calm. We can regroup for a moment before we continue," Dashu called.

I pulled the chain and felt my team do the same behind me. If anyone could make it through this barrier alive, it was us. I couldn't help but glance up as the barrier's shadow overtook us, as the roar of the moving water filled my ears. The barrier seemed endless from this angle, a thing moving past the clouds, eternal.

And then we plunged into the dark.

Water buffeted me from all sides. I let my breath out, took in another. The light tingle in my belly had diminished, the god gem nearly spent. The god arms were dissipating into the mist. I fumbled for the pouch of red gems at my side, managed to pull one free and slip it between my teeth as Thassir did his job as arbor, hauling at the chain with enough strength for the both of us.

Before I swallowed, I felt it again. That swell of power within me, just out of reach. A banked ember, waiting for a breath to bring it to life. The red gem slipped down my throat, began reacting with the aether in my blood. That whiff of power winked out, a star retreating from the dawn.

I pulled, felt my fingers slip against the sharp edges of barnacles. I found myself holding my breath without meaning to, long practice and the water around me, thick as a downpour, causing my instincts to kick in. I put my head down and breathed. Here, in the midst of the Sanguine Sea, I couldn't tell if that briny, seaweed scent was the aether or just everything around me. I focused on laying one hand in front of the other, using all my strength and will to get us through this barrier as the ship rose and plunged through waves I couldn't even see.

The world around us stilled, the splash of water against the deck reducing to a fine mist. I blinked, breathing heavily. We were in the lull, surrounded on all sides by the barrier. The cracks in the surface below must have forked, joining again to form an eye in the midst. It was larger than I'd expected, big enough to fit at least ten boats like Falin's. The barrier ahead of us was opaque; I couldn't tell if the distance to the other side was longer or shorter than the span we'd just crossed.

"Your hands." Thassir dropped the chain behind me. It clattered to the deck as he pried the fingers of one hand loose. My fingers were curled into claws; I couldn't quite seem to make them open on my own. The palm beneath was streaked with blood.

I pulled my hand away from his, wiped my palm on my pants, which were just as soaked as the rest of me. It left red streaks – though the clothes were ruined anyways. "I'm fine. We rest a little before we go on." My legs buckled and I struck a foot out, forming a steadier stance. My other hand was still holding the chain. A quick glance behind me found Alifra and Dashu slumped to the deck, the loose chain coiled in a tangle behind them.

Everything here was in shadow, the sea dark as a night sky. Thassir shook his wings, water droplets flinging in every direction. Alifra lifted a hand to shield her face, but didn't even manage a groan. She pulled the filter from her mouth. Water dripped from her russet curls, running in rivulets down the sides of her face. Dashu looked as sullen as a dog in a bath, his clothes clinging to his wiry frame. Alifra put a hand on his shoulder and he patted it.

"How much farther?" I asked her.

She shrugged. "No one could tell me how broad the barrier is for certain, but I think we're through the worst of it."

The ship lurched.

I stumbled to the side. Thassir crouched, his claws digging into the wood. All four of us looked at one another, as though one of *us* had somehow caused the boat to tilt.

The sea around us felt ominous, the water surrounding us a hungry, waiting thing. "The goods don't always make it through."

Alifra shook her head. "They do not."

We'd all assumed it was because of the barrier, the churning sea. Something large moved in the sea beyond the boat. A slick shape breaking the water, a puff of mist, and then it dove back into the depths. I thought I caught a glimpse of eyes. More than two. "A whale?"

Thassir's eyes were glazed as he peered into the sea. "Barexi," he whispered.

Dashu frowned from his spot on the deck, his chest still heaving. "Barexi is dead. And he wasn't a shifter – why would he be in the sea?"

Something about this was making me feel a certain sort of way, and it wasn't a good way. A sense of foreboding was sneaking up on me, breathing at the back of my neck. A hint of a memory tugged at my mind. Dashu droning on, telling Alifra and me the story of a disagreement between Ayaz and Barexi.

"Barexi *is* dead." I watched Thassir's face as I spoke. "But Ayaz once cut him into pieces. It took him a hundred years to put himself back together, but he lost one of his little fingers. To a whale that swallowed it." *The whale grew into a leviathan*, Dashu had said, *and then disappeared into the Sanguine Sea.*

"It's just a whale, right?" Alifra's voice wavered, her hands finding the hilts of her daggers.

The boat rocked again. Harder. I dropped to the deck, felt the rumble of something scraping against the hull through the wood. "Not just a whale. Not anymore. A leviathan."

"How do we fight something like that?" Dashu was pulling the chain to the mast, wrapping it around the wood, ready in spite of the hopelessness of the situation. I'd only caught a glimpse, but the thing was three times the length of the ship.

Thassir closed his eyes. "I'm not as I once was. I changed myself."

I shook my head, gritted my teeth. We didn't have time for this. What use were secrets if we were all dead? I untied the rope from my waist and then moved to untie it from his. "Get that leviathan off us."

He put his hand to the side, his fingers spread, his face a mask of concentration.

Nothing happened.

Zayyel, I realized. He was trying to summon his lightning-forged blade, the one the stories spoke of. Something cracked in his expression, like his insides were crumbling to sand. I wasn't sure if it was the bond, but I understood something of what he felt – that sense that he'd lost something through his own actions that he could never get back.

Dashu cleared his throat.

As soon as Thassir looked up, he tossed his flower-hilted blade to him. "Don't lose it."

Thassir caught it, the sword's edge glinting.

I shoved another red gem between my teeth and lifted the chain again, ignoring my bloody palms. "I'll get us to the other side." I swallowed, and the aether was there around me. I breathed it in.

"You can't fight this thing," Thassir said to Dashu. A head broached the surface of the water, horns like stalagmites atop its mouth, a webbed crest flowing down and into the water, a multitude of eyes staring out from slick skin. He saluted Dashu with his own sword. "But now *I* can." He leapt into the air, his damp wings spread, and then dove into the water.

32
Lithuas
161 years before the Shattering

Unterra - a home in the second territory

When a Langzuan inventor was close to creating a movable-type printing press, it was Lithuas who came to visit him in the guise of a hopeful assistant. She advised him, took care of the tasks that might otherwise hinder him, and when he'd finally completed the first press, she took him to her bed. The Bringer of Change had always found pivotal times to be particularly exciting. She disappeared shortly after and returned two years later with a baby son in tow, whom she left with the inventor. All accounts say he was a devoted and doting father, though the movable-type printing press was the last thing he ever invented.

Around her, glasses lifted, cheeks a polished pink even beneath a layer of bark or fur. Kluehnn stood at the end of the room, his own glass raised to the sky painted on the ceiling above them. "You've all done well," he said. He looked larger than Lithuas remembered, although that was perhaps just the steps he stood on, the spiraling horns on his head grown a little longer in the interim years. He wore a voluminous gray robe, eyes stitched into the trim lining the opening. A black satin sash held it shut, overlaid with a black leather belt. A knife hung from each hip. "To justice served." His voice echoed through the cavernous room, repeated in a gentle murmur from the lips of so many gods. Lithuas said the words with them, putting her glass to her lips and letting the wine slide down her throat.

She'd helped in the final execution of the plan, joining an expedition to Aqqil, impersonating the Emperor's husband and murdering the leader himself. Every country above had been thrown into chaos. It had been a long time since she'd felt so alive. She wished she could dig into her mind and pluck the memory of that night free, capturing it in some place where she could observe it whenever she wanted. The surprise in the Emperor's eyes, the blood spurting from his chest, the shouts, the confusion. Sometimes the changes she brought into the world were slowly gestated, birthed over a span of decades.

And sometimes they happened all at once.

Lithuas slipped through the crowd, searching for the faces she knew best. It took her some time to find the other elder gods – not because they were scattered throughout the palace, but because they were all in one place. All of them except her.

She found them in the gardens, voices alternately hushed and raised, hands cutting through the air, Nioanen's golden wings ruffling and settling, twitching and pulling close. A cat greeted her at the arbor that led into the roses – a mortal world import – winding its orange form around her ankles, its purr a soft rumble against her leg.

Cats were one of the few creatures that existed both in Unterra and the surface world, but Lithuas knew this was not a real one.

"Hello, Irael," she said.

He pranced a little in place, paws kneading the grass beneath his feet. "Lithuas." His whiskers trembled. "It's good to see you."

She peered at the group in front of her – Ayaz, with his golden scales and cutting gold eyes; Velenor, her dark skin contrasted against the white petals of her dress; Barexi, his black nose as wet as his eyes, his antlers rising toward the moon; Rumenesca with her long brown fingers and tufted black ears, her hair the color of autumn leaves; and Nioanen, his countenance as stormy and threatening as the looming clouds on the horizon.

"I wasn't invited."

"It wasn't a formal meeting." Irael licked a paw before springing back to join the others. "No invitations were sent."

She followed him toward the elder gods, their heads close, their words quick as the rush of a snow-melted stream.

"He has the support of all the younger gods," Barexi was saying. "They want to believe that this will keep us safe. But the roots of the Numinars are still dying. The mortals above may be disorganized, they may be scrambling, but that won't stop them from cutting the remaining trees down."

"So we were supposed to do nothing?" Ayaz hissed. His tail moved like a snake in the grass. "I'm not saying Kluehnn was justified, but he did do something."

Velenor let out a soft snort. "Ayaz, have you thought that perhaps you're a bit biased? Cutting down the mortal leaders seems like something *you* might have suggested."

The scales on his cheeks lifted. "I won't apologize for who I am, but don't insult me. I think things through."

Rumenesca noticed her first, the furrow between her brows deepening, a crack in the bark of a tree. "Lithuas."

They all turned to look at her. Their stances shifted, shoulders turned toward one another. She felt, suddenly, as though she were being shut out, like they no longer thought she belonged. She'd taken Kluehnn's side when the rest of them had declined to get involved, and now that she and Kluehnn had successfully carried out the assassinations, they weren't quite sure what to make of this shift in power.

In a few steps, Irael changed from a cat into a young man, red hair ticked with black at the ends. Nioanen moved a wing aside to allow him space, and Lithuas saw the way his gaze lingered on Irael's face. Not that Irael noticed.

"Recklessness is sometimes the only way to institute change," she said. "If you spend too long on calculations, often the moment passes and you are left lingering in the same spot. We've punished the mortals. We've demolished their leadership. It's more than the six of you would have done."

Nioanen crossed his arms, a movement that might have intimidated any of the younger gods, but Lithuas stood tall, staring him straight in the face. She watched his fingers clench and unclench and knew he wanted to summon his blade, Zayyel. He was always more comfortable fighting than he was navigating politics or interpersonal relationships. Probably why he'd made a life out of standing up for the downtrodden. There was always a fight to be had there.

"You have something to say to me, Nioanen?"

He pressed his lips together, and for a moment Lithuas didn't think he'd speak. When he did, his voice was a low rumble, barely loud enough for her to hear. "Where did Kluehnn come from? What does he really want?"

Irael chimed in. "As far as we know, he popped up out of nowhere, ingratiated himself with you, and, using your power and connections, started a war with the mortal world."

Lithuas scoffed. "It's not a war."

"Isn't it?" Velenor spoke up. "What else would you call it? You and Kluehnn have led the gods to assassinate their leaders. What is this if not an act of war?"

She couldn't believe she was hearing this. They were not elder gods, they were *old*, past their prime and their time, moving so slowly as to be completely ineffective. They said what she did was wrong yet offered no solutions of their own. How easy it was to criticize! "It's not war. It's *punishment*. If this was ever a war, it was started by the mortals when they cut down the living Numinars. They're not just changing the world above, they're changing ours too."

Velenor reached out and touched Lithuas's arm, her fingers soft and warm. "We have our role in this too. Remember the pact we made, that we bound all the gods to. We have to accept some blame."

Lithuas pulled her arm out of the goddess's reach. "No. I won't be guilted into sacrificing myself. Guilt is useless. It does nothing."

Rumenesca stepped into the center of the circle, confronting her. "What will you do now? You've wrought your change. What's next?"

"Let the mortals stew in the world they've made. Let them think about what they've done to deserve the wrath of the gods. Maybe the next time they go to cut down a Numinar, to burn the living branches, they'll reconsider." They wouldn't. She knew they wouldn't. The change she'd wrought was enormous, but it was temporary. Others would fill the vacuum of power. Why the urge, then, to pretend this punishment had more meaning than it did? To prove that she'd done the right thing?

Frustrated, she wheeled about and marched back down the path through the roses. If they wanted to exclude her from their little meetings, then so be it.

Velenor called after her, but Lithuas ignored her, finding the main hall again, letting herself be absorbed in the celebration. The younger gods gave way before her, smiling at her presence. They didn't worry about the far future. They didn't think she'd perhaps made a mistake. They felt this victory keenly, living in the moment. She took another glass from one of the servers, trying to drown the bitter words of the other elder gods in wine and elation.

Two glasses later found her in an alcove, resting her head against a stone pillar, her silver hair pillowing her scalp. No matter how much she drank, how many heads inclined at her passing, she felt the hollowness of what she'd done. But she'd chosen. She'd set her feet on this path and had seen it to the end. She didn't want to be like Nioanen, brooding on each action, dwelling on the consequences rather than what had been accomplished.

Yet here she was. And this was how Kluehnn found her – unkempt, dissatisfied, and restless.

He slid onto the cushioned bench next to her, his hands empty. For a moment, he just sat there, watching the others as they danced and drank. "This isn't the end," he said finally.

She lifted her head at that, loose strands of hair brushing against her cheeks. The comb at the back of her head had nearly come free. "What do you mean?"

"We're not done. We've punished the mortals, but they're not the only ones to blame for the way the world is now, are they?"

Icy tendrils crept across her heart, crystals stabbing into tender flesh. The gods. They'd failed to fulfill their duties, to propagate more Numinars. Why spend so much, though, when the mortals would only cut them down? "It's not our fault," she managed, her whisper echoing off stone.

"We have to break the cycle," Kluehnn said. He took her

hand in his. She could have sworn, in that moment, when his arm reached out, that she'd seen something move beneath his robe – the slither of something alive across his ribs. And then it was gone. "I need your help."

She cast her gaze, desperately, over the crowd of younger gods and knew that Kluehnn saw the same thing she did. She'd brought them to him. They respected her, but he was the one who led them now. They were his, they would do his bidding. He'd grown too powerful for her to stop. Yet still, beneath all her apprehension, there pulsed the need to make things different. He was right – they were caught in a terrible cycle that could only end with everyone dead, mortal and god alike. Dread and hope filled her, mingling. She felt she spoke from the lips of a corpse. "Tell me what you want me to do. Tell me how to help you."

He lowered his head close to hers, his warm breath filling the air between them. "We punish them. We punish the gods."

33

Sheuan

11 years after the restoration of Kashan
and 572 years after the Shattering

Langzu - inner Bian

By the Sovereign's decree, all citizens who have committed major offenses — such as murder, treason, or grand theft — shall be executed by banishment into the barrier between Langzu and Kashan. However, all such criminals shall also be given the opportunity to beg clemency at one of Kluehnn's dens, as Kluehnn is merciful and sees value in those society no longer has use for. Members of noble and royal clans who commit such offenses shall be beheaded in the Sovereign's court. There shall be no opportunity for clemency.

The castle felt more and more like a prison these days. Or perhaps, more accurately, it was the workshop and the castle that made Sheuan's prison. She went to the workshop to make the filters and the enforcers followed her. She wandered the halls of the castle and the enforcers watched her. Time marched on and she badly needed a way to take control of the situation.

Would the Sovereign extend the use of the filters to her, when restoration came? Somehow she doubted it. She'd already secreted several of them away, just as a safety measure. Letting her be swept into restoration would be an easy way to rid himself of her, but he could still choose to have her executed. How easy it would be for him to accuse her of theft or treason.

The way he had with her father.

She needed the information her father had found; she needed to leverage it before the Sovereign could kill her. So she went through what she already knew, how it all fitted together, as she strode through the heat-baked streets of inner Bian, two enforcers following on her heels. She'd indulged in a parasol today instead of a hat, the light dim through the painted paper. Though she supposed it wasn't really an indulgence if she had good reason for it.

The Sovereign had smuggled god gems. He'd been good at it. So good that he hadn't been caught and had gained power and notoriety for his exploits – so much so that the Hangtao clan had started sniffing around and trying to find out who he was. The Sovereign, sensing the danger he was in, had looked for an ally, one who could partner with him in taking down a royal clan. He couldn't have done it himself. And that ally was, naturally, his biggest customer. Mitoran had always taught Sheuan she should form alliances with the enemies of her enemies. And the Sovereign had gone and done just that.

He'd given magic to his enforcers. But what had he known about magic and how did he know how to use it? That was a question she hadn't been able to solve with the knowledge she had. But it was a question she was intent on answering today.

She ducked into the Reisun workshop, and to her satisfaction, this time the enforcers didn't argue with her. They waited outside, by the door.

For a while, she did as she was supposed to – constructing filter after filter. The cloth had to be layered in a certain way, the rubber seal fixed so there were no gaps. She was running low on the proprietary cloth Mull had woven from Kashani fibers. Another problem for another day. She had records of his supplier, but she'd have to be careful when she sent someone to obtain the fiber, when she sent it to a weaver. All these steps had to be obscured, or the Sovereign's spies would find her secrets without her having to spill a word.

She stopped to eat a basket of steamed bread she'd brought with her, and finished just as the sun was beginning to dip toward the horizon, the light changing from bright to a burnished copper. Quickly, before the workers left for home, she changed into a freshly laundered work outfit, shucking off the loose silk dress she was wearing.

She pulled aside the woman she'd marked a few days before as being a similar height and build, handing over the dress and the parasol before she could protest. "Go out the window," she told her. She pressed five parcels into her callused palm. "The money is yours. You can change behind my screen."

Don't give them a chance to say no. She couldn't escape Mitoran's lessons, not even now, as the Sovereign's wife. *Make it easy for them to say yes.*

The woman glanced at the coins in her palm, her eyes widening slightly, before she let herself be guided behind the screen where Mull's workbench was. Only a couple of other people noticed this exchange; most were getting ready to return home, stripping off their work outfits in the changing area, grabbing their bags from near the door. It didn't matter. There wasn't enough to tell, and the workers were exactly the type Mull liked — they kept to their own business.

The woman came out from behind the screen once all the other workers had left, dressed in Sheuan's clothing, the parasol at her side. She looked a little anxious, so Sheuan put a hand to her shoulder. "They won't care. What they care about is following me, not about who you are." She couldn't be quite sure about that, but the worker wouldn't know where Sheuan was going, so it was pointless for them to interrogate her. Sheuan gave her a hand up to the window, and then she was in the alleyway, the parasol raised, and heading toward the street.

Sheuan waited by the door until she heard a startled murmur, followed by the retreating footsteps of the enforcers. Then she ducked into the street and locked the door behind her.

The only conclusion she could come to when she ran over all the knowledge she had was that the Sovereign must still be smuggling god gems. He must be using them for whatever magic he was engaging in. And the god gems always went through a realm's government before they made their way to the dens. They had to pass through the Sovereign's possession. There was a warehouse near the dried-up lakebed where god gems from the mines were ferried to, cataloged and counted, and then sent to the dens. The Sovereign had to keep track of which clans were meeting their tithes, contributing appropriately to the mining, of course.

Convenient.

The streets were always busier once the sun had begun its descent, the air cooling to a more tolerable temperature. Servants and some clan members moved around her, completely unaware of her presence. There was something delightful about passing through a crowd unnoticed. Like she was holding a secret that only she knew.

She passed carts of wares – bolts of cloth, bundles of dried herbs, stacked pottery. Light began to shine from between shutters, casting a glow across the plastered walls of buildings. The tiled roofs faded, bit by bit, into the night sky. The castle stood behind her, above it all, a shepherd over its flock.

The taste of the air changed when the sunlight faded, going from baked clay to something dark and loamy. The faint smell of smoke lingered as she made her way to the edge of the lakebed, the charred remains of funeral fires black marks on the dusty ground. She didn't light a lantern, taking care on the uneven ground, her pulse quickening. A light at this time of day would stand out like a star against the sky, and she didn't want the enforcers at the warehouse to notice her.

The warehouse itself was a nondescript building, tucked in amongst other buildings at the edge of the lakebed, one long road passing by them all. It had a few small windows on the ground floor, more on the upper floor, and only one door. The whole thing was painted in a drab beige; Sheuan couldn't tell if that was a deliberate choice or just years of dust from the lakebed coating whatever color originally covered the walls. She ducked into the nearby rocks as a cart approached, a lantern swinging from the corner.

Gems moved constantly to and from the Sovereign's warehouse. And since gems were valuable, the warehouse was nearly surrounded by enforcers, each one armed with at least two blades, their blue jackets faded to a dusky gray by night. It wouldn't be easy to get inside. She'd considered the possibilities. She could throw her weight around, as the Sovereign's wife. It would be hard for them to say no to her, especially if she said she had been directed here by the Sovereign. But word would get back to her husband quickly, and in spite of whatever excuses she might come up with in the meantime, he'd know what she'd been up to.

She'd have to break in.

She could already hear Mitoran's voice in the back of her head as she crept toward the building. *If you have to resort to trespassing, to physical confrontation, to actual seduction, you're already losing the game. These ways are how you get caught. Act with subtlety and no one will know your true purposes.*

This went beyond that, those silly games, those morsels of information she'd fed, bit by bit, to Mitoran. She didn't have the time and she was certain the Sovereign already knew what she wanted. The key was to get to it before he could stop her.

So she circled the warehouse and watched the enforcers as they patrolled, counting them as they stepped beneath the lanterns, noting the pattern of their movements.

There. An opening, if she timed things right. The window this enforcer patrolled back and forth next to was small, the edge of a lantern's light barely reaching it. Most people wouldn't take the chance. But Sheuan was slender and quick. There was a clump of boulders nearby; she could take cover behind them. When he had his back turned, she could undo the latch on the window and slip inside. Before she could change her mind, she crept toward the rocks. It was this or the executioner's ax, she reminded herself.

This was a terrible idea. She reached into her pack, pulling out a long, thin piece of metal she'd taken from Mull's workshop. She stuffed down the fear and the uncertainty, crouched behind a pockmarked boulder, and waited.

The enforcer turned his back. Sheuan darted for the window.

It was close, but each stride felt an age-long endeavor. She kept her footfalls light, making sure she landed on the balls of her feet first, letting her heels softly touch after.

The shutters were tightly closed, a tiny gap between. The piece of metal she'd taken from Mull's shop barely fitted. Her breath gusted over her hands as she worked, her chest prickling with heat. She had to lift it up, to undo the inside latch. The metal stuck, wedged too tightly.

The enforcer would be turning around soon. He'd see her. Sheuan swallowed. She had to ignore his presence; she had to focus on what she was doing. Think. *Think!* She wiggled the piece of metal back and forth, trying to work it free, to work the latch. There. Something inside lifted. The shutter swung open. She put a foot to the wall.

A hand grabbed her wrist.

For a moment, all she could do was stare into the eyes of the young man standing there, his other hand on the hilt of his blade. She flitted through possibilities in her head. If she tried to fight him, he'd subdue her, perhaps even kill her. She couldn't seduce him – there was no set-up for this and she was in worker's clothes besides. If she went with him quietly, if she told him who she was, she'd be at the Sovereign's mercy.

A fourth option sprang to mind. She pulled her hand in, tugging him close, whispering into his ear, "I am a worker at Mullayne Reisun's workshop. I'm not here to steal. You must have heard the rumors. Let me go into this warehouse, let me leave, and I'll give you his invention. The one that will save you from restoration. Do you want that?"

He didn't move, and when she'd counted in her head to five, she knew she had him. She'd been right, then. Rumors were spreading among not only the nobles and the royals, but the Sovereign's own enforcers. Among the commoners. She understood the strategy – doling the filters out in waves, seeing who was willing to do what in order to gain his favor. But he'd bring Kluehnn down on them all if he wasn't careful.

The enforcer's fingers loosened. "Go," he said quietly.

She didn't need to be told twice. She pulled herself up and through the window, carefully closing the shutters behind her.

The inside of the warehouse wasn't lit by any lantern. Crates were stacked in neat piles, a faint glow emanating from between the wooden slats. She didn't try to lift the lids; they were all tightly secured. Each footstep stirred up dust, the musty smell filling her nostrils.

Several desks sat in one corner, ledgers lined up on a shelf next to them. She leafed through a few of them. Nothing unusual. Nothing strange. Just lists and weights of gems from the crews paid for by the different clans. Accounting of tithes.

This wasn't what she'd hoped for. Every instinct in her body screamed at her to hurry, to leave, to get out of here before the enforcer lost his patience. But she had to be careful. She had to be methodical. Her heart beat a staccato in her chest as she began, painstakingly, to canvass the warehouse.

The stacks of god-gem crates. The desks. The ledgers. Nothing else.

She kicked at the dust on the floor, frustrated.

The dust.

Her gaze found a patch of floor oddly free of dust, except for what she'd tracked over it. Three floorboards. As though someone had wiped them clean. Or had *lifted* them, letting the dust fall free.

She knelt, feeling around on the ground. These three floorboards didn't quite sit flush with the others. She pulled out the piece of metal, wedged it between the boards, and with a soft creak, the wood lifted.

A hollow space existed beneath, a dark hole lit by a faint blue glow. Sheuan lifted the other two boards, trying to keep the movements quiet.

A set of stairs disappeared into the hole. She knew the buildings of Bian had been built on the ruins of others. The Shattering had destroyed many of the old cities, and no one had bothered to rebuild them. They'd simply built on top of them, slowly burying the past.

She descended, feeling her way to each stair before putting her weight on it. The blue glow was stronger at the bottom. Her eyes quickly found the source – a box on a table, the lid slightly cracked. She couldn't tell without a lamp how large this space was, or what else it contained. So she went to the box and opened the lid.

It was filled to the brim with glowing blue god gems.

He *was* still smuggling gems. Sheuan thought of her father, his star anise scent, the smudge of ink on the side of his hand, his quiet consideration of each problem the Sovereign had set him to. He wouldn't have cared about this. If he'd known, he would have simply looked the other way. The use of god gems by mortals wasn't legal, but it was common enough among the clans. Her father wouldn't have risked his life over something like this when he himself had purchased black-market gems to sow in their fields, to help the crops grow.

She picked up a handful of the gems, holding them aloft like a torch. Their light pierced the darkness, showing her a large room hewn from stone, pillars holding up the floor above. There were ledgers down here too, and a row of empty cells, metal-barred doors hanging open.

And there, in the opposite corner, was an altar.

She crept toward it, a deer drawn inexorably toward a wolf. There was only one god – one *true* god. It was the bargain Tolemne had made with Kluehnn, long ago – one the mortals kept so that restoration could save them all. Worship of other gods wasn't just illegal; it was forbidden. She knew it happened sometimes, desperate people who hewed to old ways. And her education had included mention of the elder gods, just so she would know. There were still buildings that had their faces stamped on the endcaps of roof tiles.

The seven elder gods stared back at her from the carved altar — Barexi, Ayaz, Rumenesca, Irael, Nioanen, Lithuas, and Velenor. Sticks of incense stood in front of each image. She leaned in close. Only five had been lit, and recently, the pungent scent drifting toward her as she examined the ashes. For Barexi, Rumenesca, Irael, Nioanen, and Velenor.

Those for Ayaz and Lithuas remained pristine.

What did it mean? This seemed to be proof of worship. If the Sovereign worshiped the old gods, did that mean he had learned from a god how to use gems? A chill settled into her chest. This was certainly information he could have executed her father for. If her father had leaked it, the Sovereign would have faced Kluehnn's justice.

She was running out of time. The evening was young, but dinner would begin soon, and she could only think of so many excuses. She rushed back up the stairs, replaced the floorboards, and returned to the window. The enforcer was waiting beneath it when she opened it.

"Here." She stuffed one of the filters from her satchel into his hand. "Tell no one."

And then she was off into the night, her mind reeling. She found an alleyway as soon as she returned to inner Bian, stripping off the worker's clothes and leaving them in a refuse pile. The tunic and pants she wore beneath were simple, but still of fine enough quality that she wouldn't be questioned on her return.

The streets of inner Bian were emptier now, all the lamps in the buildings lit. She hurried back toward the castle. She could leave a letter with her mother about the warehouse, the altar beneath the floorboards. If the Sovereign threatened to execute her, she'd still have that information, held somewhere else, ready to be released. She had to be measured about this. She had to be smart. She turned the last street toward the castle and nearly ran straight into an entourage.

"Well, this is a surprise." The Sovereign stood behind two stone-faced enforcers, his dark eyes raking over her. In spite of his words, he sounded not the least bit surprised. "My wife, in the streets of Bian, at night, by herself. What *exactly* would you happen to be doing here?"

34
Hakara

11 years after the restoration of Kashan
and 572 years after the Shattering

The Sanguine Sea – the anchor point between Langzu and Pizgonia

Tell your council that the clans of Langẓu send the following message: The current trade treaties between Piẓgonia and Langẓu state that only the finest-quality tea from Piẓgonia will be shipped across the anchor to Langẓu. You put tea that was not good into the double oilskin. The tea contained older, broken leaves and even some particles of dust. What do you take us for? Why do you treat us with such disrespect when we have paid for the best, sending our hard-earned money through that terrible barrier? You will restore the money we paid for the tea in full, and we reserve the right to strike medicinal herbs from our agreements if the next shipment is not of fine quality.

Alifra let out a little breathless laugh as she watched Thassir disappear beneath the waves. I pulled, the breath tight in my chest, and she and Dashu scrambled to the chain, putting their filters into place before taking it up behind me.

It was harder without Thassir at my back, his strength seemingly limitless. But the boat lurched toward the far barrier, the chain drawing taut. I tried to keep my gaze on that barrier, but I couldn't help looking at the spot where my arbor had dived into the ocean. I could feel his presence in my mind, moving farther away and into the depths.

Something flashed in the water, a bright white light that hurt to look at. I counted in my head as I pulled. We were nearly to the other side. All I had to do was hold my breath until we could make it into the aether. Most people tried to avoid aether, and here I was, in desperate need of it. I could feel each pull seeping away my air, pulling it to my muscles. My throat spasmed and I clamped down, pressing my tongue to the roof of my mouth. Not now. Not yet. Not until we were through.

A crashing sound came from the starboard side. The leviathan broke the surface, Thassir on its back, his wings slick black and dripping, Dashu's sword half embedded in its flesh. The beast's shadow stole what little light we had on deck. I found my gaze focusing on the extra fins at its sides, the barnacles clinging to its skin.

It was going to fall on the stern.

I yanked on the chain as hard as I could, as fast as I could. Dashu and Alifra must have seen it too, because I heard them grunting from behind me as they put the full force of their weight and effort into getting us out of the leviathan's path.

It splashed down just behind us, one fin slapping against the stern and tilting the boat dangerously into the air. A stray thought wandered into my mind as I clung to the chain, nearly hanging from it. What was Falin going through below decks?

And then the ship fell back toward the water and I pulled again, my arms burning, my lungs aching. Spots swam in front of my eyes. We landed with a splash, the bow dipping before leveling out again, water sloshing onto the deck.

I focused on the wall of mist before us. I had to hold my breath until we reached it. If I let the aether out of me now, we'd be just three mortals trying to haul an entire ship. We'd never make it. One hand over the next. I told myself just to get to ten pulls, and then when I'd finished those, coaxed myself into ten more.

What if we made it to the wall without Thassir? Would he still be able to follow? I felt his presence in my mind, still there, still alive. Everything in me screamed to take a breath, to suck the sweet air into my lungs, to calm my clenching belly, my tightened throat. A sense of calm washed over me, my hearing dimming. My mouth felt stuffed with cloth. I was going to pass out and we were still half a boat-length away from the barrier.

"Hakara!" Dashu called my name as I fell, my fingers still wrapped around the chain. I tried to pull again and found my arms useless. I wouldn't give in. I couldn't give in.

My cheek met the wood and still I tried to pull.

A face rose from behind the rail, black hair dripping, wings sodden. He grasped the side of the boat, grimacing, and then hauled himself back onto the ship. Without even thinking about it, I took in a sharp breath. My vision cleared as Thassir strode toward us, Dashu's sword in his hand, the blade streaked red. I thought I saw the flicker of a silver flame before I blinked and it was gone. Suddenly, being on the deck felt like the silliest thing in the world. I struggled to my feet before he could get to me, taking the chain firmly in my grasp, like I hadn't been about to pass out at all.

Behind us, the beast let out a long, low sound.

I could barely draw enough breath to speak, but I managed, "It's still alive?"

Swiftly, Thassir handed the sword back to Dashu and seized the chain. "Take a moment to breathe. I'll get us to the barrier."

I lifted my hands from the chain and set them on my knees, trying to balance as Thassir, Alifra, and Dashu yanked at it. The misty wall rose before us. I plunged a hand into my pouch of red gems, swallowing one more. A quick glance at the water showed me three eyes, blinking in the surrounding darkness.

Aether took the bow and then it took us. I breathed it in and found my strength again. I stopped counting handholds. Each time Thassir and I worked together, I felt unstoppable, invincible. A by-product of the bond between us, or just of working with an elder god?

Before I could settle into the question, we burst into the light. I heard Dashu and Alifra collapsing to the deck behind me, their breaths rasping. I squinted against the sun, a warm breeze licking at my salt-drenched skin.

Alifra tore the filter from her face, sucking in the fresh ocean air. "Didn't think I'd ever get to do that again." She eyed Thassir. "It really *is* you, isn't it?"

He let go of the chain and it rattled against the floorboards. "Don't look at me like that. I'm not that elder god." His black wings shook, water raining onto the deck.

Alifra gave him an odd look. "But you *are*," she said slowly.

He glowered at her, and when that didn't seem to work, he stalked off to the prow. The shoreline of Pizgonia appeared in the distance, a line of gold and green above the darkened ocean.

Falin burst from the hatch. "We made it?" When Dashu nodded, he rushed toward the ship's wheel. "Unfurl the sails, you idiots, or we'll crash into the anchor on Pizgonia's side!"

We all jumped to obey. The ship lurched to the side once the sails were loose, the anchor knocking twice against the hull before we skated past.

Talie emerged next, stretching on the deck and then rolling onto her side in a patch of sunlight, a breeze ruffling the white fur of her belly. I wouldn't have been able to tell the difference between her and a regular cat if I'd not already known.

"Yes, yes," I said, knowing that if I knelt to pet her, she'd bite, "I'm glad you made it through too. Now go make yourself useful and make sure there are no mice aboard."

She merely yawned.

The shoreline of Pizgonia approached more quickly than I expected, the wind brisk and warm. The golden line I'd seen from a distance turned out to be a broad sandy beach, strangely shaped trees dotting the land beyond. Their trunks were wide and squat; the leaves gathered at the top of branches formed almost a geometric pattern. A city of buildings in red and gold rose above the beach, the architecture oddly square, devoid of the curving tile rooftops I was accustomed to.

It was just as grand as Xiazen, maybe even more so, and I didn't know anything about it.

This was the first time I actually missed the presence of Sheuan's cousin, Mull. I would have bet he knew some of the language, even though the continents had been separate for hundreds of years. My gaze slid over my comrades and stopped on Thassir.

Wait.

The gods always knew before I opened my mouth that I spoke Kashani; I'd never run into a god who hadn't spoken my mother tongue as though born to it. It was one of the gifts the gods were granted – the knowledge and ability to speak any language. I crept toward his position at the prow.

Black feathers rustled as soon as I came within five paces. "You are . . . staring at me."

"You can feel that?"

He ignored the question. "What is it you want, Hakara?" He said it lightly, without rancor, but without curiosity either.

"We're not going to be able to dock without questions, and we can't answer those questions. Have you been to this city before?" I waved over Dashu, who came at a trot from the other side of the ship. "Gathering information," I called to him.

"The last time I was here, it was called Gorina," Thassir said. "City of a Hundred Moons."

I beckoned Dashu closer. "Is that what your stories say?"

He rubbed his goatee and squinted at Thassir. "My uncle told me Go-reen-a."

"Well, your uncle was mistaken. It's Gorina. Something was lost along the line."

Dashu frowned. Gods below, we didn't have time for this to devolve into a disagreement about oral histories. "We'll find out soon enough which of you is correct. Why the epithet?"

Dashu shrugged, letting it go. "The wells and fountains. It's said there are a hundred of them, and at night, they each reflect the moon."

"So now we sort of know the city's name and we know it's got a lot of fresh water. Helpful." We had no idea what requirements the place had for foreigners docking at their port, or how they would treat visitors from across the barrier. "Thassir? Do you sense her?"

He scanned the shoreline. "No. She's stopped shifting. She's in hiding."

Right. So we needed to find whatever resistance had formed within the city, and we had to find a way to warn them. None of us spoke the language except Talie and Thassir. That meant

I'd have to send Talie out into the city, knowing that Lithuas was lurking somewhere within. "Can Lithuas sense Talie if she shifts?"

Thassir shook his head. "No. That ability is linked to a blood pact between the elder gods. She won't be able to sense Talie. But the godkillers can."

Alifra joined us at the prow. "We're here to renegotiate trade terms before Langzu is restored. It's what they would expect." She pointed at Thassir. "Obviously we needed an altered to help us get through the barrier. He learned the language from a scholar." She looked to me. "You'll be the Langzuan representative. Thassir will translate. The rest of us are sailors." She studied her salt-stained clothes. "It's the best we've got."

"And Talie goes into the city to search for both the resistance and Lithuas."

The calico padded up the stairs to the prow. "I'll do it on one condition."

We all turned to look at her.

"Thassir comes back with me. The gods are finally fighting back, and we need help. He will at least hear us out."

Falin's brow furrowed, but he didn't ask any questions. Wise move, not getting caught up in this.

"That is acceptable," Thassir said slowly.

The closer we got to the city, the more it was apparent that our strange ship had not gone unnoticed. A retinue of guards greeted us at the docks, halberds in hand, a row of archers behind them, their bows trained on the deck of the ship. Their skin was varying shades of golden brown, from a medium bronze to the rich dark of a tree hollow. Each wore a light beige robe topped with an orange cowl. A stylized sun was embroidered on the front of each robe.

I stood at the rail. "We are here to renegotiate trade agreements between Pizgonia and Langzu," I called out in Langzuan. Thassir, next to me, shouted to the guards below in a language I didn't understand, the vowels rounder and the consonants strange to my ears.

Someone emerged from between the guards, a young man in a steel helmet. He spoke in a clear voice, beckoning to us.

Thassir nodded, tucking his wings behind him. "He says to follow him to the palace's guest house, where we will be made comfortable before negotiations with the council." A crowd had gathered by the docks, people eyeing us past the guards. No wonder – we must have looked a sight with our strange clothes and strange faces.

We lowered the gangplank and disembarked, but not before Talie leapt to the dock, swerving between feet and legs and disappearing into the crowd.

The guards closed in around us as we moved toward the city. A wall surrounded the perimeter, rising above the sandy beach and the crashing waves, crenelations revealing more guards walking atop the walls. The gates we passed beneath bore a decorated arch of carved stucco; it shaded us briefly from the heat of the sun. The city beyond stole my breath. Streets were paved with flat stones, alcoves between buildings painted in bright murals. And I seemed to find, tucked away in every alley and small, shaded square, tiled fountains in beautiful patterns, the water trickling out of spouts carved into the shapes of various animals. Struts and reeds above kept the brightest sun out of the streets below. A low hum of activity echoed off the rust-colored walls.

A crowd followed us through the streets, and every so often, a guard had to push away a citizen who had become a little too curious. Several managed to slip in and out of the crowd, keeping pace with us.

A woman caught my eye, her face veiled in midnight blue

but for her eyes, a tall hat upon her head, draped in the same blue. She studied each of us in turn as she walked just outside the perimeter of the guards, sliding ahead or behind each time the streets became too narrow. A group of children ran ahead of her, feet slapping against the stone. I didn't know much about this continent we'd landed on, but I could smell a suspicious situation before most could. I drew in close to my companions.

She lifted a hand before I could speak a word to them.

Veiled men and women dropped from the tops of buildings or flowed in from alleyways, swords raised. They slipped beneath the halberds of the guards.

In the next moment, the veiled woman stood by Dashu. Another of the ambushers grabbed my arm. Dashu pulled his sword free from its sheath. To my surprise, the veiled woman seized his hand and, in a movement I couldn't follow, took the weapon from his grasp.

"Agashu Indaya!" someone called from the crowd. The cry was taken up by others, passed as though from one set of lips to another. The guards stopped fighting back.

Someone dropped a bag over my head.

My instinct was to struggle, to claw and kick and free myself from whoever thought they could take me alive. But I'd been here before, in this very same sort of spot, even if the bag smelled different. A bit sweet, with a pungency I didn't recognize. "Don't fight back!" I called to my companions. "I think they may be who we're looking for."

"Risky gamble, isn't it?" Alifra's voice drifted through the din.

A grunt of assent from Thassir.

I felt us being rushed through the streets, turns I couldn't keep track of, quick flashes of heat against my shoulders as we moved from shadow to sunlight to shadow again. And then the warmth of the day disappeared as we were led down a set of stairs into the dark.

This felt so familiar. Except this time, I wasn't tied to a chair.

Several more turns, whispers I didn't understand. And then we finally came to a stop in a cool and silent space.

Someone lifted the bag from my head.

We all looked at one another and then around at the room. We were in a basement, signs of a pre-Shattering civilization scattered around us. An old, flaking painting was lit by a lantern against one wall; a few metal beams lay across the floor.

The veiled woman stood opposite us, twenty or so warriors arrayed behind her. "Leave us. Close the door behind you." The draping on her hat swung as she turned her head. They obeyed without so much as a question. We stood there in the dark, waiting.

One woman. We could take her on. Alifra, next to me, shifted, as though she knew my thoughts. Why would she want to be alone with the five of us? She wasn't even looking at us, Dashu's sword in her hand as she ran her palm along the length of it. She lifted it to eye level, studying the white enamel flowers on the hilt. "It's been a long time since I've seen this."

Dashu gripped his empty scabbard, his brows low over his eyes. "That sword has been passed through my family for generations. You know of it?"

She laughed, then said something in the very same tongue I heard Dashu often muttering to himself. His face paled. "I more than just know of it. I *made* this sword."

Thassir took a hesitant half-step forward, his face alight with the sort of hopeful curiosity I usually only saw on children's faces. "Velenor is supposed to be dead. Is it really you?"

She unwound the draping of her head covering, revealing not the structure of a hat, but two long antelope horns. With graceful fingers, she pulled her veil down. Her skin was dark as onyx, glittering by the flickering light of the lanterns, the faint glow of a god's aura casting a competing light. "Yes, friend. It's been a long time."

35
Hakara

11 years after the restoration of Kashan
and 572 years after the Shattering

Pizgonia - Gorina, City of
a Hundred Moons

How is Kluehnn able to maintain himself in more than one body while other gods do not? If one aspect of Kluehnn dies, another takes its place, yet if a god dies, they are truly dead. Is this some magic the other gods do not know? Or if they know it, are they simply not skilled enough to enact it? Or, and this is the one that terrifies me, is it so abhorrent a process that no one else will undertake it even under pain of death?

I should burn this paper.

It seemed we hadn't found the resistance; instead, the resistance had found us. I watched Thassir and Velenor talking in the corner, unsure of what to say or whether I should interrupt, feeling a little like I was party to a conversation I shouldn't have been able to hear. Two elder gods, catching up. It felt more than a bit mad.

Velenor reached out to touch his feathers. "That's different."

He shrugged his wing away. "It doesn't matter. Lithuas told me you were dead."

"She told me you were dead too. That she'd let me live as long as I didn't interfere with her plans or Kluehnn's. So I went south, to where his influence wasn't quite as strong."

"But it's growing."

"Yes. Once Langzu is restored, he'll focus all his attention on us."

Dashu had his sword in hand again, gazing at it as though it had been made anew. He'd known it was valuable. He hadn't known it had been forged by an elder god.

I tapped my foot, wondering if or when they'd get to the real issue.

"Have you been well?" Thassir asked.

"Well enough. I'm not leading the Godless here, nor am I a part of that resistance movement. I'm outside of it, in a manner of speaking. They think of me as a folk hero, one who supposedly passes her knowledge down to the next generation. So I've existed here for hundreds of years, always veiled. They know me as Agashu Indaya, the veiled rogue."

I couldn't take it anymore. I stalked toward them. "Lithuas is here." I locked gazes with Thassir. "He knows. And if you were part of this blood pact he's mentioned, you'll be able to sense her too when she uses magic. She's been infiltrating the resistance movements of each of the realms, subverting them to find corestones. And Kluehnn uses these to enact restoration. We have the two of you now, here in one place. We have filters that can protect mortals from aether. There is an *army* of gods waiting for Thassir to lead them. If we take out

Lithuas, we disrupt Kluehnn's plans and have a real chance to strike back."

Velenor shook her head, and my heart dropped, a sick feeling in my belly. "I can protect the Godless from Lithuas. But please, leave her be and go back to Langzu."

I didn't know what to do except shout. "She has *murdered* countless people! I'll grant that you may be able to protect this realm from Lithuas and Kluehnn, but you cannot protect all of them. What do you think is going to happen? You have some pretty little side agreement with Lithuas, and then Pizgonia is the only realm left among a sea of restoration? How do you think this ends?"

Velenor didn't meet my anger with her own. Her large, dark eyes regarded me with the patience of a mother with an overwrought child. "I understand that is the truth. But in the end, Lithuas is not who you think she is."

"A murderer?"

She let the air between us cool, her breath a winter breeze. "She took a wrong turn and doesn't know how to walk her way back. Have you never made mistakes, not been the person you should have been? She thinks she is doing what's right. Did you know that when she spared my life, she wept?"

"She did not weep when she spared mine," Thassir said beneath his breath.

"Nioanen" – he flinched at the use of his real name – "your relationship with her was different to mine. But she and I – we were once as close as sisters. I will fight for her life. I cannot do anything else, even if it means losing mine."

Only words, yet it felt like she'd stabbed me clean in the heart. Rasha. The bond in my mind tugged, the citrus-fresh feel of it making me ache. All I'd wanted was to cocoon her into a safe place, to keep her from suffering. Even now I could feel that instinct tug at me – that need to protect her.

No. This was different. It had to be different. "If we kill Lithuas, we don't just delay Kluehnn's plans, we bring them to a halt. He'll have to find another way to obtain the corestones. I'm going to try, even if you won't help me."

I turned to Thassir. He stood by the wall, near that cracked painting, and I could see now, this close, that it was a painting of Nioanen in his full glory, his golden wings spread, Zayyel in his hands. He claimed not to be that god anymore, but I didn't know what to believe. The seven elder gods had ruled Unterra together, not separately. He'd known Lithuas for far longer than he'd known me. "And what about you?" I could feel myself teetering, *needing* desperately for him to be on my side. "Would you stand in my way as well, now that you know Velenor's mind?"

He opened his mouth and hesitated. "I . . ."

I'd needed him to be unequivocally on my side, to bolster my certainty, and instead he hesitated. It was all I needed to know. I whirled, grabbed one of the lanterns, and stalked deeper into the ruins, keenly feeling the stretch of both my bonds, with him and my sister. I'd let myself be swayed by hope – that was my mistake. Dashu was right, as were all the stories children told one another in each unrestored realm. The gods were selfish, they were cruel, they were unkind. Lithuas had set this all in motion. Thassir had let it all happen. And even Velenor held herself apart from the Godless, doing meaningless work so she could tell herself she was making a difference.

What would make a difference was putting an end to Lithuas. Yet Velenor didn't want to, and Thassir *hesitated*.

Carved reliefs flashed past, mosaics of tile, depictions of historical events long gone, from a world that no longer existed. I couldn't win this fight without Thassir, and even though we'd found ourselves circling one another, trying to understand the path forward, I still couldn't quite trust him. There were things he wasn't telling me, and I held the bone-deep suspicion that he'd always hold his ties to the other gods above any ties he held to mortals. To me.

He could have stood against Kluehnn, if only he'd tried.

He could have tried.

36
Mullayne

11 years after the restoration of Kashan
and 572 years after the Shattering

Langzu - the den northeast of Bian

Very few mortals have ever been to Unterra, though all describe a strange area between the last aerocline and emergence into the land of the gods. "The place of floating", they call it, where even those without wings can fly.

Mull wasn't built for subterfuge. He'd thought it clever, asking to use the latrine ditch and then sneaking off somewhere else. And maybe it was. But what he hadn't thought through was what to say if he was caught.

So something of the truth slipped out of his mouth. "I was looking for something."

The godkiller who stood before him was one of the most intimidating women he'd ever seen. She was a full head taller than he was, her dark eyes narrowed in suspicion, her hands ending in claws. One horn curved up and around the side of her head. Her long black hair hung around a wound on the other side, where her other horn should have been. It wasn't bleeding anymore, but the skin there was pink and scabbed. She didn't give any indication that the wound caused her pain. There was a stain on the skirt of her robe, one that looked like old blood. "You were looking for something. It does not appear to be the latrine ditch." Her voice was a low hum, thick with menace.

He swallowed, almost expecting her hand to lash out, to seize him by the front of his convert's robe. It took him the longest moment to realize she wasn't holding a staff or a knife at his throat, but . . . a crutch? He tried to move away from the wall, to obscure what he'd actually been doing. But he still wasn't used to the strange strength of his limbs, their unfamiliar shapes. He stumbled over a stone.

The godkiller caught him by his forearm with her free hand, setting him back on his feet.

He really *had* thought he was going to saunter into this den and it would give up its secrets to him, just like that? "I'm not used to this body," he found himself saying. "I haven't been in it for very long."

Her narrowed eyes softened, the set of her mouth a little less harsh. She made sure he was steady before she let go and then leaned back on her crutch. "I remember what it was like, being newly altered. Everything was strange. You'll get used to it." She sighed, some frustration she didn't see fit to share. "What are you doing out here? You're meant to be tending to the books. And don't tell me you got lost."

There wasn't really any plausible story he could tell, was there? Maybe it didn't matter. Surely the godkillers had a pittance of curiosity in them, didn't they? Didn't everyone? He pointed uselessly at the carvings on the wall. "They say things. They're leading somewhere. I used to be a scholar." It was enough of the truth to explain his presence down here. The whole den was littered with these carvings. It had been easy to find one outside the archives. Some of them spouted what seemed to be complete nonsense. Children's rhymes. Some of them gave a tantalizing insight into the world of Unterra – a description of some lush plant, or some strange animal. But each of them included instructions at the end that led him to another carving.

They'd been leading him deeper down, into parts of the caves he was sure the converts weren't supposed to go. What lay at the end of these instructions? The tomb, he hoped.

She took the lantern from his hand, held it up to the engraving, and squinted. "Can you ... read that?"

"It's Old Albanoran. I learned it later in life, but I'd already learned Albanoran, so it wasn't too hard to pick up. There was a pretty big leap between Old Albanoran and Albanoran, occurring sometime close to the Shattering, which makes sense – it was an upheaval for everyone, and those tend to have a strong effect on the ambient culture."

She didn't take her gaze away from the carvings. "And are those and Langzuan the only languages you know?"

He opened his mouth to respond, and then remembered, at the very last moment, that he wasn't supposed to be Mullayne Reisun, scholar, inventor, noble. "Well, I ... I think that's quite a lot of languages."

She whirled on him, seizing his wrist, her face close to his, her sharp teeth bared. "I just spoke to you in Kashani, and you answered in it too. You were a prisoner, a murderer, the lowest of the low. Where did you get an education?"

He'd done it now. Perhaps instead of taking lessons in languages, he should have begged a lesson or two from Sheuan in subtlety. She was always pretending to be someone else, and here he was, unable to pretend to be anyone but himself – and that wasn't what he needed right now. "I was a noble." It was the only answer he could think of. "Nobles can still be murderers."

Her grip didn't loosen even marginally. "You think I don't know enough about your country to know that nobles who commit crimes get their heads cut off? They wouldn't have thrown you into a wagon to take to the barrier." She made a small sound of disgust, as though she couldn't *believe* he'd given himself away so easily. "Come with me."

He didn't exactly have a choice, as she hadn't let go of his wrist. She handed the lantern back to him and began to limp up the tunnel, pulling him behind her. Even with her apparent injuries, he felt like a wayward cub, being dragged back into shelter.

How did Sheuan always seem to get along with everyone she met? "What's your name?" he asked. Surely there was a more elegant way to introduce yourself to someone, but if there was, he didn't know it. And it probably didn't involve one of the parties hauling the other around by the wrist.

"Rasha," she said, to his surprise. So maybe it *was* that simple.

"I'm Mull." He didn't think it would matter if he gave her his real name. He'd come to realize that no one in the den really cared who he was – as long as he did what he was told and stayed put.

She only grunted. What would Sheuan have said to that? He had no idea.

Rasha seemed content to thump along in silence, stopping every so often to stretch out her leg. The missing horn and the wounded leg seemed recent, and he assumed she must have received both injuries fighting against the gods. He'd always seen the godkillers move in groups of three, but she didn't have a blade at her side and she wasn't in any condition to fight. So Kluehnn must have sent her to the archives so she could recover.

She didn't seem happy about it. He caught glimpses of her grimace, of lowered brows, and every so often her claws would prick his skin as her grip tightened, as though some unpleasant thought had just occurred to her.

When they at last returned to the archives, the place was empty. "The others have gone to the mess hall for dinner," Rasha said. "You'll have to go without."

He didn't dare protest.

She led him to a crate, let go of his arm, and cracked the lid open with her claws. Stacks of papers lay inside, scattered like refuse. He caught glimpses of several different languages, all of which he recognized.

Rasha pointed into the crate. "Read them to me."

There was something subversive about the demand. A godkiller wanting to know what was going on in the archives? And no one else was here. She wasn't doing this under any command; Kluehnn already knew what was happening in this room. All Mull wanted was to get out of this room again, to wander the tunnels with a notebook, recording every phrase Tolemne had carved into the walls. But he didn't have leave to do that. He licked his lips. She didn't have a dagger at her side, but the crutch and the claws looked dangerous enough to him.

Sheuan would have handled this better. He wondered what exactly she was doing now, whether she was safe. "What if I don't want to?"

Her lips set into a line. "Read them to me. Or I'll tell everyone here that you're a spy. And I don't even know if I'd be lying."

37
Hakara

11 years after the restoration of Kashan
and 572 years after the Shattering

Pizgonia - Gorina, City of a Hundred Moons, in the Godless hideout

The construction of the anchor between Pizgonia and Langzu happened so long ago that disputing how exactly it was built has become a bit of a hobby amongst scholars. The pieces have so often been replaced that nothing of the original remains, so any clues that might have been apparent there are now lost. Some think that surveyors must have had some advance notice from Kluehnn that the Shattering would occur, that they determined where the Sanguine Sea would be divided and placed the anchor before the Shattering. Others think that the builders used large whales to carry the chains through, as these creatures are capable of moving through the barrier. And yet others suppose the involvement of gods in its construction, though these suppositions are quickly hushed by scholars who are wary of drawing Kluehnn's ire.

I found myself in the depths of the ruins, my cheek pressed to the cold stone of one of the walls as I tried to cool my temper. I didn't know what I should do next. Gather Dashu and Alifra, try to find Lithuas? See if Talie would join our plans? She'd been born to this world at least; she didn't have the same misguided loyalty to Lithuas that the elder gods did.

The relief I'd set my cheek against was too distorted at this angle for me to understand it, but I caught a glimpse of a hand holding something just above the ground. Carved rays extended from it.

I frowned and pulled away, rubbing the indentations it had left on my face. The lantern swung as I lifted it to the relief, metal creaking. The top and bottom of the lantern were decorated with geometric patterns that cast triangles and dots along the floor.

Carved shapes of people dressed in strange clothing covered the wall. One knelt, something held in her hand. A glowing stone. When I moved in closer, holding the lantern flush with the wall, I could see flecks of old paint clinging to it.

Multiple colors.

A corestone. She was either burying it or uncovering it – I couldn't be sure which. Another panel stretched next to this one. With hesitant steps, I followed the passage. A scorpion, feeling the vibration of my footsteps, skittered away. The next panel showed the woman holding the corestone high. I hurried to the panel after that. In this one, she brought it to a man with antlers. He reached for it.

In the next, the god had the stone at his lips. He was swallowing it. Just the way I'd done. I pressed a hand to my belly, feeling a slight tingle in response. I didn't quite understand. Was this how gods used corestones? Was that how Kluehnn had planned to use them?

I took another step and found chunks of stone at my feet, the floor littered with dust. When I lifted the lantern to the panel, I found only a gouged-out piece of rock. This wasn't the work of an earthquake or some odd accident. Someone had deliberately destroyed this panel. And the next one. And the next.

"I hope you don't mind that I followed you." A rich voice echoed from the tunnel walls.

I whirled to find Velenor behind me. I'd been so immersed in the reliefs that I couldn't be sure how long she'd been standing there. She was an elder god. They probably had ways of sneaking around I didn't know about.

"What if I said I did? Wouldn't really matter, would it?"

She gave a little shrug, trailing a hand along the stone. "These things are more complicated than you would like to think. People and gods are not who they seem to be at first glance."

I crossed my arms. "Let me say again – Lithuas has murdered countless people."

She stopped just short of me. "And Nioanen has not."

Was she trying to make some comparison between them? I didn't want to kill Nioanen, did I? "I've been working with him. If I don't trust him completely, it's only because he hasn't shown himself worthy of trust."

"Worthy." She let the word sit in her mouth. "But he cannot ever prove that to you, can he?"

"Killing Lithuas would go a long way," I muttered. She was right, though. He couldn't erase his past, even if he'd so desperately tried. But I didn't owe him my trust either. I stared at the panel in front of me. The corestone at the god's lips, the rays of light shining from his mouth. "Whatever pact you all made, it has to do with this, doesn't it?"

"A blood pact binds everyone involved, and if the ones who make it are powerful enough, they can bind others as well, against their will. I could speak of our pact, but if I did, all the surviving elder gods would die." She opened her mouth and then closed it, shook her head. "That is all I can say."

I dug around in the ashes of my anger, found the embers cooled. "What was he like? Nioanen? I've only known him as Thassir, and he is stubborn and terrible and sometimes ... he is kind." I'd said too much. I could hear it in my voice, the way my tone went suddenly gentle.

"He was not so different then, though he was much warmer, more welcoming – at least on a surface level." Her finger found one of the god's antlers, and she traced the branching points. A short laugh escaped from her mouth. "There were so many rumors flying around in those days – it was a game to us, who was doing what and who was sleeping with whom. So many gods vied to find a place in Nioanen's bed, which only made him more reluctant to take a lover. Not that he held himself completely apart, but those he did choose were not discreet. He garnered a reputation he did not want. None of us thought he would ever partner with anyone, not for any real length of time, except he did finally find his way toward Irael. Irael had loved him for over a hundred years, but it took Nioanen longer to realize they'd always been more than friends."

It felt like someone had struck a large drum right next to me, the vibration of it filling my bones. I remembered his raven-dark eyes, the despair that had settled around him like a blanket. "He said he lost everything."

"They had a son. They hid. I don't know when Lithuas and Nioanen found one another again, but it must have been after the Shattering and after Kluehnn created his godkillers and after those godkillers hunted down Nioanen and his family. I assume they are dead – he would never have left them otherwise. He is nothing if not devoted."

I thought of his cats, the way he'd focused all that devotion on them – something he could control. Until we'd met and I'd unintentionally jolted him from his solitude. How strange, to be him, to realize that even his cats were half of them gods, waiting for him to spring back to glorious life. I wasn't even him and I felt the desperate weight of it.

I didn't *want* to understand him, to give him any grace for what he'd done.

"Gods have fallen in love with mortals in the past." Velenor's tone was too casual.

A bitter laugh escaped my lips before I could stop it. I shouldn't be speaking this way to one of the seven elder gods. They seemed to be popping up everywhere these days, though, so perhaps I could be forgiven. "And how many mortals have fallen in love with gods? Oh, I imagine a great many have thought they were in love." I eyed her lithe form, her liquid eyes, her skin as dark and smooth as onyx, flecks like freckles glittering on its surface. "I'm certain you make it easy to fall, looking the way you do. But really – how could mortals love those who are so distant, who hold themselves so superior, who will protect their own over the countless lives of the mortals? We must be like chaff to you." I couldn't quite understand how mortals ever worshiped the gods, how they ever cared about them.

She turned the full force of her doe-eyed gaze on me, and it took my breath away. The strong shape of her jaw, the curve of her lips – I couldn't look away. "We are not superior," she said, her voice soft. "I am just as broken as any mortal. As is Thassir." Delicate fingers touched my cheek. "As are you. Sometimes we need others to heal. We don't have to do it all alone."

I wished I hadn't spent my anger so frivolously before, when I needed it now, my heart yearning to turn my face into her touch, to give over some of my burdens to someone more powerful than I was. To give in to blind trust.

Her brows lowered slightly as she touched me. And then the air filled with the scent of the ocean, sending me back to the chilly, silent mornings of my youth. I breathed in without thinking. Just a small taste against the back of my tongue, a sip. The corestone in my belly burned into life.

She jerked away, her eyes wide. "You should be dead."

"I've been told that a lot," I said, trying for lightness.

It was as though she hadn't even heard me. "He must have done something to it. You shouldn't be alive."

I'd never felt so keen a sense of dread as I did then. It wasn't the creeping sort of dread, but the sharp and cutting kind, a knife wedged into the gaps of my spine. What exactly had Thassir done? I thought of his mouth pressed to mine, the thickness of the aether that poured past my tongue. I'd been dying, yes, but he hadn't thought to ask my permission for whatever magic he'd enacted to save my life – he couldn't even tell me what he'd done.

The sounds of clashing metal carried through the tunnel. A shout. Both of us whirled, running back the way we'd come without stopping for discussion.

We'd been followed.

38
Rasha

11 years after the restoration of Kashan
and 572 years after the Shattering

Langzu - Kluehnn's den northeast of Bian

I have seen a terrible thing with my own eyes, and I know not what it means. A wall of black smoke has emerged from the barrier on one side of our realm, and it is traveling across the land, enveloping everything in its wake. I ride ahead of it on a series of horses, as each tires and cannot continue any longer. No one knows what the wall is doing – if it is swallowing our land and people whole, or if this is the promised restoration from Kluehnn. I have slept in fitful starts, dreaming of it running me down.

Yet dream must soon become truth, because the closer I draw to the southern border and the barrier that exists there, the more I understand: there is nowhere left to run.

I massaged my leg, trying not to hiss in pain each time I moved my hand over the spot Kluehnn had stung me. Each time I stepped on the leg, the wound burned like the first day I'd received it. I shifted on my cushion, glancing out the archives window over the foothills below. Everyone had left for dinner and I'd smuggled some persimmons and dried fish from the kitchen. "Read more," I commanded Mull. I leaned back against the wall and took a bite from a persimmon. I'd cast my robe off and it pooled on the floor. The setting sun cast a pleasant warmth across my bare shoulders.

Mull sat cross-legged across from me, a sheaf of loose papers in his hands. He lifted it so the fading light from the window fell onto the paper.

I scowled, pushing his hands down. "Use a lantern if you need to. No need to draw attention."

"Attention from who?" He peered out into the wilds. "We're up the side of a mountain."

I wasn't going to tell him that there were shapeshifting gods nearby. I wasn't going to throw my lot in with them, and if they got a hold of those pages, I knew who Kluehnn would blame. It was my job to guard the archives, after all. "Read," I repeated.

He cleared his throat and began to translate into Kashani. That had been my idea. There were fewer converts in this den who spoke Kashani, so it gave me one more small, insulating layer against being caught. I listened to the cadence of his voice as I finished the persimmon, watching the sun descend into the horizon. These pages spoke of a dalliance Barexi had with a mortal, a scholar of great renown. She had been the one to end their relationship, as she knew Barexi would live many long years that she would not.

I stopped him. "Is that what it says? Specifically? 'Many long years'?"

"It's as close a translation as I can manage. Why?"

"Why not say 'immortal'? The gods cannot be killed except by godkilling blades. Did those blades exist back then, too?"

The gaze he cast me was filled with a fraying patience. I had so many questions; I couldn't seem to help from speaking them aloud. A memory surfaced – me following on Hakara's heels, asking her about the diving, how she practiced her breathing, what she saw under the water. Her exasperated sighs as she told me it didn't matter, that if she did her job right, I'd never have to see what lay under the ocean's surface. I'd held my tongue but had kicked a rock, sullenly. My toe ached in remembrance.

"I don't know the answers to the questions any more than you do. I've never seen these pages before. I'm learning along with you," Mull responded for perhaps the fifth time.

I picked up a piece of dried fish from the basket between us, setting it between my teeth to chew. The rich, salty flavor of it leached across my tongue. I waved a hand at him. "Continue."

He kept reading, describing a child the woman bore, his doe-bright eyes and the small two-pronged antlers at his brow. This wasn't the first accounting he had read to me of mortals and gods mixing. Their children had some god traits, some mortal ones. I found it endlessly fascinating, that this was, at one time, just accepted. That gods sometimes roamed the surface and loved mortals, that some of their children lived and died under the warmth of the outer sun. Some gods took their children back to Unterra with them, and so far, the stories didn't say what happened to them. "Does this section mention the Shattering?"

He flipped through the pages. "No, not this one."

There were more mentions of the gods on the surface after the Shattering, and that was what really made me think. The crow I'd spoken to said the gods had been driven from their homes. Was this the catalyst for that exodus? Everything I'd been taught said that Kluehnn had enacted the Shattering, had made it so that the realms could be restored one at a time.

I shifted and winced. My leg had grown stiff; it froze in place. I tried to stand, to stretch it out. Even grasping at the wall, I nearly lost my balance. Sweat beaded at my forehead, the pain suddenly so sharp that it made my throat clench; the persimmon I'd just ate felt like a bad idea all around. I wasn't sure how I'd managed the climb up the mountain to talk to the crow after I'd first been injured. Shock, perhaps. Or maybe that climb had made it all worse.

A warm palm grasped my arm. Mull. "Bone or flesh?" he said, his voice quiet.

"Flesh," I said from between gritted teeth.

He gestured to my leg. "May I?"

I nodded. He took my calf in his hands as I grabbed for my crutch, pulling my leg slowly straight. His fingers found the indentation on my thigh where Kluehnn had stung and then bitten me, pressing to work out the knots. "I don't know much, if anything, about medicine, but I had a friend ... *have* a friend. She had spasms. Sometimes this would help."

Slowly, my jaw unclenched, my shoulders loosening as the pain dissipated.

"Who hurt you?" Mull asked. "Did it happen during one of your missions to kill a god?"

"It was Kluehnn." I wiped the sweat from my brow. "His aspect."

Mull said nothing, only worked his hands over the wound one more time. Outside, the wind picked up, the sun a sliver between two hills. He still had his hands on my leg when he finally spoke again. "Is that who you follow? A god who hurts you?"

I jerked away. "It was my own fault. I'd failed him. He punished me." I'd placed myself at his mercy when I'd taken Millani's hand and followed her, so many years ago. If this was what he chose to do with me, then I deserved it. Didn't I?

He took the sheaf of loose papers, stacking them and placing them back into the crate. "It just ... it doesn't feel right."

"Is that so?" I bit back. "Then who have you worshiped?"

He shrugged, the fur on his neck standing briefly on end before settling. "I've never really been devout."

Oh, of course. He was a noble, one of the clans, at the top of Langzu's government and society. That always afforded a person certain privileges. "You don't know what it's like. Kluehnn runs this realm, he runs every realm, he is the one true god and the rulers of every realm have never said anything otherwise. The rulers continue to live in whatever system they've built and they live comfortably. It's the people at the bottom who must be devout, because they have to be in order to survive. It feels like the only option." The words poured out of me, hot oil onto a fire. I wasn't sure why I was saying it, except that it felt true. "How grand, that you can afford not to care too much. Empires are built on such foundations – people not caring. It was the same in Kashan, it is the same here. So don't speak to me of who I worship and why as if you know a better way."

He kept putting away the papers, though by his hunched shoulders and twitching ears, I could tell I'd given him something to think about.

"I'm going outside to get some air and stretch the leg. Finish up here. You can have the rest of the food." I swept away from the window, leaving Mull to complete his task.

Naatar and Khatuya were still gone. Each time I returned to our room, I felt their absence. It was too quiet when I tried to sleep, my breathing echoing off the stone walls. I hadn't realized how much comfort I'd taken from them until I was alone, with only Mull to keep me company. I tested my leg off the crutch as I made my way up the tunnels. It still hurt when I put weight on it, but it hurt a little bit less. I was letting myself become too familiar with the convert, too comfortable. He'd arrived here under false pretenses – not a prisoner, but a noble, in search of answers. Well, now he was altered. I didn't know what that meant for his clan prospects. Probably nothing good.

For now, our goals aligned.

The horizon was a light blue by the time I emerged, the firmament dark and pricked with stars. A breeze tugged at my loose hair, whispering over the wound where my horn had once been, the flesh sore. I'd have to start moving soon without the crutch, if I wanted to regain my status as a godkiller, if I wanted to be sent with Khatuya and Naatar on their next mission. I could do it, but it meant moving so much slower. Being left behind was unbearable, wondering what they were going through, wondering how much weaker they were without me and if they would make it back alive.

My thoughts wheeled away to the documents Mull had read to me. If the increase of gods on the surface coincided with the Shattering, then it aligned with what the crow had told me about the gods being driven from their homes rather than launching an assault on the surface. Unless the Shattering had ruined their home and they'd sought to replace it with ours.

There were too many possibilities, too many things I still didn't know.

I took a lantern from a hook near the entrance and passed guards who nodded at me in acknowledgment, though they no longer bent at the waist. I was something between – not a godkiller, not a convert, not even an acolyte. Until Kluehnn restored me or cast me down, I existed in a strange space. Yet I couldn't bring myself to push aside my questions, to devote myself fully to earning back my place.

The climb was hard, my leg giving way several times, though I caught myself with my crutch. Finally, when I was halfway up the peak, the crow found me. I'd had to come farther this time, and I'd paid for it.

It watched me from a rock as I leaned on my crutch, breathing hard. My leg was on fire. I rotated my ankle just to be sure I still could. There was only one way out that I could see – one way that would ensure the safety of my cohort as well as my own.

Kluehnn had decided he was the one true god, that he was the only one who should be worshiped. It was blasphemy to speak to other gods – but what if it was only blasphemous because Kluehnn could think of no positive outcome? The gods now had all been born on the surface. What if things had changed? "I want to make peace," I said. My words seemed to fill the air, louder than I'd intended them. "If the gods are organizing against Kluehnn, that can only mean an all-out battle. There would be losses on both sides. If we found a way to send you back to Unterra, would you take it and promise never to return?"

The crow bobbed its head. "That's a start, but only a start. If we can come to an agreement – you and me – what then? My people will listen to me. Will yours?"

"If we can write a treaty that allows Kluehnn the surface, he will reward me, I'm sure of it. The dens can kill all the gods, but only at great cost to ourselves." Khatuya and Naatar were out there, under this same sky, hopefully still alive and on their way home. "He cares about us – his converts, his altered, his godkillers. Kluehnn, above all else, still loves his people."

The crow regarded me with its black eyes and said nothing.

39
Mullayne

11 years after the restoration of Kashan
and 572 years after the Shattering

Langzu - the den northeast of Bian

There is a joke in Cressima that goes something like this: "How do you get people to attend the funeral of their least favorite aunt? You tell them they are not allowed to go." People are somehow always willing to go places they are warned off for their own good. Every time a realm is restored, goods and people continue to move through the barrier for around five years, after which the restored realm stops trade and communication with the unrestored world. The barrier becomes a silent place. Yet there are those who are too curious to leave these things alone. They go into the barrier. They never come back. So what happens to them? Are they imprisoned for not respecting the wishes of the realm? Are they killed? Does the barrier swallow them before they even get to the other side? These are the questions that haunt scholars in the dead of night.

Mull eyed the godkiller robe on the floor as he considered his options. Rasha had left in a rush, clearly upset by what he'd said. He hadn't quite intended to upset her, but he couldn't deny it had worked to his advantage. She'd forgotten her robe, and he was here, in the archives, alone.

If she'd gone for a walk, she might not return for a while. The other converts would finish eating soon. So he didn't have long to think things over. If he took her robe, there was a good possibility she'd return before he made it back. But that didn't necessarily mean she'd catch him with it. If she'd forgotten the robe, she could have also forgotten where exactly she'd left it, and he could sneak it back into her possession without anyone being the wiser.

Perhaps he was overestimating his abilities, though. He had to be more cautious than he'd once been.

But he wasn't likely to find a better opportunity to go deeper into the den. Yes, he was learning things from these discarded pages, but the reason he'd come here was to find the tomb of Tolemne's family, and he couldn't do that while he was working in the archives and reading pages for Rasha.

He had to take this chance.

Glancing about to make sure he was alone, he leaned over and seized the robe. Rasha was taller than he was, and, even in his altered form, sturdier. He felt a bit like a child trying on his parents' clothes. The hem nearly brushed the floor; he had to tie the sash tight to keep the robe from hanging around his body like a shapeless blanket. On the fortunate side, it covered his convert's tunic completely.

He made sure the crate of pages was back where they'd found it, all remnants of the makeshift meal they'd shared cleaned up, the cushions returned to their places. He seized a lantern from the entrance of the archives as he left and hurried into the tunnels.

The last carving he'd seen was deep down, near a fork. He had to double-check one of Tolemne's engravings to remember the correct path to take, but then he was back at the spot again, breathless.

Each convert he'd encountered had only bowed their head as he'd passed, barely even looking at his face. At least being altered afforded him the privilege of passing as a godkiller. Small favors. He'd only just begun translating this carving from old Albanoran. He lifted the lamp, mouthing the words to himself. The beginning was a reiteration of what he'd seen on Tolemne's Path before the whole thing had collapsed on him. Trust only what was written in stone.

A thrill moved through him; he felt the fur on his arms rise, a strange sensation that only slightly resembled the feeling he got when his hairs had prickled. This body was stronger but still unfamiliar. He wondered when it would stop being so, when all the memories of his old body would feel stranger than this one. The reiteration was further confirmation that these carvings had been made by Tolemne, that he'd made them after returning to the surface, that they led to the tomb of his family.

The gods have on occasion played with time, accomplishing such miracles as bringing someone back to life or turning an adult back into a child. It's a difficult feat, which is why it is so seldom mentioned in our histories.

Played with time? If they had manipulated the histories of living people, Mull wondered what else they might have done. He thought of the books, the way he'd never heard of those missing pages he was reading to Rasha. Could they, perhaps, change the books? He ran a hand along the lower lines of the text. *Take the left tunnel, one hundred twenty steps.*

He obeyed. No one else walked these passages; all the sounds he heard traveled down to him from above. The way forward was silent and dark.

He found the next carving exactly where it was supposed to be. He lifted his lantern to peer at it and sucked in a breath. Two phrases stood out to him immediately: *my lineage* and *gods*.

It took him a little while to decipher the rest, though he'd been getting quicker at this. *I can trace my lineage back to the gods, to Barexi's dalliance with a scholar. There is a god's blood in my veins and I wish I could rip them out. I asked them for help and they denied me.*

All except one. But it didn't say that. That part would be on the next carving. That was how the stories always went. All the gods denied Tolemne. Except one. Kluehnn. And Tolemne initiated the god pact with him, the one all mortals abided by.

The last part of the engraving gave him his directions: *Down, down, keep going down.*

Rasha might be returning to the archives soon. But he couldn't turn back now, not yet. He was getting close to something, he was sure of it. He followed the tunnel, past trickles of water flowing over the walls, past the hint of some bioluminescent moss. He must be getting close to the first aerocline this deep. He lifted the lantern, careful of his steps. The spare filter was always tucked close to his skin, with him at all times. He'd use it if he had to.

Just as he'd braced himself for this possibility, he ran into a wall. He placed a hand on the stone. This was the way Tolemne's words had sent him. Why would they send him to a dead end? He felt the rock, wondering if he was missing something, a sick feeling rising in his throat. All this for nothing? His dead friends, his alteration, the confines of the den.

Wait.

It wasn't quite a wall. His lantern outlined the edges of a large, flat stone. He felt around the perimeter and found a crack. Air sifted through this space, the slightest breeze against his hand. He brought the lantern close, peering into the gap.

There was something there. A room behind this rock. The tomb? Someone had blocked the way. The edges of the stone were rough beneath his palms as he wedged his fingers into the crack, as he pulled. He thought he *almost* felt it move. But almost was not what he needed right now. He stared at his hands, disgusted. He'd hoped to find a reason to use his new strength, some way to glean some more slivers of gratitude for this transformation. Pointless.

He needed help.

His relationship with Rasha had smoothed over the days they'd spent together, the times they'd broken into the crates and read the discarded pages. Silences between them felt almost companionable. But he remembered the disgust in her voice when he spoke of his ability to not care, to hold only a vague sense of devotion. She'd told him a little, haltingly, of how she'd come to the den. She'd been hungry, a child, with no one to care for her.

He should have been thinking of that when he'd spoken so carelessly. Their realms of experience were so vastly different. Mull's father had been from the Sim clan, and that was the closest Mull had ever come to any sort of hardship. A brief moment in time, after the execution of Sheuan's father, before his father had married into the Reisun clan. Mull hadn't even been born yet. And even that hardship was worlds away from Rasha's experience. That hardship meant perhaps not being able to afford the latest fashions, rather than lacking food and shelter.

Would he have become devout if he'd been in her position? Without anywhere else to turn? He liked to think he would have come up with another way. He'd always found other ways. But then he wouldn't have had any of the resources he'd always had access to.

He found himself floundering in this thought as he climbed back toward the archives. Was who he was, everything he'd accomplished, truly just an accident of his birth? No, that couldn't be right. Look at his brother. Kiang had so little curiosity in his bones, so little desire to break free from the path their parents had set for him.

It made him feel a little better. So ... at least he wasn't Kiang? Gods below, was this what he'd fallen to? Comparing himself to his brother so he could feel the slightest bit smug? No wonder Kiang always found him insufferable.

He'd turned into the tunnel toward the archives, nearly at his destination, when a godkiller approached from the opposite direction. He was lithe, patterned with small patches of scales, a brown tail undulating behind him. A bandage was wrapped around one hand, the scrape of claw marks marring the eye on his leather breastplate. A violet glow emanated from the dagger at his side. Mull swept his gaze to the floor, quickly.

Panic squeezed his heart. He shouldn't have been afraid. He had the hood up and low over his face; he'd prepared for exactly this situation. That was why he'd worn the robe.

But he didn't have a dagger. That should be fine, right? They couldn't always wear their daggers. Surely at some point the blade needed sharpening, or the hilt needed a new wrapping.

The scaled altered glanced at him and then away as they drew closer. Mull had to stop the instinct to bow, to move away. He had to get back into the archives and hope that Rasha hadn't returned yet.

A hand shot out, blocking his way.

He ran into it before he could stop himself, and cursed his lack of dexterity. Would a godkiller have been so caught out?

The scaled man was peering at his face. "I don't think I know you."

"I'm new," Mull tried, doing his best to sound gruff. "Transfer from another den."

The godkiller nearly pulled his hand away, but then glanced down. His gaze fixed on the old stain, a faint blotch a hand's span below the sash.

"That's not your robe. That's Rasha's." The hand tightened around the collar of Mull's robe. Brown eyes met his, the pupils slitted. "And you are no godkiller."

40
Sheuan

11 years after the restoration of Kashan
and 572 years after the Shattering

Langzu - inner Bian

Vendors refusing to accept ration tickets, or asking for more tickets than is warranted, has become an issue in Langzu. We distribute the tickets monthly, and the vendors at sanctioned markets are required to take them, but they complain about the hassle of redeeming them. Twice a month is not enough, they say. They hate having to line up to exchange the tickets for money from the Sovereign's enforcers, and this takes time from their work. However, I do not think increasing the frequency of redemption events will solve the problem.

"Sovereign," Sheuan muttered. She inclined her head to him, her mind racing. She was caught out, alone in the night air of the streets. What possible excuse could she have that made any sense? It wasn't as though she could say she'd stayed late at the workshop making filters. She'd slipped away from the enforcers set to ostensibly protect her. And she knew inner Bian like the back of her hand; she couldn't say she'd gotten lost. Detained? But by who? She had to have an excuse for privacy.

Ah, wait, she had just the thing. Her heart raced and she tried to reframe the feeling in her veins from fear to a slight anxiety. "I hesitate to say in front of others. Please, can we speak in your rooms about this? Back at the castle?"

Two of the enforcers closest to the Sovereign held lanterns aloft, illuminating their silver armbands and the smooth lines of his face. His expression might have said he was concerned, but she caught the gleam of triumph in his gaze. She had him. "Where were you? Answer me."

She inclined her head again, the picture of a deferent wife to the most powerful man in the realm. "I went to see a physician. I wanted to go alone, so I found a way to leave the enforcers behind. It was a private matter. A womanly one."

He didn't look unsettled, like some men did when womanly medical issues were mentioned – he only looked bored. "Yes? What was it? The volume of your monthly flow? And did the physician tell you everything was fine?"

She glanced at the enforcers as though nervous to reveal any information in their presence. Several of them shifted from foot to foot, avoiding her gaze, embarrassed. "Well, it wasn't that. He said he wouldn't know for certain until a few weeks more. But since you and I . . ." She trailed off.

It was like placing a hand on a dog's back when it hadn't heard you approach. The Sovereign flinched away when it finally came together in his mind. And this time, his expression was easy to read, his brows low, his jaw slightly slack. He was annoyed, yes, but perturbed too.

Sheuan wanted to laugh, but she stuffed the sound down her

throat, burying it under caution and fear. As though she'd let herself become pregnant by him, at this time. That was one of the first things Mitoran had taught her – what herbs to take to prevent that, and how much to mix into her tea. If he already held power over her, imagine how much more he would hold if she were carrying his child.

The annoyance she understood. She'd given him a very reasonable explanation for her disappearance; if he asked after the doctor, he'd look overzealous. But she wasn't even sure he'd thought that far ahead. It was the clear discomfort he'd shown that piqued her curiosity. He'd told her himself: he hadn't been intimate with many people over the years. Perhaps they'd been mostly men, and maybe this wasn't a worry he'd ever encountered before. They'd only been together once, but once could have been enough.

Shouts rose in the distance. The enforcers' heads whipped about. Someone screamed. The distant clash of metal.

Sheuan felt all the hairs on her arms rise at once. Something bad was happening. The Sovereign beckoned to her, and then she was cloistered in the middle of the enforcers.

An enforcer jogged up to the others, breathless. "A riot. Outskirters in the inner city. They started raiding the merchant carts and stalls. Some of them are trying to set fire to the estates. We need to get you back to the castle. Now."

The Sovereign's special enforcers closed in around them.

She'd been so preoccupied with the reason her father had been executed, she hadn't kept a close enough eye on the situation in the city. Restoration had been delayed, the winter rains hadn't yet arrived, and crops were failing. The Sovereign was still handing out ration tickets, but those tickets purchased fewer and fewer goods these days. She should have expected riots.

Even if she had, she wouldn't have expected them in inner

Bian. Somehow she'd always thought violence would be confined to the outskirts.

"Take as many enforcers as you can find," the Sovereign said to the man who'd run up. "Arrest any rioters who are trying to destroy property or set fire to buildings. Send someone to warn the noble and royal families, and get the guards out in front of their estates."

"The looters?"

"Leave them. We have to prioritize and shut down any destruction first. We need to get this under control and make sure it doesn't get any worse."

The man nodded and darted away.

Sheuan was already making a mental map of the city in her mind. She'd arrived from the direction of the lakebed. Outer Bian ringed inner Bian in a half-circle, on the opposite side. They should be able to make it up and into the castle before danger struck.

That was assuming the rioters had planned none of this, that they were just reacting to the poor conditions, that this had all just sprung up as randomly as a grass fire. The Sovereign's shoulder jostled hers as they made their way down empty streets. The sounds of breaking wood and screams grew louder. She breathed in deep, letting it out in one long, controlled movement. They had to move toward the riots to get to the castle. The scent of smoke drifted in the wind.

Some other part of her mind flitted back to the conversation she'd just had with the Sovereign and his strange reaction. Why would he be so worried that she was pregnant? Wouldn't most people in his position want a child for their legacy? The Sovereign had no heirs, had done nothing more than dangle marriage as bait before other prospective suitors. She'd cornered him into it. Still, she would have thought a child would be something he wanted, especially with the filters protecting his chosen from restoration. The man's hair was nearly all white. He was older than her father had been, and Sheuan was a grown woman. He wouldn't live forever, and then what would happen to the organization he'd built? She had no illusions that he'd pass the whole thing on to her. What, then, was his endgame?

All she knew for certain was that with the development of these riots, he'd want restoration to occur sooner rather than later. Which meant he'd want her to make more filters.

She was so buried in these thoughts that the chaos surrounding them became nothing more than background noise. They turned into an alley to avoid a group of rioters storming toward her mother's old estate. And when that group passed, they moved into the main street, only to be forced into another alley.

Were they getting any closer to the castle? She thought she recognized the walls of the nearest building.

And then they stopped, and Sheuan ran her face into an enforcer's broad shoulder. For a moment, all she could do was study the silver embroidery on silver cloth, an eye and a cherry branch. She'd always thought it some ridiculous reference to the power of Kluehnn combined with the Sovereign's power. But here, this close, she noticed a small design difference. Kluehnn's eyes were always depicted symmetrically, rays emanating from the center. This one was asymmetrical, like a normal eye, bereft of rays. Her nose hurt. She put a hand to it. No blood.

Her gaze lifted over the enforcer's shoulder. A group of rioters stood at the mouth of the alley, blocking the way out. They looked tired and gaunt, but some held makeshift weapons high. A few, she noticed, had swords. Swords they must have taken from the bodies of enforcers. She glanced behind. Another group of rioters, closing in.

They were surrounded.

41

Hakara

11 years after the restoration of Kashan and 572 years after the Shattering

Pizgonia - Gorina, City of a Hundred Moons, in the Godless hideout

There are a few statues that were reconstructed after the Shattering that depict mortals carrying strange weapons. They generally consist of a long barrel, about the circumference and length of a person's forearm. At the base are several chambers into which jars are fitted. One bas-relief, uncovered in the ruins of Albanore, shows something bright, with carved rays, being ejected from the end of the barrel.

This projectile, in the next frame, sends an entire building toppling to the ground.

The room we'd occupied earlier was empty, the door hanging open. Sounds of fighting emanated from beyond. "The entrance," Velenor gasped out. "There are fewer godkillers here than on the northern continent, but they are still here."

I let her run ahead of me and through the door, uncertain of the turns we'd taken to get to our current location. "If you're not their leader, who is?" I called out. Lanterns and stone whipped past us.

"One of the council members." She halted at a fork so quickly that I ran into her. Her arm shot out, steadying me. "Help the Godless. There's a back entrance to these ruins. I need to leave and get to the palace. The council are here for their quarterly meeting. This is likely a distraction, something to keep the Godless occupied while Lithuas goes after their leader. I have to protect her. Go left, take the first left." And then she was gone, disappeared down the right-hand tunnel.

Cursing, I hesitated for only a moment before darting to the left. Dashu and Alifra were there, and Thassir as well, and I was their bruiser. They might have each been formidable on their own, but the four of us together were much more effective.

I took the first left and found myself in the midst of a nightmare.

The space beyond was wide and sloping, the ceiling high enough to give even Thassir clearance at my end, narrowing along the other end so that most people had to duck to fit. Light streamed in from an open hole, the makeshift wooden stairs leading to the street already partially destroyed in the fight. Several cohorts of godkillers pressed forward into the ruins, the flash of blades and glowing violet mixing with sprays of crimson.

I spotted Alifra trying to get a clear line of sight with her crossbow from behind the ranks of Godless, Thassir with a borrowed sword in his grip, Dashu sliding through the gaps like water through cracks, his sword leading the way.

"Thassir!" I called. He might not have been able to hear me, but I knew he could sense my presence, the bond between us loosening. I dipped into the pouches Velenor had given me, swallowed gems without looking, and drew my sword.

Thassir summoned the aether to meet me, and I sucked in as deep a breath as I could hold.

The Godless parted to let me through, another of them near the front of the line, her limbs clad in smoke. I wondered, briefly, if we were the same everywhere. Did they also have a pest, a vine, and an arbor, but by different names? Or had they formed some other strategy? I didn't have time to dwell on it. I focused on the godkillers ahead of me, new strength flooding into my body.

For once, it was an advantage in a fight not to be tall. I could stand free of the ceiling here, while my opponents were forced to keep their knees and necks bent. Two of them focused on me – one with brown and black-barred wings, the other with red, stony skin. I tracked the movement of their blades, parrying instead of jumping back. Didn't want to give them more space to work. I pressed the winged godkiller back toward the entrance, and she hunched over, teeth bared. The stone-skinned one took the opportunity to attack my right side.

A crossbow bolt landed in her left eye. She screamed, clawing at the bloody ruin it had made of her flesh. I leaned down and slid my blade across the back of her ankle. She collapsed to the ground, unable to hold her weight in the narrowed space.

One feathered wing shot out, battering my shoulder, trying to force me to give ground. I thrust at the wing, but my head was starting to swim, my lungs burning. I caught only feathers and not flesh. I could feel Thassir moving in the crowd behind me, trying to get to the front lines, to my side. His size was a disadvantage in this enclosed space. He'd practically be on his knees if he made it as far as the entrance.

I couldn't breathe – not yet. I sidestepped a swipe from the godkilling blade, trying to put the groaning body of the fallen godkiller between me and the winged one. Same gray robes, same embossed eyes on their armor. It seemed I could travel half a world away, yet godkillers hadn't changed a whit. Velenor had said Kluehnn didn't have as strong a hold on the southern continent. I wondered if these were all the godkillers he had at his disposal here. They'd have to have traveled from restored lands – a nearly impossible trek.

I parried two more blows, thrust my blade at the winged godkiller. He easily flowed around the edge of my sword. I had my enhanced strength and speed, but the need to breathe was becoming all I could think about.

A warmth at my side, the touch of a hand. "I'm here." Thassir's voice in my ear.

I let the aether out in gasping breath, taking a moment to hang my head as he stepped between me and the godkillers. It felt natural, letting my guard down completely, trusting him to be there for me no matter the danger. I caught glimpses of the fight, saw two Godless getting cut down by godkillers. They hadn't expected this ambush and it wasn't going well for them. How many times had they faced godkillers? Velenor couldn't have prepared them the way Lithuas would; she wouldn't know their strengths and weaknesses as well, their style of fighting. And she wasn't leading them.

The Godless who'd swallowed the gems lay on the floor, shadowed by the fight still occurring over her body, blood from a gaping wound on her neck seeping into dusty stone.

The corestone. *He must have done something to it.* What exactly had he done? I didn't feel much different, except when I fought, when I breathed in the aether and felt the vastness of the corestone just beyond my reach.

The god gems used up that aether before it could reach the corestone.

I couldn't put things together, one after another, the way Mull seemed to do so easily, following suppositions like strings tied together through a forest. But I had the strength of my instincts, and I could follow those, even if I wasn't sure where they were leading me.

Could they be leading me into a bear's den? Certainly seemed to do that more often than not, but at least I knew the bear was there.

I reached into the pouches at my side, scooping out nothing but air, cupping it to my mouth. And Thassir – reliable Thassir, who always seemed to anticipate my movements and my needs – summoned the aether to me.

I breathed in the smell of mussels in a bucket, the scrape of a knife against the inside of an abalone shell, the cold of water seeping past my hair to my scalp. The aether dissolved into my blood, became a part of me, and found the corestone in my belly.

It was an oil-soaked torch catching fire in a darkened room. The burning I remembered feeling in the Kashani den returned, my veins pulsing with heat. But it felt contained, safely observable from behind glass. And when I reached toward that stone, that vastness of power, I felt myself falling into it, becoming part of it.

My fingers tightened on the leather hilt of my sword. I stepped around Thassir's protective wings and into the fray.

Was this what it felt like to be him? I moved with ruthless precision, my body two steps ahead of my mind. Every flinch, every twitch the godkillers made seemed magnified by my gaze, slowed down. How easily they gave away each movement, each attack! I swept their blades aside, barely noticing the strength of the impact. My heartbeat thudded in my ears – slow, steady, inexorable.

Dashu would have despaired of my footwork, but that didn't matter. I gutted one godkiller straight through her leather breastplate, took another's head clean off. I felt filled with molten metal, my skin sensitive to the slightest shift in the movement of the air.

My blade gave way before I did, the metal shattering on the stone behind a godkiller as I cleaved him in half. I whirled and killed another with the sharpened stump, piercing her heart. She stared at me as she died, and I wasn't sure what she feared more – me or the death that swiftly took her.

I slayed another, and another. And then warm hands were on my shoulders, wings surrounding me. "Breathe. Hakara, you have to breathe."

Thassir, his gaze filled with worry and regret and loss.

He hadn't lost me. He shook me, teeth bared. "*Breathe.* Damn it, Hakara!"

I sucked in a breath and felt, suddenly, how close I'd come to the edge. The fire in my veins drained out. My knees shook just before my legs collapsed beneath me. Every part of me felt weak and useless.

Thassir caught me before I hit the ground. His voice shook. "You pretended to take the gems. You didn't. You used the corestone."

I'd wanted to be sure, to know whether that feeling I'd had in earlier fights was a fluke or something real. We'd been losing – what was I supposed to do? Just let us die? If I had a power in me that I could access, then I would do it, no matter the consequences.

"What did you do to it? How am I still alive?" I could barely hear my own voice.

He opened his mouth and said nothing. Not meeting my eyes, he reached out and brushed the hair from my forehead, tucking a loose strand behind my ear. There was something devastatingly gentle in his touch, and it made me remember what I'd said to

Velenor – that he was kind. Dashu and Alifra hovered nearby, though they did not approach. The fight must have been over. We'd won. *I'd* won.

Slowly, strength returned to me. "Fine. You may not be able to tell me what you did to it, or what I did when I swallowed that stone. But Thassir, you also cannot stop me from using it."

42
Rasha

11 years after the restoration of Kashan
and 572 years after the Shattering

Langzu - Kluehnn's den northeast of Bian

How could mortals all be content with the bargains their ancestors made? Of course they wouldn't be. Mortals are discontent, contrary creatures, always disagreeing with one another. Where there is order, some always feel compelled to create chaos. Someone says the world is round? There will always be someone willing to squint at the horizon and say it must be flat. So in each realm, a resistance to the god pact arose, a faction whose sole purpose was to break it.

I sat on the rock next to the crow, watching the sky deepen into night, my arms around my legs, my chin resting on my knees. "The gods used to wander the surface before the Shattering. They used to come up, become a part of our stories, and then disappear below again. After the Shattering, they came to the surface in greater numbers."

"I can't say I know exactly what happened," the crow said. "I wasn't there. I was born in Albanore, before it was restored. I've only shifted a few times since then. My parents forbade it. So the history of the gods, even just the feeling of being a god – I don't know it well."

"What happened to your parents?" I thought I knew the answer already, but some part of me needed to hear it, to know for sure.

"The first two times I shifted, nothing bad happened, so I thought I could do it again. I wanted to swim in the Bay of Barexi, to see what lay at the bottom. So I shifted into a shark. I found ruins, the remains of artifacts, twisted pieces of old, dark wood. I spent all afternoon there. And when I returned home, my parents were both dead. Godkillers. My luck had run out, and they'd found my parents instead of me."

I didn't know what to say. "I'm sorry" felt like a lie. I was a godkiller; I'd killed gods just like the crow's parents. So instead, I made my own confession. "My parents died when I was young as well. One from illness, the other one from walking into the barrier. My sister cared for me."

The crow cocked his head. "And is she still alive?"

The bond was a constant thing in the back of my mind, a subtle tug, a string glued to the inside of my skull. I felt it, following it southward. I couldn't be sure how far it stretched. "She is. Somewhere. Far from here, I think."

He didn't ask me any other questions about her, and I felt an odd swell of gratitude for that small courtesy. I couldn't explain, didn't want to. I traced a circle on my shin, aware suddenly that I'd forgotten my robe.

"There are many of us," the crow said. "More than Kluehnn thinks there are. I don't think he understands how many shapeshifters have eluded his godkillers, simply by refusing to change, by taking the shapes of animals. If he makes war upon us, he will find we are not so easily killed."

"You're trusting me with too much." If I told this to anyone else in the den, they would tell Kluehnn, and he would readjust his plans. He'd have an advantage.

The crow blinked. "I'm trusting you with what I think you can handle."

There had to be another way, one that didn't burden me like this. "If I can find a path to Unterra, a way to funnel the gods back there, would you agree to be shut away from the surface? Surely there must be at least one still open."

"I think I could get the other gods to agree to that. Please understand: we've lived in hiding for centuries. We are generations from our parents. Our stories are different from yours; they say Kluehnn drove us from Unterra."

I still felt that defensive urge to say he was wrong, that the gods flooded the surface in a bid to subdue the mortals. But what did I know, in the end? Everything the converts had been ordered to excise from the archives told a different story. Was Kluehnn protecting us – or himself? Now that was true blasphemy, but I held the thought, examining it in all its ugliness. I couldn't say it was untrue, not without knowing more.

In the end, he'd still given me a place to exist, to live, to work. He'd given me the friends I held dearer now than any family, who had survived with me through the trials. He'd given me food, shelter, water.

I would be dead if it were not for my faith. I would have had no meaning without it. I held these two thoughts together, weighing them, feeling the unease of the opposing feelings they conjured. Suspicion and doubt, love and trust.

The crow hopped a little closer, feet scraping against stone. "Would Kluehnn agree, if you found a path and we brokered such a deal?"

I cast him an annoyed glance. "I already said he would."

He polished his beak against the rock. "If he does not agree, I should tell you – we have ways to make him think twice about continuing this pointless war. If he throws the bulk of the god-killers against the forces we are assembling, he may win, but we will make you pay dearly for it." He reached beneath one wing with his beak, pulled out a small piece of blue chalk. "Take this."

I didn't extend my hand. "What would you have me do with it?"

"If there is a time the den might be vulnerable, mark the stone above the latrine ditch, the largest one. We will see it. We won't kill anyone, I promise you."

"Why should I trust you?"

"What do you know of gods and promises?"

"If you break one, you die." It was in all the old stories, this limitation, as it often came into play in the games between mortals and gods. "But you could be a willing sacrifice." In spite of that, I unfurled my fingers. The bird dropped the chalk into my palm, and I stretched my legs, slipping it into a pocket. It felt like a piece of hot iron against my thigh.

"May we meet again, Rasha." The crow leapt into the air. I watched it go, marking the direction it flew in, trying to keep my gaze surreptitious. North, further into the mountains. When it had disappeared into the night sky, I picked up my crutch and hobbled back down toward the den.

The workers would have retired from the archives by now, but I still had to close the shutters, blow out the lamps, and make sure everything was in order before I went back to my room. Menial work.

At this time of day, the tunnels were warmer than the air outside; returning to them felt like returning to an embrace. In spite of the chalk in my pocket, I couldn't quite imagine turning against Kluehnn, against the people I'd been raised among. Even if no one would be hurt. Yet I'd still taken the chalk. Just in case, I told myself.

Someone was waiting for me in the archives when I returned. His hand was bandaged, his armor scratched with three deep furrows, but he was here, and he was alive.

"Naatar," I gasped out, breathless. My gaze darted around the room. "Khatuya, is she—"

"She's alive." Naatar lifted a man from the ground by the collar. It took me a moment to process who it was. His black-ticked fur blended into the walls, and I didn't recognize him at a glance, not when he was wearing a gray godkiller's robe. My robe.

Mull.

"This convert stole your robe," Naatar was saying. "He was arriving here from deeper in the den. I don't know where he'd been or what he used this robe to get access to. He must be punished by Kluehnn."

I could feel everything fraying at the edges. I hadn't realized how cloistered the space was that I'd built with Mull. In it, I'd felt safe to question things I'd been told were true, to dig into the precepts and how they might have formed, to learn things of our history that were being forcibly removed. And now all of that was violated, my two worlds clashing in a way that could only end in bloodshed. "I let him borrow the robe," I said, before I could think of anything else.

"Borrow it?" The scales on Naatar's forehead puckered as his brow lifted.

"He's helping me."

"Helping you do what?"

I didn't know what I could tell Naatar and what I couldn't. When we'd been out in the wilds of Langzu together, he'd always been the one to step in between Khatuya and me, to stop our fights before they could really start. It meant I didn't actually know where he stood. Did his opinions align with mine, or with Khatuya's? Did he also think questioning was blasphemy? Or did he see more nuance in our place in the den, in Kluehnn's place in our world? If I wanted Mull to live, I had to take a chance. And I surprised myself by wanting him to live. "He's helping me find the truth. I've found pages. They're not just sorting things here in the archives, they're removing pages from the books. I think they're replacing them. There are probably other crates in here with new pages, fresh ones, with other information. Things are being hidden from us." I couldn't bear to say what lurked in my mind – that *Kluehnn* was hiding things from us.

Naatar was injured. He could have been killed. If those claws had dug just a little deeper ... He was frowning, his black topknot swaying as he shook his head. "You've gone mad."

It would have sounded crazy to me, before I'd met the crow, before I'd uncovered these secret histories, but now I wondered if there was a way to make peace, and I felt small again, wishing and hoping that Hakara wouldn't go diving in the sea.

Did that make me weak?

Naatar was still holding Mull, who shook in his grip, an autumn leaf shivering in the wind. "The truth is what Kluehnn tells us it is." His voice turned pleading, and this was what stabbed a thorn into my heart. "Put your head down, keep to your work. Kluehnn has always favored you. He will return you to your place, he will give you a new blade. You can fight with your cohort again." Just as it used to be. "Kluehnn has given us everything; is it too much to ask us to trust him?"

The doubt flared. "So ... what? Someone does something kind for you and it means they are beyond reproach?"

I regretted the words as soon as they left my mouth. I knew

what he was thinking, because I was thinking it too. I'd once saved Naatar's life. During our second trial, I'd killed another neophyte to save him. I'd betrayed another neophyte. What did he owe me for that?

He took a half-step closer, Mull dragged along in his grip. His lip trembled – with anger or fear, I wasn't sure. "He is a god. The one true god. The god who has changed and is changing the surface of the world. Who is changing us."

My voice was small, the howl of an injured cub. "What if I didn't want to be changed?"

He stared at me, and I stared back – I wasn't sure for how long. When he leaned in, I could smell his breath. "No. Someone who does something kind for you is not beyond reproach. But they certainly deserve better than this sneaking around." He let go of Mull, who stumbled back.

"Don't tell Khatuya," I begged him. "She wouldn't understand. Please."

He didn't even acknowledge my words, storming out of the archives as though fleeing his fate.

43
Rasha

11 years after the restoration of Kashan
and 572 years after the Shattering

Langzu - Kluehnn's den northeast of Bian

By decree of the Albanoran ruling family, any traveler passing through our fair capital must surrender their books to be copied by our scholars. Before departing, you may collect your books at the Royal Academy. We appreciate your contribution to our vast library and to the education of scholars throughout the realms.

I didn't know what to say to Mull. I took my robe from him and let him go back to the room he shared with several other converts. Naatar was right, I couldn't stay on this path of doubt. I had to re-commit to my faith. I had to earn back my dagger. I could protect my cohort by being at their side, leading them to victory. What did I think I was doing here in the archives, reading pages not meant for my eyes? I wasn't a scholar; I'd never been a scholar.

Unwilling to face Naatar again, I curled up on a few cushions by one of the windows in the archives, surrounded by the smell of old parchment and ink. Fitfully, I drifted off to sleep.

I woke in the early-morning hours. A cold breeze brushed my legs. Hakara was slipping out from beneath our blankets. She was going down to the sea to dive. This time, she might not come back. I reached for her. "Hakara, don't."

I knew how she'd respond. A last squeeze of my hand. A kiss to my forehead. But then she'd be gone and I'd be in the tent, where she told me I was safe.

I wasn't safe. We were never safe. My heart clenched. I knew she needed to protect me, I knew that if I pushed against that, I'd be taking away the best reason she had for being brave, yet I chafed against it. Before Mimi had died, I'd protected her too. In smaller ways, yes. But I still needed Hakara in that way, I still needed a sister, and she'd abandoned me.

My hand groped at empty cushions.

I rolled onto the hard ground, coming fully awake. The archives were dark, the quiet of the tunnels telling me it was still night-time. It took me a moment to orient myself. I wasn't in Kashan. I was in Langzu, and it wasn't time to open the shutters, not yet. The air outside was still too moist and would damage the books. Unsure of what else to do, I rose to my feet, testing the weight on my leg. It held, so I left the crutch by the window and wandered toward the room I shared with Naatar and Khatuya.

I'd have to face him sooner or later and I'd not had the chance to see Khatuya yet. I didn't know if he'd told her what I'd said, but I couldn't avoid my cohort forever, and better to have these conversations in the privacy of our room.

I opened the door, expecting darkness.

A lantern was lit, the light low. I caught the outline of

Khatuya's bare back, her rough brown skin beaded with sweat. She was moving on her bed and hadn't noticed me.

And then I saw Naatar's scaled hands on her waist. She bent low over him, a moan in her throat.

I felt frozen in time, every detail of this moment excruciating, my heart a drumbeat in my ears. Khatuya's head turned. I didn't know what my face looked like, what expression was painted across my features.

I was stumbling away, unsure of what I was doing.

She gasped and pulled the bedsheet over her body. "Rasha! Rasha, wait..."

The door was shutting behind me and I was running, trying to put distance between myself and what I'd just seen. While I'd been here in the archives, reading forbidden pages, they'd been out in the wilds together. Without me. Something must have happened between them.

Was it love, or just the closeness of a cohort? Was it a closeness either of them had thought to include me in, or had I always been an afterthought, unknowingly on the outside? They'd known one another before I'd joined them, they'd been friends. That had apparently blossomed into more.

And here I was, a bystander, an unwelcome intruder. I'd thought we'd become a cohort of three, that we were all on equal footing. Apparently not. My toes caught in a crevice. I couldn't get my injured leg in front of me in time. The ground rose to meet me. No one was awake yet to see me fall. I lay there, fresh new pain radiating up my leg. The idea of returning to the field with Naatar and Khatuya felt foolish. I was healing, but I wasn't ready yet. They'd be sent out again before I could earn another blade.

I'd be stuck here, with Mull, who didn't even like me. He might have been altered, but I saw the way his gaze kept flicking toward my horns, lingering on the one Kluehnn had eaten away. I wouldn't ever be his friend – to him I would always be a monster. To my sister, I'd always be a girl who needed protection.

And to Sheuan, the only person who had made the two sides of me fit peacefully together?

Someone to love, briefly, and then leave behind. I was always going to be left behind. I dragged myself to my feet, my leg burning. It held my weight, though my knee threatened to buckle. Without knowing where else to go, I limped back to the archives and lit a lamp.

A figure stood by the window. I couldn't make out his features, but I knew his silhouette. Mull. "I couldn't sleep," he said. "I owe you an explanation."

I'd forgotten, in my turmoil over Khatuya and Naatar, that he'd taken my robe. I seized my crutch from where I'd left it, unwilling to sit, not right now. "Tell me."

"I'm not here to spy, no matter what you might think. I came here to find a tomb. The tomb of Tolemne's family. I've found his writing on the walls of the den, and I think the tomb is somewhere in these tunnels."

I couldn't make sense of it. "You came here just to find some dead people's resting place? You risked your life for that?"

"I'm a scholar. My friends died because" – he licked his lips – "we were searching for Unterra. There weren't two aeroclines. There were three."

I scoffed. "There are two."

"Yes, and the gods and mortals never mingled, never had children together. That's what the books say, isn't it?"

I had no retort for that. A large part of me yearned for the days before I'd spoken to that god in the forests of Kashan. The days before I'd lived with doubt.

He let out a sharp breath. "There are carvings here that match the ones made along Tolemne's Path. One of the carvings on

Tolemne's Path says that he was headed here, to the tomb, to write the truth of this world. The writing here leads me down to a stone that blocks the way. I think the tomb is behind it, but it's too heavy to move by myself."

He left the last words hanging in the air, an unspoken question. I should have shut it down then, refused to speak to him again, focused on my work, as Naatar had bade me. But if I were truly alone, and Kluehnn was lying to me, then why not? Why not do this? Find the truth? I closed my eyes, and the image of Khatuya and Naatar was there behind my eyelids, together, sharing something I never could. I shook my head, trying to force it away.

"I'll help you. We go now. While the den is still asleep."

I followed Mull at a limp, my heartbeat thudding like the hooves of racing horses. My mind seemed to float somewhere above me as we made our way down the tunnels, Mull stopping every so often to touch words that had been etched into the walls, muttering to himself. He stopped at a fork before leading me down the left-hand tunnel. "The next one says that Tolemne can trace his lineage back to Barexi. He's not pleased by the information. He did not like the gods."

"Understandably," I whispered back. "They all refused to grant him a boon."

"Except one," Mull said.

"Yes."

He stopped at the end of a tunnel, fitting his fingers into a crack in the wall. "The stone is here. I can get my fingers behind it, but I can't move it."

I obliged, setting down the lantern and moving next to him, reaching over his head to find a spot I could grip. I gave an experimental tug. He was right. The thing was heavy. "Together. If we do this together. One ... two ... three!"

Both of us pulled. The stone moved with an echoing,

grinding sound. I gritted my teeth, hoping no one had heard. Did Kluehnn's aspect ever sleep? I wasn't sure. "Lift. Lift!" Mull strained, and the stone moved silently. We let it rest when we'd opened it enough that we could wedge ourselves through the gap.

Mull ducked inside first, before I could caution him that we didn't know what lay beyond. Creatures sometimes lived in the deeper tunnels, ones I'd never seen on the surface. But the man was frustratingly single-minded. He didn't even have the benefit of a light. I grabbed the lantern and hurried after him.

The space beyond was larger than I'd expected it to be. The wall opposite had been carved into a facade, complete with pillars and a darkened entryway. A geometric design decorated the area above the doorway, bookended on either side with seated wolves.

The other walls were covered in more writing I didn't recognize. Mull was already tracing it with his hands, too impatient even to wait for the lantern.

"'The surface is barren'," he read. "'There is not enough water, not enough food. Every day is misery. They keep burning the Numinars, and that living wood fills the corners of the sky with lingering black smoke. We are choking on it.'"

He traced some carvings lower down. "'My wife died first. And then our children. All while I searched for a way to Unterra, to ask the gods to fix the surface. They refused.'"

"What about Kluehnn?" I asked, casting my gaze over the facade. I lifted the lantern, trying to see what was inside without walking into the tomb.

Mull stopped, his hand moving over the carving again. "Tolemne's wife and children. They died *before* he went on his expedition."

I waved dismissively. "These carvings sound like the ravings of a madman. He was confused. Maybe he came down here and got lost."

He pointed to the tomb. "There's a whole tomb carved here. You can't get lost and then do that. That's ridiculous. First you'd run out of fuel for your lamps. Then you'd run out of food and water. Do you think that is the work of one man?"

I shrugged. "Maybe someone else carved it before he got here."

A disgusted sound left Mull's mouth. "Think about it for more than just one moment." He swept past me and toward the entrance of the tomb.

"Wait, you don't know what's in ..." He was already gone into the dark.

Cursing, I followed him, lifting the lantern to light the walls. Except for a few small cave spiders, the tomb was blessedly empty of life. A couple of shelves had been chiseled into one wall, and four urns had been placed there, names carved above. Mull beckoned me over. "His wife," he said, pointing to the one at the top. Then at the shelf below. "His two daughters and his son."

I peered at the top shelf. There was an empty space next to the wife's urn. "And Tolemne himself?"

Mull scratched at the fur on his chin. "According to the texts, Tolemne remained in Unterra and was entombed there when he died."

We both stared for a while at the urns. I touched a shelf but didn't dare touch any of the urns themselves. It felt a little too close to sacrilege to do so. "If there's anything else down here that you want to see, you should do it now. We need to get back out of these tunnels before the den wakes up."

Mull took the lantern from my hands without asking – a privilege he was used to, I was sure – and turned to the rest of the tomb. It extended into the darkness, the walls lined with some more etchings. He ran his hand along the stone as he explored. I followed him a few paces back. The air here smelled of damp earth and dust.

He suddenly stopped, swinging the lantern around – first to a short phrase carved into the wall, and then down toward his feet, where an opening descended into the ground. "We must be deep."

"What is it? What does that say?"

He put a hand beneath each word as he spoke them. "'I made a bargain.'" Then he pointed to the hole in the ground. The air at his feet shimmered, the space beyond distorted.

I knelt, dipped a hand into the shimmer. It was slightly warm, and thicker than the air we stood in now. The first aerocline. When Mull crouched next to me and held the lamp next to the hole, I could see some of the space beneath. There were carvings down there too, but I couldn't make out their edges past the distortion of the aerocline. "I wonder what's down there," I murmured. I realized, startled, that I'd forgotten about my encounter with Khatuya and Naatar, those morose thoughts overtaken by curiosity, by the thrill of this discovery.

"You don't have to wonder." He took a deep breath before pulling something out from beneath his shirt and fastening it over his nose and mouth. Some sort of cloth contraption. "Wait here."

Before I could stop him, before I could ask him what in all the depths that thing was, he'd slipped down into the hole. Beneath the first aerocline.

44
Hakara

11 years after the restoration of Kashan
and 572 years after the Shattering

Pizgonia - Gorina, City of a Hundred Moons, in the Godless hideout

The city of Gorina is a marvelous thing indeed! Built on the coast, fresh water flows from an inland oasis through numerous aqueducts, filling the fountains that make the city so famous. It may be gauche of me, as a tourist in this fair port, but I took a walk through the winding streets at night, a cup of sweet date brandy in one hand and a warm pigeon-stuffed flatbread in the other, and counted out each of the hundred moons reflected in the fountains throughout the streets and alleys.

Velenor returned to the hideout later that evening, her face veiled again, horns hidden by winding cloth. She spoke first to the Godless, checking in on their injured, embracing the grieving while whispering soft words of comfort. Then she took them aside, questioning them one by one.

I waited, more than a little impatient, my knees drawn to my chest, my back against a wall. Someone had stopped by with some dense, sweet pastry that tasted like honey and dried fruits. I'd gulped it down before returning to my sullen watchfulness. I couldn't understand what she said, and I wasn't about to ask Thassir. Gods, the man was a wall. How apt a comparison – he was tall, impenetrable, steadfast. He expressed himself just as well as a wall, too.

I should sleep, but all I could think about was the sadness in his eyes when he looked at me. My hand closed into a fist. I couldn't stand it. Each time I caught his gaze, I felt like I must be dying, or dead already. It was enough to make me want to punch him. Except that would be so very like punching a wall, too. The only one I'd hurt would be myself.

Finally, Velenor made her way to me, just as my own shoulder started to feel like a decent-enough pillow. When I scanned the room, I didn't see Alifra or Dashu. They must have retreated somewhere else to sleep.

She squatted in front of me, peering into my face. "You did quite a number on the godkillers – it was all most of the Godless wanted to talk about."

I shifted, grimacing as bones and muscles screamed in protest. "It was the least I could do."

She waited, as though expecting another answer, but when I said nothing, she sighed. "No one attacked the council member. I went to the palace, climbed the wall, and shadowed her all afternoon. Nothing."

"Lithuas probably orchestrated the attack to infiltrate the Godless, so if she didn't replace the council member leading them, she might have replaced someone else."

"That's what I thought," Velenor said. "Both Nioanen and I were distracted. We wouldn't have noticed her shifting through the blood-pact bond. So I am speaking to each of the Godless in turn. None of them so far are Lithuas. I know her like I know myself."

"And the Godless in other places? She could have gone elsewhere."

"That's true. But we cannot do anything about it now except to keep vigilant." Her fingers brushed my forehead. "Get some sleep. Let me do my work. Worry about it tomorrow."

I set my jaw. "I'll worry about it tonight." But maybe I was more tired than I thought, or there had been magic in her touch, because I found my head sinking toward the ground without my permission.

I woke to the flicker of lamps and a rolled-up shirt beneath my head. Had I put that there, or had Velenor done it? A fresh sword in a patterned scabbard had been placed to my right. I pulled the blade partially free, testing my finger against the edge. Sharp. A purse of hexagonal coins lay next to me as well, along with a note: *The least I could do for the distance you traveled and the perils you faced.* Perils? Maybe it was just the roughness of life on the road and then living as a miner, but I didn't know anyone who used words like that. Velenor must have left the note as well. I squinted. It was written in Kashani, besides.

I rose, fastening both sword and purse to my belt before finding my way toward the entrance to the Godless hideout. Someone had placed a ladder in the ruin of the stairs. But that wasn't the first thing I noticed.

Alifra and Dashu stood beneath the wooden trapdoor, Dashu with a hand on the ladder, Alifra with her arms crossed. I felt as though I'd wandered into something I shouldn't have.

"You two are up early. Or late? I'm not sure, is it morning yet?"

They both jumped, and neither were people I knew to startle easily. Dashu spoke first. "It's morning."

I jangled the coins. "Someone needs to find Talie, see if she's spotted Lithuas anywhere. And if it's morning, might as well grab a bite to eat while we're at it." I imagined the pastry I'd eaten last night, sitting like a piece of wet clay next to the corestone. My stomach growled in protest. No more of that – had to find something substantial. And looking for Talie would get me out of this miserable hideout where I'd have to face Thassir's silence and doleful looks.

The Godless guards above fell back in awe as we emerged into an abandoned warehouse, their gazes focused on me. What in all the realms had I done *exactly*? I could only remember flashes of the fight the day before, most of my memories consumed by the way I'd felt – the fire flooding through me and the power I'd so freely accessed.

Outside, the sun had barely crested the horizon, swathing the eastern sky in rosy gold. Dashu and Alifra fell naturally into step behind me. I could smell food stalls nearby, the scent of frying meat and spices carried on the wind.

I let my nose guide me, the quiet of the morning reminding me of my time back in Kashan, Maman roasting skewers of goat over a fire as Mimi packed her medical bags for work with the horses. Maman let us run free on those mornings, with fair warning on what to do if we ran into any wolves. "Make yourself big," she'd say as she turned the skewers, pulling one off the fire to inspect it. "Shout, wave your arms. They'll run away." She gave us both knives to tuck into our belts, and then we were off into the wilderness, expected back by lunchtime for lessons. Until then, we spent hours skimming over the plains with our arms spread, pretending we were eagles, building fortresses from sticks and stones we then defended from imaginary enemies.

When Mimi had died, when Maman had left us, I'd confined Rasha to the tent in the mornings, too afraid to lose her. *Take care of your sister,* Mimi had said to me before she'd died. It was the only thing that had kept me going. The only real purpose I had.

Alifra and Dashu were talking behind me, quickly and quietly. I swallowed and tried to make out what they were saying, trying to distract myself from the silence. No good could come of thoughts like these, not when I had two loose gods in the city to find. Better to focus on what lay ahead.

"It doesn't have to mean anything," Alifra was saying. "You're the one who's making it into more."

Dashu's urgent whisper. "Tell me you don't feel anything for me, then. Tell me we're just friends. Tell me it was a mistake."

Alifra said nothing for a long time. I nearly missed the turn into the market, waiting to hear if she would respond, trying to pretend I'd heard nothing. Had their relationship stepped into something more when I hadn't noticed? I'd been so single-mindedly trying to hunt down Lithuas, distracted by thoughts of Rasha and Thassir.

I thought of the way Dashu had taken Alifra's hand before we'd raided that den in Kashan, the tender way he'd spoken to her and told her to grieve then, when he'd always told everyone to grieve later.

"I could never think of any time spent between us as a mistake," she finally responded.

Were they holding hands now? Gazing at one another lovingly? I risked a glance back, pretending to notice the beauty of an archway mosaic. No. Definitely not. They stood arm's length apart, staring at one another and very deliberately not closing the distance.

"That's it then?"

"It's all I can give you right now. And don't pretend differently – it's all *you* can give *me* right now."

He leaned in, and amidst the bustle of the market, I lost track of their conversation. It really wasn't my business anyways. I found the stall I'd been smelling, where two people were working to cook and dole out flatbread stuffed with spiced meat and some vegetable I couldn't identify. I watched how much others paid and then handed over the right amount in coin for three.

My comrades crowded in next to me as we ate, having decided that whatever argument they'd been having was over, or at least delayed. I was used to spice, but whatever was used to season the meat made my eyes and nose water. Still couldn't seem to stop eating it, the fragrance an incredible blend of heat and herbs. Oil dripped out the side of my flatbread as I reached the end of it. I shook out my fingers. "Look down the alleys for Talie. She'll still be in cat form."

Alifra eyed a tabby that ran across the street in front of us. "Doesn't seem to be a shortage of cats here."

Now that she'd said it, I saw them everywhere, looking for handouts or scraps, meowing at strangers, chasing one another across the struts and reeds that shaded the streets. We wandered away from the market, glancing down side streets.

One alley in particular was filled with cats. Someone had put out bowls of food and water for them, and the animals had picked the bowls nearly clean. There, lying in a beam of sunlight, was a scruffy-looking calico.

I wanted to think it wasn't Talie, that she was instead prowling on the struts and reeds overhead, peering at every face and listening to every conversation. And then she rolled over, yawned, and opened her eyes.

"Oh. It's you."

A nearby cat hissed upon hearing her speak.

I strode closer, cats scattering before me, and knelt at Talie's side. "Did you find her?"

She licked one paw. "No."

I watched her brush her paw over her ear. "And exactly how hard did you work?"

"Harder than you."

Dashu, from behind her, said drolly, "I doubt that."

Her tail swished as she rose to her feet. "I searched the city all night. Cats are nocturnal, remember? What were *you* doing all night?" I glanced back at Dashu and Alifra and watched the color rise to his cheeks. Alifra remained coolly disinterested. Nerves of steel, that one.

"Anyways. I saw and heard nothing. She may not even be here anymore. We've lingered here for long enough with nothing to show for it."

I gritted my teeth. "It's been *days*."

"We should go back." She pressed forward before any of us could protest. "I've followed you here, I've done as you've asked. Now consider what *I* ask. The gods have gathered in Langzu. The Unanointed brought them hope that there was a chance to fight back. You know what could bring them even more hope? Two of the elder gods popping up alive. Can you imagine? Kluehnn may be powerful, he may be split among many aspects, but in the end he is still one god." Her ears flattened against her head. "And so is Lithuas."

I thought of the stillness of the ocean, the uncertainty of my purpose, the painful memories flooding in. "No. We came here to find and kill Lithuas. We cannot keep changing track."

Talie followed us back through the streets to the Godless hideout, but not before she rubbed against my legs and asked sweetly for one of those meat-stuffed flatbreads I'd been eating. She could smell it on my hands, you see, and wasn't it rude to buy some for my comrades and not for her? I grudgingly acquiesced, though as the sun rose, I could feel the pull of fresh urgency.

I had to carry her down the ladder of the hideout to where

Velenor and Thassir were clearing up the aftermath of the battle. There were others in the room beyond, but Velenor saw us and discreetly closed the door. Talie made a beeline for Thassir as soon as I set her down, shifting to her original form. Alifra glared at her, but she only shrugged and gestured to the bloody remains of the godkillers as she backed toward the corner he was stacking loose weapons in. "What are they going to do, rise from the dead and hunt me down? They already know where this place is."

I wanted to watch, to see how he'd react to her demands, but Velenor approached, her face veiled in midnight blue. She shook her head before she even came within earshot. "I finished questioning everyone. None of them are her."

I pressed the heels of my palms to my eyes, my voice sounding strange with the pressure. "That's not good enough. We have to find her. I'll scour the entire city if I have to." I lowered my hands, glaring at her defiantly.

She met my gaze with her level own, and I was reminded of the look Maman gave me when I made wild claims about being able to knife a wolf in the gut instead of scaring it away. Both she and Thassir turned at the same time, their gazes fixed on the wall.

"Lithuas," Thassir growled from the corner. "She shifted."

I stared at the wall they were looking at, as though I could discern anything at all from it. "Where?"

Thassir was moving to the ladder. "She's either at the docks or back on the Sanguine Sea. We misjudged this, Velenor. She didn't come here to infiltrate the Godless, not yet. She's played us."

"She must have found a corestone here," Velenor said. "She'll take it back to Langzu, force restoration."

I gritted my teeth – it was what I'd feared. We'd come such a long way, through the ocean barrier itself. I wanted to kill her and be done with it, to return home triumphant, not with this sense of unease swirling inside me.

Thassir seized the ladder, and then his eyes met mine. In a mere moment, he'd melted from shaking anger to a doleful helplessness.

I tore my gaze away.

I'd crossed an ocean to find an elder god and had found one I hadn't expected. But now, at least, I knew what I was capable of with the corestone in my belly. If I met Lithuas again, I wouldn't have to trust Thassir, to rely on him in any way. I had the knife I'd taken from my sister. I had the strength.

I would kill her.

45
Sheuan

11 years after the restoration of Kashan and 572 years after the Shattering

Langzu - inner Bian

During Ayaz and Barexi's infamous disagreement over the mortals they were curating, Ayaz could have killed Barexi when he crept into his room at night. Only a god can kill another god, if they do so with intention. But Ayaz, when he made those thousand cuts and scattered the pieces of Barexi's body, only intended to teach him a lesson.

Given the fact that the first thing Barexi did upon re-assembling himself was to interrupt Ayaz's plans within the Aqqilan Empire by assisting a doctor in finding a cure for the nettlepox plague, the lesson Barexi was left with may not have been the one Ayaz intended.

It did not escape Sheuan that if the Sovereign hadn't found her, she'd be in a plain outfit in inner Bian, able to move through and around the rioters without drawing their attention. And now here she was, trapped in the middle of a bevy of the Sovereign's special enforcers, very clearly a target.

The Sovereign seized the arm of the nearest enforcer, a woman with broad shoulders and close-clipped black hair. "We need to clear a path."

She hesitated, her gaze darting to Sheuan. "Sovereign, we don't have—"

"Never mind that. Do as I've asked."

The woman's lip firmed up and she nodded, her hand dipping into a pouch at her side. She lifted something to her mouth. A faint glow, and then it was gone. She'd *swallowed* it.

Sheuan observed all this, absolutely mystified.

The enforcer strode toward the rioters at the mouth of the alley as the other enforcers shifted, focusing on the flanking group.

One against all those men and women? Sheuan counted four, probably one or two more behind them. It was hard to see in the dark and over the Sovereign's shoulder.

An odd-smelling breeze brushed past Sheuan's ear. She caught a faint whiff of ink, of star anise. And then something *happened* to the woman. The blue of her jacketed arms was encased in darkness. It happened so quickly that Sheuan couldn't be sure exactly what was occurring. One moment the woman moved toward the rioters, pulling her sword free. In the next, she was casting them aside as though they were wooden puppets. Each stroke of her sword sent a rioter flying back. One, two, three, four, five. They barely had time to react or regroup. If they'd put up a fight at all, Sheuan hadn't seen it. So it seemed the magic the Sovereign used to pull information from others wasn't the only magic he possessed. She'd heard the hesitation – was this just not a magic he used that often? Was it too obvious? Too scarce?

But then the way was clear, and the enforcers behind them carried them on, one of them gripping Sheuan's upper arm.

The streets beyond were a haze of panic; she couldn't tell who was running from something and who was running toward something. The faint light of a fire limned the rooftops to the west.

"This way," one of the enforcers said. Two more turns, and the castle rose above them. Enforcers stood in formation at the base of the ramp leading up to it, guarding the only way in. They flowed to the side as soon as they saw her and the Sovereign, re-forming as soon as they'd passed up the ramp.

"I should have expected this." The Sovereign's voice was low and cutting. "I'll have to move quickly. My enforcers are highly specialized fighters," he said to her as they swept into the entrance hall.

She slipped a hand around his arm before he could leave her. Was that all the explanation he was going to give? Please. As though she'd believe that what they'd done could only be attributed to skill. "Thank you. For getting us out of there." Only a gentle pressure, hoping for more.

He looked down at her fingers. "I have to talk to my Minister of Arms. Make sure this riot is put down quickly."

She tried not to let her annoyance show. "Of course. Can I do anything to help? Re-evaluate the rations? It may be time to release more of our stores. We should look to the cause, try to stem the problem there."

He waved a hand as he strode down the hall. "Yes. Fine."

She didn't dare glare daggers at his back, not when there were still others in the hall. The rations were tight these days. There'd been a fire in the farms to the west, and it had wiped out a good deal of their crops, including some mature fruit trees. They had extra grain stores. Sheuan already knew that if they released the stores to bring rations back to what they'd been, the entire supply would only last a couple months.

But maybe that would be enough to tide them over until restoration finally came. She went to her rooms, drew up the order. She'd pass it to the Sovereign's desk for review.

And then she went to the window, watching the fires glow, the sounds of shouts and fighting now faded away. It would be hard to put out the flames. They'd try, but it would probably burn out a few buildings before they managed.

She woke with her cheek pressed to the windowsill, one arm sore from where she'd splayed it above her head. The scent of smoke and petrichor filled the air. She had vague memories of hearing the patter of rain, feeling a drop or two of wetness on the top of her head.

Bian looked so different by day. Smoke still wisped above some buildings, but she could see the wet cobbles of the street. It had rained a little in the night, no doubt helping the efforts to put out the fires. The whole night before swam through her mind, one scene flashing after the next. The Sovereign was smuggling god gems. His special enforcers were *eating* them. The gems gave them some sort of magic. The Sovereign had an altar to the old gods, and cells for holding prisoners. She had no doubt this was where he interrogated people before execution. Her own father had likely been held there, at least briefly.

The thought made her shiver. She was so close – to both answers and her own death. All she had to do was to slip up once, and she'd be facing the cold stone of the executioner's block. She'd come close twice the night before, and had she been only a little less clever, a little less lucky, it would have been over.

There was one more place she could keep digging.

Quickly, she changed out of the worker's clothes and wiped the dust from her face and hair. It wasn't as good as a bath, but time was everything. She slipped on one of her finer dresses, a sleeveless light blue silk with a high collar and a flowing skirt.

Two enforcers stood outside her door. Fine. It didn't matter to her. "I'm going into the city."

Before they could make any protest, she strode down the hall and to the stairs. She passed through the Sovereign's main hall, the one where he held his parties, the glassy eyes of strange, dead animals staring at her as she passed. Her gaze caught on his chair, the one he sat in to hear petitioners. Dark wood, carved with the elder gods. The only evidence of the elder gods in the entire castle, one that was permitted by society because the chair was a valuable antique, said to pre-date the Shattering.

One of the enforcers darted forward and wedged his way between her and the main doors before she could reach them. He bowed his head. "It may still be dangerous out there."

"And I have the workshop to attend to and someone to visit. Surely there will be no danger with you by my side."

She reached past him and pushed her way out onto the ramp.

The modest house she'd purchased for her mother lay just inside inner Bian, nestled near the wall separating the two parts of the city. The gates had been closed, she noticed. Someone could make their way into inner Bian by walking into the dried lakebed, but they'd be spotted quickly in that empty, rocky expanse.

Again one of her enforcers tried to stop her, bowing his head several times, as though that might soften her determination. "This is not the house of a noble or royal clan. There is no seal on the door."

"Nor is it a physician, nor a merchant. This is the house where my mother lives, and though she may now be clanless, there was a riot in our city last night. Would you truly stop me from checking on her well-being?"

The Sovereign would likely see it as a weakness, this visit, something that should be dissuaded and punished, but Sheuan didn't care. She knocked sharply on the door and waited. Footsteps sounded from inside.

Her mother opened the door, hair drawn back into a tight, neat bun. She was dressed cleanly, though the cloth was of middling quality; a few stitches on the embroidery had clearly come loose at some point and then been snipped clean, leaving an empty space behind.

Some silly part of Sheuan wanted to throw herself into her mother's arms, completely disregarding the fact that her mother might feel the pinfeathers on her back, or the strange bones that pressed beneath. It *was* a silly thought. There was perhaps only a slight chance that her mother would even open her arms, and the whole thing was likely to end in some sort of awkward half-embrace, with her mother's hands limp at her thighs.

She smiled ruefully at the thought and inclined her head — her mother was a venerable elder, after all. "May I come in?"

Her mother stood to the side to let her pass, and Sheuan's gaze focused on the veins on the back of her mother's hand, the green protrusions like overflowing rivers, the age spots like sinkholes. The enforcers moved to follow her, but her mother shut the door firmly in their faces without explanation. Sheuan couldn't see whatever expression her mother had shown them, but she knew from being on the receiving end of her ire that her glare could stop a person in their tracks and give them the sudden sinking feeling that they had done, or been about to do, something terribly rude.

"I don't have tea," her mother said. "Not the kind you would be used to now, in the castle. But I can serve you mint."

The cheapest, the easiest to grow. "That's fine," Sheuan said. "I like mint."

Her mother brewed the tea herself and then sat with her at the table in the adjoining room. "Why are you here?" She stirred the tea with a chopstick, replaced the lid, and then sat back on her cushion. The morning light filtered in, hazy, the neighboring building blocking any direct sun.

"There was a riot last night. Can't I check on my mother?"

She snorted. "That's what you told the enforcers, girl. Don't think you can tell me the same thing."

Sheuan wrapped her hands around her empty cup. "I did worry about you. I *do* worry about you."

Her mother shook her head. "I am just one person."

Gods below, she could be so stubborn. But Sheuan hadn't come here to start yet another argument. She rose, swinging the shutters on the window quietly shut. The small room darkened. Her mother watched her as she sat back down, her gaze wary.

"I went to the Sovereign's warehouse. I found something. Something that would get him into trouble with the clans. And with Kluehnn."

Her mother made a clicking sound with her tongue, grabbed the teapot, and poured into Sheuan's cup. The liquid was a thin green; it hadn't steeped for long enough. She leaned forward through the curls of steam. "This is a stupid thing to do, Sheuan. I told you not to go digging before, and still, look" – she waved a hand – "you go digging. Ah, why can't you listen to your elders? We've been here, alive, for longer than you have. You think you know everything. You think you know what's best, and then you stumble into every sinkhole life has to offer while we shout at you to stop for a moment and look at the path ahead."

"Then *tell me* what lies ahead."

"Your head on a block and the ax above your neck." She sat back, huffing out a breath. "You think I want to see you executed too? You think I *want* to see the same thing happen to you as happened to your father? You both went into that big castle with big plans."

Sheuan's temper frayed. "And what am I supposed to do? Abide by everything you've told me to do? We would have fallen into ruin no matter what you did. It was what the Sovereign wanted."

"So you think you're cleverer than me? The Sovereign doesn't *want* you as his wife. He sees it as convenient. When you are no longer convenient, you will no longer be his wife. You will be dead."

Sheuan knew she was right. She'd told herself the same thing, more than once. So why did it hurt when she heard it from her mother's mouth? She didn't *want* her mother to spout lies, to tell her the Sovereign saw her as anything more. So what *did* she want, exactly? "I know he sees me as a tool, and not as a person. I've spent all my life being treated that way, as something to be used for the good of the clan. You think I don't know the feeling?"

"Oh, Sheuan." The pity in her mother's gaze was almost more than she could bear. "I see every individual in the clan that way. No one else has complained. Only you."

"Did I not matter more?" They weren't quite the right words, she knew it as soon as she dug them up, but they were close, so close to the truth.

"How selfish would that be of me, if I put my daughter above everyone else?"

"I still wanted you to. I still *needed* you to!" Instead, she'd had no one who'd loved her in the way she'd needed, someone who would care to dig beneath and know her. That secret self she'd always had to hide for the good of her family. And her mother had praised her for it. The only person who'd ever cared to dig beneath had been Rasha – so very, very briefly.

Her mother sipped from her tea, calm as the sea after a storm. "You have always had that roiling beneath the surface, that need to take, take, *take*. Always such a needy child."

If this was a fight, Sheuan could feel herself losing. She scrambled for some semblance of decorum. This outburst only proved her mother right. "Did you ever consider that maybe I behaved that way because I never really got what I needed from you? Father was executed and you thrust me into a role I wasn't prepared for. There was never any softness to you. Any give. You owe me. You owe me this. What was my father doing in the days before his execution? You know something and I have to know it too."

For a moment, her mother only pursed her lips as she regarded her. Then she rose from her cushion, went to a chest in the corner, and lifted some blankets aside. She pulled out two stone tablets from beneath it, stacked one on top of the other and bound with twine. "It's written in an older form of Langzuan, more elaborate than the one we use today, but you should still be able to understand it." She passed the tablets to Sheuan. "He was reading these the day before he died."

She took them. A quick glance highlighted the names of the elder gods. A piece of parchment was folded and placed beneath the twine. With shaking fingers, she pulled it free and opened it.

It bore only two words, in her father's handwriting, the smudge of ink from his left hand marring the bottom of the page.

The scar.

46
Mullayne

11 years after the restoration of Kashan
and 572 years after the Shattering

Langzu - the den northeast of
Bian, Tolemne's Tomb

Aqqila once existed simply as a country, though it stretched long fingers out in trade. When the neighboring country, Montiyano, sought to change the terms of trade, Aqqila declined to negotiate. Montiyano attempted to assassinate Aqqila's queen, which led directly to a year-long war and Montiyano's conquest. Aqqila's queen married a prince from Isegin, and a subsequent series of skirmishes and further political alliances led to the spread of Aqqila's influence — as far east as the western edges of Albanore.

Like all empires, the Aqqilan Empire eventually toppled, though it prospered for over six hundred years.

Mull had said the whole thing with the sort of bravado he imagined Jeeoon would have done. *You don't have to wonder. Wait here.* But as soon as the first aerocline closed over his head, he could hear his pulse pounding in his ears. The sensation of the aether moving through fur was so much more unnerving than it had been with just the sparse hairs of his arms.

The filters had all slowly failed as they'd walked Tolemne's Path, as the aether had grown thicker. Not that he felt it was something he needed to mention to Rasha. She didn't like him. He knew how she saw him – some scion of a rich family, feckless, falling into the den and its secret places by accident rather than any real design.

This, at least, she couldn't say was an accident. This was by design – the design of his filter, more specifically. And yes, they'd failed before, but he was simply dipping below the first aerocline for only a moment, and he'd actually tested it under these sorts of circumstances.

Sweat beaded in the small of his back and he scratched at the tickling sensation. His tunic stuck there. It seemed no matter what he told his mind, what soothing rationalizations he made, his body had different ideas.

The cavern here was small, so he could barely stand up straight, and there was a tunnel branching off from it, leading into the darkness.

"Mull?" Rasha's voice traveled to his ears, muffled.

"I'm fine. Give me a moment." He lifted the lantern to the walls. These ones were covered in even more etchings. All the practice he'd had with Old Albanoran, reading those pages to Rasha, came in handy now. He didn't have to write the phrases down, cross-reference them with his books or mark words for further consideration. The translations came easier.

There are three aeroclines before Unterra. The closer one gets to Unterra, the lighter one gets, until everything shifts.

He remembered the way their hair had lifted past the third

aerocline, though he wasn't sure if any lightness he'd felt was real or just a figment of his aether-addled mind. He ran his hand along to another carving.

The gods are each strongest in one of four abilities, though only the shapeshifters can truly shift. Past that, there are the makers, the changers, and the augmenters.

And another.

The consumption of Numinar syrup staves off aether sickness and can improve one's own abilities. This allowed us descendants to move along the path to Unterra.

He felt drunk on this information, all of it whirling in his mind like flecks of gold in a cup.

Along these tunnels is another path to Unterra, which Irael used to frequent.

Another path? In Langzu? He couldn't know if the way was still open; it had been ages since the Shattering, since Tolemne must have carved these words into the wall.

I cannot survive up here. I must go back.

His breathing quickened. Did Tolemne go back? All the way back to Unterra? There was writing farther down the wall, farther down the tunnel. When he lifted the lantern, he couldn't see the end of it. He followed it, and then stopped, a phrase jumping out to him.

He knew that phrase. He'd seen it written on one of the pages he'd read to Rasha.

Barexi was struck by the mortal Taminus, so much so that he fell in love with her.

And below it, a similar phrase.

Barexi was struck by the mortal Taminus, so much so that he decided to teach her.

He wasn't sure what it meant.

"Mull?" Rasha's voice, so faint he could barely hear it. How far had he wandered? He looked back the way he'd come and couldn't see the hole he'd entered through, or even the cavern he'd entered into. Only more tunnel.

I don't think they're all dead. The elder gods. I think some have escaped.

Something wasn't right, but he couldn't quite be sure what. Suddenly, all he could think about was Imeah, wandering off into the dark. Alone.

He never should have left her. He should have gone with her, no matter what she'd said of the truth. The only truth that mattered was that he loved her and she loved him, and everything since that moment had felt like some shade of reality, a tree reflected on a pond.

If he followed this path, would he find her?

He reached to scratch his back and stumbled, nearly fell. Caught himself on the wall, his hand pressed to the stone. Took a deep breath. And froze.

No wonder he'd been thinking of Imeah. He could nearly taste the scent of her floral perfume on the back of his tongue, infused in the soap she used to wash her long black hair. "Darling," she would have said to him, her lips pressed into a mocking pout, "have you thought about the conditions you've been keeping that filter under?"

Pressed against his sweating skin, folded in half, pulled and pushed every which way.

He lifted his hand to his face. The rubber was flush against his skin. But as his fingers explored, he found the hole. Small, but there, a tiny puncture in the cloth just above the seal.

He'd been breathing in aether and walking farther into the deep. He tried to slow his breathing, his pulse racing. The more aether he took in, the worse it would be. He needed to calm himself, to go straight back up to Rasha.

His gaze caught on the carving he was touching.

The elder gods made a blood promise to one another long ago, when the mortals first began to kill the Numinars. It linked them to one another, so that if any one of them revealed the truth, they all would die. And then they bound the rest of the living gods. Now they call them corestones, but they are not stones.

They are seeds.

He traced the edges of the words, fingers following each curve and line. The last line of the last word trailed down, past his line of sight. He knelt, found the bottom of it, his heart pounding.

Something was wedged into the end of that word. He closed his fingers around it, his head swimming. Without knowing exactly why, he pulled.

The thing came free, and he held it in front of the lamp, Imeah's scent thick in his nostrils.

It wasn't a chisel, or even the end of one.

It was a claw.

47
Rasha

11 years after the restoration of Kashan
and 572 years after the Shattering

Langzu - Kluehnn's den northeast of Bian

Long ago, in Montiyano, after it became a province of the Aqqilan Empire, there lived a famous archer known for her accuracy with the bow and arrow. As she grew older, she entered fewer and fewer competitions, but continued to boast. When a younger archer challenged her, laying a goodly sum of money on the line, the general public sat up and took notice. During the first challenge, attended by over five hundred people, the famous archer missed the target entirely. "I am sick," she said, waving away the younger man's protests. "Challenge me when I am feeling better." At the next challenge, over six hundred people attended, and the famous archer arrived drunk. She struck the stem off a pomegranate instead of the fruit itself. "Was hitting the fruit the challenge?" she said. "I thought we were meant to hit the stem. Challenge me when

I am sober." At the third challenge, nearly one thousand people attended, and the famous archer took aim, striking the very center of the target. "See?" she said. "I did not make an empty boast. Pay up." The challenger, who had hit the target each time, judged the mood of the crowd, who knew the famous archer and did not know him, and paid the sum.

Who acted more the fool? The famous archer or the challenger? Whichever you choose says more about you than it says about them.

"Mull?" I peered into the hole as the light from the lantern grew more and more faint. Of course he'd leave me here, like this. I could probably feel my way back to the tunnels where lanterns hung, but it would take me some time, at which point I might be discovered.

And then what? Kluehnn would never let me earn a godkiller blade again. I waited for the dread, the anger. It was there, a darkness clawing at my heart, but it wasn't quite as shattering a thought as it usually was. I was numb, still trying to process Khatuya and Naatar. Their coupling didn't have to change anything between the three of us, did it? Yet I felt it already had.

"Mull?" I tried again.

Nothing. Altered had a stronger resistance to aether than any mortal, but he'd been down there for quite some time. I could barely see light emerging from the hole now. He'd said he would only be down there a moment, and now I had no idea where he was, how far he'd gone. He'd seemed so confident that the contraption he'd placed over his nose and mouth would protect him.

What if it hadn't? Even an altered would now be starting to feel the effects of aether. I remembered the way it had made my head swim, the way I'd had to work to keep my wits, the itching of my arms, that drunk feeling that everything would be fine.

I didn't owe Mull anything. He'd always be afraid of me, he'd never understand me or what I'd been through. He had come here to search for a hidden tomb, for truths that were probably better off buried. I tapped a claw against the floor. I should leave. I should go back to the archives.

Instead, I found myself swinging my legs into the hole. I sat on the edge for a moment. Was the light growing stronger? Was he now headed back? I took a deep breath and lowered myself into the cavern.

The walls were covered with strange writing I couldn't understand. Mull was there, stumbling over stone as fast as he could, one hand on the wall to balance himself. He held the lantern in a death grip, as though he knew that if he let go, he'd never find it again. His eyes were wide, the cloth over his nose and mouth fluttering in and out with each breath.

I knew what aether sickness looked like. I should have questioned his contraption and whether the thing still worked, or had ever worked at all. I marched toward him and grabbed the lamp from his hands. He flailed at me as I seized him under the arms, one of his claws scratching my cheek. I grimaced but kept my breath held. Wouldn't do for both of us to become addled, not right now.

My lungs aching, my leg threatening to give out with each step, I hauled him back to the hole and hoisted him out. Quick as I could, my stomach spasming, I set the lamp up above, grabbed the sides of the hole, and pulled myself out past the first aerocline. Cool, fresh air brushed my cheeks, the scratch on my face stinging anew. I sucked in a deep breath, the aether still clinging to my clothes and smelling faintly of a dung fire.

Mull lay on the floor, gasping. He reached to his face with one trembling hand and tore the filter off. "He wrote the truth.

He wrote the truth down there, so much of it. There are three aeroclines – three, not two. The gods ... they made a pact. The pages I read to you. It's all there. In that cave going down into the dark. All the way to Unterra."

He was speaking nonsense. It would take him at least a day to get the aether out of his system. He was supposed to be working. I'd have to make excuses for him, figure out how to hide his condition.

"Sheuan, I'm sorry. This is my fault."

My heart dipped. *Sheuan?* I'd tried not to think of her, to leave her behind as she'd left me, but just the mention of her name brought it all crashing back. The night we'd spent together, wrapped in one another's arms. The callous way she'd left. This wasn't the time to question him, though. I picked up the filter, the lantern, and my crutch. "I can't carry you. If you value your life, you've got to get on your own two feet."

"My head," he muttered.

Once the dizziness completely faded, the headache would take over. I couldn't bring myself to sympathize, not when the den would be waking up any moment. "Altered have stronger resistance. On your feet, Mull."

For a moment I thought he would just lie there, pathetic and sad and sick. But somehow he found a reserve of strength and pushed himself to stand. "Lead the way," he managed.

Sighing, I extended a hand. "You can lean on me, for a little way at least."

He waved me away. "No. I can do this."

Together, we hobbled back out of the tomb, stopping to replace the stone that had covered the tunnel. Slowly, the pain in my leg faded away as we moved toward the archives. "Who is Sheuan?"

He only moaned. I tried a different question. "Is there another way? To Unterra?"

He leaned for a moment on the wall, and then pushed away, his breathing heavy. "Yes. The writing said the tunnel we were in led to Unterra. I don't know which twists and turns it takes, but it leads there. According to Tolemne, it was a path Irael used to take."

So there was another way. The agreement I'd spoken of with the crow was something that could actually happen if Kluehnn agreed to it. I turned that thought over in my mind. What if godkillers could be used to help the populace through restoration instead of merely being focused on killing gods? I doubted that all gods would abide by an agreement to return to Unterra, but this was a start. There'd be fewer to fight.

"I think I'm going to be sick." Mull's voice was thick.

I reached out and seized his arm. "Not here," I hissed. "Hold it. Get behind your screen. I'll bring you a bowl and clean it up. But if someone else has to clean it up, Kluehnn will know."

He swallowed.

We made it back to the archives. I found a bowl, and waited as he emptied the meager contents of his stomach. I tossed it out the window just as the first workers began to arrive in the archives. Gods, Mull was going to be absolutely useless today. I was surprised I'd gotten a response from him about the path to Unterra. I was going to have to find the herbs that would help the aether sickness pass. They'd have most of them in the kitchens. It wouldn't taste great, but that wasn't my problem.

I turned to find Khatuya standing in my way, the sick bowl still in my hands.

I didn't know where to look or what to say, a flush rising up my chest in spite of my best efforts. "I-I shouldn't have walked in without knocking."

She gave an impatient little tap of her foot. She was dressed now in her robe, the godkilling dagger at her belt. "I'm not here about that. And it's your room as well. We can talk about the knocking. Later."

The flush colored my cheeks, made my face hot. Which meant that tryst between them hadn't been a one-time thing.

"Kluehnn wants to see you."

My innards turned to ice. Had someone noticed us returning from our early-morning adventure? Had we not replaced the stone in the correct spot? Or had someone heard us? There were so many things that could have gone wrong. And here, in the den, there was only Kluehnn's justice. The aspect was responsible for the well-being of our den – the rewards and the punishments, doled out as Kluehnn saw fit.

I brushed past her, finding my footing was steady enough without the crutch. Whatever discomfort hung between us could wait. I spared a quick glance for Mull, hunched over his books. He looked miserable but alive. The herbs would have to wait as well. When Kluehnn summoned someone, you went.

Kluehnn's aspect had already emerged from below when I went to meet it. It waited, sitting on its haunches, the uppermost set of human arms folded over the mouth at the base of its neck. All five of its eyes darted in my direction as I entered. Its barbed tail swept across the stone floor. I shut the door carefully behind me, trying to keep my hand steady. The last time I'd been in here, Kluehnn had taken one of my horns. He'd hurt me. I couldn't imagine what more he'd do to me now.

"You are much improved," he said in his low, rasping voice. "Good."

Relief made me weak. I struggled to keep my feet under me, my knees steady. If this was what he greeted me with, then he didn't know what I'd been doing. "I can fight again." It didn't sound like my voice – it was too clear, too confident. Inside, my stomach roiled. If I kept on with helping Mull, with talking to the crow, I would be caught. Yet I couldn't seem to stop myself.

I had to. I had to stop.

Kluehnn was speaking, and I'd missed half the words. "Of course, rumors are rumors, but these are disturbing enough that I think I should handle them myself. I'm putting together a retinue to accompany me to Bian, to the Sovereign's castle. I want you with me."

It was an honor, more than I could have hoped for, given my transgressions. I prostrated myself, ignoring the ache in my leg. "Thank you." I waited, the space at my belt still empty, questions still swirling in my head. Rumors? Rumors of what?

But I knew this about Kluehnn: he did not appreciate questions.

His claws scraped against the floor as he rose. I watched his feet click closer. "I will not give you another blade, not yet. But if you acquit yourself well, you can expect to be returned to your cohort when we arrive back at the den. Until then, I'm sending Khatuya and Naatar out again. Even without you, they're formidable, and one of my godkillers has seen the gods' encampment. I will send other cohorts with them. We need to press the gods, find out how many of them there are, and what their defenses are like."

I remembered my conversation with the crow. There were more gods gathered than Kluehnn thought. They'd hidden their numbers. I wished I still had the sick bowl with me. If I didn't tell him, he'd send my friends into terrible danger. If I told him, the fragile peace I was trying to broker would never exist.

My mouth was so dry. I licked my lips and dared to lift my head. "What if we didn't have to fight?"

Kluehnn's eyes narrowed. "You suggest we let the gods overrun the surface? I made a bargain with Tolemne. I said I would restore the land above, I would protect the mortals. Should I abandon that promise?"

It would kill him, as it would kill any god who broke a promise. "No," I said quickly, bowing my head once, twice. "Of course not. I only wondered if there was a way to peace."

"Peace?" He snorted. One back hoof scraped against the floor. "With the gods? What do you think would work that hasn't already been tried, my child? Any peace we made would be a chance for them to grow in numbers again, to rest, to gain an advantage." He lowered his head, cocked it to the side. "Is that what you want?"

I sat back on my heels. "No. No, of course not." I bit my lip. There was part of me that knew I should leave it at that, but I had to know. "But what if there was a way still open to Unterra? What if we could send them back, seal them away?"

His lip curled back, showing sharp white teeth. "I thought you had become strong, yet here you are, trying to solve the problems of the gods – your enemies. Let me be clear: there is no way back to Unterra, and even if there were, the gods would refuse to walk it. They do not *want* peace, they want conquest. They want all mortals dead." He stalked from one end of the small cave to the other, his tail whipping behind him.

I flinched back and hoped he didn't notice.

"There can be no peace," Kluehnn snarled, the filaments on his back waving about. "Not until all the other gods are dead."

"I'm sorry." I bowed again. "I did not mean to make you angry."

The waving filaments went still. He stopped, reached a hand out to touch my cheek. He stroked the scratch Mull had left me with the pad of his thumb. "Ah, Rasha, I know. Sometimes the fiercest hearts are formed around a gentle core. You must burn it out, harden yourself. There are those who would seek to use you, to turn you to their advantage. You cannot allow it. You must not. I thought you'd put these sorts of thoughts aside after the trials."

He shook his head, as though admonishing himself. "I will let you fight again when we return. That will help. Killing an enemy can be purifying; it can strip away the uncertainties. It is either us or it is them, and perhaps you need a reminder." He pulled away. "Now go. Ready your pack and tend to your duties. We leave for Bian tomorrow."

I retreated, bowing, letting the door slam shut in my wake.

There was something startling and final about that scrape of metal door against stone, the echoing of the sound through the corridors, the fading of it.

Khatuya and Naatar were embracing when I returned to our room, even after my timid knock. Naatar took my hand. "Khatuya and I ... we've known one another for a long time."

I pulled away. I didn't want him to explain – like they were adults trying to explain their relationship to a child. All I wanted was for nothing to change between us, though it clearly already had. So I forced a smile. "I'm happy for you."

"Kluehnn is sending us after the gods. Without you," Khatuya said from behind him. Always blunt and to the point.

"I'm to attend him as he visits Bian. When we return, he will give me a blade again."

We stood there for a while in silence, and then Naatar clapped me on the shoulder. "That's good. That's good news."

I fled as soon as I was able.

Mull was slumped over the books when I arrived back at the archive.

I pushed his shoulder, handing over a cup of foul-smelling liquid. "Drink this. It will help."

He sniffed, gagged, but choked it down.

"You have to pull yourself together. I'm leaving tomorrow for Bian, to see the Sovereign."

His face paled. "The Sovereign. *Sheuan*." He seized a piece of parchment, began to write. "Please. If you see her, give this to her. She's my cousin."

Now that I looked, I could see a resemblance between them. This was my Sheuan he was talking about then, not someone else. I watched, not sure what to say, unable to read what he'd written. "I'll be with Kluehnn's aspect at the castle. I'm not there for a pleasure visit. Why do you think I might see her?"

He folded the letter, handed it to me. "Because she's married to the Sovereign."

48
Lithuas
63 years before the Shattering

Unterra - Irael's Path

Velenor spent years teaching the Aqqilans how to fight, but she always also lingered in Isegin, known for its beautiful flower gardens containing plants imported from many different realms. Although Isegin's integration into the empire was a peaceful one, when the Iseginians eventually rebelled, generations later, the empire burned their flower gardens to the ground. Perhaps, Ayaz said to Velenor when he caught her weeping, if she'd wanted to protect her flowers, she should have taught them to fight.

L ithuas's silver hair floated around her shoulders, buoyant in the aether of the third aerocline. Other, younger gods stood at her sides and behind her, weapons in hand, their auras glowing more faintly than the bioluminescent algae that dotted the tunnel walls.

She thought she could still feel the warmth from the inner sun at her back, smell the large, lush blooms that covered the cave Irael often took to the surface. She'd not walked his path before. She had her own path, in her own territory, but hers required shifting shapes several times, and Irael's was large enough to accommodate an army.

That was what they were. An army. It was time she admitted that to herself.

It was time she admitted other things as well.

She heard his footfalls before she saw him. Kluehnn approached, his army giving way as he arrived at her side. She caught a glimpse of his antlers from the corner of her eye. If she stood just so, and looked steadfastly to where the tunnel rose into a cavern, she could pretend he hadn't changed.

It was strange to pretend. Comforting, but strange. She was the Bringer of Change, shouldn't she relish this? Shouldn't she relish all of this? When Nioanen had refused to come to her side, to support Kluehnn, the gods had split into factions. They'd had their petty skirmishes – who didn't remember the way Ayaz had cut Barexi into a thousand pieces? – but this was different. This wasn't one god against another. Always the elder gods had kept the peace, refusing to drag others into petty squabbles. But now, at Kluehnn's behest, she'd done so deliberately.

"We keep harrying them," Kluehnn said from next to her. "We drove them from their homes and now we will drive them forth onto the surface."

"Where they will rally," Lithuas reminded him. "They are slow now, with their children in tow. When they get to the surface, they will find support with the mortals, they will find a place to keep their children safe, and then they will meet us." Forgetting herself, she turned her head.

There was another eye below his right one, blinking in time with the other two. A third antler had grown from the center of his forehead, joining with the others, forming a cage of thorns atop his head. He was taller, and when he thought she wasn't looking, and he moved quickly, she saw the outline of other hands beneath his voluminous robe.

She'd never asked him what kind of god he was, where his strength lay – was he an augmenter, a shapeshifter, a maker, or a changer? It wasn't the sort of question someone just asked at parties. But she'd caught him with the shimmer of blood at the corner of his mouth, and it was then that she began to understand – she had made terrible mistakes.

Nioanen had been right, not that she would ever admit it.

"You think they will find support with the mortals?" Kluehnn's voice was thick with amusement. "Walk ahead with me, Lithuas."

She obeyed, even though each move he made filled her with a strange sort of dread. She'd gotten used to obeying. These gods she'd gathered, who she'd convinced to take up Kluehnn's cause? That was just the thing – it was *his* cause, and that was who they followed.

When they were out of earshot of the rest of the army, he spoke again. "Not all the mortals above relish cutting the Numinars, using their magic. Some of them never see the results of that magic. Some of them only suffer the consequences. Suffering is a weakness, you see. Those who are suffering are looking for someone to blame. Right now, they blame those who are doing the cutting. But how easy would it be to turn that blame on the gods? They prayed and the gods never helped them."

She remembered the mortal who'd traveled all the way to Unterra. He'd been desperate, half delirious, asking the gods to grant him a boon. He needed them to fix the surface world.

Of course, that had been right before they'd all made the blood pact. They could not continue to sacrifice for a world above that thought nothing of the intertwined relationship between the surface world and the one below. If the gods let the knowledge of the seeds die, let them become merely strange and powerful stones, they effectively cut the mortals off.

An imperfect plan, she saw now.

They'd turned the mortal away. There was nothing they could do without breaking the pact. The mortals had made terrible mistakes and the gods could not fix them. She wondered now – what if they'd tried? Bah, they'd be caught in the same cycle they'd once all been trapped in. Nothing would get better.

Yet by initiating this change, everything had become stagnant.

"Is that truly the responsibility of the gods?" Lithuas ventured.

The eye on his cheek moved independently of the other two, rolling around to look at her. It blinked. "Is that what you believe? That the gods held no responsibility to the mortals?"

She could feel herself changing. It was easier to yield to him. She gritted her teeth. "We hold responsibility to one another. We may live above and below but we all exist in the same place."

All three of his eyes lifted to the stalactites overhead; he gave a small, annoyed shake of his head. "This won't help anyone. Once we reach the surface, go to the mortals in disguise. Whisper in their ears. Tell them the gods have come to take their lands. Tell them that we have followed to stop them, that we need their help."

"That won't be enough."

Kluehnn shrugged. "That's not all I'm asking you to do."

She waited for the rest of his plan, a sick feeling in her stomach, knowing that she would help him execute it. If she killed Kluehnn, his followers would kill her. She wasn't Nioanen, who found purpose in protecting others. Once she was dead, then what? They'd continue on this mad quest.

"I spoke with Barexi before he turned against me. It's so easy to get someone like him to talk if they think you're interested in every gritty detail. I asked him about manipulating time."

"It's difficult, and not something the gods have done often." She knew whatever words she said wouldn't dissuade him; he was simply explaining things, yet she couldn't stop herself from the feeble attempt.

Kluehnn tapped a clawed finger to his chin. "Yes, but what caught my curiosity was that the stories always speak of the gods sending mortals back in time, undoing injuries, making them younger, making them forget. Why do they not send objects back in time?"

Lithuas shrugged. "It's never been quite as useful. Sending something non-living back in time doesn't change its current properties."

"And that's exactly what Barexi told me. But look at you all, stagnating, so few fresh minds among you. I'm younger, I can see possibilities you cannot. The immutability of objects is an *opportunity*, not an impediment."

He waited, and she knew he wanted her to ask – what did he want her to do? But she had some pride left. She wouldn't play the part of a sycophant so wholeheartedly. And the younger gods were always more impatient. She pressed her lips together, determined to wait him out. When he finally spoke again, without her prompting, her triumph was short-lived.

"Bring me back books. Steal them from libraries, from the homes of the nobility. We will not simply whisper into their ears. We will whisper into their minds."

Her scoff was part derision, part surprise. "You cannot possibly change all the books."

His gaze settled over her shoulder, to where his army rested, ready to advance and to drive their brethren to the surface. "I don't have to. Spin me a pretty enough tale, and there will be plenty of mortals who want to believe the gods are solely to blame for the mess of the surface world. Who wishes to believe their own people are at fault? The purpose is not to obliterate all mention of the truth. I give them two different truths, and they will choose the one they find more comfortable. All I must do, my dear Lithuas, Bringer of Change, is to sow doubt.

"And that will bring me the rest of my army."

49
Hakara

11 years after the restoration of Kashan and 572 years after the Shattering

The Sanguine Sea

Sailors from both Pizgonia and Langzu claim there is a monster lurking inside the barrier near the anchor, and it is this monster that sometimes ransacks the goods. Both the council of Pizgonia and the clans of Langzu are skeptical of this claim and strongly believe that any ransacking is done either by the sailors themselves or by pirates.

I hated every moment of our leaving, though we made it quick. This whole trip felt like it had been an enormous waste of time. I found myself focusing my anger on the continent itself, furious that they had food and water and fewer godkillers on their lands. They'd found ways to thrive in this desperate environment, and from the contented looks on many of the faces I encountered, they thought of restoration as a distant thing, something that might happen in the far future.

Velenor pointed out sights to me as we passed through the city to the docks. The gardens, where water was carried by aqueduct to the green plants, a place everyone was permitted to enjoy. The towers of the palace, where council members – one elderly person and one young adult from each province – met quarterly to make realm-wide decisions. Pizgonia considered the wisdom of their elders to be as crucial as the fire of their youth, she explained to me.

"And what of the people in between?" Alifra asked without receiving an answer.

Velenor swept a hand inland, to where she said conical buildings stood in the desert, collecting water in the chill mornings of winter, where it turned to ice and stayed cold into spring and sometimes summer. She spoke of all these things with pride, this place she'd come to think of as home.

And Dashu, Alifra, and I? We had no place like that. My gaze had slid to Thassir and Talie. Then again, I supposed they didn't either.

Falin hadn't been exactly happy to see us again, though he was eager to be on his way back to Langzu, burdened with goods enterprising merchants had loaded onto his ship with a promise of some of the profits. He spent most of his time in his cabin, probably counting out his future earnings. From his mutterings about altered folk, filters, and the barrier, he had bigger dreams than I'd expected from someone who'd named their boat *The Birdeater*.

The way back through proved not to be quite as difficult as our first crossing. We'd secured a sheep carcass to serve up to the monster in between, and it left us well alone. Not that it was easy. We ended up back on Langzu's side so drenched and exhausted we couldn't speak.

Or maybe none of us wanted to. I was avoiding Thassir as much as Dashu and Alifra were avoiding one another. Dashu had taken to sleeping on the deck, as had Thassir. I wondered if Alifra also lay in her hammock at night staring at the ceiling, unsure whether I was awake. The ocean stretched out before us, other ships near us moving to and from the anchor, Xiazen on the horizon.

And here I was, trying to stave off my thoughts. The Sanguine Sea only made me think of Rasha even more, so I'd holed up in the cabin with a set of cards I'd found in a sailor's hammock, laying them out on the floor in front of me, playing for both myself and an imaginary opponent.

Dashu and Alifra were on the deck somewhere, probably studiously avoiding looking at one another. And Talie had turned back into a cat. She slipped through the spaces of the ship, content with the silence. Falin seemed as eager to be rid of us as we were to get back to land.

The door to the cabin creaked open.

Thassir took up the entire space, his wings obscuring the hall beyond. I'd thrown open the shutters, and the smell of sea spray filled the room, the wind ruffling my hair.

"May I join you?"

"No."

He entered and closed the door behind him anyways. Seemed he was taking a page from my book. I could practically *feel* his mopey gaze on the top of my head.

"Stop looking at me like that."

"Like what?"

"Like I'm a ghost, and not the kind you're frightened of. The kind you miss." I felt my throat closing up, and continued in spite of my misgivings. "The kind you wish was still alive." The breath I took felt as filled with relief as the ones after I'd used the god gems. I'd said my piece. Now it was his turn.

He sat down across from me, folding his legs and wings. Still took up too much damn space. I shifted away a little, to avoid the brush of a feather against my shoulder.

"I wish you could tell me exactly what's going on."

He let out a sigh that smelled of sweetness and musk. "I wish I could too. I hope you figure it out, even as I hope that you don't."

He lifted the hand I'd laid out and began to play.

I gestured at the cards. "I already know what cards you hold."

He shrugged. "I don't care."

We played a few rounds, all of which I easily won, my mind only half on the cards, the painted figures, the feel of the lacquered surfaces beneath my fingers. "You said you had a family. That you had a son."

To my surprise, he didn't stand up and leave, he didn't shout – he didn't do anything except lay down his next card. "Yes. Irael was... he was special to me. It took me a long time – too long – to see he'd been there all along, through centuries, waiting for me to see the same things he did. That together, we were happy." He said nothing as I played another card to defeat his. He drew a card from the stack, grunted. "And then, when I finally understood, when I finally *saw* him, we had so little time. Kluehnn had driven us from our home. We were on the surface. We tried to make a life out of it still. We nearly succeeded."

I felt as though I shouldn't move, afraid that if I did, I would break whatever spell this was that let him speak to me so freely.

"In the end, Kluehnn shattered the world into realms, he restored the first one, and he sent his godkillers after us. They took Rumenesca first. Then they took Irael. And they took our son. I failed Irael so many times in the years I knew him – by never quite seeing him the way he saw me. When the godkillers came to our home, I thought I could protect my family. I was strong enough, but it didn't matter. In the end, I made a mistake, and they took them both."

The next card he laid down beat mine, and I drew another. "It's not your fault. You can't wallow in it forever."

He lifted an eyebrow, a strange amount of levity in this moment. "Can't I? I *am* a god."

"I should never try to forbid you from healthy actions, lest you refuse them out of your own stubbornness."

"Not unlike yourself. And your sister? Do you never wallow in that?"

"It wasn't my fault. I'm at peace with it."

"Are you?" He moved a card to the end of his hand, considered, and laid it on the floor. "You bonded her. That suggests there is something there you cannot let go of. You say your parents died, that you took care of her. I have been a parent. Even when my son was alive, I had ... regrets. Many of them." His eyelashes fluttered, limned with silver by the window's light. "You have none?"

His words speared some deep and secret part of me, a part I'd been trying to push away. I'd already dealt with the truth, the fact that I'd had a chance to turn back in the barrier to try to reunite with Rasha. Yet I found, when he spoke, when I was forced to stillness, there were still sad and unpleasant parts of me lurking just beneath the surface. I began to toss a card onto the stack, but Thassir grabbed my wrist. "No. You didn't even look at it."

Did he feel the beat of my pulse beneath his palm? I tried to pull away, half-heartedly. "What does it matter? It's just a game."

"I want better for you, Hakara." The edge of his wing brushed my bare arm, the soft pressure of feather against skin.

I shivered but didn't draw back. "If only I could want that for myself." I tried to say it lightly, but the words fell like stones from my mouth. If I wanted something better for myself, I wouldn't be placing my other hand on top of his, brushing a thumb over his knuckles, caught between prying his fingers from my wrist and letting them stay. Slowly, I lifted his hand to the level of my eyes, studying the veins beneath the surface of his skin, the hairs lifted all along his arm. I listened for the sound of his breath in this small space and heard nothing except the stirring of the sea and the thundering of my own heart. He was waiting. I wasn't sure – didn't think I could ever be sure – but I felt carried along, magnetized, pulled to an inevitable conclusion as I pressed my lips to the back of his hand.

A sharp intake of breath, and then he huffed out a strangled, impatient sound. It stirred a heat within me that had nothing to do with the corestone.

I dropped the card, tugged him toward me. This was a stupid, terrible thing to do. There wasn't a world where we made any sense – an elder god and a mortal, both filled to the brim with stubborn, vicious thoughts. But then his arms tightened around me, the cards scattering beneath our knees. His wings circled us, enclosing us in a private space where everything felt suddenly as though it might work, the outside world shut away.

I wasn't sure how to move on from this moment, how things might change, how they already had. Every move I made seemed weighted with too much meaning. We'd kissed once before, but I'd been dying then, half out of my mind. This felt so different, so strange. I tilted my head back, daring to press my lips to the base of his throat, wanting to sink into his warmth.

One of his hands lifted, his claws tangling in my loose hair. His mouth found my forehead, breath stirring the hairs on the top of my head. His chest rumbled as he spoke. "We don't have to do anything more than this."

In answer, I reached behind his broad back, undoing the cloth-knot buttons of his shirt, letting my cheek rest against his chest, marking the rhythm of his heart. I slipped my fingers beneath, sliding the shirt from his shoulders, hearing it pool on the floor behind him. He kissed a fiery line down my neck, pulling loose the ties at the front of my tunic. I couldn't look at him, not directly. It was too much like looking at the sun. Skin met skin, and I was trailing my fingers across his collarbone, letting my tongue follow in their wake. He tasted like salt and faintly of berries warmed by the sun. My other hand clenched, nails lightly scratching his lower back as I pulled him closer. He let out a low moan and my breathing quickened.

The longer I stayed here, pressed against him, the more I felt things shift between us. There was him, and there was me, and this thing between us unfurling new and tender leaves.

I froze.

Like a plant. A tree. Between the relief I'd seen on the wall and the power I'd accessed when I'd fought the godkillers, I'd just assumed the corestone was a greater form of god gem. Some rare, strange crystal that contained even more magic.

But perhaps that wasn't all it was. I remembered Utricht teaching me about the god gems, referring to them as something like seeds. Maybe they weren't actually seeds. But maybe corestones were.

"The corestone isn't a stone. It's a seed."

Thassir's nose nudged at my hairline, an infinitesimal gesture. He couldn't confirm or deny what I'd said, but I felt him waiting, his wings tightening around us.

"The Numinars are gone, but there are still seeds. The seeds grant someone great power when combined with aether." I stopped. "But you don't want me to use it."

His hands settled gently at my waist, stroking the skin over my hips, making it hard for me to think. If he didn't want me to use it, then it was harming me in some way.

"Velenor said I should have been dead. You've done something to help protect me from it, but that was all you could do – help."

The burning sensation. "It gives me power, but it takes, too. If I keep using it, I'll die."

The softness of lips against the shell of my ear. "Do you understand why I can't bear to look at you? You *will* keep using it. You've never taken the time to stop, to think about who you are and what you want. The pain you keep putting aside – it's a part of you."

No. Pain wasn't a personality trait. It was a feeling. "I can shut it out, I can separate it away." The warmth of a kiss at my ear lobe. I found myself sinking deeper into his embrace, desperately wanting. "You say I put aside my pain, but I can't be like you. You live in your grief every day, you let it consume you. And if you can't see a way past it, to finally stand up and put everything on the line, then what use are you to me?"

He pulled away, and I couldn't avoid his gaze, the pain and the desire here in the shadow of his wings. Without thinking, I tilted my chin up. He kissed me softly, hesitantly. The gentle press of his lips was enough to undo me. I wound my fingers into his hair, wanting to bring him closer again, feeling the muscles of his shoulders shift as he tensed. He gritted his teeth, his expression a grimace. "Is that all I am? A thing to be useful?"

I swallowed, wishing more than anything for the heat of his mouth against mine again, to take my words away. I could say that was all he was, and we would both know it wasn't true. But it would still hurt him, would force us apart. I needed that space. I thought he did too. We had too much to do, too many places we needed to go. Instead of speaking, for once in my life I paused, thinking, trying to find words that were true. I pressed my forehead to his, wishing I could convey my thoughts and feelings with a touch. "Everything you did, everything you didn't do – it's led us here. What do you think the future should be? I don't know what your hopes are. They can't center around me. I'm mortal. Whatever this thing is that we have, it's going to end. It's pointless. There has to be more. I can't be your anchor to this world." The way I'd once made Rasha my anchor, the only thing that mattered.

His hands tightened once, then let go. His wings settled at his back, leaving me feeling cold and exposed. "Is that it, then? Are you ... rejecting me?"

Gods below, why did he have to sound so sad? I didn't know. There was so much more to figure out than this.

A clash from above. A panicked shout. Alifra's voice. "Hakara! Attack!"

50

Rasha

11 years after the restoration of Kashan
and 572 years after the Shattering

Langzu - Kluehnn's den northeast of Bian

In quiet corners of the world, in basements, in cellars, in secret places in the woods, people still light candles for Irael, for Nioanen, for Rumenesca. They still believe the elder gods are alive somehow and are convinced this dangerous worship brings them good fortune.
What a beautiful delusion.

The early-morning air was cold; rain had fallen across the mountains in the night. It made the latrine ditch below me smell terrible. I opened my hand, the blue chalk in my palm. I couldn't keep denying the truth, and the truth was that Kluehnn had lied to me, and was continuing to lie to me. Naatar thought that whatever Kluehnn did, he had good reasons behind it all.

I wasn't so sure.

If the crow spoke on behalf of a significant group of gods, and they were all willing to return to Unterra, then that meant peace was possible. For whatever reason, Kluehnn wasn't interested in pursuing it.

The lives of my cohort hung in the balance. If I marked the rock, if I let the gods know that Kluehnn's aspect would be leaving, that godkillers would be leaving, and the den was vulnerable, they would launch their raid. They would do whatever it was the crow had said would make Kluehnn think twice about war. It would mean fewer gods for Khatuya and Naatar to face. It meant that maybe, Kluehnn would listen to me.

I marked the largest rock, quickly, and then tossed the chalk onto the ground.

If it rained again before they found it, then it was just fate, doing what was right. I'd done my part. I'd made my decision.

The letter Mull had given me still weighed in my pocket. I'd thought myself inured against any further hurt from Sheuan. She'd left me – what more could she do? Yet knowing she was *married* now dug sharp fingernails into my cracked heart and peeled pieces of it away. Somehow it made sense, her marrying the Sovereign.

I wondered if she loved him, if she'd known this was what she was going to do before she'd left Kashan. But she'd asked me to go with her. Surely that had meant something to her, the way it had to me. Or maybe this was something she always did, the way some people gathered lost pups.

I hoped I would see her, I hoped I wouldn't. Either way, I felt I'd be disappointed.

Everyone was finishing preparations to leave by the time I made it back to the road leading away from the den. A covered cart took up most of the road, probably confiscated from a nearby farm. Two oxen were hooked to the front of it, their eyes rolling as their noses lifted into the air. Three cohorts of godkillers surrounded the cart and the oxen, and the animals could smell them. We weren't mortal, and neither was Kluehnn.

I hesitated at the edge of the group, as servants loaded supplies onto the back of the wagon, unsure of my place.

A pale hand emerged from inside the wagon, one eye peering out. A finger crooked. "Ride with me, Rasha."

I obeyed, though I couldn't help the dread clinging to my spine. The interior of the wagon was a step up, the dark cloth stretched over the top letting in only a small amount of light. Kluehnn's aspect swiped a tongue over its teeth, a coordinated movement by both mouths, as though it had just finished eating.

"It's a long journey. You don't need the crutch anymore, but you should rest your leg a little. When we return, I want you to be ready to fight."

I bowed my head and sat, wondering if I'd be able to lift my gaze this entire trip, or if I'd have to instead memorize the whorls and knots in the wood. I'd rather be out walking with the other godkillers. Strange – back when we'd been in Kashan, I would have leapt at the opportunity to spend so much time with an aspect of Kluehnn. I'd have thought it an honor. Now, though, all I could think about were the small betrayals I'd committed, the lies I'd once believed as truth.

He was sending Khatuya and Naatar to fight without me, for the second time. If I deserved his ire, then I would take my punishment. But it felt unfair to punish them for what I'd done.

The way he was punishing the living gods for the sins of their ancestors?

"You seem troubled."

Now I was glad of my gaze on the floor. "I'm just thinking about my cohort." That much, at least, was the truth.

"Recite the precepts to me, child." The wagon creaked, the wheels beginning to roll. "You will feel better."

I didn't.

He let me walk next to the wagon occasionally, when I begged to stretch my legs. But mostly he wanted me inside with him – day after long and wretched day, as the mountains turned to golden foothills and then to flat plains. He watched me eat my meals, his five eyes flicking at me and then away as I tried to be surreptitiously quick about shoveling rice into my mouth. The aspect did not eat and I dared not ask him why.

I slept inside the wagon, lying awake late into the night, listening to the sound of Kluehnn's breathing, always aware of where he laid his barbed tail.

It took sixteen days to reach Bian, even at a quick pace. The aspect had taken to sleeping most of the day and night toward the end of our trip, as though it had tipped into hibernation, conserving its energy and strength. I sat inside, feeling mostly alone, my mind wandering, tracing back everything I knew and thought I knew.

The archive. The books. The pages cut free, the bindings taken apart. The room with the yellow gems where the books came to rest. The gods had made a pact. I didn't know what it all meant. I wished I'd been able to stay at the den, to question Mull when he'd felt better.

By the time the buildings of Bian rose out of the cracked earth, I felt a little like someone had shaved away pieces of my mind into curling strips, scraps discarded on the side of the road.

Kluehnn's aspect stirred, one hoofed foot twitching. "You can get out. Tell them to go straight to the castle. The enforcers can take the cart to the stables. I want all my godkillers with me, including you, Rasha."

Grateful, I hopped off the back of the wagon, stretching my stiff leg and luxuriating in the feel of the sun against my face. It was late morning. They'd have to serve us lunch, and tea, and I tried to focus on that instead of my wayward, treacherous thoughts.

I'd never been to Bian. The outskirts melded into the surrounding grasslands, the buildings seeming to gradually grow in height and size until they stood in the shadow of the wall between the inner and outer city. The lower half of the plaster walls was coated in brown dust; a few broken shutters caught my eye. The cobbles here were rough and unsteady beneath my feet. The wagon rattled over the stones all the way up to the wall.

The gate was closed.

It took some pounding by one of the cohorts, and shouting that we'd come from Kluehnn's den, and did they not pay fealty to the one true god? But the doors finally opened, a retinue of wary-eyed enforcers giving us only the narrowest bit of space to pass into inner Bian before shutting the way again.

The difference between inner and outer Bian was stark. The cobbles became smooth, the buildings mostly free of dust. I spotted several estates, the gates to their courtyards stamped with the seals of the clans. One looked as though it had recently suffered a fire, half of the main building burned away, exposing the wooden struts beneath. Several other buildings bore broken shutters, the empty space covered with translucent paper. I frowned. An accident? Or a purposeful attack? It would explain the closed and guarded gate.

The castle rose above it all, rooftops layered one on top of the other.

Someone must have sent a runner ahead of us, because the enforcers stood at attention at the bottom of the ramp, one out in front, set to greet us. She wore a silver armband over her upper arm. All the enforcers bowed as we approached.

The wagon came to a halt, and the back half of it creaked as Kluehnn's aspect slipped from beneath the cloth.

It was no less terrifying by day, in the open city, than in the cloistered darkness of the cave. All eight of its limbs seemed to stretch as it stood to its full height, its eyes cast down upon the enforcers as though they were nothing but insects blocking its way. The filaments on its back writhed, each seeming to move of its own volition.

The enforcers fell before it, from simple bows to foreheads touching the ground.

The aspect's rasping voice took on two separate tones, both mouths speaking at once. "I am here to meet with the Sovereign. You will take our wagon to your stables and you will host us here in the castle. It has been too long since I have myself seen Langzu's great city of Bian."

Without waiting to see if they would obey, the aspect started the climb up the ramp, cloven hooves clipping the stones. I followed behind, aware of the enforcers scrambling, trying to figure out what they should do next. The two by the doors paled as we approached, one putting her hand on the great handle while the other only trembled.

So only one door had swung open by the time we reached it, the other enforcer gathering himself enough to seize the other one, pulling it wide while Kluehnn stood there waiting.

He stalked into the entrance hall.

There was no one there to greet us. Through a carved square arch, I could see the great hall. The glimpse of a dark chair caught the corner of my eye, figures I couldn't quite make out carved onto its surface, a red cushion its only adornment.

The aspect's bulk moved between me and the arch. The two cohorts spread behind me; I glanced to find them with their hands on their daggers. Kluehnn rose onto his four hind legs, pale flesh out of place in this castle of delicate, fine things. "I will meet with the Sovereign alone. Search the castle from top to bottom for any evidence of someone trying to subvert my will. Go."

That meant me as well. I hesitated a moment before sweeping past the aspect into the great hall, searching for a set of stairs.

Sheuan. She'd walked these halls, feet touching the same floorboards I now walked upon. She could be here, sharing the same space, the same air as me.

And if someone here was subverting Kluehnn's will, she was likely to know about it. If it wasn't her doing the subverting. It was one of the reasons we would never work, could never work. She was a politician, through and through, and nothing she'd done had disabused me of the notion that they thought primarily of themselves. For maybe a brief moment, when I'd inhaled her breath in that tent, when she'd twined her fingers in mine, we'd had an understanding. In that moment, we'd been one.

But time and distance had separated us. She would never understand me and I would never understand her, not truly.

I passed the chair, giving it a wide berth without knowing why. This close, I could see that the carved figures were the elder gods, one curved in and around the next. The glassy eyes of stuffed dead animals stared at me from the walls – some of which I recognized from restored Kashan.

The servants' stairs lay a little ways past the chair, concealed behind a wall lined with potted plants. I dared to cup the green leaves of one. In this hot and dry realm, the air smelling faintly of smoke, the beauty and lushness of restored Kashan felt so far away.

I passed two servants on my way up, both of whom flattened themselves against the wall to let me pass as soon as they saw my gray robes, whispering Kluehnn's precepts as they bowed their heads. I knew that at least one of the cohorts would head to the uppermost level, straight to the Sovereign's rooms, to search there. Sheuan would have separate quarters on the same floor as the guest rooms.

I opened doors as I passed them, peering quickly inside before moving to the next. The third room I opened greeted me with darkness, the shutters closed to keep out the heat. The scent of ginger, mingled with a faint floral smell. I knew that scent. Without meaning to, I inhaled deeply, living again in that moment when she'd kissed me in the tent, her hands firm but gentle.

What was more cruel? To betray someone you loved or to never love them at all?

What I'd felt for her wasn't love, it was the shadow of a dream I'd thought I could hold when the sun rose, only to find it slipping inevitably from my grasp. I left the door open behind me as I ransacked the place. Kluehnn hadn't told us to be gentle, or neat, or kind – and I knew his mind. If I left anything untouched, he'd fault me for it. So I stripped the bedspread, unbuttoned cushion covers, pulled out drawers. All I found were books and clothes, all of them smelling like *her*. My claws caught on the edges of cloth, scratching marks in fine wood.

How could all of this matter more to her? Just things. She'd spoken of her clan, of her family, yet she'd left them behind as well – all to marry the Sovereign.

I peered into the dresser, now emptied of drawers. Behind and below, in the hidden space, was a satchel. I stilled. If this were hidden, then it held secrets. Carefully, I pulled it free and sat on the edge of the bed, the blanket strewn at my feet.

I'd been angry when I'd turned over the room; now all that heat had fled, leaving me cold. Sheuan had known who and what I was, and I'd known who and what she was. I couldn't pretend otherwise, no matter how much I wanted to.

And now I potentially held her life in my hands.

I opened the satchel; I couldn't do anything otherwise. I had to see, had to *know*. A few clothes. I dug beneath them and felt something else. The edge of something rubbery. I pulled it free, lifting it to the light from the door.

A mask. Meant to be fitted over the nose and mouth.

No. A filter. Just like the one Mull had worn.

51
Sheuan

11 years after the restoration of Kashan
and 572 years after the Shattering

Langzu - inner Bian

Ayaz, the Cutter, often compared his interference with the mortal world to his favorite pastime of gardening; in particular, the pruning of trees. Some branches were dead, he said, and some hindered the overall growth of the tree. It was the justification he gave for murdering the wayward son of an Albanoran royal family, for manipulating a bureaucracy into doing away with half their regulations, and for stealing the funds meant to go toward building a bridge to a marshy isle in Pizgonia.

In all fairness, the murder of the royal son led to his younger sister taking the throne as an effective leader, the scrapping of the bureaucratic regulations led to unprecedented economic growth, and the failure of the bridge saved the nests of a rare bird that began a colony on the isle.

Ayaz always liked to say he did not cut without reason.

The castle was in an uproar when Sheuan returned, a hill of ants onto which someone had poured a glass of water. In spite of the recent riot, there were only two enforcers still at the foot of the ramp, their eyes wandering like flies let loose in an empty room.

"Tell me," Sheuan said without slowing to stop.

"Kluehnn," one of them had the presence of mind to gasp out.

That was all she needed to know. He was *here*. He'd not announced his presence, nor had anyone known he was coming. He must have traveled from the den, his aspect under some sort of cover. It wasn't unusual to see cohorts of godkillers moving throughout Langzu on the hunt, so no one had really taken notice.

She could hear more of the commotion when she reached the top of the ramp, the two doors into the castle still open, the enforcers guarding them milling about as though unsure what to do. Kluehnn was a threat, but they also owed him their allegiance, their faith. What an odd position they'd found themselves in.

But she didn't have time to empathize. "Close the doors," she snapped as she passed them. "You want the whole city to hear what's going on? And there's no point in letting all the cool air out. Don't make me do your thinking for you."

The doors shut behind her, the enforcers suitably chastened. One stood in the entrance hall, silver armband gleaming in the light that leaked through the shutters. She saw, through the arch behind him, a godkiller searching the great hall.

"The Sovereign is in his study," the enforcer whispered. "He needs to speak to you right away."

This was what she'd warned against, it had happened, and she still found herself caught by surprise. There wasn't any good way to prepare for a hostile visit from a god. She found the main stairs thankfully empty, and practically flew up them. The Sovereign's study was on the south side of the building, overlooking the dried-up lakebed.

She found him inside, pacing the length of the room. Someone had pulled nearly all the books from the shelves. He stepped on papers as he paced, swept onto the floor like layered snow. A shattered teacup lay by his desk, the gold enamel glinting in the sunlight.

He was afraid. She could see it in his tight shoulders, his clenched jaw, the quick rhythm of his steps. "They've taken over the cellar of the castle and they've set up residence there, I don't know for how long. The aspect wishes to meet with me." He straightened, regaining a small part of his dignity. "Perhaps you can go instead."

Was he really trying to send her in his place? When he was in residence at the castle now? "Sovereign" – she inclined her head – "would Kluehnn not think it an insult if the leader of Langzu sent his wife in his stead? I am high-ranking, but I am not you."

He licked his lips, and she saw the sweat beaded below his nose. "Of course. It must be me. Go. Make sure there are no filters to be found anywhere. I can't . . . I couldn't stop the god-killers from searching the premises."

How strange, to hear him admitting this powerlessness to her. For a brief moment, she wanted to reach out, to touch his face. He wouldn't like it. He'd find some way to make her pay for it later, once he'd found some equilibrium.

Assuming, of course, that they got out of this alive.

Sheuan went, her heartbeat pattering in her chest in spite of her best efforts at calm. Panicking never did anyone any good. She had a filter in her room, hidden well. Likely no one would find it, or if they did, they wouldn't understand what it meant. She had to hope for that.

The scar. Her mind turned to the note her father had left, so thin on any real details. The tablets, which only described the gods' countenances and their epithets. Barexi with his antlers and sleek brown fur, Nioanen with his golden wings, Ayaz with his scales and his tail, Velenor who glittered like stone beneath the light of the sun, Rumenesca with her pointed ears, claws, and fox-like coloring. Silver-haired Lithuas. Red-haired Irael.

What did the note mean? How did it meet with the clues she'd found beneath the warehouse – the blue gemstones and the altar still in use?

The wood creaked beneath her feet as she made her way through the hall, servants only glancing at her before continuing with their tasks. If that was what the Sovereign's study looked like, the rest of the castle was likely a shambles. They'd have their work cut out for them.

Sheuan's family was scattered, her husband ready to execute her when he found her more threatening than useful. So needy, was she? Always grasping, wanting attention. Wanting the warmth of a love that didn't pick and choose parts of her. She hadn't gotten that from her family, from her mother. So instead she'd sought power, to use her gifts for herself and see how high she could climb.

She had power now, but even the slim pieces of affection she'd had from her mother were gone. There was nothing left, not even crumbs – all she had was her position and the mystery of her father's execution. What had he realized right before he'd died, before he'd had the chance to tell anyone else? She could feel herself walking in his footsteps, unsure of where the ground grew thin, the place her father had fallen from without a rope to keep him safe.

They had to find a way to satisfy Kluehnn, to reassure him that the Sovereign was still loyal and acted only in good faith. That any rumors that had reached his ears were unfounded, the hopes of desperate people yearning for an end to this slow, terrible decline. She'd have to send servants to the clans the Sovereign had already doled out filters to, to remind them that if they spoke up, they'd receive no more, that Kluehnn would confiscate the ones they already had. And if Kluehnn didn't find any filters, he'd have no proof that the Sovereign was doing anything untoward.

A servant stood outside Sheuan's door, her face pale, her lip trembling. Not a hint of relief when she saw Sheuan, only a darting of her gaze to the inside of her room and then back to her mistress. The door was open.

Sheuan felt her blood run cold. They'd already ransacked her room, then. She hurried to the door, unsure of where she was placing her feet, her head a haze of fear.

Someone was sitting on the bed.

Rasha's face was narrower than when Sheuan had seen her last, the remnants of a healing scratch on her cheek. One of the curling horns atop her head was missing completely, the hair falling around a pink and shiny scar. Sheuan was so involved in studying her appearance that it took her a moment to see what the godkiller held in her hands.

The filter.

52
Rasha

11 years after the restoration of Kashan
and 572 years after the Shattering

Langzu - inner Bian, the Sovereign's castle

The first inventions created to extract magic from Numinar fires were small, simple, and horrifyingly inefficient. An oven was used to burn the branches, which first had to be cut into smaller pieces. This oven did not have a door (imagine how much magic was lost by this one omission alone!). Instead, a narrowing chimney with a rough ceiling caught some of the magic while the smoke escaped. The fire was quenched and the magic was subsequently captured in jars for later use.

From illustrations showing large-scale burning and black smoke, we know this process was later industrialized, the living branches burned, and the mortals stopped separating the smoke from the magic.

Sheuan.

"Shut the door," I told the servant. The woman obeyed, her hand shaking. My eyes adjusted to the dimmer light. In spite of myself, I drank in Sheuan's appearance like a woman who had been deprived of water. Her clothes were simple but finely wrought; her hair bound halfway up with a golden comb. I remembered the feel of it between my fingers, damp with her sweat.

"You're here," she said, still frozen by the door.

"And you never expected to see me again." I'd examined this thought in the quiet of night, when I remembered the way her body had fitted against mine. At those times, I'd only felt sad, slightly wistful. But now the words, spoken, left my mouth with the heat of the forge. My faith might have been shaken, one of my horns eaten away, but I had yielded to each challenge and remained, somehow, unbroken.

"Don't say that like you're angry with me." There was something plaintive in her voice, and I could see, the way I had in the tent – the vulnerability beneath the grasping, that desperation for connection she couldn't quite acknowledge, that she did her best to always turn aside.

"How am I supposed to feel? Happy? Relieved?"

She lifted a hand and then let it fall back at her side. "Don't think I'm not glad to see you again."

"What else am I supposed to think? You left me without a second thought. I told you everything I'd been through. I admitted it to you, someone I'd known for a few short days, when there are so many others I haven't told. And you still left, knowing how I would feel." It felt good, to vent these feelings as they swam up from beneath some buried rock.

She ground the ball of one foot into the floor, her fingers curling into fists. "What was I supposed to do? There was no great happiness in store from us that I turned aside. You could not leave your den and I could not leave Langzu."

I still remembered the acute pain of her leaving, though I'd known that was how our brief encounter would end. "You could have cared. You could have turned around. You could have said you were sorry."

"I was hurting too!"

I gave her a long look. We both knew she could close that pain away, lock it into a box. She was older than me, she was more experienced, she'd broken hearts before and had no regrets. "Well. Here you are. Where you wanted to be. Was it worth it?"

"Rasha..." Her voice was a whisper. She moved closer, as though pulled against her will.

I gestured to the room, to the castle surrounding us. She'd gotten everything she'd wanted. And what did I have except my doubts? Except a certainty that whatever happened between me and Kluehnn and my sister and the crow, it would all end badly. "You're married to the Sovereign. People respect you now. You're not beholden to your family or your clan anymore. You're in a place you can maneuver things to your will."

She dared another step closer. "I never deserved you."

I let out a soft snort. "That's not why you left the way you did. In the end, you thought you deserved everything."

"It's not that I thought I deserved everything – I thought I deserved *something*."

"At whose expense?"

She closed her eyes and took a deep, shuddering breath. Her hands found one another, fingers twisting together, her gaze flicking to the wall. "Maybe there is truth in what my mother said to me. I need too much, so I took. But you aren't my mother, you never owed me anything. I took and I didn't think about what I was leaving behind. Not really." Her gaze found mine. My stomach flipped. "I am so deeply sorry."

The heat in my chest cooled, though I stirred fruitlessly at the embers, lingering on the image of her proud back as she'd walked away. How could she so easily find the gentleness in me? It didn't feel fair. I held up the filter. "How do I know you aren't just saying these things because of what I've found? I'm not as naïve as I once was. I know this is what Kluehnn has come to find."

Sheuan let out a breath. "You don't. You have to trust me."

"I've tried that once already."

She must have moved a step or two when I'd not noticed, because she stood over me, so close I could smell the scent lingering on her skin. I found myself craning my neck to meet her eyes, two dark pools that threatened to drown me if I let them. Her jaw moved as though she wanted to say something, her lips parted, ever so slightly.

I knew that she was considering closing the distance between us. She wouldn't have been Sheuan if she hadn't noticed the way I leaned toward her, the quickness of my breath. There was safety for her in this, in the control she'd always hold over me. I couldn't bring myself to reject her fully, because some sad, stupid part of me still hoped she would change, that she'd want me more than she wanted everything else. Yet I also knew that even if she did choose me, I wasn't in a place to be chosen. I was still in the den, and I'd tangled myself up with Mull, with the gods, with secrets I didn't know how to process.

A different kind of heat flooded through my body as I thought about the touch of her hands, her lips. We were alone – who would have to know? Maybe it wouldn't kill me this time, to part with her. Maybe I would be the one to turn away and not look back.

No. That could never be me. Yet I decided I didn't care. If pain was the price, so be it. I would let her inflict pain.

And then she lifted her hands and took a deliberate step back, without even looking at the filter. Her gaze was locked on mine. "This isn't how I want to treat you. Not anymore. Maybe, finally, my luck has run out. I have to be at peace with it, if it means I can finally start putting things right between us."

She looked so utterly broken in that moment. I'd thought myself the weak one when we'd first met, but she'd gotten everything she'd thought she'd wanted and it had shattered her. "What would we be putting right between us?" I could barely breathe past the ache in my chest. "Is there anything there at all? Can there *be* anything?"

"No." It was the flatness of her tone, the way she tried so hard to pretend this didn't matter to her, when I could tell how deeply it did.

I surged to my feet. The touch of her hair beneath my fingers felt as ephemeral as a morning mist. Without another thought, I pressed my lips to hers, our bodies aligning, my other arm, the filter still in my grasp, snaking around her waist. It was different from when we'd kissed in the tent; it was the same. I'd made that choice without knowing the full consequences. I made this choice knowing that this moment might be all we had.

She pulled back, the warmth and softness of her body leaving me. Her fingers touched my cheek where Mull had scratched me. "I don't deserve this."

"No," I agreed, turning my face into her palm, pressing my lips to the inside of her wrist. "You don't." I wrapped a hand around her wrist, pulling her into me. She let out a soft little moan. I stopped it with a kiss. And then another. I couldn't seem to stop. If this was all I would get, then I would take my fill of it.

Her hands found my face, one pressing at the back of my neck, the other rising into my hair, fingernails light against my scalp. She stopped as her fingertips brushed the scar. "Does it hurt?" She was breathless, her heartbeat a steady thump against mine.

I shook my head. "Only a little."

Something changed in her face, her expression suddenly thoughtful.

I let go of her, bringing my hand and the filter between us. "Take it. Hide it."

Someone else might have taken a moment to consider, to ask if I was sure. But Sheuan merely slipped the filter back into the satchel.

There was something else I was supposed to do. The letter. Of course. I'd completely forgotten about it. I dug into my pocket, pulling it out. "And here. Mull wanted me to give this to you."

She tucked it into the satchel on top of the filter. "Mull? You saw him? Is he well?"

I hesitated, unsure of what to tell her. "He's whole and hale." I took her hands, kissed her gently, thinking of what I should say – that her cousin was now altered? She seized me by the front of my robes, deepening the kiss until all thoughts of Mull fled.

The door creaked open.

53
Sheuan

11 years after the restoration of Kashan
and 572 years after the Shattering

Langzu - inner Bian

In Montiyano, before and during the existence of the Aqqilan Empire, they played a game called obelisks, which consisted of a heavy stone board and carved stone pieces. While there are no lasting descriptions of how the game itself was played, there are two recorded instances of someone using this stone board to bludgeon someone else to death.

She should have been more cautious. She should have locked the door behind her. Not that it would have mattered, but the turning of key in lock might have given them a moment to pull apart, to look as though they didn't know one another.

Instead, the Sovereign entered the room to see Sheuan still in Rasha's embrace.

He lifted a brow, the door open behind him, as they extricated themselves, fingers suddenly tangling in clothes, catching in hair.

"This isn't what it seems," Rasha began. Ah, Rasha. She should have left things to Sheuan. The rosiness of her cheeks spoke the truth louder than any words could have.

Sheuan stepped firmly in front of the godkiller, letting her hand trail on the woman's arm. This was her problem, the issue *she* had created. "I only wanted to know if godkillers were as skilled in other areas as they are at fighting. She obliged my curiosity."

What she was saying didn't fool the Sovereign one bit. Something about him was different. She couldn't quite put her finger on it until her eyes adjusted to the brightness of the sunlight from the hall. His hair. Had it been this way when she'd seen him downstairs, or had he managed to color it in the moments they'd been apart? It was dark now, the silver gone.

It made him look different, and so much younger. There was a strange uncanniness to his appearance, one that made her feel ill at ease. She couldn't quite understand why. People in the inner city often dyed their hair to look younger.

Why would he have made this a priority, with the riots, and Kluehnn here in their very castle?

"So," he said, and Sheuan's analytical thoughts fled, "you, a married woman, thought nothing of kissing someone else? Is that what you think of our marriage? Is it just a sham to you?"

"No, of course not." Sheuan lowered her gaze, wishing she could take another step away from Rasha without making it conspicuous.

A tinge of amusement colored his voice. "Should I then question, if you *are* pregnant, whether the child is mine?"

She felt the sharpness of Rasha's gaze against her cheek. What? Was she not supposed to sleep with him? They were married, after all. Yet it still felt somehow uncouth to mention this in front of her.

Gods below, what a mess she'd made. Of everything.

"Or perhaps I should berate Kluehnn for bringing such an element into my home – one that would tempt my wife away from my side."

Sheuan risked a glance at Rasha's horrified face. It would not go well for her. "No." She lifted her chin. "If there is any fault, it is with me."

"So noble," the Sovereign said, sounding slightly bored. Sheuan could tell from the way his gaze wandered, from the bed to the wall to the shutters, that he wasn't truly invested in this conversation. He just couldn't help himself, could he?

The sound of footsteps emanated from the hall. The Sovereign glanced out the door. His entire demeanor changed in an instant – from lazy annoyance to attentive fear. He gave way as they approached, shrinking to stand inside the darkness of the room.

Kluehnn's aspect filled the doorway, and Sheuan's mouth went dry. She couldn't even imagine the softness of Rasha's lips – and she could generally conjure up a number of imaginings at a moment's notice, no matter the situation, a skill that was endlessly useful when she had to pretend at so many different facades.

All she could do was stare at the creature before her: flesh pale as the burgeoning moon, multiple legs lining a caterpillar-like torso, the face at the pinnacle a distorted mockery of a human's, the mouth too wide, the teeth too sharp. Another mouth lay beneath the face, just below the collarbone. Stomach-churning filaments rippled in rows along the aspect's back, a millipede turned onto its back. Four arms and four legs moved at its sides, the bottom four ending in cloven hooves. It took her more than a moment to even *see* the cohort of godkillers behind it.

"Rasha," the aspect rasped out, "did you find anything?"

"No."

Sheuan might have believed her had she not taken the filter from Rasha's own hand and hidden it back inside her satchel. She was impressed, in spite of herself.

Kluehnn turned to face the Sovereign. Every single muscle in the man's body tensed. He bowed, quickly, his face turned toward the floor, and did not rise. It was the most humble Sheuan had ever seen him.

"I will be sending godkillers to be permanently stationed here. The nave in the cellar has been in disuse for too long. When they return, they will stay, and I will modify the lower level to my liking so there is a proper nave here in Bian."

"Yes, Kluehnn." The Sovereign didn't so much as lift his gaze. "As it pleases you. Let us provide you with food and drink before your long journey back to the den."

"Bring it to the lower level. Rasha. With me."

The aspect left, its multiple feet clicking against the wood, one after another, all the godkillers following in its wake. It wasn't until the sound of footsteps had faded that the Sovereign lifted his head. He glanced down the hall, his lips pale. "We will speak of your transgressions later," he said, without looking at Sheuan. "As soon as they're gone, go to the workshop. Make sure all the extra filters are hidden. And make more of them, as quickly as you can."

Sheuan was afraid of Kluehnn, of his aspect, but something about the way the Sovereign reacted to him told her that his own fear ran deeper. Why? Did it have something to do with the altar, with the tablets her father had been studying before he died?

"Wait," she called out, before he could leave. "If Kluehnn places godkillers here in the palace, and restoration hasn't yet occurred, you will be caught. *We* will be caught."

He looked at her then. "Then I will have to ensure restoration occurs soon, wife." His mouth twisted on the last word, and then he was gone and Sheuan was alone.

She locked the door this time, opening one of the shutters to let in some light, though the sun was hot against her skin. She put the satchel back in its hiding place, drew out Mull's letter, and replaced the drawers.

Cousin, a great many terrible things have happened to me, but I am still alive and well. I cannot waste time or parchment on those things. What matters is this: the gods have organized and are forming an army to stand against Kluehnn. And I found Tolemne's Tomb. I am still making sense of it. But a carving says some of the elder gods may still be alive.

Yes, Sheuan knew Lithuas was still alive, and working with Kluehnn. So that was a pointless dead-end. But he'd said "some" not "one". There was something frenzied about the writing, as though it had been done under duress or illness. So unlike the neat and steady handwriting she was used to seeing from Mull. She felt like she was seeing a puzzle half put-together, unsure of what the overall picture was, only the shape of it.

If that's true, then they could help lead the gods against Kluehnn. If you can find them.

54
Hakara

11 years after the restoration of Kashan
and 572 years after the Shattering

The Sanguine Sea

Pizgonia was once ruled by a council of elders, one from each province. But year after year, the youth of the realm complained that their elders moved too slowly, were less invested in the future, did not have an understanding of the problems the new generation faced, and were too stuck in old ways to see clearly. One account, from an irritated elder, says they all just got tired of the complaining and changed their governance (one cannot be sure if this was written in jest or seriousness). Today, the council consists of one elder and one youth between the ages of twenty and thirty-five from each province. It's far from a perfect system, but it has held for over a hundred years.

Thassir and I darted for the stairs, him bare-chested, me desperately tying my shirt closed again. I got there first, his wings a hindrance in the enclosed space. As soon as I stepped into the light of day, someone knocked me over. We both fell to the deck.

For a moment, all I could feel was an intense confusion. I recognized Dashu's face – his sharp cheekbones, his goatee, his dark brown eyes. I lifted my hands instinctively, though I wasn't sure why. And then I saw the glint of a knife in his hands. His mouth stretched into a grin.

I grabbed for his wrist and found his strength greater than mine, the blade lowering toward my belly. Toward where the corestone lay.

Not Dashu. Lithuas.

Clawed hands seized her by the shoulders, tearing her away from me. She flowed into her natural form as she tumbled across the deck, rising in a smooth movement, her feet firm beneath her. I reached for the sword at my side and swore. I hadn't exactly been expecting to fight aboard *The Birdeater*, so I'd left it by my hammock. I pulled the godkilling knife free instead. I was better with the sword, but this was the sort of weapon I needed to put her down.

Thassir stood at my side, claws at the ready. I reached for my belt again. Right. Gems weren't there either. Well, we could manage without. Hopefully.

Alifra came hurtling toward Lithuas from my right. "What did you do with him?" she screamed, her knives drawn. "Where is he?"

She threw herself at the goddess with a ferocity I'd never seen from her before. Always, Alifra had hung back in our fights, acting with a cool head, strategically, picking off enemies or hassling them at just the right time. Now she fought like a raccoon caught in a trap. Her russet hair, tied back, bobbed as she moved, her blades flashing. Even Lithuas seemed taken aback.

Thassir and I strode forward together, moving toward and around the fight, judging best where to find an opening. We were without Dashu, and perhaps Thassir was diminished from his state as an elder god, but the three of us could still take her on, I was sure.

Lithuas shifted, two more arms sprouting from her ribs, both seizing extra blades from her belt and thigh. She seemed somehow able to hold all three of us off at once, backing toward the prow of the boat, putting the captain's cabin at her back. Where was Talie when we needed her? Probably snoring in a hammock – it *was* daytime after all. I was going to give her an earful if we got out of this.

I hammered at Lithuas's defenses, the glow of the violet gem drawing patterns in the air. Every blow I tried to land she turned aside. Even Thassir set his jaw, earning only a slash across his shoulder for his efforts.

"Tell me where he is!" Alifra darted in, thrusting a dagger through the upper part of one of the goddess's primary arms. Lithuas grunted but didn't relent, switching her sword into a single-handed grip. She could just shift again, give herself another arm.

The door of the captain's cabin opened with speed, slamming into Lithuas's back. Falin tumbled past, having put his whole weight into it. Lithuas lost her footing and I swept in under her guard, knocking one of her knives away. Thassir seized the arm holding the sword and I pivoted around her, holding the godkilling blade to her neck.

She went deathly still, her chest heaving. Her remaining hand opened, the knife clattering to the deck.

I nodded at our erstwhile captain. "Look at that, Falin. Who's not getting involved now? You've just clobbered one of the seven elder gods."

His face turned the color of a cloud at mid afternoon. "I don't want any part of this. Just didn't want her to come after me next."

I let the blade part Lithuas's skin, a shimmer of blood appearing at the wound. "She won't." Everything had happened so quickly. Now that we were at a standstill, I felt Dashu's absence keenly. When had Lithuas taken him? How long had she been aboard? "Tell me where Dashu is."

She let out a throaty laugh. "So you can kill me?"

I should have killed her. Shouldn't have stayed my hand, let this become any sort of standstill. Just the quick cleanness of her blood spilled on the deck. We'd find Dashu. We had to. And this was more important than one man's life.

I leaned my mouth close to Lithuas's ear. "Bringer of Change, they called you. Is that why you joined with Kluehnn?"

She wriggled a little in my grasp, but found it firm. Thassir dug his claws into her wrist.

"Lithuas," he said. "I know what you told me, all those hundreds of years ago, before the Shattering, before you and Kluehnn drove us from our home. You believed in what he said. That the crimes of the mortals deserved punishment. That our crimes deserved punishment. Have we all not suffered enough? You changed during your years with Kluehnn. Is it not time to change again?"

"Change? Like you? Is that what you wish? For me to weaken myself? Look at you, Nioanen. What in all the realms have you become? I *let* you live and this is how you repay me? You wish to kill me now, when you have the advantage and not me? Fine. Do it."

I clenched my jaw. "He's not the one holding the knife."

"What a pathetic way to die," Lithuas said beneath her breath.

"At a mortal's hand." No matter what had happened in the interim, no matter what the gods had suffered, she still hated us. Was this all that existed in some of the gods? Hate for the mortals? But what did I have in return? I certainly hadn't thought highly of them, even if my thoughts toward them weren't as poisoned as Dashu's. What would happen when we returned to Langzu? What if the gods followed Thassir and they defeated Kluehnn? Could he hold them back from wanting to kill the mortals who'd spent hundreds of years hating them and turning them over to the godkillers?

Thassir made no attempt to stop me. He would let me kill her, if I deemed it necessary. It was what we'd crossed the barrier to do. What we'd fought for. My gaze found Alifra's, and the terror in her eyes was enough to stay my hand.

A little bit disgusted, with both Lithuas and myself, I eased the blade from her skin. Someone had to start being merciful, and it looked like that sad sack of shit was going to be me. I started with something simpler. She'd said it would be a shame to kill such an artist as Dashu. "Is he still alive?"

She hesitated, but seemed to decide that withholding every scrap of information wouldn't go well for her. "He's alive."

I rubbed at the back of my neck, looking to the ships that slowly passed in either direction. "She put him on another boat."

Alifra finally sheathed her knives, her hands trembling. "I think she meant to ambush you, Hakara. I went to talk to him, and he didn't seem to remember that we'd argued. She must have stolen aboard with the goods in Dashu's form, when everyone was distracted with the fighting at the hideout. We thought she intended to take over the Godless, but she made the move we least expected. We ... we were lucky. This could have gone differently if Dashu and I hadn't been at odds." She lifted a hand to her throat. "Oh gods, what if those were the last words I said to him?"

I eyed our prisoner, an idea occurring to me. "We tie her up. We take her with us."

Thassir frowned. "And how do we stop her from doing magic? She could easily shift and escape."

I reached into my pocket and pulled out one of Mull's filters. "You can summon aether all you want, but if you can't breathe it, you can't do magic, can you?" I strapped it on over her head as Alifra found some rope. "It keeps the aether out." Damn near cleverest idea I'd ever come up with.

Alifra tied the rope a little tighter than necessary, keeping both sets of Lithuas's arms behind her back. "And Dashu?"

Our team was broken. We'd been broken again and again; I couldn't seem to hold them together. I put a hand on her shoulder. "He's alive. I believe Lithuas that much. She'll have sent him somewhere back in Langzu. Probably to a cohort of godkillers and then into the depths of a den. If she was so fascinated by his fighting style, they won't kill him. They'll want to study him. You should go find him, get him out. I won't keep you here." Xiazen loomed in the distance, the sails of the docked ships like flecks of white paint scattered across a wash of blue. I knew what it was like, knowing someone I loved was in danger, being too far away to help them. I wouldn't do that to her.

Alifra swallowed. "No. We can't afford to split any further. We need to see this through together. We take Thassir, Lithuas, and Talie to their brethren. We get back to the Unanointed, see if we can convince them to ally with the gods. Dashu..." Her voice broke. She swallowed. "If anyone can survive in a den of godkillers, it's him. He wouldn't want me to come for him, not now, with so much on the line. I stay with you." She nodded to Thassir, her face grim. "And you."

"Fine." I brought my fingers together in a fist, tried not to think about the brightness of my bond with Rasha, growing looser by the moment. "When we raided the den, when we took that corestone, we started this war. Now we finish it."

55
Rasha

11 years after the restoration of Kashan
and 572 years after the Shattering

Langzu - inner Bian, the Sovereign's castle

King Wallam of Cressima was convinced that the hot peppers eaten in the south of Langzu were poisonous to one's health, unless one was Langzuan. He was so taken with this idea that when a woman on the street insulted him, he sentenced her to death by consuming one such pepper. It took quite some time to obtain these peppers in Cressima, by which time King Wallam's wrath had waned, but he insisted the execution be carried out. She did not die after consuming one pepper, nor did she die after the second, nor the third. Frustrated and bored, Wallam declared that she must have Langzuan blood running in her and pardoned her. She went on to marry a Langzuan woman and together they made a healthy living importing hot peppers to Cressima and incorporating them into traditional Cressiman dishes.

I caught only glimpses of Sheuan before we left the castle, tastes that lingered, crumbs on the tongue of someone starving for more. But I could not find any way to beg some time to myself. Even had I been able to, I wasn't certain I could find Sheuan alone, or even if I should, given that her husband had caught us in an embrace.

I might only cause more trouble for her.

There was nothing I could do in Bian, so I climbed into the wagon with Kluehnn and began the long trek back to the den. He was more irritable than on the way here; when he wasn't sleeping, he snapped at me, telling me I should have looked harder in the castle, that I should have followed the other cohorts instead of searching only one room. I bowed at each criticism, urging him to see only what I wanted – soft Rasha, obedient Rasha, who had grown used to following others, to being their reason and never her own.

He tired himself out on these occasions, and I escaped the confines of the wagon, walking beneath the night sky, grateful for the sight of the moon for at least a little while. One day blended into the next, and I found myself yearning for the conversations I'd had with Mull, or even the crow. The other cohorts avoided me, never addressing me by name.

A messenger arrived as we approached the foothills. He came running toward us, never stopping or slowing down, his antlers stark against the early dawn sky. Kluehnn was asleep in the wagon, so I'd taken the chance to slip away again, my leg sore but holding.

All six godkillers drew their blades, gems lighting their faces from below in soft violet. I reached for my belt and found the space empty again, tried to turn the movement into brushing my palm against my robe – as though it didn't matter to me that I was the only godkiller here without her blade.

He stopped short of us, and one of the godkillers raised her hand to bring the wagon to a halt. The altered leaned over his knees, breathing heavily. "I have news," he said. This close, we could see the gray convert's clothes he wore, the eye stitched onto the chest. The cohorts slowly sheathed their blades. I waited, my shoulders tense. I'd left that chalk mark on the stone. I'd let the gods know that the den would be vulnerable.

What had they done?

"We were attacked," the messenger gasped out finally. "The gods. There were more of them than us. They ransacked the den."

I wasn't sure if Kluehnn had heard the messenger's voice, or if the stopping of the wagon was what had woken him, but he poured out the back, his filaments waving, the extra mouth just below his neck baring its sharp teeth.

"What did they do?" he hissed. "What did they take?"

The messenger fell to his knees, bowing before the aspect. "They went into the deep places. They took the bodies your godkillers bring back to the den."

The sky had lightened in the time we'd watched the messenger approach, as we'd waited for him to catch his breath. I could see the smoke now, rising from the mountains.

Kluehnn let out an echoing howl. All the hairs on my neck and arms stood on end. I'd *caused* this. I'd loved Kluehnn and I'd betrayed him, because I loved my cohort too. Because nothing was making sense anymore and I was grasping for a buoy at sea, trying to find reason again.

I squinted at the smoke, trying to figure out where it was rising from. Not the den. The gods had taken the bodies, and they were *burning* them. Something in my head clicked into place – it all made sense, though I couldn't quite see how. They had to burn the bodies, and it wasn't just to honor their dead. They had another reason. I could feel the reason burgeoning on the back of my tongue, like a word I couldn't quite remember.

Kluehnn roared again. He hadn't eaten this entire time.

He hadn't eaten.

The girl with the horns, a meat hook through her shoulder. The sucking sound of a mouth and teeth working flesh from bone.

I wasn't sure exactly how I knew, but I knew that he needed those bodies to eat, and they'd taken them and burned them and now he was so terribly, desperately hungry.

He climbed back into the wagon. "Get us back to the den as quickly as possible. Rasha, with me."

I followed him inside, my stomach roiling. As soon as the curtain shut behind me, he spoke again.

"There is a traitor among us. Someone told the gods we would be gone. That *I* would be gone. You must find that traitor. And while you do that, I will deal with the gods. We will attack now, and I will call for more godkillers from other dens for a second wave. The gods cannot hide forever. If there are shifters, they will have to take other forms again to fight us unless they want to watch all their comrades die."

"Kluehnn." I let his name roll off my tongue with reverence, though all I felt now was fear. "They have done this to provoke you. Shouldn't you wait for more godkillers and *then* attack?" The messenger had said so himself – there were more gods than the den had accounted for. If Kluehnn sent the cohorts against that army now, so many godkillers would die.

His barbed tail lashed, and I stiffened. "We must kill the gods, enough to replace the bodies they took. I cannot let this attack go unpunished. Are you questioning me? Your faith?"

I bowed, pressing my face to the floor. "No. Of course not." Even as I said the words, I doubted. He wanted to replace those bodies so he could eat them. He would make mistakes. Terrible mistakes. Ones that might cost Khatuya and Naatar's lives. "I will find the traitor."

"See that you do." His voice was a low growl. "And quickly."

The converts were walking among the injured when we arrived back at the den, checking bandages and offering up the white steamed bread with its grainy paste – Kluehnn's sustenance. I noticed, with relief, that there were no bodies laid out on the ground.

The crow had kept his word. I wasn't sure how much of my relief was because that meant he was still alive.

Kluehnn's aspect slid from the wagon and past the various injured godkillers, retreating into the deeper parts of the den. The sun had risen fully now, and sweat gathered in the small of my back as I squinted against its light. I hadn't been away from the den for that long, but everything felt different.

I should have gone first to Khatuya and Naatar, to regroup with my cohort, to find out what had happened during the skirmish, but I found my feet instead moving toward the archives. The room was quiet but for the scratch of pens and the turning of pages.

He was there, behind his screen, fingers moving over the lines of a book, looking as though he'd never suffered from aether sickness at all. The fur on the back of his neck was smooth; he'd not heard me approach. He leaned his head into his palm, and then he saw me.

"Rasha!" He sprang to his feet. We stood there, both unsure of exactly what we should do. Then he extended a hand. I took it, and he wrapped both our hands in his ink-stained palm. "We should talk."

"Yes, we should." The sweat on my back had cooled, my robe sticking uncomfortably to my skin. I was the traitor. I was the traitor Kluehnn wanted me to find. I couldn't see any reasonable way out of this. If I didn't hand in the traitor, he would punish me. If I did, he would kill me. "Not here. In private." I had to think of a way around this, and maybe Mull could help. I knew I'd have to make a choice at some point – between my faith and the relationship I'd begun with the gods, but I didn't know enough yet. I didn't know the truth, and Khatuya and Naatar were still here. How could I leave them behind?

He followed me from the archives toward the room I shared with my cohort. Kluehnn would be gathering the godkillers in the nave, and they'd be getting ready to fight. I had a moment, and our room should be empty. "I gave your letter to Sheuan," I said as we turned through the tunnels. "I told her you were well."

He scratched at the fur on one arm. "Well enough."

I opened the door to my room and froze.

It was not empty.

Kluehnn's aspect took up nearly the entire space. It loomed over Khatuya and Naatar, who bowed before it. All its terrible eyes swiveled toward me. "You think I'd leave *you* to root out the traitor? You think I could trust you that much after I had to take away your blade? That I wouldn't ask my own questions?"

One clawed arm shot out and seized Naatar. He let himself be dragged to his feet. "This one told me who the traitor is." Kluehnn's gaze landed over my shoulder, to where I could feel Mull's presence, his breath quick against the back of my neck. "Someone who came here as a convict and immediately started digging in places he did not belong. A spy."

Everything was falling apart. I hadn't been able to choose, not yet, and so my choice had been made for me. Naatar was pale, the brown scales standing out against his cheeks. I caught a glimpse of fear in his eyes before someone seized Mull.

Another cohort of godkillers, here to take him away. And

I couldn't speak out, couldn't say anything, lest I be dragged away too.

"Enter, Rasha, and close the door behind you."

I obeyed, my mouth dry, wondering exactly what Naatar had told him. If this was my fate, I knew I'd go to it willingly, unsure of what else to do.

When the door had shut, Kluehnn let go of Naatar's arm. The three of us stood there uncertainly. I wanted to reach for them, to take comfort in my cohort, but it had been so long since I'd last done that. We'd saved one another's lives, we'd come out of the trials together, yet we'd still been drawn apart. I'd thought our bond immutable.

Time could change anything.

Kluehnn's lower mouth licked its lips. "I know you helped him. The spy."

I fell to the floor. "Forgive me, Kluehnn. I did so only because I was worried for my cohort. You've been sending them out without me. There are two of them and there should be three to stand against a god. They are strong, but I . . . I am not. Not without them." I didn't understand myself – how I could go from searching for the truth to this sniveling, obedient creature who cared only for the safety of her cohort and nothing else?

"You think that trip to Bian was the test? You think I would give you back your blade for simply sitting alongside me and searching a castle? After you betrayed me by letting your sister go free? No."

He turned, lifted something from the table at my bedside. It was another godkilling dagger, the glow of the gem dim by lamplight. "This is yours. Rise. Take it."

Confused, adrift, I pushed myself to my feet. I nearly expected to feel the sting of his tail as I took the dagger from his grasp. Why would he give me a blade again if he saw me as helping a spy?

"Your reasons are good, Rasha. Your heart is in the right place. But you've allowed yourself to be led astray. You want to keep your cohort safe? You want to ensure they keep their lives?" He moved so he was between me and Naatar. Khatuya stood next to me, though I didn't dare look at her face. Not right now, when I couldn't know what my expression might betray. "You want so badly to be sent out into the world, to prove yourself through violence? You've grown so restless here that my answers are no longer acceptable to you and you've sought out others? Then let me give you a task to calm your busy, busy mind. You will go out into Langzu with Khatuya. You will find your sister, no matter what it takes. You will kill her and bring back proof."

One hoof tapped the floor. He rose onto his four hind legs, his head scraping the ceiling. "And if you fail, I will kill Naatar."

56
Rasha

11 years after the restoration of Kashan
and 572 years after the Shattering

Langzu - in the wilds

Just between you and me, Dagino, while I admire the explorers who have managed to delve deep into the honeycomb of tunnels beneath our feet, and I am happy they have brought us descriptions of the bioluminescent flora that lives beneath the aeroclines ... why the fuck have none of those adventurers thought to cut some of the vegetation free and bring it back? I swear, they are a different breed than you and me, who are rich with curiosity about the plants and creatures that share this world with us. The explorers go there, they come back (sometimes), and for what? So they can say, "I have been there?" I will never understand their lack of thought about anything other than this.

My bond with Hakara pulled us south, farther and farther away from the den and from Naatar. We'd been given the best provisions and more money than I'd ever seen in my lifetime. We were to take as many wagons and horses as possible, to rest well in inns. He'd marked two other dens that we could stop at on our way, along with a note that we were to be given the use of two cohorts. The gods hadn't killed anyone during their raid, but they'd injured a fair few, and Kluehnn wasn't willing to spare anyone from the den near Bian. If he made this mission easy for me, he'd whispered in my ear before we'd left, and I *still* could not complete it, then I would have no one to blame but myself.

I already blamed myself.

My gaze found a crow on the afternoon we left, circling above. Khatuya caught the direction of my gaze, her lips pressed. Then she shook her head, scooped up a rock, and threw it at the bird, screaming out her frustration.

Mull was imprisoned back in the den and Naatar was firmly in Kluehnn's grasp, waiting to find out his fate. I'd made such a mess of things, and *still* I had so many questions – ones I knew my god would not and could not answer.

Khatuya treated me with silence for the most part. It was like traveling with those two cohorts to Bian – she barely looked at me, refused to use my name. I wasn't sure what she was thinking. But I knew how she was feeling, and I'd never seen her so angry, not even with Shambul, the boy who'd bullied us all before we'd left him to die.

Finally, when we'd passed Bian and were on foot for a bit, I dared to speak to her directly. The sun beat down on the back of my neck, the walking making my leg ache. "I don't know how to make this right."

She wheeled on me. "You should have told me what was going on. I didn't know what you were doing in the archives. You didn't *tell* me! Naatar confessed to Kluehnn, and you didn't even tell *him*, you just let him find you with that spy and asked him to keep your secrets. From everyone. From me. And you *know* Naatar. You know he would do anything to keep us from fighting. He tells me everything, but he would not tell me this. And it's your fault." Tears streaked her rough brown cheeks, though I didn't think she even knew she was crying.

I wasn't sure how to tell her that in those moments – when Mull and the crow had let me sit with my doubts, had allowed me to question – I'd felt more like myself, like the person I'd always wanted to be. Someone who wasn't afraid to dig into her faith, even if it meant she found her faith or herself lacking.

Khatuya was lifting her hands as though in supplication. "Why didn't you tell me? You should have trusted me. We were your cohort, we were meant to trust one another, even with the hard truths. It was the only way we got out of the trials together, and alive. You said you'd get us all out, and I trusted you even when it looked like you'd betrayed Naatar. I put so much trust in you, Rasha, and you couldn't do the same for me."

Was she truly so blind to everything she'd said to me? "I never told you because I knew how you'd react. You want to know the hard truths? Fine. Kluehnn is *lying* to us. I found another way back to Unterra, in our very den, and he didn't want to hear it. Did you know the gods want to go? They don't all want to fight. We could send them back to their homeland if we only let them pass peaceably through the den. Kluehnn says he cares about us all, that he loves us all, but he would send us to our deaths instead of coming to an agreement with the gods."

She stalked toward me, until I could see the whites ringing her irises. "The gods *lie* to you. Kluehnn doesn't. How can you believe that? This is why we are forbidden from speaking to the gods. What have they done for you? Nothing. Kluehnn and the dens have done everything. You wouldn't have a family without him. You wouldn't have a place where you belong. You wouldn't even be alive."

Her words cut me deeply, because they were true. I wouldn't have anything, and I knew how this all made me look – ungrateful and petty. "Do I owe him my unquestioning faith in return?"

"*Yes!* It's the bargain we all made. Is it that hard for you to just do as you're told? To trust the one god who has always been there for you?"

"He hurt me. He took my horn." I pointed to the empty space on my scalp, where the skin still itched.

"And you deserved it!" She thrust her face toward mine, her hands in fists.

Khatuya had no idea what I'd been through while Kluehnn had been sending them off to fight the gods. I knew she had to care. I trusted that she did. "Of course it's been hard for me to do as I was told. I love you and Naatar. It killed me every day knowing you were out there fighting alone while I was trapped in the archives. You know why I first talked to the gods? Why I wanted to make a bargain with them? If we could stop fighting, it meant you would be safe."

"We cannot be safe until all of them are dead."

"I don't think that's true."

She stared at me, her face close to mine, strands of hair come loose from her braid, brushing against her cheeks. "Is this because of me and Naatar?"

"What?" I leaned away. "No."

"It's because we have something between us, isn't it? Something you're not part of."

I gritted my teeth. Yes, it had shaken me. Yes, it had spurred me toward helping Mull. But that wasn't the only reason, and she wasn't *listening*. "If you ever cared about me at all, then know I'm telling you the truth about this. There are books that Kluehnn is altering, changing to say other things, sometimes the opposite of what they said before."

"And how would no one notice?"

I lifted my hands. "I don't know! He's doing something with them. But there's more – there's a tomb. There's writing by Tolemne in there. It says he didn't stay in Unterra. It says he came back to the surface and that his family was still alive when he left. It says the gods had children with mortals and that Tolemne was one of their descendants. It says there are three aeroclines."

"And did you read these things yourself?"

I faltered. "Well, no. Mull translated them."

"The *spy* translated them, and you would believe him over your own god?"

I grabbed her shoulders. "Listen to me for just one moment! Kluehnn is lying. He is *lying*. I saw the books with my own eyes. What reason did Mull have to lie to me?"

"To turn you from your faith!"

"So he risked his life and spent all this time mistranslating things just to get me to turn against my god? I'm not that important. None of us are. And if Kluehnn loves me so much, why did he hurt me so much? Even if I deserved it? I don't know if the gods have told me the truth, but I know that Kluehnn hasn't."

Khatuya bared her teeth, white against the oak-brown of her skin. "You say that one more time..."

"I am here, doing what you want. I am telling you the hard truths. Kluehnn lies."

With a shout, she attacked me. It should have been an easy fight for someone like me, with my superior strength and height. But Khatuya, when she was angry, fought like a cornered bear. She wouldn't let up, she wouldn't stop hitting and kicking and biting. And I didn't want to hurt her. I seized one of her wrists, and then the other, and still she came at me, undeterred, her fingers curling so her claws could mark my skin.

"Stop!" I cried out. Our feet kicked at the road, sending up clouds of dust. A cart moved in the distance, heading south.

"Or what?"

There was no Naatar here to come between us and say reasonable words. I didn't even know what he would have said in this moment; he was already angry with me. Khatuya on the other hand was a spitting fire, oil tossed onto a burgeoning flame.

I pushed her away and she pulled her godkilling blade free. I unsheathed mine just in time to block her attack. There was nothing graceful about the movement. It had been a long time now since I'd held a blade. Too many things had happened between then and now, and I'd not even had the chance to spar. Khatuya pressed her advantage, darting back and swiping at my arm.

A thin line of red welled up, my robe cut cleanly by her blade. I'd never been the full focus of Khatuya's anger. Why did she think I should have told her the truth when this was simmering beneath at all times? She didn't trust me. Naatar didn't trust me. Kluehnn and Mull didn't trust me.

What did I have, without that? What lay beneath, if I stripped away all those relationships and my faith besides?

I screamed back at her, no longer caring if I hurt her. I may have taken the first step away from our cohort, but she'd wandered the rest of the path without stopping to see if I was still there. All that mattered to her was that I obeyed Kluehnn. I whipped my blade about, cutting through the air as though it was doing me some wrong by standing between me and her. Khatuya leapt back, and I pressed my longer reach. She stumbled.

Just as she did, my injured leg caught a rock. I went down with her, my knife falling from my hand. I seized her hand with the blade, landing on top of her. Her eyes were unfocused, and I slammed her hand against the ground – once, twice – until her fingers opened and I threw her blade into the grass.

Her other fist met my cheek.

It was a glancing blow, with her non-dominant hand, but the world still turned briefly red, my ears ringing and the sky spinning above. She wriggled out from beneath me even as I tried to hold her still.

"You want to make things right?" she gasped out. "You don't tell me all these things you think you've learned. That doesn't help either of us and I don't want to hear it. The only thing that will make it right is killing Hakara. We follow your bond, we kill her and get this over with."

I pressed my hand to my cheek and rolled onto my feet, choking on the dust from the road. All my certainty, my anger fled. "I don't know if I can."

"It's the only way we'll save Naatar. You have to."

# 57
Hakara

11 years after the restoration of Kashan
and 572 years after the Shattering

Langzu - Xiazen

Langzu used to be a wetter place when the Numinars were still alive. Back then, there was a vine found in the southeast forests with seeds that had a very particular taste. But the last of the fruits were harvested 124 years after the Shattering, and now we only have descriptions of what they tasted like. Spicy, they say, tangy and light, with a floral aroma. These seeds were common in the cuisine of southeastern Langzu, and just like that, nearly an entire repertoire of dishes was wiped clean because there was no clear substitute for this spice.

Talie showed up again just as we approached Xiazen's docks at sunset, yawning as though she'd had the best sleep of her life while we'd been *fighting* for our lives. I had the brief satisfaction of watching her back arch, her tail poofing into a bottlebrush, when she saw Lithuas.

She did a little sideways hop, her ears flat. "Is that *her?*"

We'd bound her to a chair on deck, her silver hair in disarray beneath the filter. "It is indeed, little one," she responded. "Are you certain you want to be on the losing side?" Really should have gagged her before putting that filter on. Seemed I could only have one good idea per day.

My bond with Thassir itched at the back of my mind, but not nearly so much as my bond with Rasha. I wasn't sure when was the best time to tell my comrades that she was headed our way. We'd have to encounter her on our way to meet with Talie's gods in the mountains near Bian. Even if we somehow managed to avoid her, because of the bond we'd be leading her and Kluehnn first to the gathered gods and then to the Unanointed.

The tension of these fast-approaching decisions hung like a weight about my neck, one I wasn't sure how to unburden myself of. I still had time, but not enough of it.

We gathered our belongings, Alifra looking as bleak as I'd seen her the night before our raid on the Kashani den. "I did not say kind things to him, Hakara," she said, her gaze on the docks as Falin went to secure the ship. "We left one another in disarray. I wasn't sure how to repair our relationship. We have always been friends, and I let that change, and it made everything strange between us." She looked at me, her expression helpless. "I know how he is. If we were together, he would want to continue his legacy, to teach these stories to his children, and there are so many stories. I don't know if I could burden someone else with that without giving them the choice, the way his uncle did with him. I never really got to explain to him."

"You'll get to. I promise."

She laughed then. "When you say it, I almost believe it. But you shouldn't make promises you can't keep."

I thought of Thassir, the blood pact between the elder gods, the way promises could force uncomfortable and painful compromises that no one wanted. "Maybe you're right. But it's a promise I want to keep."

Falin tied the boat up. I tossed him the rest of the coin Velenor had given us and clapped him on the shoulder. "I hope you find your crew waiting for you safe and sound, and you make so much money you don't know what to do with it."

He hefted the pouch of coins and let out a grunt, eyeing Lithuas as we guided her off the ship, a broad hat over her head, a robe about her shoulders, and a veil covering the filter on her face. That was all the goodbye we got from him, but I couldn't blame the man for wanting to live an enclosed life, focusing on what was in front of him instead of the larger problems of the world.

We spent the night at an inn in Xiazen, taking turns watching Lithuas as the others slept. Talie offered to take an extended watch, as long as someone carried her the next day so she could sleep. I fell into bed in our shared room, completely and utterly drained, the seafood stew I'd eaten for dinner making me feel heavy.

In the morning, as we walked the road out of the city and toward Bian, I took note of the charred hillsides, burned trees blackened skeletons against a cloud-streaked sky.

"My sister is coming," I said into the quiet. "Today."

I'd slept, but I didn't know if she had. I wished I could reach through the bond we shared, tug her closer, whisper in her ear. I wished we could put aside everything that had happened to us in the time we'd been apart.

Thassir let out a sigh as Alifra rounded on me. "You didn't think to tell us earlier?"

The basket she carried let out a low growl, and Talie's head nudged the cover open. "The godkiller you fought in the lakebed? Do you know if she's bringing anyone else?"

I shook my head. "I only know where she is, and she's getting closer."

She ducked back into the basket. "This could be bad."

"Should we throw the blades away, as you promised?" Alifra said, putting a hand to the godkiller blade at her belt.

I touched my own dagger, the one that had once belonged to Rasha. "They'll have gotten new ones by now. Let me talk to her alone."

Thassir shook his head. "Absolutely not. She may be your sister, but she's made it clear that she's a godkiller first and foremost. You want to talk to her? We all go."

Alifra gestured to Lithuas. "And bring an entire elder god with us? This isn't sounding like a good idea either."

I lifted my hands. "It's better than leaving her behind and hoping she doesn't work her way free. Maybe there aren't any good ideas, just ones that are less bad. We all go. Not to fight. To talk."

The clouds in the sky darkened the farther up the road we traveled, my bond with Rasha slackening, the feeling in my head like the relieving of pressure when I floated to the surface after a dive. One cold drop struck my head, then another. The moisture sat atop the dusty road, gathering into the wagon tracks. And as more rain fell, the dust became mud.

A line of figures appeared before us, stretched across the road. I counted. Six of them.

"I want to talk!" I shouted across the distance, before anyone could get any silly ideas about crossbows and bolts. "We have Lithuas. She is working with Kluehnn. He'll want her back. We are here to negotiate!"

Heads bent toward one another, though I couldn't hear what, if anything, they said through the worsening storm.

And then one figure stepped forward. I squinted through the

rain. Rasha? "Only Hakara approaches. We meet in the middle. No weapons drawn."

It was her. My heart lurched, but I managed to keep my voice steady. "Fine." I lifted my hands from my belt, glancing back at my companions. "Stay put unless she attacks. I want to see if we can resolve this peaceably."

We strode toward one another, our bond going quiet in my mind.

One of her horns was missing. It was the first thing I noticed, the sick feeling in my stomach threatening to spill into my throat. A scar marked her scalp where it had been, the skin shiny and purple. "Rasha . . . are you well?"

Her eyes narrowed. "You're here to negotiate, not to ask after my health. So negotiate. Give us Lithuas and we'll let you leave here alive."

I wanted, more than anything, to ask who'd done that to her, what had happened. It felt as natural to me as breathing – and maybe that was the problem. I'd told our Mimi I'd take care of Rasha, and to me that had meant only one thing: keeping her safe. I hesitated, knowing I had no real intention of negotiating. We couldn't give Lithuas over to Kluehnn. "It shouldn't come to this – a fight. We've each spared one another once now."

"Yes." Her words were clipped. "Which means we no longer owe one another anything."

I let my eyes close briefly, the rain pattering around us, seeping past my hair to my scalp. I'd kept moving this entire time, convinced that if I only pushed harder, tried harder, solutions would arise. And for the most part, they did. But this – I didn't know how to fix this.

For the first time since I'd been a child, I stopped running. I let myself be still.

The pain washed over me, at last catching up. Losing Mimi

and then Maman, losing Rasha. Did we truly owe one another nothing? Here, in this moment, every beat of my heart the throbbing of an opened wound, I knew it wasn't true. I'd pushed all those memories away, making a new narrative for myself, focusing on one thing: finding Rasha. I loved her, I wanted the best for her, but it didn't mean I'd been right.

"Maybe you don't owe me anything, but I owed you more. I had more of a responsibility than to just protect you. I should have listened, I should have raised you to learn to protect *yourself*. Instead, I left you with no sense of who you were or who you could be without me."

If I'd done things right, maybe Rasha wouldn't have felt the need to turn to Kluehnn and the godkillers, to fill in the hole I'd left in her life. I could forgive myself for not going back, for leaving Rasha behind. But this? It wasn't me that needed to forgive. It was her.

I kept my hands spread, the rain soaking into my tunic. "I owed you more than I gave you. I tied up your identity in mine, and you are, and have always been, so much more than that."

Something in her expression shifted, though the wariness didn't disappear. I couldn't expect it to, couldn't expect to just show up here and say the right words and for everything to suddenly be right between us. "Why *are* we fighting? Look at the gods. They are selfish." She gestured to the spot where her horn had once been. "All of them."

I couldn't hope, yet this wasn't the way she'd reacted the last time we'd spoken. This time she said nothing about Kluehnn, about how he was the only one who spoke the truth.

She unfurled a hand toward me. "We can go. Just you and me."

Wouldn't say I wasn't tempted. I wanted to fix things between us, to see if there was anything left to fix. But I had more responsibilities now – to my team, to the Unanointed. Mimi had told me to take care of Rasha. I couldn't be like Thassir, letting one promise rule the rest of my life. Yes, the gods were selfish, but in the end, so were mortals. All we could do was to try to do the right thing, to move forward, to recognize that each new moment was a fresh opportunity to change.

"Rasha." My voice nearly gave out, the rain louder than my words. "I wish I could."

Someone shouted from behind me.

I whirled to find two godkillers rushing toward Thassir, who was still holding Lithuas. One of them leapt for him.

The other drew a small knife from his belt and threw it. It pierced the filter on Lithuas's face, casting it away.

In the next moment, she'd shifted to an eel, slipping from Thassir's grasp. In another flash, she was Lithuas again, blade in hand, silver hair damp with the rain.

I pulled my sword free, just in time to meet Rasha, a fresh godkilling blade in her hand.

Maybe one day I would get tired of fighting. Maybe one day I *would* give up. But it wasn't that day. Not yet. And if they wanted to try to take the corestone from me, I'd ensure they'd have nothing to take. "Thassir!" I called. A quick gesture of his hand.

Just a sip of aether, the scent of the ocean sliding past my tongue. It was enough.

The corestone burned within me.

58
Rasha

11 years after the restoration of Kashan
and 572 years after the Shattering

Langzu - on the road from Bian to Xiazen

The Queen of the Aqqilan Empire and the Prince of Isegin went on to have six children, five of whom grew up to be exceptionally accomplished. The eldest took over rule of the empire, the second-born became the best swordswoman the world had seen, the third-born a renowned natural scholar, the fourth a legendary musician, and the fifth a shrewd businessman. The sixth son looked at his older brothers and sisters and, according to the stories, threw up his hands and said, "What is there left for me to be exceptional at?" Instead, he spent his days smoking bung-rou imported from Langzu and playing games of Montiyanan obelisks, which he was only marginally good at.

I tried to think only of Naatar as I fought, held helpless in Kluehnn's grasp, waiting for us to return with evidence that Hakara was dead. Yet here was Hakara, in front of me, her sword flashing and wet with rain, and she'd told me she was sorry, spilled out her regrets. All those silent mornings, when I'd reached for her, asked her to stay, and she'd left me alone to fear the consequences. She'd always made a joke of it, always told me not to worry, as though words could chase away fears. She hadn't even taken my fear of her going to the mines seriously.

I'd never let myself be angry about it, just as I'd never let myself be angry about Kluehnn's lies. Now I felt that rage bursting within me. No one had ever trusted me with the truth – that Hakara might not come back from a dive, that the other gods were not a monolith. Did they not see me as worthy of the truth? Was I always just to be a paper puppet, moved about by others for their own purposes and their own stories? I'd thought I'd escaped that, only to end up in the hands of someone else.

Hakara had always seen everything she'd done as necessary. If she told me to stay in the tent, I was to stay in the tent. She was the end authority in our relationship.

Just the way Kluehnn was. But Hakara, reckless and foolish as she'd been, had never hurt me the way he did. Even now, as we fought, I could feel her holding herself back, blocking my blows but not following up. Her heart wasn't in it.

Was mine?

I gritted my teeth, a shiver at the back of my neck. It was too late for apologies, too late for mending things. No matter what Kluehnn had done, no matter what lies he'd told me, Khatuya and Naatar were my friends. Khatuya hadn't wanted to listen to me, Naatar hadn't either, but they were just as blind to Kluehnn's flaws as I'd been. Neither of them deserved to die for it.

The other godkillers rushed to my side just as I felt fatigue begin to weaken my limbs.

The winged god stepped in front of Hakara, claws brandished, giving her a chance to breathe. Eight of us, and now Lithuas too. I didn't know what the others made of that. Their one true god, working with an elder god? It was blasphemy, yet she barreled toward the winged god with her sword drawn. They clashed just as one of the godkiller cohorts circled, trying to find an opening to attack.

He thrust out his wings, battering them, forcing them back, though not without a knife catching on the end of one of the wings. I darted forward, trying to find Hakara behind him. A bolt whizzed past my ear. A cat was running across the ground toward us.

It registered for a moment – strange behavior for a cat – before that cat *shifted*. A panther the size of a small pony roared, claws kicking up mud as it leapt for one of the godkillers.

I lifted my blade, determined in spite of the presence of another god. Were we not godkillers, after all? I spotted Khatuya, engaging with the russet-haired woman.

And then Hakara burst from beneath one of the god's wings, her sword held tight in one hand. She was *glowing*, a golden aura surrounding her. She cut down one of the godkillers in three blows. I didn't make it there in time, but caught her next thrust before she could attack another of that cohort. Our blades locked.

I could see a vein throbbing in her neck as she held her breath, the glow of her skin more visible up close. "What did you *do* to yourself?"

She only gave me a sad half-smile before retreating behind a black wing and gasping in a breath. I was faced with the teeth and claws of the panther as Lithuas and the winged god fought. The two remaining godkillers in that cohort joined me. For a moment, it was like fighting with Naatar and Khatuya again, every glance an instruction, a communication.

It quickly became clear that though this shapeshifter god was large and its claws and teeth terrifying, it hadn't done much fighting. It leapt too far forward, snarling and snapping at one of the cohort. I shifted from one foot to the other, springing forward to plunge my knife into the god's shoulder.

The cat screamed, flowing out from beneath us as it retreated, and I pulled my knife free. I noted its limp with satisfaction, keeping loose on my feet, aware that the russet-haired woman still held a crossbow. I didn't know how Khatuya fared. I pursued the cat, but was brought up short by Hakara again, breathing heavily but still in the fight.

"You think to face me like this?" I hissed out, striking away her sword. "Without your godly strength or speed?"

She said nothing, only stood steady between me and the panther. She was too slow this way, too weak.

"I don't want to hurt you," she said. She thrust and slashed, each blow only designed to test my defenses. "Don't you remember those days we used to spend out on the plains? The invisible enemies that we fought together?"

It hit me harder than any blow, that she remembered, that she still thought of those times. "We were different people then."

"You may bury those pieces, but they are still there."

I blinked away the rain that threatened to drip into my eyes, batting her blade aside, finding an opening and thrusting. She jumped away only just barely. So incredibly foolish. She would let me kill her, all because she was afraid of doing me harm. There was a part of her that still wanted to treat me like a child. "Are they? You think there is any world in which we are sisters again?"

She shook damp hair from her face. "I hope there is."

"Fight me!" I lifted my free hand and shoved her. She could have taken my hand off at the wrist if she'd tried, if she'd used those gems. She stumbled back, her feet catching in the mud. "You think I still need to be protected?"

Hakara gritted her teeth. "I don't believe you'll kill me. I can't believe it."

And there was the truth of it. I wasn't sure I could either, and the thought filled me with despair. In the heat of battle, the need for survival pressing down on me, I could do any number of terrible things. But she didn't want to hurt me, and without that, I wasn't sure how to hurt her. Naatar was back in the den, his life in Kluehnn's hands. In *my* hands.

I whirled away from her, found the winged god two steps behind me, engaged with Lithuas. I thrust my dagger into his side.

He staggered away, a groan of pain shuddering from his throat. When I pulled the blade free, shimmering blood spurted from the wound. "Then I will kill everyone you care about."

"No!" Hakara shouted.

In an instant, she was there, holding her breath, her skin once more aglow. Her sword flashed through the air like lightning. This time, when I blocked her blow, I felt the weight of her strength pressing against mine. She shoved me back and was there again before I could blink, her lips pressed together, her brows low over her eyes. She lashed out.

She defended the winged god with the same ferocity she had once contained when defending me. I felt each blow I stopped vibrating down into the marrow of my bones, my arms quickly tiring. Each time I leapt away from her sword, I felt the slice of the blade's breeze against my skin. It caught once against my leather breastplate, cutting a scar across the eye.

I lifted my dagger to block a blow, my fingers numb. She struck it clean from my grip. It skimmed the grass, clipped a rock, and settled down the road, out of reach. Her breath was still held, the pulse at her neck steadier than I'd expected.

Maybe I'd been wrong. Maybe she *would* kill me. There was

a moment, when she lifted her sword, when I felt at peace with that idea. I wasn't Kluehnn's anymore, and I couldn't be hers. Perhaps this was always meant to be my fate. Perhaps it was what I deserved.

And then someone barreled into her, knocking the breath from her. A quick, violent skirmish I couldn't quite follow, two figures rolling in the mud and the rain. Hakara took in another breath, the aura emanating from her skin.

I saw then the brown of Khatuya's rough skin, her white teeth bared as she raised her dagger – all before Hakara thrust her sword into the godkiller's chest.

Everything in my world went silent but for a faint ringing in my ears. I caught glimpses out of the corner of my eye – Lithuas subduing Thassir, the panther cornered by godkillers against a boulder, the russet-haired woman shooting one last bolt before tucking her crossbow away and pulling her daggers free.

My focus narrowed to Khatuya. Not Khatuya. I was running for her before I could stop myself. She was on the ground, the sword freed from her body, her chest heaving out last breaths.

Her gaze caught mine as I stood over her. "You should have trusted me," she gasped. "I would have listened. I would have gone to the ends of the world for you. I would have questioned everything, if you'd ... if you'd only let me in from the beginning."

Her eyelids stopped fluttering, her mouth going still, rain dripping into like it was just one more hollow to fill.

Hakara hovered two steps away, breathing fast, her bloody sword held in a two-handed grip.

She'd killed her – my comrade, one of my cohort. Khatuya and I were closer than friends, and now she was dead. I lifted Khatuya's dagger from her limp hand, ready to face off against my sister. I would make Hakara pay.

59
Hakara

11 years after the restoration of Kashan
and 572 years after the Shattering

Langzu - on the road from Bian to Xiazen

Here is the thing about oral histories: they work well so long as there are enough people to hold them. Information can be cross-checked, verified, and consensus can be reached. No one need hold more information than they can handle. But over the long years, the Aqqilan people have diminished as realm after realm has undergone restoration. Now the few left must carry the burden once meant for so many.

This wasn't where I'd wanted to end up. Hadn't wanted to kill her friend. Hadn't wanted to kill any of them. I watched Rasha's expression shift, and I wasn't sure if this was a thing we'd be able to mend.

Lithuas was pushing Thassir back; he was barely able to defend himself, the wound in his side still bleeding. In that moment, when Rasha had shoved her dagger into him, I'd felt the shock of it as surely as though she'd thrust the blade into me. It felt like a violation, a thing that shouldn't ever happen – this intentional harm of someone I cared about.

And I, unthinking, had done the same thing right back to her. Only I'd killed the person she cared about.

Rasha screamed and leapt at me. I looked to Thassir, hoping he would still have the strength to know what I needed from him.

Another small sip of aether. I held it, felt it reacting with the corestone. I could feel a reserve of power behind a wall, one I couldn't quite access. And Thassir refused to give me that access. Frustrated, I fought off my sister's furious attacks. Her dagger slipped through my guard, catching my forearm. A sting, the warm sensation of blood dripping to my elbow.

Thassir faltered.

It was this that broke me open more than anything else. I'd been so angry with him for all the things he hadn't done, the differences he could have made long in the past. He was supposed to be the Defender of the Helpless, and he'd let that go. I'd focused on this instead of the incredible loss he'd suffered. He'd become less than himself, unwilling and unable to cope. I'd wanted him to be like me – screaming in defiance in the face of everything, putting myself on the line over and over, not caring about the value of my life.

And that wasn't always the right way. I'd done what I thought was right, yet I'd let so many people down. So had he. But we were both trying to fix those mistakes. I'd wanted grace for my mistakes, and I hadn't given him any for his.

I put all my strength and my magic into shoving my sister back. I took a breath, my throat aching, head pounding. "Thassir, I need you!" I shouted.

His raven-dark eyes met mine. Something ground into place, the rusty teeth of our hearts finally aligning.

Without exactly knowing why, I called out his name. "Nioanen!"

He straightened. His wings snapped out. The black of his feathers cracked like the dried earth of Langzu. It flaked away with the breeze, whirling into the rain, dark specks of ash mixing into the water and mud.

The feathers it left behind were gold, shining with their own light. Lithuas fell back at the sight of them, and Nioanen extended a hand.

A bright blade, wreathed in lightning, appeared in his palm. Zayyel.

I felt a fraction then of what people must have felt so many hundreds of years ago when they saw him. A being of golden light wielding a crackling white sword. Fearsome and beautiful.

The wound in his side still bled, but this time, when he summoned aether for me, I felt the thickness of it in my throat. My belly burned with the corestone's power, my veins alight. I couldn't care about what effect it might have on me in the future. Right here, right now, Alifra was in trouble and so was Talie.

Nioanen and I gravitated toward one another as we fought Lithuas and Rasha until our backs met, his feathers brushing the back of my neck. I took a moment to breathe, and my sister leapt at me. "Alifra! Talie!" I called. "Hold on!" A moment of air, and then another breath of aether.

Rasha snarled as she attacked, and I was still only holding her off, even with the corestone. I didn't want to kill her and I couldn't see a way to incapacitate her. We wouldn't make it.

I was going to have to choose — my sister's life, or the lives of my comrades. The burning of my belly seemed to extend into my chest, a slow and fiery ache.

Hoofbeats came up the road. Someone slid from horseback just short of the fight, cloaked all in midnight blue. She tore the hood from her head, the veil from her face. Velenor. In one smooth movement, she'd drawn her sword. Velenor was not Dashu, but she'd forged his sword, she'd taught his ancestors how to fight.

"Lithuas!" she called as she approached. She took down one of the godkillers attacking Alifra, pivoted and sliced a wing from another that had slashed a cut across Talie's nose. "It's time to put down your sword."

I could feel Nioanen rallying behind me, the flash of his lightning blade sparking at the corners of my vision. Rasha's face went still as Velenor approached, her attacks weakening. I knew the effect Velenor could have on people – her glittering skin, her luminous eyes, the grace with which she moved. Even when she lifted her sword, there was something soothing about her, a lullaby sung from a mother's lips. The closer she came, the more I could feel the presence of the three elder gods together, like the heat that emanated from a bonfire.

Lithuas hesitated. "Velenor. You were supposed to stay in Pizgonia."

"And I might have," she said, "if I'd never realized you'd left more of us alive. I'd always thought it was just me, that fighting would be pointless. And now I know – no fighting is pointless, not when it can bring hope to others. If no one makes a stand, no one ever will, because who wants to stand alone? So drop your sword, Lithuas. You spared us for a reason."

I rushed to help Talie and Alifra, my breath still tight in my chest, taking advantage of the distraction. Didn't know if Velenor would convince Lithuas of anything, but my friends needed me. I slammed into one of the two remaining godkillers fighting Alifra, hamstringing one. Alifra darted away from the last one, pulling her crossbow and taking aim at the godkillers harrying Talie.

Lithuas's laugh sounded behind me, mingling with the

pattering rain. "It's too late. I might not have killed any of you, but I have killed countless other gods in Kluehnn's name, and even more mortals. No one wants me on their side."

I was fighting a godkiller whose face was nearly covered in mottled brown and black scales, dagger whipping about as ferociously as his tail. I heard a cry of pain from behind me, across the muddy road, and knew Alifra had hit her mark.

We could win this. My belly spasmed and I let the aether go, sucking in a lungful of air. The burning in my belly and chest didn't diminish. I thrust at the godkiller. He sidestepped, but my aim was still true, my sword piercing his leather breastplate a handspan above his hip. I felt the blade exit out his back. Not close enough to center to hit anything vital, but I'd hurt him.

A hand grabbed me from behind, pulling me back, an arm wrapping around my neck. A godkilling blade rested against my collarbone.

"Hakara." Rasha's voice in my ear, strangled. Her other hand seized my wrist, keeping my blade from reaching her.

"I didn't want to kill your friend." A crawling sensation filled my chest, something tickling at my ribs. "She would have killed me."

A moment's hesitation. "I know. But ... the other of my cohort. Kluehnn holds him in the den. I'm sorry."

She was doing this against her will. I wriggled in her grasp, trying to get free, to look her in the eye. We could handle this together, if only she'd let me try.

Wait. Sorry? What was she sorry for?

She let go of my wrist, grabbed my other hand. For a moment, I wasn't sure what was happening. The blade was no longer on my neck. I tried to twist, to lift my sword.

Something struck the end of my left hand, like someone had somehow managed to punch me there with a hand gloved in hot iron. I glanced down, found my little finger gone, blood pouring from the wound. My finger was in her grasp and she was pulling away, and I couldn't even think, my ears ringing.

Lithuas had dropped her sword. She and Velenor were speaking but I couldn't hear their words. Nioanen appeared in my narrowing vision, grabbing at my injured hand. I'd dropped my sword. Pain finally flooded in, a deep and throbbing ache. My knees gave out and he lowered me to the ground. "Help Alifra and Talie," I said, pushing him away. "I'll live." I could barely get the words past my tongue. Nothing felt real.

Every drop of rain fell against skin that felt suddenly too sensitive, bursting with pain. But as I let my head fall back into the grass, the rain falling into my open eyes, I felt something that disturbed me more than the missing finger.

My heart thudded in my chest, a quick rhythm. But next to that pulse was another one. Slower and fainter, but steady all the same.

A twin heartbeat that was not mine.

60

Rasha

11 years after the restoration of Kashan and 572 years after the Shattering

Langzu - on the road from Bian to Xiazen

There was a boy, fickle and sweet
Who met a foal that wanted to eat
The boy reached in his pocket and what did he find?
An apple to feed this foal of mine

The foal grew into a horse, the boy into a man
A steed and a warrior who fought and ran
The man reached into his pocket and what did he find?
An apple to feed this horse of mine

There came a battle, one that couldn't be won
And when the dust cleared and all was done
The foe reached into the man's pocket and what did he find?
An apple to feed this ghost of mine

I knew, no matter what I did, this battle wasn't ending in my favor. So I ran.

I was the only one left, and by the time they finished with the other godkillers, I would be too far away. They were all hurt except Velenor, and she'd be too busy tending to the rest of them to put up a chase. Hakara's finger still lay warm in my palm.

It was the only way Kluehnn would believe that I'd killed her.

The rain increased to a downpour, obscuring the road from view. I could still feel the bond with Hakara in the back of my head, stretching with each step I took away from her. She'd make it through this. I wasn't sure I would.

I was going back into the den, to a god who'd nearly killed me the last time I'd failed him. I'd learned too many of his secrets, and I had no idea what Mull had told him while I'd been gone. The man was a scholar, not a hardened fighter used to enduring pain.

But Naatar, who loved Khatuya, who never wanted us to fight – he was there in the den and he didn't deserve whatever Kluehnn was doing to him. Every time I turned, I still expected to see my cohort with me. Rain gathered dust, running in muddy rivulets down the hill I climbed. The grass was damp, brushing against my knees. I leaned against a tree at the top, taking a moment to catch my breath.

There was something comfortable about believing in Kluehnn, in letting him tell me what to do and how to live my life. All I'd had to do was to make one choice – to take Millani's hand after I'd been transformed – and the rest had flowed naturally from there. There was no natural flow to what I was doing now. My faith was broken; my cohort was broken. I was not strong the way Hakara was, fierce and unbending. But I was still strong and Naatar needed my help. Somehow the bond we'd built mattered more than the one I'd built with Kluehnn. He was always aloof, mysterious, strange. But my cohort? We'd been through everything together and we'd come out the other side. And now Khatuya was dead.

My hand tightened around the finger as I remembered the pact Khatuya, Naatar, and I had once made, before our third trial, when we'd faced the dzhalobo. Before we'd become a cohort. A pact that was more important to me now than anything else.

I found myself humming – a tune I thought I'd forgotten. The lullaby Hakara had once sung to me at night, the same one I'd sung to Sheuan before we'd spent the night together. A song about a boy and his horse and a pocket of apples. I'd thought this tune a weakness before, but the music bolstered me, strengthened my faltering heart.

We go in together. We leave together.

None of us leaves any of the other two behind.

61
Mullayne

11 years after the restoration of Kashan
and 572 years after the Shattering

Langzu - the den northeast of Bian

Avagnith the adventurer went to the depths of the world, to Unterra, and returned after a length of ten years. Hers is the only verifiable account we have of a mortal returning to the surface after finding their way to the land of the gods. She said she missed her friend and could not bear to be apart from him any longer. They became lovers, yet even as they did so, Avagnith was putting her affairs in order. She gave away her finest jewelry, signed her home over to a friend in need, and wrote letters to everyone she cared about.

And then, six months after returning to the surface, she quietly died.

Mull's prison was filled with meat hooks. The lamp outlined the sharpness of the metal, glinted off the shimmering god's blood on the floor. The room was empty now except for him, the door solid metal and locked from the outside.

The lock turned.

Dread filled him. Sometimes, when the lock turned, it was just a meal being thrust into the room before the door clanged closed again. Sometimes, it was Kluehnn. There was fear in the uncertainty, in not knowing if he was getting the aspect or food.

The aspect did, at times, emerge from the hole in the corner of the room, and Mull was served two meals a day, so that at least meant, probability-wise, if the lock turned it was likely food.

But probability didn't ease those feelings of dread. He couldn't reason his way out of them, and the fact that reason held no sway in this dark, bloody room made the whole experience a thousand times worse. He'd come to the den thinking he could face any obstacle and overcome it, and now he knew there were obstacles that were far beyond him, that he couldn't overcome no matter how hard he tried. He was altered, he was alone, he was imprisoned – and he couldn't change anything about any of these facts, much as he wanted to.

A hand appeared around the door, and then another, and the tension at the back of Mull's neck exploded into a paralyzing fear. He didn't know how the godkillers and the converts could stand it, bowing before the aspect, making themselves vulnerable in such a way.

His breathing quickened and he seized a meat hook from above. It was a play he'd made before, but he never executed an experiment only once.

The god flowed into the room, teeth bright by lamplight, filaments reminding Mull of nothing so much as the last stray hairs on a bald man's head come to life. The aspect seemed a mockery of life. There was nothing beautiful about it, nothing that spoke of generations of trial and error. It was an amalgamation of terrible, incongruent parts.

He lifted the meat hook, and the aspect only laughed, the sound echoing from stone. "Must we, Mullayne Reisun?"

It crouched so all its hands and feet touched the floor, and crept to him with the speed of a centipede. Mull swiped the hook; the god caught it in one hand and wrenched it free.

In the next moment, he'd cocooned Mull in a cage of hands and cloven feet, claws scratching at his throat, threatening more than just scratches. "What did you tell the gods?"

"Only that you were powerful, but you were leaving the den. Everyone knew." Everyone knew – *including Rasha*. He'd given up so much more than he'd intended: his name, his clan, his purpose in coming to the den, his encounter with Hakara and her crew.

He'd thought, in those daydreaming moments at his desk, that he would stand against torture, that he'd have the mental and emotional fortitude to feel pain and then be able to compartmentalize it, to examine it with intellectual detachment. Instead, he'd caved almost immediately, telling the aspect nearly all it wanted to know.

He just wasn't who he'd thought he might be. There'd been comfort in never having been challenged in this way, because back then, he could tell himself there was a chance he'd react with valor. Instead, he'd found the depths of himself, and they were not nearly as pristine as he'd once imagined.

He'd let his friends die. He'd let himself be permanently altered. He'd been caught.

Once, these had all seemed impossibilities, and yet here he was. Kluehnn was going to torture him, one way or another. He'd committed too many sins against the god to escape with his life. The least he could do was to keep Rasha from losing hers. Maybe she'd do something more worthwhile with it than he had.

"What else did you tell them?" One claw pierced the junction of neck and shoulder, digging in so deep it scraped against his collarbone. "What do you know?"

He couldn't even think of a convenient lie. He would have told Kluehnn anything, if only he could think of something that made sense. So he divulged the most secret information he knew. "I read about the pact you made. The corestones."

Kluehnn's eyes narrowed. "The seeds."

The door scraped open. Kluehnn's head whipped about.

A cohort of godkillers entered, dragging two bodies behind them. "We found them trying to spy near the den," the godkiller at the front said, her pronged horns catching the light. "Forgive the interruption."

Kluehnn said nothing, only waited as they hung the naked bodies on the hooks. As soon as the door closed behind them, he let Mull go – so quickly that he landed hard on the ground, his shoulder aching. By the time he had rolled to a sitting position, the aspect was already at one of the bodies, both mouths fastened on the god's leg.

A low shock rippled through him. Kluehnn was *eating* the god. But when Mull stopped to separate his emotional reaction from his thoughts, it all made a strange sort of sense. Why would they keep the bodies instead of burning them, even if a god's body never decomposed? How would this room not become crowded? A part of him had just assumed they would throw the bodies into the pit when they ran out of space, but now that assumption seemed silly.

A crunch of teeth on bone echoed through the cave, and Mull curled into the corner, letting his mind tumble forward, away from the fact that something very horrifying was happening only a few steps away. If this was what the aspect lived on – and he had never seen it eat anything else – then of course the gods would take the bodies when they raided the den. Of course they would burn them. It wasn't just about honoring their dead. It was about weakening Kluehnn.

If he didn't have enough to eat, he'd have to attack. Pont had often despaired of ever teaching Mull to brawl, so he'd done the next best thing – he'd given him books on military strategy, both to help with his Cressiman and to at least be able to honestly tell Mull's parents he was teaching him how to fight. Some of that knowledge had filtered into Mull's brain, because he knew that forcing an enemy into a position where they had to attack gave you an advantage. It made them predictable, and predictability meant you had the leisure to respond in a way that would give you the upper hand.

Mercifully, Kluehnn did not return to questioning him when he'd finished eating his fill. He left the room, the two gods still hanging, one with his leg partially chewed away.

The lock turned.

The first thing Mull did was search the bodies. He found nothing useful. He sagged to the floor, his knees just shy of the puddle of shimmering blood. When he lifted his gaze again, all he could see from this angle was the gruesome, jagged thigh bone Kluehnn had left behind, jutting out from flesh.

When Kluehnn came back, he'd eat again. And when he ate, he'd be vulnerable.

Mull reached up and felt the end of the bone. Sharp as the point of a blade. He pulled. The body only swayed in response to the pressure. He lifted his other hand, digging his claws into flesh.

These were not the most dignified moments of Mull's life, and all told, they were moments he hoped he would quickly forget. He tried to tell himself it was just like butchering a chicken – an activity he'd only completed once, to understand the underlying structure. For all his scholarly detachment, the cold, slimy feel of dead flesh made him want to retch.

He swallowed his bile. He used his new strength, his new claws. He cut away the tendons and pulled the bone free. Then he snapped off one of the jagged pieces.

Sleep took him before he could enact the second part of his plan. The next turning of the lock caught him unawares, laid out on the floor. He was lucky. It was a meal – a thin porridge with unidentifiable bits of meat and woody vegetables. He ate it quickly, keeping the bone close. He was unsure whether it was day or night; all he knew was that he needed to stay awake if he wanted to live. He stood next to the door, the sharp-edged bone tucked into his waistband, the shard between his fingertips.

He found himself nodding off even while standing. The aspect would still be hungry – it would have to still be hungry after not eating for so long. Mull propped himself against the wall, blinking.

The lock turned again.

The sound woke him fully, his heartbeat quickening. Just as the door opened, he shoved the shard of bone into the space that appeared between the hinges. Then he leapt back, just as the door closed on the shard. He couldn't be sure if it had held, if it had stopped the door from latching, but he couldn't check either.

Kluehnn flowed into the cave, his presence pushing Mull back and away from the door. The aspect let out a low, harsh laugh. "Did you think you might escape? Jump on whoever came to serve your food? You're no warrior, Mullayne Reisun." With a snort, it went to one of the hanging bodies. It didn't move with the same urgency as before, the edge of its hunger sated. Mull touched a finger to the end of the sharpened bone at his waist as he watched Kluehnn latch onto the arm of the nearest dead god.

The aspect paused, drawing back, shimmering blood on its lips. "You're a clever man. Should I keep you alive, do you think, or should I kill you? I can never trust you to be loyal to me, even though you cave beneath the slightest pressure. And clever men are always dangerous."

Mull edged closer to the door, not daring to look at it. In the end, his cleverness hadn't made him better than anyone else. He'd aimed it toward selfish desires, convinced that his pursuits were helpful to everyone. He was making mining more efficient, he was uncovering hidden histories, he was searching for a cure for Imeah. He'd been blind to the larger world – no wonder Sheuan had thought through the implications of the filters before he had. And this was where it had all gotten him – his pride, his selfishness, his gods-damned cleverness.

He had to remake himself. If he had grown fat off his cleverness, the profits of his workshop, then this den was his chrysalis, and he would emerge changed. Cleverness was nothing without wisdom, and the wisdom he'd gained was hard-earned.

If he escaped. He needed to escape.

Kluehnn returned to eating and Mull took a sliding step toward the door. One more step, and he could reach out and take the handle. He had to be careful. He'd seen the aspect move, knew that it was much, much quicker than he was, even in his altered form.

Kluehnn froze, all eyes pivoting to focus on Mull, and then on the door. Everything sharpened, the sound of his own breathing harsh in his ears.

They moved at the same time.

Mull pulled the shattered bone free and reached for the door. Kluehnn's footsteps thundered across the stone floor, a terrible mix of clicking hooves and slapping hands.

The door opened. His shard of bone had kept it from latching.

But Kluehnn was there, towering over him, trying to get between him and the way out. Mull stabbed at the creature blindly. The shard of bone sank into one of its eyes, and the aspect screamed. One clawed hand still made it around Mull's guard, seizing the top of the door, trying to push it closed.

A thought drifted to the front of Mull's mind.

He had to remake himself.

All those carved messages in the tomb – written in stone and not on malleable paper, like the books he'd been instructed to mark. The etchings could not be changed. Tolemne didn't stay down in Unterra after returning there. He came back to the surface. He buried his family after he'd returned, not before. *I cannot survive up here. I must go back.* So he'd gone back to Unterra and become someone else.

The claw in the wall, the pact between the elder gods. Tolemne had carved that into the stone. If all the gods were bound by it, then Kluehnn shouldn't have been able to speak the truth of it without dying. The seeds, he'd said. Unless he wasn't a god at all.

Mull leaned close as he pulled at the door, his whisper barely audible past his strained breathing. "You say you are the one true god. But that isn't true, is it, Tolemne?"

The aspect recoiled, its hand slipping from the door. Mull yanked it open, slipped out, and slammed it shut.

The aspect howled, the sound muted by the metal door. Mull ran.

No one stopped him; they stopped those who were going deeper into the den, not those who were going up. He caught confused glances, hand lifting a moment too late.

He had to dodge one set of hands before bursting into the light of day. There were altered in the rocks. They would skewer him with crossbow bolts. But he couldn't stop himself from running. At least he'd die under an open sky.

The beat of wings sounded next to his ear. A bird landed on his shoulder, claws digging into his fur. "Keep running," a hoarse voice said. "We'll get you out."

And then the crow was flowing from his shoulder, changing into an enormous gray wolf with raised hackles and teeth as long as Mull's fingers. It loped alongside him as two other birds fell from the sky, shifting into wolves that ran up the mountainside.

Shouts and screams echoed from the rocks. The whimper of an injured animal.

"Get on my back," the giant wolf growled.

It felt like a dream, stranger than the ones Mull usually had, which generally involved books and tea and the solitude of quiet places. He seized the fur around the wolf's shoulders and pulled himself onto the creature's back.

It darted away from the den and up into the mountains. Mull had the presence of mind to press himself flat, to become a smaller target. A bolt whizzed above his head. Every moment felt etched into memory, as though his mind wanted to make sure that if these were his last seconds, he'd understand each detail of them. The roughness of the wolf's fur beneath his fingertips, the rasp of his breath in his throat, the wind lashing tears from his eyes.

Kluehnn was Tolemne. He was *Tolemne*. The thought ran circles in his mind. There was so much he still didn't understand. What had happened to the man? How was he still alive, his consciousness split into aspects? What had he done when he'd gone back to Unterra?

If Tolemne had gone to Unterra to plead with the gods, and none of them answered except Kluehnn, that meant that none of the gods had offered him help. The only one who'd helped Tolemne had been himself.

They stopped at last in a valley between two mountains, a small, verdant spot watered by the morning mists. A camp had been erected here, tents lined up in neat rows. People and animals began to emerge from the tents to greet them. The people seemed to shine with an inner light, skin and fur glowing in the late-afternoon sun. Gods. Two other wolves emerged from the mountains, one stopping to lick at a bolt that nestled in its side. Mull slid from his mount's back.

The wolf turned its head, brown eyes meeting Mull's. "Your friend Rasha spoke of you. She said you had information, that you'd been to the depths of the den."

Mull tried to set his thoughts straight, unsure of where to begin. "I do. There's another path to Unterra in there. Irael's Path. You could go back. You could—"

A voice emerged from among the gods. "No. They could not."

Mull's heart seemed to thud to a stop, the air crystallizing in his lungs. He *knew* that voice.

Imeah stepped from between the gods. She didn't walk with a cane. She stood tall, her black hair loose. "I made my way back, darling," she said, her lips curving into a smile.

He wasn't sure when he'd moved, but then he was holding her, their heads resting on one another's shoulders, their breathing aligned. "You're well. You're *well*."

"It's not what it seems," she said, her arms still wrapped around his back. "And I have so much more to tell you – about what happened when you left me, where I went, where I have to go. But know this: the gods cannot go back to Unterra."

He wanted to say he didn't care, but he couldn't be the same person he'd once been. "Tell me then. What does it mean? What must we do?"

She finally pulled away, her hands on his shoulders. "The Unanointed stopped restoration. They brought the gods out from hiding. It means the real war is beginning."

62
Lithuas

10 years before the Shattering

Langzu - Ruzhi

Ruzhi once nestled securely in the mountains, sure-footed as a goat. The first disastrous flash-flooding of the city occurred 463 years after the Shattering and has occurred thereafter in decreasing intervals. In this first flood, buildings were carried down the slopes, smashed into the gorge below. Trees that had once thrived on the mountainside died, their roots rotting, no longer able to hold mud and debris in place. And what did the citizens of Ruzhi do? They have rebuilt each time, because this is certainly easier to do than to move somewhere else. In spite of the periodic flooding, Ruzhi is more resistant to drought. There is no safe place in Langzu, but at least this is the sort of unsafe that everyone already knows.

The city of Ruzhi smelled of pine sap and the crispness of sweet persimmons. Lithuas climbed the sloping street before her, stopping every so often to lean heavily on a cane. Some shapeshifters only took on the appearance of the shape they inhabited, but in this way, Lithuas and Irael differed greatly. Lithuas inhabited a shape fully, with all of its foibles and aches. Irael flitted from shape to shape like a dream, each more fantastical than the last.

Which made Lithuas a much better assassin than Irael would ever be.

She could feel the world changing along with her, day by day, with every god she hunted and killed. She'd seen Kluehnn's experiments in the depths of Unterra. Soon, he would shatter the world and bring forth his own children. Children he could use to hunt gods on his own.

He would still need her. She lifted her gaze to the peak of the mountains. Ruzhi lay nestled in a valley between two of them, benefiting from the way the morning mists were trapped by the peaks, the moisture rolling down to gather below. This place wasn't safe from the changes wrought on the surface, though the three clans that had their main estates here thought themselves inured. She could see, when she squinted, the future of this city. When some of the pine trees died, when rain became a deluge, washing mud down the sides of the mountain. They'd have to rebuild, again and again. The grand temple, the castles, the history – these things would fall, the meaning behind them lost. They'd replace the temple with a nave for Kluehnn, each iteration of their castles less grand and less ornate, not feeling they had another choice as they waited for his promised restoration.

Her cane thumped against the stones of the street as the city woke. Shutters above her were thrown open, the faded red-painted plaster of the buildings glowing crimson by the light of the rising sun, dark brown roof tiles glinting. Jewel of Langzu, they called it.

She'd heard Ayaz was here, peddling the gemstones that were one of the few remnants of the Numinars. She'd never really understood the Cutter, his obsession with clean lines and efficiency. Likely he'd say the same of her, that her focus on change above all else was rather messy. But that was as far as their disagreements went; they quickly turned to other matters without ever coming to blows. Not like Barexi, whose desire to hold on to every artifact, no matter how cluttered that made his library, was anathema to Ayaz. Barexi – whom she'd killed, watching his blood spill onto the ground.

Desperation drove Lithuas forward, made her forget, for a moment, that she didn't just appear as an old woman – she *was* one.

A man with a cart laden with peaches stopped as she stumbled, seizing her arm before she could fall. "Careful, grandmother," he said. "Rushing may save you time, but dying spends it all at once."

It was an old saying, so old that even Lithuas wasn't sure where it had originated from. She nodded her head to the young man and pulled away, afraid that if she spoke, she'd tell him that she wasn't afraid of dying. It was others dying she was afraid of. She still believed in much of what Kluehnn wanted to accomplish, in restoration and changing the world. But the murder of the gods – she didn't want this.

Her knees ached. She hadn't changed form since Bian, knowing that if she did, Ayaz would sense her coming. She'd gathered all the information she'd needed there, flitting from room to room as a fly, listening to conversations and piecing things together. He'd be at the market, seemingly selling pearl and tortoiseshell combs. And if one asked the right questions, he'd duck into a nearby tea shop and bring out his rarer wares. She wasn't sure how long he'd stay in Ruzhi before he moved on.

The street widened and leveled, stalls clinging to the sides of buildings, spilling over into alleys, where customers had to step over refuse to reach the wares they wanted.

She bought a few persimmons, partially so she'd look just like someone browsing the wares, and partially because the taste reminded her of the tintean berries in Unterra – which she desperately missed.

Plucking one from her bag to bite into, she turned into an alley. Light filtered down from the narrow gap between the roof tiles above; condensation born of the morning mists dripped every so often from the bottoms of the gutters, darkening the stones at her feet.

Ayaz was there, and her rapid heartbeat calmed.

If she hadn't known him over all the long centuries, she might not have recognized him. He'd stripped the scales from his face, the skin beneath pale and slightly pockmarked. Here, in the darkness of the alley, his eyes looked golden brown rather than gold, his white hair with its streaks of black pulled into a tail.

Another man sat behind the stall, hunched on his stool, carving a fresh new comb out of dark wood.

She slowed to look at the combs, eating her persimmon as she browsed. She picked up one with her face carved at the top – the face she usually wore. "People these days do not appreciate the old gods." Her voice was thin and reedy. She set the comb back down, choosing a mother-of pearl one with the eye of Kluehnn etched onto its surface. "The new religion is catching. Soon it may be all there is."

Ayaz cocked his head at her, and she saw the serpent in him considering whether he could swallow his prey. He wore a voluminous robe; she wasn't sure if his tail was lashing beneath it. "Is that what you want, grandmother?"

She tossed the comb back onto the table. "He promises magic

on a grand scale, but there is a part of me that would miss the more subtle magic of the elder gods." She shook her head, really feeling the role she'd chosen. "I am too old for all this change."

Ayaz's hands came together and he bowed, followed it with a nod. "Ah, I know how you feel."

Lithuas let the silence hang, hoping he'd follow through. Look how harmless she was, just an elderly woman with a cane. And see? She'd had the money to buy a whole bag of persimmons. She took a last bite of the one in her hand before tossing the stem aside. Her gaze lingered on the combs.

He cleared his throat. "I may have just the thing for you, if you'll step into this shop. Lei, watch the stall for a moment."

"Well, you have my curiosity." She followed him down the step. He had to duck to get through the side door, but he held it open as she passed into the tiny space of the tea shop. The proprietor glanced back from his spot at the front counter and gave Ayaz a brief nod of acknowledgment. They must have had an arrangement.

Lithuas tried not to let her gaze wander too much, to the herbs hanging from the ceiling and gathered into small clay jars. It smelled *wonderful* in here. Tea was one of the few things she felt mortals actually got right, and that made her feel a bit fonder toward them than she might have otherwise. To most mortals in Ruzhi, this was just another tea shop. To her, it was a treasury.

Ayaz lifted the flap of his satchel, removed a folded handkerchief, and held it before her. "The Numinars may be gone, but there are pieces of them left behind, deep underground." Carefully, as though he were uncovering the delicate carapace of an insect, he unfolded the handkerchief. A glow emanated from within, and Lithuas thought, with an ache, of the brightness of a Numinar on the places where the bark had worn smooth. She would never see the grandness of those broad trees again on the surface. This was the problem with change – it always meant leaving things behind.

A rough, uncut gemstone lay on the cloth, cupped in Ayaz's hand. A soft red light emanated from it. "The roots of the Numinars emit sap, a sap the gods drank to help sustain their powers. While the roots may have mostly rotted, the sap has remained, crystallizing into these stones that still have magical properties."

With her gaze fixed on the stone, all she could think about was how cleanly and quickly Ayaz had turned to this huckster lifestyle from one of godly decadence. He might not have been the Bringer of Change, but he was more smoothly adaptable than she'd given him credit for.

She turned to the proprietor of the shop. "Leave us."

"This is my shop, and—"

Lithuas didn't raise her voice or turn from Ayaz. "Leave us if you value your life." She let her tone fall into her normal register, and something about it must have stirred the hairs on the back of the man's neck, because she heard the front door open and close.

Ayaz was looking at her with narrowed eyes, knowing something wasn't quite right but not sure what that was.

She grabbed his wrist before he could reach for his knife. "I am here to warn you," she said.

"What a funny way to do things." His hand snapped shut around the gem. "Warn me and then kill me. What use is the warning, then?"

"If I'd wanted to kill you, I would have done it already. I could have taken you unawares."

"The way you did Barexi?"

She hadn't even used subterfuge with Barexi. She'd only stated that she wanted to talk, and Barexi – who'd never had a deceitful bone in his body – had believed her. One swift move, and her sword had jutted from his chest, the light fading from his eyes. Only a god could kill another god.

Though Kluehnn was working on changing that. With her help.

Ayaz dropped the gem to the floor and pulled his knife free. He was quick, but Lithuas was quicker. She took a step away, her old woman's form melting into her true shape, silver hair flowing down her back, sword in hand. "Please, we both know we're not evenly matched," she huffed out.

His gaze flicked to the door.

"Don't even try it."

He shrugged his shoulders, though he didn't sheathe the knife. "Fine. Let's say I believe you. What have you come to warn me about?"

She couldn't fight back against Kluehnn. She had come to accept that. If she did, she would die and all the events she'd set in motion would continue as though she were still alive. But this way, by still working with him, she could enact the changes she wanted and could, perhaps, save some people in the meantime.

"He has sent me to kill the gods, but he is developing a way to kill them without a god's help." Or without further help. Her wrist ached in response to the memory of a blade parting her skin, the blood dripping down her hand, the intent to kill throbbing with every beat of her heart. She lifted her blade so the point was level with Ayaz's chin. "Here are your options. You can fight me now, and lose."

"Or?" He didn't look sad, the way Velenor had. His gaze was merely considering, calculating.

"Or you go into hiding. You don't interfere with my work or Kluehnn's. I'll tell him that you're dead."

"Why spare me? Did you spare others?"

"I didn't have the chance." A lie, but better that Velenor didn't know Lithuas was sparing her brethren. Better to keep them isolated, for their sake and for hers.

The end of his golden tail swung out from beneath his robe. "It can be hard for a god to hide."

"Cut off your tail. You can even keep it if you really think you'll have use of it again one day. Remove the rest of your scales. Continue selling the sad remains of the Numinars, if that's what you want to do."

He sheathed his knife then, steepling his fingers and placing them beneath his chin. She didn't lower her guard. She knew Ayaz could be tricky. "Well I appreciate the warning," he said. A deep breath in and then out. "So. You said we cannot interfere with your work or Kluehnn's. What of the mortals? Am I allowed to get involved in their affairs?"

Ah. She sheathed her sword. Lithuas understood the need for an outlet. This was Ayaz, though. Hopefully she would not regret this. "Do as you will with them."

63

Sheuan

11 years after the restoration of Kashan and 572 years after the Shattering

Langzu - inner Bian, the Sovereign's castle

To Wensama Juitsi, Minister of Archives, I, the humble Minister of Trade, seek your help in swaying the Sovereign toward investigating the disappearance of trade items at the anchor. We have all assumed there is no monster, but then what is causing the losses? The Sovereign does not seem to think it worth the effort. If you and I worked together, however, we might get Ashi Risho, the Minister of Austerity, on our side. I know — she's a tight-fisted, miserable woman, and no one likes her except perhaps the Sovereign. Which means we need her support.

For a span of twenty days after the aspect had left, the Sovereign kept mostly to himself. Not that Sheuan minded. She went about her business and did her best to avoid her husband. She knew that when they finally did talk, he'd be in a foul mood. Who wouldn't be? Kluehnn had upended all his plans in one fell swoop. And as soon as the new godkiller cohorts arrived to be permanently stationed at the castle, the Sovereign would be as watched as Sheuan was now.

Perhaps he'd devise some clever plan – that seemed to be his way. He still had the support of the clans, though that support might fray when the godkillers descended on inner Bian. Anyone worth their weight could identify a power struggle, and they'd seek to find advantages in it.

The scent of rain was in the air by the time Sheuan returned to the castle from the workshop, her two enforcers in tow. She let them follow her, unsure what her next move would be, where she should dig now. It felt like she had all the pieces to this puzzle, but no matter which way she turned them, she couldn't seem to quite make them fit together.

She climbed the ramp and felt the first patters of rainfall cold against her scalp. They needed the rain, but it also often occurred in sudden deluges, washing out the dried earth and flooding the crops. It wouldn't necessarily make their lives any easier.

"Sheuan," one of the guards said at the doors. "The Sovereign wishes to see you in his study."

She shook herself from her thoughts and ducked inside the entryway. She supposed she couldn't avoid the man forever, and though she knew he'd be angry, she might as well get this over with. Maybe he'd let something slip about her father. Something she could use. For now, she'd settled on the idea that he'd known about the Sovereign's worship of the elder gods.

It didn't feel like the whole story.

She climbed the steps to the next floor, slightly annoyed that the enforcers followed her there as well. Was she not to be given a moment's peace, even in her own home? Would she always be in this escalating arms race with them, with her finding ever more clever ways to escape notice while they increased their defenses? It wasn't exactly the life she'd hoped for.

She had to go to her mother, tell her exactly what she'd found in the warehouse. And she'd put a letter in a safe place for Mull. Assuming he was able to make it out of the den alive. Probably she should leave another letter for someone in the royal clans, to be opened upon her death. Maybe Nimao. At least then, someone else would know, and she could threaten to release the information widely if the Sovereign tried to have her executed.

She stepped into the Sovereign's study, leaving the enforcers outside. He was lingering by the window, watching the rain begin to fall past the overhang of the roof, drumming against the tiles – a silvered curtain between them and the lakebed. If it rained for too long, it delayed the burning of bodies, left the southern side of the city dealing with the terrible stench of decaying flesh.

"You wanted to see me?"

His voice was sharp when he spoke to her, as she'd expected. "How did word get out about the filters, about what I was doing? How did Kluehnn know?"

She strode closer to him, to show him she was not afraid, that she had nothing to hide. "I didn't tell anyone, if that's what you're asking."

His hair was still dyed that ridiculous shade of black, the gold in his brown eyes dulled by the overcast sky. "I was *careful*."

She stood only a pace away from him now, and still he didn't look at her. "You think I would tell someone, that I would bring Kluehnn down on our heads with my life on the line? Who would he have been more likely to punish? You, the ruler of this country? Or me, your wife from a dead clan, who was caught *making* the damned things. You wanted to distribute the filters as you saw fit, you let the clans jostle for favor, as you always do, and someone among them couldn't keep their mouth shut. It was your own sloppiness that caused this, not mine."

To her surprise, he stayed silent, his jaw clenching. Was he still angry with her, or was he angry with himself? She'd never seen him like this, defeat etched into the lines of his shoulders, the looseness of his hands. Instinctively, she reached out, closing the distance between them. She touched him as a wife would – a reassuring caress, her fingers against his cheek.

He caught her hand.

There was strength in his grip, far more than she'd expected. Without knowing exactly why, she tested her strength against his, knowing she'd grown stronger since the feathers had begun to sprout from her back.

She broke free, sliding a hand beneath his robe, pulling him in close.

He *hated* her, she could see it in his gold-flecked gaze. But hate was something more than indifference, and maybe it heated his skin the way it heated hers. She thrust her hand around his back, loosening his robe from the tightness of his belt. Her fingers brushed the scar.

The scar.

The altar flashed in her mind, the incense lit for the elder gods – all except Lithuas and Ayaz. It wasn't an altar of worship, as she'd thought. It was an altar for the dead, to honor those who'd passed. But no incense lit for the living. Not for Lithuas, and not for Ayaz. The Cutter.

He'd carefully cut away at the clans, excising the elements he knew wouldn't work for him, keeping the ones he knew would make him strong. He'd done such a good job of hiding in plain sight – until he'd reached a little too far. He'd gotten lucky, though. Kluehnn hadn't recognized him.

The way Sheuan recognized him now. "It's *you*," was all she managed.

He seized her again, his grip firmer this time. He turned her about, hands rough, searching her, though she wasn't sure for what. She tried to pull away again, unsuccessfully. "Ayaz."

He shook her. "Don't you dare. Do not say that *name*."

Gods below, this was what her father had discovered. The tablets with the descriptions of the gods, the scar he must have seen on the Sovereign's back. Of course the Sovereign would have framed him for this, would have gotten rid of him as quickly as possible. A brief ache of grief for what could have been, if only her father hadn't been so recklessly clever.

The way she'd been.

Ayaz's hands found her back, stilled. His fingers traced the outlines of feathers, the strange bones that pressed against her skin.

Without another word, he took her by the wrist and dragged her toward the door.

"Where are we going?" Her voice was oddly steady, though her mind could only settle on the executioner's block, the sharpness of a blade against her neck.

The enforcers moved to follow them, but he waved them back. "No. Stay at your posts."

She tried again to break free when they reached the first floor, but his grip was like iron. One of the elder gods. How could she not have known? He'd not reacted to her like anyone she'd ever encountered. So many missed opportunities, ways to find this out without exposing herself. To settle into the darkness, unseen, ready to pounce.

He took the set of stairs to the windowless lower level, where the servants stored curing meats and root vegetables. It was dark down here, and for a moment she considered screaming. What exactly would that accomplish, though? Who would come running to help her? Absolutely no one. How painfully obvious to her now, that she'd wrenched herself free from the grasp of her mother and her clan only to land herself in a place where she had no support. She'd leapt, but she'd leapt too far.

He passed the root cellar and went to a locked door. So quickly Sheuan wasn't sure what she was seeing, he broke the lock, seized the lantern from next to the door, and pushed his way inside. The space was vast and quiet, the floor beneath her feet rough and damp. The floorboards above creaked as a servant passed through the main hall.

The godkillers had dusted off the altar at one end of the unfinished room. Near the altar was a pit. They drew closer and she could see the mark of claws, as though it had been freshly dug. Was this where he would murder her?

When she craned her neck to see how deep the pit was, all she could make out was a cloud of black smoke.

"Do the filters work? Do they work as you promised?" the Sovereign hissed at her. The golden rings in his eyes glinted. He set the lantern on the ground and took one of the filters from his pocket. He'd kept one on his person. He pulled her in close, deftly pulling the filter over her nose and mouth, cinching the strap tight. "Do they protect against restoration?"

"Yes," she said, her voice muted and frightened to her own ears.

There'd been no way to test it. Theoretically, Mull had said it would work. Theoretically.

She felt his hand at her back, between the itching pinfeathers. The shove took the breath from her lungs, and she fell into the hole.

The hole in the Queen's nave in Kashan had been shallow. As in Kashan, she didn't fall far. She stumbled to her knees, the smoke stinging her eyes. This time, sensation didn't leave her. She stood surrounded by the swirling smoke, and each breath she took was clear of it. She could feel her hands, her fingers against her palms, the strange coolness of the smoke against her skin.

What would he do with the results of this experiment? Did he have the means to help restoration along? If he saw restoration as a way of cutting away what he didn't want, to further his personal ambitions, then he needed the filters. He needed them to work. She thought of the letter from Mull, still in her pocket.

She had a choice. She could preserve herself, as she'd thought she wanted to. She'd been the blade that had protected her family from ruin, and when she'd proposed to the Sovereign, she'd thought she was done protecting others. Her mother had pushed her into that position without ever taking a moment to find out who Sheuan was or what she *wanted*.

But not wanting to be the blade that kept her family in power – it didn't mean she cared for no one. In spite of everything, all her failures, the way she'd fumbled her way through these schemes, she still loved her mother, her family, Mull.

Rasha.

She could save herself, or she could protect others, finding a way back into a community. One she'd chosen. And wouldn't this be the ultimate trick? Manipulating a god? Sheuan felt her lips curve into a smile as she lifted the filter and breathed in the smoke.

Everything faded into pain. Bones lengthened and re-formed, flesh moved to accommodate new shapes. She had no mind; she was only a body, and that body was on fire.

She came back to awareness with her hand gripping the side of the hole. She watched, as though from a distance, as her other hand met the first, and she pulled herself up and out. The filter was still on her face; she'd at least had the presence of mind not to tear it off.

"You *lied* to me!" Ayaz was screaming. "You *lied*!"

She was calmer than she'd expected to be, her body still aching. She twitched and found black-feathered wings at her shoulders, a band of white on the undersides. The air inside the filter still smelled faintly of smoke, tinged with ink and star anise. She pulled it from her face, letting it rest against her collarbone. "I didn't lie. I told you it would theoretically work. I'm not my cousin. We had no way to test it until just now."

She flexed one wing, trying to stretch out the new muscles. She wouldn't be able to sneak through the city anymore. What would someone like Nimao think of her now? Oh, he'd probably find this development even more attractive, knowing him. "There's only one thing we can do."

Ayaz ran his hands through his hair, and she watched the withering of his expression as all his carefully laid plans fell apart. "I don't know what that is." Strangely, she felt no awe of him. Now that she knew who he was, she thought she understood him a little. An elder god, living among mortals, convinced of his superiority and yet alone. Desperately alone. No matter how solitary he might have been in the past, there was still comfort in knowing others like you were out and about in the world. Instead, his kind was hunted. He'd watched the fall of his people and the rise of Kluehnn and the godkillers. What a terrible thing to live through.

And now that she'd broken him down, it was time to build him back up.

She pulled Mull's letter from his pocket, noting that her hands did not have claws. Her fingers looked the same as they had before. She'd have to get a glimpse in the mirror at some point, to see exactly what had changed. Ayaz didn't take the letter from her hand, so she seized his wrist, pressed the parchment into his palm.

"There is an army of the gods, gathering. With restoration delayed, and Kluehnn distracted by the Unanointed, they've had the chance to regroup. You're Ayaz. You're one of the elder gods.

"Lead them."

64

Hakara

11 years after the restoration of Kashan and 572 years after the Shattering

Langzu - on the road from Bian to Xiazen

There are always points in history where people feel stuck, the forward progress of society a wheel with a stick caught in the spokes. But if enough pressure is applied, if even one person is forceful enough, the stick can be broken and momentum restored.

The rain turned into a miserable downpour, my hand throbbing terribly with each move I made. I could barely breathe through it. Nioanen had torn his shirt free, and he'd used this to bandage my wound. I gritted my teeth, trying to ignore both the sensation of my bond with Rasha stretching and the strange twin heartbeat in my chest.

I strode over to Velenor and Lithuas. Nioanen was behind me, tending to Talie, Zayyel dissolved back into the air. Alifra had made it through, yet again, without a scratch.

Lithuas stood by the side of the road, her sword nestled in the grass. She was the soggiest, saddest-looking elder god I'd ever had the misfortune of seeing. They were speaking in low voices, Velenor soft and coaxing. "We can protect you from him, if you'll let us."

"No. You can't. You mean to fight him. How can you protect me?"

"We can try."

I shook my head as I approached, water dripping from my hair. It was an effort to speak. "We doesn't include me. You want to break with Kluehnn? You want to start making things right? Where did you send Dashu?"

She glanced up at me, silver eyes a dull gray. "All the way back to Kashan, where we have more resources. In the den just past the barrier."

A weight in my chest eased. If we knew where he was, then we could find him.

She licked her lips. "Don't you want me dead?"

I glanced at Khatuya's body. Rasha's friend. Her black hair was plastered to her forehead, the rainwater now spilling from her open mouth, trickling over the grooves of her bark-like skin. "May seem strange to someone like you, but I've had enough of killing for today. You spared Nioanen. You spared Velenor. Maybe we spare you."

"I won't fight for you," she spat back, though her venom was mild.

I shrugged. "You and Nioanen can handle this," I told Velenor. I grimaced, a fresh wave of pain washing over me. Funny how pain could just take over a person's body like that, from just one tiny severed finger.

Velenor nodded. "I'll offer you the same bargain you gave us. You disappear into exile. You don't interfere. See how it feels,

Bringer of Change, living a life without real purpose. Maybe someday, when you're done with that, you'll come back to us."

Lithuas gave me one last, angry look before leaping into the air and shifting into a bird. We watched her go. Alifra joined us, one hand on her hip, her buoyant hair flatter in the rain. "We should find a place to regroup. There's a village ahead of us, with an inn. It'll be small, and we'll have to share rooms, but if Talie shifts back into a cat, we should be able to make it work."

Nioanen let me lean against him as we walked, and for once, I didn't feel resentful of the help. Maybe I was just too tired. "You won't be able to hide for much longer," I told him, half delirious as we walked.

His golden wings shook. "Maybe I'm done hiding."

Alifra paid the innkeeper enough money to avoid any questions. We ducked inside and hurried to two adjacent rooms, and somehow I ended up alone with Nioanen. He dug into my bag, found some clean bandages, dried and re-dressed my wound, his hands gentle. He helped me get out of my wet clothes and beneath the warm sheets of one of the two beds. I shivered, fighting against sleep, knowing there was more I had to say to him.

"Defender of the Helpless, eh?" I said, my tone light.

This time, when I said it, he didn't flinch. He caught a feather of one of his golden wings between his fingers, pulling until it slid free. "I suppose, in the end, that is who I am." He rose to go, but I grabbed his hand.

Without meaning to, my touch turned to a caress. Our fingers twined together, his thumb rubbing at my palm. "Velenor told me I should be dead." I couldn't look him in the eyes, not when we were this close. I knew if I did I would fall into them and I wouldn't be able to think. "At first I thought you must have done something to the corestone inside me, to keep it in check, to keep it from killing me. But then I remembered that Nioanen's . . .

your greatest magic was augmentation. You didn't do something to diminish the corestone's power. You did something to *augment* me. The glow when I use it." I swallowed. "It's like a god's aura."

"Hakara." Again, that tone in his voice, like he was afraid of losing me. He was immortal. I was not. He was always going to lose me.

I pressed a hand to my chest, still aware of that twin heartbeat. "It's a seed, and seeds grow. I can feel it. It's sprouting roots." The carving in the ruins, the god with the corestone at his lips. "The gods once swallowed them, to become the trees."

He let out a sigh.

I watched his face as I spoke. "You used to take them into your bodies willingly. You used to die, to become one with the trees. But when the mortals cut them down, used them for their own whims, you became less and less willing to do so. You stopped. You made a pact not to speak of it, to hide the information, to let it be forgotten."

His touch was light against my palm, his gaze on the floor. "If the mortals could be so selfish, why couldn't we?"

I squeezed his hand until he looked at me. I was afraid of falling into that gaze, of losing all reason, of never coming out – but I could never let myself be ruled by fear. "We have to make this right."

A thousand years of grief stared back at me. "There is no way to make this right. All of us tried."

I set my jaw. "Fine, fine. So we'll just try different things than you did." I'd stopped running. I understood myself better now, understood my flaws, the way I'd let them hurt the people around me. Maybe grief wasn't a thing I could shut away, but it wasn't a thing I needed to let swallow me either. It was simply a part of me, beating alongside everything else, just like the corestone sprouting roots inside my chest. I could use it to shape myself, or I could let it shape me.

He leaned in close, kissed my forehead with a tenderness that made me inexplicably want to cry. "You are terrible."

"First things first—"

"You are in bed. You need rest."

I ignored him, waving my injured hand, immediately regretting it. I let it sit back at my side, trying to forget it existed, sucking a breath in past my teeth. "Well. That may be true, but we need to find Mull, extract him from that den, find out what he knows. Rasha is acting under duress. We need to get her out as well. And we rescue Dashu."

"Just that?"

"Well, there's fighting Kluehnn and all his godkillers. After I rest." I already felt pulled into the mattress beneath me, my mind sinking. "You'll see, we'll find a way. Our world is broken, our team is broken, but all we have to do is put it back together."

His voice was light. "Is that all?"

"You and all the elder gods may have tried to make things right, but *I* haven't. And you've got to let me have a crack at it too, haven't you?"

A hand brushed the hair from my cheek. Something warm and wet struck my hairline, trickling past my ear. "You can accomplish all this after you rest?" The humor in his voice was tinged with sadness. "Then you had better sleep, Hakara."

I slept.

Acknowledgements

To my readers – thank you so much. Everything I write is only one half of a vision, and without readers, no book is truly complete. I'm so grateful I get to continue the adventures of these characters, to show you the middle of their story, and then to continue on to the end. I also get to go another year without having a "real job", which I will forever be thankful for as long as this lasts!

Thank you to my family, who always keep me grounded through the crazy process of writing a book. To John, who is always so supportive and is just an A+ human being in general. To my kids, who remind me to exist in the moment. And to the rest of my family, who form a network I know I can consistently rely on.

Thank you to everyone at Orbit, without whom this book would not exist. In particular, my editors James Long and Brit Hvide, cover designer Lauren Panepinto and cover artist Sasha Vinogradova (who consistently knock it out of the park!), the map artist Rebecka Champion (you made my scribbles into something beautiful!), copy-editor Jane Selley. Thank you to Ellen Wright and Nazia Khatun, whose work as publicists is both mysterious to me and absolutely essential.

Thank you to my agent, Juliet Mushens, who is exceptionally sharp and knowledgeable.

Thank you to all my friends and online communities who put up with my panicked ramblings and half-baked ideas. And to my in-person writing friends, who make this whole process feel less lonely. I love our Zoom writing sprint sessions and our food court business talks. I will always make time to grab dumplings with you all.

RAISING READERS
Books Build Bright Futures

Thank you for reading this book and for being a reader of books in general. As an author, I am so grateful to share being part of a community of readers with you, and I hope you will join me in passing our love of books on to the next generation of readers.

Did you know that reading for enjoyment is the single biggest predictor of a child's future happiness and success?

More than family circumstances, parents' educational background, or income, reading impacts a child's future academic performance, emotional well-being, communication skills, economic security, ambition, and happiness.

Studies show that kids reading for enjoyment in the US is in rapid decline:

- In 2012, 53% of 9-year-olds read almost every day. Just 10 years later, in 2022, the number had fallen to 39%.
- In 2012, 27% of 13-year-olds read for fun daily. By 2023, that number was just 14%.

Together, we can commit to **Raising Readers** and change this trend. How?

- Read to children in your life daily.
- Model reading as a fun activity.
- Reduce screen time.
- Start a family, school, or community book club.
- Visit bookstores and libraries regularly.
- Listen to audiobooks.
- Read the book before you see the movie.
- Encourage your child to read aloud to a pet or stuffed animal.
- Give books as gifts.
- Donate books to families and communities in need.

Books build bright futures, and **Raising Readers** is our shared responsibility.

For more information, visit **JoinRaisingReaders.com**

Sources: National Endowment for the Arts, National Assessment of Educational Progress, WorldBookDay.org, Nielsen BookData's 2023 "Understanding the Children's Book Consumer"